Praise for **DOUG COOPER's**

Outside In:

Winner of the 2014 International Book Award for Literary Fiction
Winner of the 2014 USA Book News Award for Literary Fiction
Winner of the 2015 IPPY Bronze Book Award

"Rarely does an author capture the frenzied descent into drug and alcohol abuse as Doug Cooper does in his tumultuous novel, *Outside In*. A story of disillusion drowned in excess, tempered by the decisions we make to survive another day. A searing debut."

—Stephen Jay Schwartz, *Los Angeles Times* bestselling
author of *Boulevard* and *Beat*

"This modern take on finding oneself shows readers what can happen when you completely lose control and become someone you are not. It reminds us all of Shakespeare's counsel, 'To thine own self be true.'"

—Weldon Long, author of the *New York Times*
bestseller *The Power of Consistency*

"*Outside In* takes readers on a wild ride with the final destination being a rediscovered sense of self."

—Colleen Hoover, author of the *New York Times*
bestseller *Slammed*

"A buoyant story of one man's willingness to sacrifice everything in the name of self-discovery."

—*Kirkus Reviews*

"[An] insightful coming-of-age story."

—*Foreword Reviews*

"…the relatable tale of one man's quarter-life crisis that will resonate with readers of all ages."

—*Red City Review*

"Brad Shepherd's teaching career wasn't exactly promising to begin with, and when it ends suddenly, he takes his unexpected freedom as an opportunity to escape to the freewheeling Put-in-Bay, Ohio, where he immediately begins experimenting with alcohol and drugs, hooks up with people his parents would definitely say were the wrong sort, and generally starts on a downward spiral that can only end in disaster. Is Brad wracked with guilt over a student's death, the incident that ended his teaching career? Will he find a way to pull himself out of the abyss and find the man he truly is? This is a coming-of-age story about someone a decade older than the genre's usual protagonist, and it's quite good—nicely written with a cast of realistic characters (the seductive girl, the affable druggie, the street musician who takes the younger Brad under his wing) and situations that would fit into a more traditional YA novel but that carry a little adult baggage. A very good first novel from someone worth keeping an eye on."

—David Pitt, *Booklist*

"Doug Cooper writes authoritatively about the ease with which circumstances conspire to ensnare a promising young teacher into a lush life of sex, drugs, and rock and roll. It remains to be seen how easy it will be for him to get himself out— or if he will just become another bleached-out lotus-eater in the Florida sun. A charismatic cast of characters populates this promising novel from a rising talent."

—Stuart Smith, CEO, Central Recovery

THE INVEST MENT CLUB

DOUG COOPER

This is a Genuine Vireo Book

A Vireo Book | Rare Bird Books
453 South Spring Street, Suite 302
Los Angeles, CA 90013
rarebirdbooks.com

FIRST TRADE PAPERBACK ORIGINAL EDITION

Set in Minion
Printed in the United States

10 9 8 7 6 5 4 3 2 1

Publisher's Cataloging-in-Publication data

Names: Cooper, Doug, 1970- , author.
Title: The Investment club / Doug Cooper.
Description: First Trade Paperback Original Edition | A Vireo Book | Los Angeles, CA,
New York, NY: Rare Bird Books, 2016.
Identifiers: ISBN 978-1-945572-00-5
Subjects: LCSH Gambling—Fiction. | Casinos—Fiction. | Sex-oriented businesses—
Fiction. | Friendship—Fiction. | Blackjack (Game)—Fiction. | Las Vegas (Nev.)—Fiction. |
BISAC FICTION / General
Classification: LCC PS3603.O58262 I58 2016| DDC 813.6—dc23

For all those who give and never expect anything in return.

Chapter One

Date: Friday, January 17, 2014

Dow Jones Open: 16,408.02

Never split tens.

The words flashed in their eyes and formed on their lips. A nervous fingering of chips followed. Except for third base, the last, and most important, seat at the table. He controlled the fates of the other players, a role he seemed to enjoy. His stout digits remained steadfast, cupped over the stack of ten black chips measured to split the hand. Never had a doubt. Once he saw the house had a five of hearts, he knew his play.

My left hand slid to the shoe, eyes directed toward first base. "Twelve."

The brim of her faded green military cap angled downward, concealing her eyes and half of her tawny face. Her hat was more fashion than function, this girl had never served, at least in the armed forces. Her body, though, was all function. Lean and mean. Definitely put on this earth to move. It was just a question of if that was in the vertical or the horizontal.

She waved her hand over the cards, never lifting her gaze from the table. "I'll stay. You're going to bust." She was there for one purpose: to make money. Played every night. Never for less than $25 per hand and often as high as $200 when she really got rolling. I wouldn't say she was unfriendly or mean. Just had an edge to her. Wanted to be left alone and not have to talk to anyone.

Next to her in seat two, a burly man, about six foot two or three—somewhere in his late sixties—nodded approvingly. He had a half-inch gray flattop that with each tilt of his head revealed a thinning patch on top. "Good girl," he said. "You don't have to have great cards; just need the dealer to have worse ones." He plucked a red five-dollar chip off his stack and placed it next to his bet. Holding up his index finger, he said, "One card, down please."

Sliding the card from the shoe without revealing the value, I said, "Down and dirty." Directing my attention to his neighbor, I nodded at the seventeen in front of the surgically enhanced Barbie doll in seat three. "The ol' mother-in-law's hand."

She furrowed her brow, barely wrinkling her taut forehead. "What does that mean?" It was obvious she didn't know the game, but she wasn't stupid either. Everything she did had a purpose. What she revealed at the table was exactly what she wanted the others to see to elicit the reaction she desired.

"It's a seventeen," I said, about to drop one of my standard lines, good at least a few times a night. "It's like your mother-in-law. You want to hit it, but you can't."

"Well, I don't have to worry about one of those." Her eyes sank to her cards. "So do I hit or not?"

The burly, elderly man to her right said, "Always assume the dealer has a ten as the down card, sweetie. With the dealer showing five, you don't want to hit because the house probably has fifteen and is going to bust."

"Just let her play her hand, gramps," the guy at third base said. Diminutive in stature—oh hell, I'll just say it. He was a little person or dwarf or whatever the politically correct term is these days. He played with aggression and anger. Winning wasn't enough. He wanted more. Acted like he deserved it. Like the world owed it to him. He banged back the remainder of his third cognac and motioned for the cocktail waitress to bring another one.

Nip-Tuck Barbie pushed her puffy lips out in a pout, waving her perfectly manicured fingers over her cards. "I'll hold then."

Seat four was all business. He was around fifty, black and distinguished, with a wiry frame. He had short salt-and-pepper hair on the sides and back that connected into a beard the same length but much thicker than the rest. Too methodical to be a pro, but he knew the game. He was firm and decisive. It was obvious he liked strategy and analysis. My guess was accountant. His face was too kind to be a broker or a banker. Wasting no time, he pushed his fingers outward from his clenched fist over the cards. "I'm good with eighteen."

The waitress delivered another cognac to the little guy at third base. He took a green twenty-five-dollar chip from his growing stack, which was almost as high as the one on his shoulder. He downed the drink in one gulp. "Bring me another," he said. His eyes were drooping with each drink. He ran his hand through his wavy, reddish-brown hair and pushed the $1,000 black stack next to his bet. With his index and pinky fingers extended like a two-pronged fork, he said, "Split 'em."

I tilted my head to alert the pit boss. "Checks play. Splitting tens."

Gramps said, "Come on, junior. You're going to take the bust card and screw the table."

The pit boss walked over. "Splitting tens. Go ahead."

I pulled the first card from the shoe, hesitating before revealing its identity. "You sure about this?"

He pressed his index finger repeatedly into the felt. "Flip the damn card."

It was an ace. "Twenty-one."

He pointed at the second ten. "Paint it."

I pulled a queen from the shoe. "Split again?"

"Nah, I'm good with twenty," he said. "I don't want to be greedy."

"Too late for that," the Accountant in seat four said.

I knew what was going to happen before I even played my hand. I had seen it too many times before. One asshole screwing it up for everyone else. I revealed my down card. A king of spades. "Dealer has fifteen."

The Accountant rubbed the bald patch on the crown of his head and shifted back in his chair. "Would've busted if you hadn't split."

"Come on, need a big one," Lean and Mean at first base sneered.

I flipped the next card to add to my fifteen. An ace of clubs. "Sixteen," I said. "Not going down easy."

"Six or higher, six or higher," Gramps said.

I pulled the next card, peeking under the corner to delay their unfortunate fate before flipping a three of hearts. "House has nineteen."

I scooped Lean and Mean's last four green chips from the bet circle.

She ripped her hat off in disgust, her thick black hair and crescent eyes now visible, and glared at Junior. "You're such a dick."

I placed my hand on Gramps's down card.

He pleaded for a ten. "Monkey, monkey, monkey."

I turned over a six of diamonds. "Seventeen." I snagged the two red chips from his failed double and redeposited them into the house bank. Returning to Nip-Tuck Barbie, in one motion I collected her chips and also seat four's. "Another seventeen and eighteen, not enough to beat the nineteen."

Greedily rubbing his hands together, Junior said, "But my twenty-one and twenty are. Daddy about to get paid!"

I pushed two stacks of one thousand to match his bets. "Twenty black going out."

The pit boss approved the payout.

"That's it for me," Lean and Mean said. "I'm not wasting any more money playing with this jackoff."

"Me, too," Gramps said and pushed his thirty-eight fifty to the center to cash in. "I'm done."

"Quit your bitching," Junior said, tipping the waitress fifty for the new cognac.

"But we all would've won if you hadn't split," Gramps said.

Junior tossed two of the blacks back to me. "Give me some green."

I measured two stacks of four green chips. "Check change. Two black coming in."

He combined the stacks and tossed four green at Lean and Mean and one each at the other three players, giving the last one to me. "That ought to cover it, you bunch of crybabies. That's why they call it gambling."

Lean and Mean flipped the chips back to him. "I don't need your charity."

He pushed them to the middle of the table. "Well somebody take them because I don't want them." His eyes scanned the other players, before stopping again on Lean and Mean. She put her hat back on and pulled the brim low. He said, "Heeey, wait a second. I know you. You work down at OGs, don't you? You and your girlfriend soaked me for about five grand one night."

OGs was Olympic Gardens, a mid-level strip club on Las Vegas Boulevard between downtown and the strip. Mid-level because it's not as swanky as the upper-tier places like Spearmint Rhino or Sapphire, but it's also not the bottom rung like you walked into a methadone clinic the day after New Year's. OGs biggest advantages are the location right on LV Boulevard and having male and female dancers to cater to both genders. The men perform upstairs and the women downstairs, which was obviously set up by a man, because that's how most men want to operate in their relationships as well. If patrons want some seediness without feeling the need to bathe in hand sanitizer after leaving, then OGs is the place.

Lean and Mean snatched her purse off the back of her chair and slung it over her shoulder. "I don't know you."

"Well, you should. We spent about four hours in the VIP room. Your name's, um…Faith, and your girlfriend, oh, what was her name? She was a real rock climber, that one. She had that chalk bag of coke in her underwear and kept bumping me up while she was dancing. Damn, what was her name? I kept calling her Dora the Explorer."

Gramps said, "Just drop it. The lady said she don't know you."

"What are you, her pimp?" Junior gulped more cognac.

"That's OK," she said. "I was just leaving." She turned and angled toward the door. Gramps followed her.

Nip-Tuck Barbie squirmed in her chair. "Geez, I never knew blackjack had so much drama."

Junior picked up the hundred dollars in green that he had tried to give Lean and Mean from the middle of the table. "For someone who works for tips, you'd think she'd be more appreciative." He tossed them to me. "I'm sure you'll put these to good use."

And that was how I met these five broken people—a drug-addict singer-turned-stripper; a widowed, retired New Jersey police officer; an alcoholic, divorced sportscaster; a card-counting, ex–Catholic priest; and a self-destructive, dwarf entrepreneur—who all somehow managed to wander into the El Cortez and sit at my table on a random Tuesday night.

I haven't always been a blackjack dealer, but I have always lived in Vegas—fifty-seven years. Have held just about every hospitality job this town has to offer, from parking cars to cooking food to serving drinks. What I've never done is been a big winner. Don't get me wrong, I've had my share of winnings, but they don't even come close to the losses. For every night in the black, there were two or three in the red, and the red numbers always seem to be higher than the black ones. Don't let anyone tell you different. They might say they're even, but they're well south of even; it's just a question of how far. That's why I gave it up years ago and switched to this side of the table. I can guarantee you I walk out of the casino up every night.

I've tried dealing other games, but there's just something about blackjack. I like how communal the game is. I like how strangers sit down and in no time will be fist-bumping and high-fiving. Of course there are a fair share of squabbles as well, like the one I just told you about. You see, a lot of players think they're just playing their individual hands, that they should trust their guts. But the good ones know there are rules and every decision at the table affects everyone else. I know the math says differently, that each play is an independent event and will help others just as often as it hurts. But I'm talking about the bigger play, the energy at the table, the stuff that flows through and carries us all.

Yeah, I've seen a lot in my years flipping cards. Seen players win fifteen hands in a row and lose just as many; be down to their last ten dollars and walk away up a thousand; win five grand and slink away with their pockets turned inside out. Won't say I've seen it all, though. Just when I think I have, a night like that Tuesday happens, and a story like I'm about to tell you unfolds.

Now I'll admit I wasn't present for all the stuff I'm about to share. Some of it I was and some of it was told to me, and, well, some of it I just filled in the blanks, and you're going to have to trust me because in this job I've learned how to read people and recognize problems before they happen: the colleagues headed for an affair, the social drinker on the road to alcoholism, and the newlyweds who won't make it to their fifth anniversary. Amazing what people will reveal across three feet of felt. They think they're in control, but putting a stack of their hard-earned money on the table loosens up more than their wallets. It triggers their vulnerability, and that opens up the vault to all their secrets. I just have to watch and listen, like reading an open ledger. Most tell more than I ever care to know, as much by what they don't say as what they do.

Dow Jones Close: 16,458.56

Chapter Two

Date: Saturday, January 18, 2014

Dow Jones Open: Closed

Lean and Mean, or Faith as she was known on stage and Crystal Moore on her driver's license, triple-locked the door to her four-hundred-square-foot studio apartment at the Siegel Suites on Charleston in the Arts District and flopped back against the door, relieved to be home. It really wasn't much of a home though. Her neighbors were Divorcées, drug dealers, and any other budget-conscious wanderers who didn't want to commit to more than a week at a time or answer a lot of questions. She had never really planned to stay more than a few weeks either, just enough time to get back on her feet after the bank foreclosed on her condo and the sheriff showed up to physically remove her.

Staring at the mess before her, Crystal released a steadying breath. Morning sunlight screamed through the window, reflecting off the specks of glitter still on her skin from work. The untidiness of the room seemed even worse in the light of day. Clothes covered the bed and most of the floor. A pizza box, a Carl's Jr. bag, and multiple Styrofoam takeout containers hid the coffee table; dishes filled the sink; and a growing pile of mail spread across the kitchen table. She vowed to clean later—tomorrow—after she had slept. All she could think about at the moment was that she had made it through another shift—one shift closer to the last one, when she would never have to let men grope her for twenty dollars a song. Unfortunately that day was a long way off. After the $1,000 she lost playing blackjack before her shift, she ended up hustling all night just trying to get back to even, and still fell $200 short.

Removing her green cap and vintage bug-eyed sunglasses, she tossed them and her purse on top of the cluttered table and pulled the blinds closed. The hat and the glasses along with the baggy pink velour hoodie and sweatpants she was wearing were all part of her standard pre- and postwork garb. She unzipped the hoodie and released the drawstring on her pants and walked out of them on her way to the bathroom to start the shower. It was all part of her routine. The shower took about eight minutes to warm up. Just enough time to crush up and snort a Roxy. The pill wiped away the mental traces of the night; the shower, the physical ones.

With the water running, she sat down at the kitchen table still in just her bra and panties. She fished out the pill bottle and tools from her purse and pushed the mail aside to clear a spot on the table. In a few quick motions, she crushed the pill and carved up two lines, and even faster, she inhaled them both. Closing her eyes, she waited for the Roxicodone to absorb and release her. Each breath helped erase all the touching and fondling that came with her job. It was all drifting slowly away, which meant she was almost free. She opened her eyes. Steam clouded the mirror in the bathroom and floated through the doorway. She unhooked her bra and tossed it on the floor next to the bed on her way to the bathroom.

A few minutes later, she emerged wearing a frayed, pink cotton robe. Her hair was hidden under a towel wrapped around her head. She grabbed a takeout container from the minifridge and dropped down onto the sheet-covered couch. When she moved in, if it wasn't a hard surface that could be disinfected, she had covered it. The thought of what had been deposited and absorbed into the soft fabrics in the room over the years skeeved her out.

Flipping on the TV, she shook her head and sighed when she saw the infomercial filling the screen. That night at the El Cortez, she might've claimed she didn't know Junior at third base, but the truth was, she couldn't escape him. No matter what channel she chose, between the hours of four and seven a.m., which was usually when she went to bed, his infomercial was always on.

Junior's actual name was Max Doler, and for the past year his infomercial for the Lapkin—the napkin designed for your lap—had flooded the late night programming. Complete with exaggerated portrayals of food and beverage spills, napkin failures, conspicuous groin stains and turgid testimonials, the infomercial was an instant classic. Everybody groaned when they saw it, but they still couldn't stop themselves from watching at least part of it, regardless of how many times they had seen it.

That night Crystal was no different. She plucked a pair of used chopsticks from the remnants of a previous meal in a container on the coffee table and sunk back into the couch. When Max appeared on the screen, she grumbled, "Ugh. Fucking asshole." But she wasn't put off enough to sit up and exchange the chopsticks for the remote and find another program, or maybe it was the Roxy finally taking over. She just filled her mouth with a gob of noodles and zoned out on the TV.

"*Always eating on the go? In your car? At your desk? Tired of getting food in your lap and having to explain that awkward stain? Then do yourself a favor and upgrade to the Lapkin—the napkin designed for your lap.*

"*The Lapkin is stronger than the cheap paper napkins they give you with your to-go orders. Made of state-of-the-art water-resistant material, dribbles and drops always slide easily into the spill catcher between your legs and never soak through like they do with cloth napkins.*

"*Always having to readjust your napkin or lean down and pick it up off the floor? Since the Lapkin is designed specifically for your lap, you never have to worry about it falling off as you shift during your meal.*"

A professional woman sits behind a desk. "*I was making some last-minute changes for a presentation to the board over breakfast when a glob of cream cheese and jelly slid off my bagel into my lap. I didn't have time to change and had to give my presentation with a big, ugly spot on the front of my skirt. I was mortified. But I don't worry about that anymore, now that I have my Lapkin.*" She reaches down and removes the Lapkin from the holster affixed to her desk chair.

A delivery man speaks through the window of a panel truck. "*Everything I do is on the go. Spilling hot coffee is a huge risk, not only for me, but also for the other drivers on the road. But now that my kids bought me a Lapkin for Father's Day, I don't worry about it, and they don't worry about me. Thanks, Lapkin.*"

"*Prevent those frustrating mishaps and expensive dry cleaning bills. For nine ninety-nine, you get not one but two Lapkins for your car or home. But wait. Act now and you'll get an extra set of Lapkins for the kids in the backseat or to give as a gift, and the second set is free. All you have to do is pay the shipping and handling charge. But wait, there's more. Order before midnight tonight, and get a protective holster for each Lapkin that will easily affix to the side of any car seat or furniture. After each use, all you have to do is simply shake out the contents, roll up the Lapkin, slide it into the holster, and you'll be ready for your next meal. That's four Lapkins, plus holsters, for the price of one. Over a forty dollar value for just nine ninety-nine plus shipping and handling.*"

Watching the TV, Crystal let her head drift sleepily back and forth before slumping forward. The chopsticks fell to the floor, the container still resting in her lap.

Dow Jones Close: Closed

Chapter Three

Date: Thursday, January 30, 2014

Dow Jones Open: 15,743.03

Bill Price, or Gramps as Max called him the night I first met him, had been at the El Cortez a lot the past few weeks. Every day, actually. I was on days, so I started my shift at ten in the morning, and each day he came in about two and was there until I left at six. The day shifts are the best. Still have my mornings free and am able to get home at a decent hour after work. Seniority does have some privileges. And the customers during the day are fairly normal, or at least as normal as they're going to get in this business. You catch people as they're recovering from the day before or just starting their evenings, and you're gone before they spin off too much.

When Bill gambled, he never varied his play. He always started with a hundred dollars, bet five bucks per hand, never took the side bets or insurance, and played by the book. He always hit his twelves against twos and threes, hit sixteens against a seven and above, and never doubled when he had eight. I always knew exactly the type of day he was having by how much his stack was over or under a hundred. He wasn't playing to make money or for the rush. To be honest, I just don't think he had anything better to do, so he came here and played blackjack.

On this particular day, Bill was having a pretty decent run. He was the only one at the table, and he was up thirty-five. Pretty much stayed that way for about two hours. He just rode the waves. His stack got as high as one fifty and never dipped below one ten.

Casinos are notorious for not having any clocks around. That doesn't mean it's not easy for me to keep track of the time though. All I have to do is count my breaks. I deal for forty minutes until someone relieves me, then go on break for twenty. After eight times, I'm done.

Right after my second break on this particular day, the Accountant from that first night sat down and bought in for $200, requesting both green and red chips. He wore a black T-shirt and jeans, just like on the first night. He had been a fairly regular player, but I didn't know too much about him because he didn't talk all that much. Really kept to himself. He was more interested in the game, but for the money, not the action. He was definitely there to make money.

I remember this night distinctly because it was the first night these two had played together since the splitting tens incident. I like getting players speaking to each other. That way I don't have to talk so much. I can just sit back and observe. Makes the time go by more quickly and makes it easy on me because all I have to do is deal.

I called out over my shoulder. "Two hundred going out." I pushed a stack of four green and two stacks of ten red. "Here you go, sir. A hundred green and a hundred red." Trying to make the connection between the two of them, I said, "Hopefully no one will split tens again."

The two players glanced at each other and nodded in recognition. Bill said, "Boy that guy killed the party that night. For such a little guy, he sure was a big asshole. Never understand people like that. He come in here a lot?"

I said, "A few times a week, usually later. He lives in the penthouse at the Ogden, that art deco high-rise building across the street."

The Accountant extended his hand to Bill. "Nice to meet you. I'm Lester Banks."

Bill reciprocated with his hulking paw. "Bill Price. Retired and moved here from New Jersey about six months ago. Do you prefer Lester or Les?"

"Les is fine." He pushed ten dollars into the circle. "I suspect that guy from the other night is just lonely. He obviously doesn't need the money. At those stakes he could play by himself at a high-limit table. For him to be at a five-dollar table, he just doesn't want to be alone."

I dealt a new round of cards.

Bill said, "If he wants friends, he sure does go about it in a peculiar way." He waved his hand over his eighteen to stand.

Les tapped next to his thirteen to get another card. An eight.

"Woo-wee. That should work," Bill said. "What brought you?"

Turning over a ten to go with my seven for a seventeen, I said, "Not enough." I paid out the winnings and flipped fresh cards.

Les said, "I retired as well. Moved here from Georgia. Now just donating my time at the Oasis Mission. It's a homeless shelter over in the Arts District."

Bill lifted his cup of decaf. "To enjoying the fruits of our labor."

Les didn't have a beverage. He just nodded.

Bill didn't wait for Les to ask more about him. He willingly volunteered his life story. "After thirty-seven years on the force, me and the missus had enough of those East Coast winters and packed it up. What did you do? Wait, let me guess. I'm pretty good at this. I'm going to say, an insurance salesman."

"In a matter of speaking," Les said. "I was a priest. Insurance for the soul."

"Catholic?" Bill asked.

Les nodded, wincing as I turned over a queen of hearts to pair with my jack of spades. I cleared his bet. He pushed another two red into the circle.

"No offense, but I don't know too many black Catholics and never met a black priest before," Bill said.

"There are more black Catholics than people realize in the US, about three million actually. Roughly a thousand of the eighteen thousand congregations are predominantly black," Les said. "But only about two hundred fifty black priests."

"So do you prefer Father Banks?" Bill asked.

"Only if you make me call you Officer Price," Les said. "That life's behind me."

Over the course of the evening, the conversation flowed, and the mood was relaxed, in part because these two men understood each other, but probably more so because they were both winning. Interesting how the happiness and comfort level at a table is directly proportional to how much the players are winning. A lot of people think the winning follows the positivity, and I'm not saying a positive outlook doesn't help, but in my experience, the optimism spawns from being on the plus side of the rake.

After a while, I think Bill was getting too close to some stuff Les wasn't ready to share. His answers became more concise, and he always had another question ready for Bill. Les was like this a lot with other players at the table. I had thought it was just because he wanted to concentrate on the game and didn't want to be rude, but that day it was pretty obvious. He just didn't want to talk about himself, which made me think he had something to hide. He said, "Why Vegas? If you were looking to just escape the winters, there are plenty of other places to choose from."

"It was all Darlene," Bill said, full of melancholy. "We'd been coming here every year as long as I can remember. Darlene said it was the only place she ever felt safe, where she didn't have to worry about me. Poor thing used to send me off to work every day and worry herself into a tizzy until I got home that night. I told her I was too stupid to get into any trouble. She said I was just stupid enough."

"Law enforcement jobs are always toughest on the spouses." Les winced at the six I gave him, for a total of fifteen.

Bill said, "You got that right. I said the exact thing in my retirement speech. I figured I owed it to the old gal."

"Where is she now, playing the slots?" Les asked. "Can't believe she'd let you run around here by yourself."

The longing and regret in Bill's face transformed to sadness. He hesitated for several moments. "Unfortunately she passed last month."

"I'm so sorry to hear that. My deepest condolences." Les reached over and put his hand on Bill's, surprising him. I expected him to pull away, but he relaxed. It seemed to really comfort him, like he hadn't been touched by anyone in a while.

"Thank you," Bill said, and put his other hand on top of Les's. "It was pancreatic cancer. She collapsed after breakfast one morning, and three months later she was gone."

Les reached in his pocket, removed a card, and set it in front of Bill. "Here's my number and the address of the Oasis. It's the mission I run over on California and Casino Center. If you ever want to talk, or maybe just get your hands dirty with some work, give me call. We can always use good people."

Bill picked up the card and dropped it in the breast pocket of his short-sleeved, checked button-down. "Think I might take you up on that. You're not too far from me. I'm over at the Juhl off Fourth Street."

The game faded into the background, a mixture of hand signals and an undulating flow of chips. The two men seemed more interested in one another than the game. I just dealt the cards and tried to stay out of the way.

Dow Jones Close: 15,848.61

Chapter Four

Date: Thursday, November 5, 2009

Dow Jones Open: 9,807.80

Nip-Tuck Barbie, more prominently known as Penny Market by everyone in the St. Louis sports community, had made all her major life choices by what was best for her career. She had started as a field reporter in Boise, covering the local sports teams, then moved to Tulsa for the same job in a bigger market. After two years there, she got the opportunity in St. Louis, which actually had a smaller city population than Tulsa, but the surrounding metropolitan area in St. Louis pushed its audience to almost three million.

Penny had her dad to thank for her love of sports. He was a high school football, basketball, and baseball coach and the guiding force in her life. Penny's parents had divorced when she was six, and her mom moved to Florida with a new husband not too long after. Penny had made a few trips to visit, but as she got older and had more say in the matter, she stopped going. She just didn't see the point. Her mom had her own kids with the new guy, so she just felt in the way. But more than anything, she hated leaving her dad alone. He had never remarried or even dated, at least that she knew of, so all he had were his coaching buddies and the gang down at the Eagles. When Penny did leave, she knew he would spend too much time at the club because he hated to be home when she wasn't there. With no female figure in her life, Penny knew there were things she missed out on without a lady in the house, but she and her dad always found a way to navigate the trouble spots, which usually centered around some aspect of her burgeoning womanhood. Other than that, he raised her like he would've a son, which was why she probably always felt more comfortable around boys and had so few female friends.

Penny was happy in St. Louis. It was the perfect-sized city for her. Still a small Midwest town, but with all the benefits of a big city. Next in her sights was the weekend sports anchor, followed by the same job but during the week. The only other thing she would have even considered moving for would have been if ESPN or one of the other national networks came calling. But Alec Baudin changed all that.

Penny and Alec had first met while she was covering the Blues. Alec was on an incredible hot streak. He had just completed his fourth consecutive shutout, and would be attempting to tie the NHL record of five set by Brian Boucher back in the 2003–04 season. Penny had been trying to get an interview since after the second game, but Alec refused, fearful he might jeopardize his streak. After the third game, he even stopped returning her texts.

Alec had been a journeyman goaltender the first six years of his career, never staying with a team more than two years. But this was his third year in St. Louis and first as their number one goaltender, and with the way he was playing, his agent assured him a long-term contract was coming in the near future.

Just as his repeated denials on the ice only encouraged his opponents more, his refusals made Penny more determined. But it was more than the declined interviews that sunk the hook and drew her in. It was that no one seemed to know much about Alec Baudin. Off the ice, he kept to himself. On the ice, the only thing you could see under his equipment were his magnetic green eyes, which fired a gaze out of his mask like a missile tracking device, locating the puck and eliminating the threat before it even got close. His combination of grace and physicality melted something deep inside her. She knew she wanted more than an interview.

In the third period against the Calgary Flames during the record-tying fifth game, Alec had denied all twenty-two shots. Unfortunately the Flames goaltender was also perfect, twenty-four for twenty-four. With a minute and a half to play, the Blues had a two-on-one break. The puck bounced back and forth between the players, sending the crowd to their feet. The Blues left wing faked the shot. The Flames defender laid out flat, skidding across the ice. The left wing slapped it across to the right wing. One-on-one with the goaltender, he showed the puck to the right then brought it back to the center. The goaltender split his legs, dropping his crotch to the ice, eliminating the five-hole. In one fluid motion, the Blues player backhanded it toward the goal, above the goaltender's outstretched arm. The puck clanked off the left post, careening into the corner. A collective groan rippled through the sold-out crowd.

Unfortunately that was as close as the Blues would get the rest of the night. The scoreless game went to overtime, and midway through the first extra period, a deflected shot ricocheted off one of the Flames' skates and trickled in just past Alec's outstretched glove, bringing the shutout streak to an end. Alec had missed the record books by less than an inch.

Out of respect for how close Alec had been to setting the goal, Penny didn't even attempt an interview after the game. The fans were crushed. She was heartbroken. She couldn't even imagine how Alec felt.

Down on the ice, she prepared for the postgame broadcast in front of the goal to show everyone where the missed Blues' shot hit, and how close Alec had come to tying the record. While reviewing her notes, awaiting the go-ahead from the station, her phone vibrated with a new text message in her pocket.

Still want that interview?

She typed back:

If you feel up to it. ☺ Just getting ready to go on. Come out whenever you're ready.

Unsure when or if Alec would actually show, Penny started her broadcast: "Emotions and expectations were high tonight as the Blues faced the Calgary Flames at the Scottrade Center, and fans were not disappointed as Alec Baudin went for his fifth straight shutout and a place in the record books with Brian Boucher for most consecutive shutouts. Tonight both goaltenders put on a show, with Baudin stopping twenty-seven shots and Miikka Kiprusoff from the Flames saving twenty-seven. But tonight's game came down to two ricochets in the goal directly behind me.

"With only a minute and a half in regulation, David Perron intercepted a pass and had a two-on-one break with Fritjof Stridh. After some back and forth, Perron got the defender to commit and flipped the puck to Stridh, leaving him one-on-one with Kiprusoff. Stridh faked right and came back left with a backhand that hit off the left post and was recovered by the Flames."

Penny could feel Alec's gaze burning through her. She followed it into the shadows, staring at him momentarily. With the camera lights shining in her face, she hadn't noticed that he had come out on the ice and was standing, watching the broadcast. She had never seen him out of his pads before. "I'm joined here on the ice by the man of the hour, Alec Baudin." Alec walked into the shot. His glowing green eyes ignited a spark within her, and his kind smile gently fanned the flames.

The producer buzzed in her ear. "Penny, ask a question."

She blinked a few times and swallowed hard, regaining her focus. "So, two shots in this one goal. One a near miss and the other an unlucky bounce. How do you feel after coming so close to the record books?"

"Like we say in Canada, close counts only in curling and hand grenades." Alec flashed a wry smile.

Penny laughed politely, unsure if that was a real saying or if he was making a joke. She said, "But to know you were so close has to sting a little."

"The only part that stings is that we lost. I'm pleased to have had four straight wins, and grateful to have been in the position to go for the record. The team has been playing great in front of me, and I've benefited from some fortunate bounces during the stretch. I was due to catch a few bad ones."

"After a streak like this ends, what do you do? How do you come back and get ready for the next game?"

"I'm a creature of habit," Alec said. "I'll do the same thing I always do after a game. I look forward to a nice meal, unwinding a bit, and getting a good night's sleep. In the morning, we'll watch the film and get ready for the next game. The secret is in the simple."

Penny turned back to the camera. "Well there you have it, Blues fans. Keeping it simple at the Scottrade Center, I'm Penny Market. Back to you in the studio."

The camera light dimmed. Penny handed the mic to the cameraman. Still uneasy and unsure what to say to Alec, she steadied her nerves with a deep breath and turned back to face him. "I really appreciate your coming down for the interview. Probably not your first choice after a heartbreaking loss. Sorry for pestering you so much lately."

"I'm the one who should apologize for not responding. You were just doing your job."

"Well, I don't blame you. I'm like a dog with a chew toy. I won't give up until it's in pieces."

Alec grinned. "You know, when I said I was looking forward to a nice meal, I meant with you."

His invitation stoked the smoldering fire inside her. Sparks shot to her extremities, warming her hands and feet. The surrounding ice tempted her. She wanted to lie flat and feel the cold on her flushed skin. "Tonight? I mean, I ate some stuff in the press box, but I could still eat." The words tumbled out of her like rocks down a mountain, each unconnected and following an unknown course. She was blowing it. She wanted to just say no, to make up some excuse and run away before she made an even bigger fool of herself.

"Or maybe another night," he said, dropping his eyes to the ice. "I'm sorry, maybe I crossed a line."

His vacillation quieted her unrest. Comfort replaced the searing heat. She wanted to go. She wanted to be next to him.

Chapter Five

Date: Sunday, October 7, 2012

Dow Jones Open: Closed

L es raised his arms to the congregation in the half-full Sunday afternoon mass. "The mass is ended. Go in peace."

The parishioners responded, "Thanks be to God," and launched into the recessional hymn.

Les rotated toward the altar to perform the final blessing. The altar boys assembled behind him. At the conclusion of the blessing, Les faced the congregation and followed the boys in the procession out of the church. The congregation filled in the aisle behind him.

Once outside, Les blessed each of the boys and released them to their duties. He stopped the two oldest. "Lucas, Malcolm, you two make sure the younger boys hang up their robes and all the candles are out, and then clean up the sanctuary and pulpit."

Lucas and Malcolm nodded in unison. "Yes, Father."

Les went outside in front of the church to greet parishioners as they filed out, offering blessings, shaking hands, and exchanging pleasantries.

A Puerto Rican woman in her mid-thirties approached with three children in reluctant tow and a husband who clearly wanted to be there just about as much. The woman said, "You still coming over for Sunday dinner and to bless the new house?"

Les rubbed the top of the youngest boy's head. "You know I wouldn't miss a chance for some of your cooking, Mrs. Rivera." He extended his hand to Mr. Rivera. "Congratulations on the new house. A blessing well deserved."

"Gracias, Father. We look forward to having you." He turned to his wife. "*Voy a traer el carro.*"

Les said, "I'm just going to freshen up and will be over in an hour or so." He smiled and excused himself to greet some other families waiting on the perimeter.

After the last of the parishioners departed, Les walked back into the church and went to the sacristy. Malcolm and Lucas were cleaning the communion vessels in the sacrarium. They always did mass together and had been best friends since second grade when Malcolm's family immigrated from Jamaica to be closer to his mom's sister and her family, who were also members of the parish. Les removed his vestments, taking special care to store each accessory in its proper drawer and hang the alb and cope in the cabinet. Malcolm and Lucas stood by, remaining quiet.

Les said, "Double-check all the candles for me, will you, boys? I'll be gone the rest of the afternoon at the Riveras.'"

Malcolm said, "Of course, Father."

"Thank you," Les said. "Nice service today. Good job." He left and went to the rectory next to the church.

After a shower and change into the less formal black clerical shirt and pants worn outside of church, Les gathered the objects he planned to take with him: some prayer cards for the children, a new Bible for the parents, and the container with the holy water for the blessing. Going to homes and interacting with the parishioners on a more personal basis was what he really enjoyed about the priesthood. He felt too disconnected when conducting mass and functioning as a figurehead of the Church. He needed more human contact. Holding up the container of holy water, he noticed it was running low. He would need to stop back at the church and top it off before leaving.

In the church, no one was in the main room of the sacristy. He assumed Malcolm and Lucas had finished and gone home. Placing the Bible and prayer cards on the counter, he walked toward the holy water font. Voices dribbled in from the servers' room. He called out. "Malcolm? Lucas?" He headed toward the room.

Malcolm, wearing only a white T-shirt, with his underwear around his ankles, was sitting on the bench in front of the servers' cabinets. Lucas was on his knees between Malcolm's legs, wearing only underwear and socks. An open bottle of church wine rested on the bench next to them.

Les froze in the doorway. "Boys!"

Lucas jerked back in shock, his head jolting toward the door. Malcolm grasped for his underwear, turning away from Les. He knocked over the bottle, smashing it on the floor. Wine spilled in all directions.

Les composed himself. "Get dressed immediately. I'll wait for you in the sacristy." He turned to go, then turned back. "And please watch out for the glass."

A few minutes later, heads down, Malcolm and Lucas shuffled out of the servers' room. Les had set up three folding metal chairs in a triangle in the middle of the room. He was sitting with his hands folded in his lap, facing the other two chairs. He motioned in their direction. "Have a seat."

The boys slid into the chairs, their eyes fixed on the floor.

Les said, "What do you have to say for yourselves?"

Still looking down, as if performing another part of a mass ritual, they said in unison, "We're sorry."

"Sorry for what?" Les asked. "Sorry for stealing the wine, for abusing what is intended for the sacrament? Sorry for taking advantage of the trust placed in you by this congregation? Sorry for succumbing to temptation in the house of God?"

Tears streamed down Lucas's freckled face. "For all of it, Father. We weren't thinking."

Malcolm looked up, finally connecting his eyes with Les's. "Please don't tell our parents." Not a drop of sadness or regret filled Malcolm's eyes, only fear. "My dad will kill me," he said, his eyes dropping back to the floor.

Les released a long, calming breath. Tears continued to flow from both boys. "For now, we can keep this between us until I determine the best course of action. Of course there will be punishment."

Lucas wiped his eyes and nose with the backside of his hand in a back and forth motion. "Absolutely. Whatever it takes, Father. We'll scrub the floors, pews, anything."

Malcolm chimed in. "We're so sorry. I promise. It won't happen again."

"I'm sure you are," Les said. "For now, let's get that glass and wine cleaned up. I'm running late for the Riveras' house blessing."

Lucas said, "We can manage, Father. You go ahead. We don't want you to be late on account of us."

"I think it's best if we do it together." Les stood from his chair. The boys followed, their gaze returning to the floor. He reached out and lifted their chins to make eye contact again. "Head up, boys. Of course I expect to see you both at confession this week."

Dow Jones Close: Closed

Chapter Six

Date: Monday, December 9, 2013

Dow Jones Open: 16,019.49

Max sat at his desk reviewing a profit and loss projection in his office in the basement of the Lapkin factory on Eleventh Street in downtown Vegas. The hum of the machines cutting, sewing, and packing the completed Lapkins on the production floor above could be heard through the ceiling. He knew it was probably time to move the offices to a new, nicer location, but he liked being close to the operation.

Jules, his head of Human Resources, walked in holding a document. She had joined the company as an intern when they moved the operation from his apartment in Henderson and hired their first crew of workers. It was only nineteen months ago, but a lot had happened in that time. Max had always liked and respected her because of her authenticity. She was extremely professional but still always found a way to let her personality and style come through, like her outfit that day. She had on a leopard camisole underneath a tailored two-button black jacket with red plastic rectangular glasses that accented the auburn highlights in her long, straight blond hair. It was all so subtle but unique. He could tell there was a real person in there, one he could trust. She handed him the paper that she had brought with her. "Looked over the press release draft. Made a few suggestions, but overall, you're good to go."

Max motioned for her to have a seat in one of the three chairs in front of his desk, glancing at the changes in the document. "You sure it's not too over-the-top?"

"Isn't everything you do, Max?" Jules said, sitting down in the middle chair. "But in this case, I think it's well deserved. You should be proud of what you achieved."

"*We* should be proud," Max said. "I couldn't have done it without you. Remember when we hired that first crew? We had no idea what we were doing."

"You're saying we do now?" Jules laughed, taking off her glasses and sliding them into the breast pocket of her jacket.

Max opened his bottom right desk drawer and removed a bottle of aged armagnac and two snifters. "Celebrate with a drink? Been saving this bottle for a special occasion."

"Are you asking the head of HR to have a drink in the office?"

"I won't tell if you don't," Max said, pouring two glasses and sliding one across the desk to her. He held up his glass, proposing a toast. "To the McLapkin."

They touched glasses and sipped the twenty-year-old brandy, swapping stories about those early days. Each swallow, they felt warmer and more open. Despite the trust and respect between the two, they really didn't know much about each other. That was the way Max liked it. He was always so focused on the future, he didn't see the point in talking about the past.

"Max?" Jules said, her cheeks flushed from the alcohol. She placed her empty snifter on the desk.

"What's on your mind?" Max said, adding more armagnac to her glass. Usually he was closed off to people, but with the McDonald's deal closed and the announcement about to be made, he was relaxed and feeling loose.

"Never mind," she said, shaking her head and looking away. "It's nothing."

"No, go ahead. Ask me. It's OK."

Jules steadied herself with another gulp. "It's just, you never talk about yourself."

"What do you want to know?" Max said, spinning in a circle in his office chair. He could tell she didn't know what to make of his boyish playfulness. He never let people see this side of him. He said, "Tonight you can ask me anything you want."

"Where exactly are you from?" Jules said, qualifying the question with a rambling follow-up. "I know you're not from here because I remember you telling the story in that one interview about moving here after your high school graduation because you didn't want to go to college and take on debt and the armed forces wouldn't accept you."

"Yep, it was either Vegas or the circus, the two places where freaks are appreciated."

"No, I'm serious," Jules said.

Max leaned back in his chair holding his glass with both hands against his chest and looking at the ceiling. "I never understood that question. What does it even mean? Are you asking, Where was I born? Where did I grow up? Where have I lived the longest? Where do I identify most with? Where am I living now? We're all a product of the places we've been and the people we've met, so if you're asking the question to understand more about me, to fully answer it, I need to answer all of these."

His long-winded, evasive response dampened her curiosity, and the mood. "That's OK. Never mind." She put her glass on the desk. "I think the armagnac made me a little loopy. It's none of my business."

Max didn't mean to be a buzzkill. He just viewed people as more of a jigsaw puzzle than a mystery. He didn't mind providing the pieces, or even occasionally showing a glimpse of the final version, but he wasn't going to do the work for others. The truth was that Max was born to a mother he never knew in a city he never grew up in. Because he was given up for adoption at birth, Max never felt the urge to find his biological mother or any other information except that he was born in Outer Drive Hospital in the suburb of Lincoln Park in Detroit and adopted by a young couple in Monroe, a small town of around twenty thousand people forty-minutes south on I-75 in Michigan. He said, "You sure? Really, it's OK. I don't mind answering."

Jules stood up and looked at her watch. "No, really. I get it. Today is about the future, not the past." She held her hand across the desk. "Congratulations. Thanks for bringing me along for the ride."

Max shook her hand. "It's you I should be thanking. This is the start of a whole new journey for all of us." Jules nodded in appreciation and turned to walk out. Max said, "Jules?" She stopped in the doorway, turning around. He said, "Monroe. I'm from Monroe, Michigan." He attempted to bring some of the comfort they had only moments ago back into the room. "Me, General Custer, and La-Z-Boy furniture."

Jules said, "Well, I guess now I know where you get your 'never back down from a fight, but know when it's time to kick back and relax' philosophy of doing business." She winked at him and walked toward the door, talking over her shoulder. "I'll see you in the morning."

"Good night," Max said, pouring another glass of armagnac. He scooted his chair to the desk and looked down to review the press release one more time.

FOR IMMEDIATE RELEASE

CONTACT: Iris Green, 702-555-0506

Email: iris.green@maxdoler.com

McDonald's and Max Doler Partner on McLapkin Giveaway

Oak Brook, IL—McDonald's Corp. (NYSE: MCD) and Max Doler Industries have announced a partnership to produce a special edition version of Max

Doler's widely popular Lapkin. The McLapkin will be a similar version, made of the same durable water-resistant material, and also include a holster to attach to the car seat like the Lapkin available through the infomercial and website (maxdoler.com), but with McDonald's branding.

"We recognize the time pressures our customers face," said Jesse Cash, McDonald's Chief Brand and Strategy Officer. "But providing a McLapkin for all drive-thru orders is more about safety than efficiency. If our customers choose to eat on the go, we want them to arrive safely and not worry about any accidental drops or spills."

When asked about the partnership with McDonald's, Max Doler, founder and CEO of MDI, said, "I'm loving it! Millions of customers across the world have already benefited from the Lapkin. We're excited to extend that value through McDonald's."

About Max Doler Inc.: Max Doler Industries (MDI), founded in 2008 by entrepreneur Max Doler, is the creator and producer of the Lapkin, the napkin designed for your lap, which has shipped to over 10 million customers worldwide. Based in Las Vegas, NV, MDI is a developer and owner of patents, inventions, and real estate holdings. To learn more about MDI, please visit www.maxdoler.com and follow on Facebook www.facebook.com/maxdoler and Twitter @MaxDoler.

About McDonald's : McDonald's is the world's leading global food service retailer with more than thirty five thousand locations serving approximately 70 million customers in more than one hundred countries each day. More than 80 percent of McDonald's restaurants worldwide are owned and operated by independent local business women and men. To learn more about the company, please visit: www.mcdonalds.com/us/en/home.html and follow us on Facebook (http://www.facebook.com/mcdonaldscorp) and Twitter @McDonaldsCorp.

Dow Jones Close: 16,025.53

Chapter Seven

Date: Tuesday, January 28, 2014

Dow Jones Open: 15,840.84

Crystal rolled down Fourth Street on her rusted beach cruiser, her purse nested in the front basket. Her first bicycle had been nicer, but it got stolen a week after she got it, from OGs of all places. If it had happened at Siegel Suites or outside the El Cortez, she could've understood that. But at a strip club? Who leaves the club and decides to steal a bike? A person can afford twenty-dollar lap dances but not a cab ride? Maybe the thief needed to dry the wet spot on the front of his pants before he got home. Maybe she had made that wet spot. If she had, at least she got paid.

Regardless, she refused to pay more than fifty bucks for a new bike again. The way she figured it, that was less than three lap dances. Even if the person left the club and stole her bike, she would still be ten dollars to the good. She had found this used bike at an EZ Pawn for forty. That was eight months ago. No matter what happened now, it was paid for, and she was playing on house money.

Crystal churned the pedals, picking up speed down Fourth Street. The hot evening air blasted her in the face. The tall buildings on each side of the long one-way connecting Charleston and Fremont Streets caused the wind to swirl, offering little relief other than keeping the dust off. The fronds on the Mexican fan palms lining the street waved above. The hot part of the day had passed, and everything was in transition. While many downtowns at this time of day prepared for the evening commute and rolled up the sidewalks, Vegas, like her, was just waking up.

In a few hours this now-barren street would be buzzing with cabs shuffling tourists, eager to escape the mega resorts on the strip, downtown to explore old Vegas. But for now she was alone, and she was happy. She couldn't say that too often anymore. That's probably why she started every day with a bike ride. While she might end her days being unhealthy, snorting pills, she never planned it that way. It just happened. At some point something or someone would alter her course and send her to negative town. First stop usually involved alcohol, then drugs. After that, the bad decisions seemed to come fast and furious. They were like storm clouds, never happening in isolation, just rolling in one after the other, each bringing their own inclement circumstances.

Crystal, like most downtown visitors wanting to step back in time, didn't realize the trip itself was a history lesson, with the cross streets named after early Western visionaries: Gass, Garces, Bonneville, Clark, and Lewis. She turned right on Carson, crossed Las Vegas Boulevard past the post office, and angled toward the Carson Hotel sign still perched on the mid-century modern building that was for its first fifty years a hotel, then a flophouse, but recently had been refurbished for office, retail, and restaurant space as part of the ongoing urban revitalization.

Crystal leaned her bike against the front of the building and went inside to one of the new tenants, Grass Roots, a superfood-based juice and smoothie bar. Healthy choices weren't the easiest to find in Vegas, but she had learned—when she was singing and dancing in the show at the Wynn and cared about her body—they were around. She just had to look and be willing to bypass all the $0.99 margaritas, $1 hot dogs, and $4.99 prime rib specials strategically positioned to entice people, hoping that if they indulged on one thing it would lead to others and eventually land them at the tables. She didn't need any help there. She knew that route just fine.

The female rawmixologist with a fifties poodle-cut and a tattoo of Betty Boop on one arm and a naked Brigitte Bardot covering her body with a guitar on the other rang in Crystal's order. "Holy Grail of Greens, yeah?"

Crystal smiled. "I'm so predictable, right?" She placed a ten on the bar, waved off any change and slid down the counter to collect her drink.

The other tenants of the building included a gourmet doughnut shop, a contemporary American restaurant, a flower shop, a tattoo parlor, and a sushi bar. All were connected on the inside by a central landscaped courtyard with fire pits and other communal areas to encourage intermingling of the guests. This was the new old Vegas. While the sign outside still displayed John E. Carson Hotel, with such an eclectic mix of tenants and communal aspirations, it might as well be flashing "Hipster Hang" in neon.

A group of people spilled in from the hallway leading to the courtyard. Based on their clothes and overheated state, Crystal guessed the hot yoga class in the studio upstairs had just finished. She pulled her hat low and drifted toward the wall. For someone who used to audition in front of total strangers critiquing every move, and who now stripped for a living, she had become extremely shy and antisocial, almost as if taking off her clothes had added layers between her and the outside world rather than peeling them away. It wasn't that she knew a lot of people or was trying to avoid anyone in particular. She just didn't like people too much in general anymore. They always seemed to disappoint her. It was a pretty simple equation. The less interaction there was, the less chance to let her down.

By moving into the Siegel Suites, she had reduced her world to about thirteen blocks: the five south of Charleston to OGs, and eight north to the El Cortez. All in all, her life stretched across a total of about a mile and a half. Everything she needed was in between. She rarely had to or wanted to venture outside this urban cocoon she had created to protect herself or, probably more accurately, imprison herself. Outside of her time playing blackjack at the El Cortez, picking up a to-go order somewhere, or dancing in the club, she really didn't interact with anyone, and she was completely fine with that.

Waiting for her juice amid the wailing blenders, she felt eyes on her, scanning up and down. She moved closer toward the wall. Her gaze remained fixed on the floor. No eye contact was one of the first rules of remaining anonymous, she had learned.

A woman's voice mixed with the yowl of the juicer. "Didn't we play blackjack together the other night?"

Crystal held her position and pretended not to hear, skimming her hand across the blades of wheatgrass in a pot on the counter.

The woman followed her voice, stopping right next to Crystal. "Hey there. I think we played blackjack together the other night."

Crystal realized she couldn't avoid the woman any longer. She glanced at the person making her juice, who was still adding ingredients to the blender. It would be a few more minutes before she could snag her drink and escape. Crystal looked over at the woman. It was Nip-Tuck Barbie. Crystal released a reluctant smile. "I'm sorry, were you talking to me?"

"Sure was. I recognized your hat. We played blackjack together at the El Cortez. Remember there was that drama with that midget splitting tens. He thought he knew you. I think he said your name was Faith." She held out her hand. "I'm Penny."

Crystal reluctantly reciprocated the handshake. "Actually, my name's Crystal."

"Boy, he wasn't even close," Penny said.

"No, he was right. Faith is my stage name." She eyed the person snapping the lid on her juice, ready to make a quick getaway. Unfortunately Penny was directly in her path. There was no easy egress without going through her, and Penny didn't seem willing to relent.

"I know that game, honey. I hated using my real name on air. Too many weirdos out there." Penny apparently noticed her sweaty, disheveled appearance in the plexiglass counterguard. She took the hairband out of her limp ponytail, pulled her hair tight, and refastened the band. "Geez, I look a fright. I love the hot yoga class upstairs, but I wish I could shower after." She studied her reflection, tucking a few stray strands behind her ears. "Ugh, what a mess."

Crystal smiled and made a move for her juice, which was finished and waiting on the edge of the counter, unfortunately right next to Penny's. When Crystal grabbed hers, Penny picked up the one for her and walked alongside Crystal toward the door.

Penny said, "What are you doing now? Want to go for a walk?" Penny must've sensed Crystal's answer was going to be no, because she never gave her a chance to respond. Penny just kept talking. "Sorry to be so forward. You're probably like, 'Why is this scary girl stalking me?' The truth is I'm pretty new to Vegas and don't know a lot of people." Penny opened the door for Crystal. "So how 'bout it? I was going to walk over to the Container Park and check it out."

Crystal reached for her bike. "Sorry, I rode here."

"Bring it along," Penny said, putting a hand on the opposite side of the handlebar. "Friends don't let friends juice and ride."

Crystal was used to dealing with pushy people—mostly men, of course. She could've instantly shut Penny down if she wanted to. She thought for a moment, looking at Penny's hand on her bike. "You're not really giving me much of a choice, are you?"

Penny said, "Come on, it's only a few blocks. What can it hurt?"

"OK, but I'm really not much of a conversationalist." She walked on the opposite side of the bike, mirroring Penny, her right hand resting on the handlebar, left hand on the juice, the bike a protective barrier in the middle. She felt safe with the bike between them, like at any time she could just hop on and ride away if she felt uncomfortable. After all, it wasn't like there was any real physical danger from Penny. She knew, if it came to that, she could easily take Penny, treating those surgically enhanced lips and breasts like speed bags. Her main reservation was that she just didn't trust Penny. People in Vegas weren't this friendly unless they wanted something. The question was, what exactly did Penny want?

They walked down Sixth Street in silence, the awkwardness mounting with each step. At Fremont they turned right, across from the El Cortez. Penny took a long pull from her juice. "I probably wouldn't have to be such a freak about my health if I didn't drink so much. I spend all this time and money on yoga, skin care, and organic juices, then wash it all away with vodka." She released an uncomfortable laugh.

Crystal wished she could just stop at vodka. She said, "Whatever gets you through the day, right?"

Penny motioned toward the El Cortez. "That was a crazy night, huh? Is that guy always such a dick?"

"Pretty much," Crystal said. "He acts like the world owes him something for making him short."

"From what I hear, he's doing pretty well. More like he owes the world. Did you and your girlfriend really take him for five grand?"

Still unsure how open she was willing to be, Crystal hesitated, considering the question as they crossed Seventh Street toward the entrance to the Downtown Container Park, an outdoor shopping, dining, and entertainment center made from pseudo–shipping containers stacked on top of each other with a children's playground in the center. At the entrance a thirty-five-foot green, metallic praying mantis transplanted from Burning Man blasted smoke and fire, startling both of them.

Crystal said, "We didn't take anything from that asshole that night. These fucking guys want to come into a place with naked women willing to rub up against them, have unlimited access to alcohol and whatever else they want, the option to go to a private room to do whatever they choose, and then vehemently object and play the victim when they lose their heads. Fuck that. They get exactly what they deserve. If they lose control, that's on them."

Penny, apparently sensing she struck a nerve, backed off. She looked around at the three levels of stacked containers. "Well, this is an interesting place." They strolled along the edge of the playground. Children screamed, twisting down the thirty-foot slide. "Where do you think all these kids come from? I didn't realize so many families were living downtown."

"They don't. They drive in from surrounding areas on a safari to witness us weirdos in our natural habitat." She pointed at a table next to the playground. "Want to sit down?"

Penny bristled, looking at the children. "Let's get out of the splash zone. I'm not that into kids." She angled toward the table farthest away from the playground on the edge of the lawn in front of the stage where live bands play on the weekends. Crystal rested her bike in the grass and joined Penny at the table. "You from Vegas?" Penny asked.

"God, no," Crystal said. "Is anyone? I moved here from LA to launch a show at the Wynn."

Penny continued her seemingly unending stream of questions, firing one after another. "What happened?" "Why'd you stop performing?" "How'd you end up stripping?"

Crystal went through the whole story, or at least as much as anyone would with someone whom she had just met. With each question, Crystal became more uncomfortable, squirming in her seat, breaking eye contact for longer periods of time, distracted by the slightest activity around them. She told Penny how the show she had moved for closed before it even opened due to financing issues, and she was never able to get another decent theater job, so she started dancing to pay the bills and just never stopped. She left out all the negative stuff: how her mom died so she had nothing to go back to in LA, how she got hooked on cocaine and Roxies just to get through the day, and how she blew through all her savings and lost her condo and car gambling and partying. She knew her life was depressing. She didn't need to bring others down as well, and she didn't need to remind herself of the mistakes she made. There was another level of acceptance in saying the whole thing all at once and out loud. She was OK with just sharing the causes. They were out of her control. It was the effects, the things she could change, that she didn't like to acknowledge.

"I'm sorry for all the questions," Penny said. "Old habits are hard to break." She paused, expecting Crystal to ask a follow-up question, but Crystal didn't bite. Penny continued the one-sided conversation, offering information about herself. "I used to be a reporter. Sometimes I forget I'm not anymore and snap back into work mode." Penny hesitated again, waiting for Crystal to speak. Penny shook her head. "Boy, you really aren't very good at this, are you?"

The direct question pulled Crystal's gaze from the playground back to Penny. She said, "I'm sorry. I don't mean to be rude. I told you I'm conversationally challenged. People always seem more than willing to talk about themselves and share on their own."

"But that's the story they want you to hear, the one they tell themselves." Penny drained the last of her juice, slurping as she moved the straw along the bottom, sucking up every last particle.

Crystal said, "So you think I'm lying?"

"Not at all. I'm sure what you told me is true. It's what you left out that makes a good story. Let's take me, for example. I can tell you that I used to be a TV sports reporter in St. Louis and married to a professional hockey player, that I got divorced because he didn't support me and moved to Las Vegas for a new job and a fresh start. It sounds very healthy and positive. While all of it is true, there is so much more to the story."

Crystal still didn't bite. She had had enough for the day. "You're probably right," she said, agreeing so that there was nothing more to talk about. She stood up and walked toward her bike. "Thanks for the chat. I should probably get going. Have to work later."

Penny didn't seem offended by the abrupt exit, as if she were used to people recoiling from her incessant inquiries. Crystal really didn't care if she was. She thought she was doing great just being there. It was the longest sober conversation she had had with anyone in as long as she could remember.

Dow Jones Close: 15,928.56

Chapter Eight

Date: Thursday, May 2, 1996

Dow Jones Open: 5,574.86

Darlene greeted Bill at the door with a kiss. Her slight build forced him to bend down significantly since she only came up to his chest. They walked back into the house together. He rested his hand on her shoulder, twirling the strands of her short, auburn hair that covered the nape of her neck. Regardless of the day at work he might have had, she always started off the second part of his day—the most important part—on a positive note. It always gave him something to look forward to on his way home. Bill knew plenty of his coworkers' wives jumped all over their husbands the instant they set foot in the door. The only thing ever resulting from that was their husbands quit coming directly home and stopped off at the pub first.

Immediately after the kiss, Darlene exchanged the beer and newspaper in her hand for his gun belt and locked it in the safe next to their bed. Their son Hughie was eighteen and, at six foot four, more of a Hugh than a Hughie, so the gun really didn't need to be locked up anymore, but just like their son would always be Hughie, the gun would always be safely put away when Bill was home. He suspected it also served as a sigh of relief when she shut and locked the safe. It meant they had made it through another day and were one day closer to when she wouldn't have to worry whether or not Bill would make it home safe and sound. That was what most things with Darlene were about—feeling secure.

Bill finished his beer and made it through the sports section undisturbed. Wanting another one, he got up and lumbered to the kitchen. He walked in as Darlene was lowering a bottle from her lips. "Aha! Caught you red-handed. That's one way to get me to drink less." He kissed her on the cheek. Her face was blank. He felt her body tighten. "Hey, hey, hey. I'm only joking. Have as much as you want."

"No, it's not that," Darlene said. "There's something I need to tell you."

Bill led her by the hand to the table. "Of course. Come on. Let's sit down."

Tears trickled down her face. "I wasn't snooping. I promise. I was just doing laundry. Had a load of darks to top off. I swear."

"Shhh, shhh, shhh. It's OK." Bill rubbed her back. "Just slow down and start at the beginning."

"Like I said, I was doing a laundry sweep and needed darks, so I went into Hughie's room. His duffel bag was lying open on the floor next to the bed. I could see jeans and a sweatshirt inside. I emptied out the duffel bag onto the bed." The tears gave way to sobbing. "I don't know. Maybe it's not his."

"It's OK, Darlene. Just tell me what you found." Bill's first thought was that she had found some pornography or maybe condoms. Something no mother wanted to find and be forced to face that her baby boy was growing up. She had always coddled Hughie too much anyway in Bill's opinion. He said, "Hughie's eighteen now. He'll be in college next year. We have to let him go and be his own man."

Darlene rubbed her eyes. "But this is bad. I don't know how this happened."

Bill became concerned. He stood from the table. The compassion disappeared from his voice. Only the hard edges remained. "Show me what you found."

Darlene remained at the table. It was as if, now on the threshold of the moment, she wanted to delay the outcome as long as possible, or maybe even take back everything she had said.

Bill charged off toward Hughie's room. "Forget it. I'll find it myself."

Darlene trailed after him. "Now we don't know for sure it's his. Let's not jump to any conclusions."

Bill barreled into Hughie's room. He snatched the duffel bag off the floor and rummaged through the inside. All movement stopped. His gaze locked onto one object. He tossed the duffel bag on the floor. In his hand remained a gallon freezer bag with a small digital scale, what looked to be several ounces of marijuana, and a bag of ten to fifteen grams of white powder.

Darlene stood in the doorway. "Maybe it's not his."

"I can't believe he would bring this into our house." Bill removed the white powder and held it up to the light, flicking the bag several times to check the consistency. He opened the bag and smelled the contents. "I don't think it's coke. Seems to be MDMA. The guys at the station will have to test it."

Darlene walked over and put her arm around him. "Come on, we don't have to involve them."

"Darlene, I'm a police officer. I can't pick and choose which laws to enforce."

"But you're a father first," Darlene said. "Can't you for once put your family before the job?"

"Why do you think I go to that job and risk my life every day? To provide for this family, to send him to college." Bill stood, dropped the bag of powder into the freezer bag, and tightened the seal. "If it got out that I covered up a crime like this, I could get suspended or maybe even lose my job and my pension. Is that what you want?"

The tears returned. "Of course not. At least let's wait and hear what he has to say."

"Call him. Now. Tell him to get his ass home immediately." Bill tucked the freezer bag under his arm and marched out of the room.

Thirty minutes later Hughie walked through the door. Bill and Darlene were sitting at the table, the freezer bag of drugs between them.

"What's so urgent?" Hughie's eyes darted to the bag. "What were you doing in my room going through my stuff?"

Darlene rushed over and threw her arms around Hughie, looking like she wanted to protect him more than to comfort him. She said, "I'm sorry. I didn't mean to. I was just doing laundry."

"Have a seat." Bill stood and paced into the kitchen, unsure if he could be so close and control himself. "So you admit it's yours?"

"It's not a big deal. Just some weed and Molly." Hughie sat down. "Me and a few friends went in together. It's for a party down at the shore this weekend."

"Not a big deal?" Bill's voice boomed. "You bring drugs and a scale into a police officer's home and think it's not a big deal?"

Hughie scowled. "Of course this is about you. You're not really concerned about me. Just what it might do to the reputation of the great Bill Price."

Bill stormed over to Hughie and lifted him out of the chair, pinning him against the wall. Their stares locked. Both knew Hughie could break away if he wanted to.

Darlene shrieked. "Stop it before someone gets hurt."

Bill released Hughie and stepped back. "Do you realize that with those amounts and a scale, you could get hit with intent to distribute and face five to ten years?"

Hughie said, "Relax. I'm not a drug dealer. I told you, it's just for a party. Why do you have to assume the worst?"

Bill plucked the bag off the table and shook it in his son's face. "You think I'm making a big deal out of this? You want to see how serious this is?" He seized Hughie by the arm and pushed him toward the door. "You have the right to remain silent. Anything you say can and will be used against you in a court of law. You—"

Darlene chased after them. "Bill, what are you doing? You're arresting him? This is a family matter."

Bill stopped in the driveway and turned back toward Darlene. "If he thinks I'm blowing this out of proportion, he can hear it from others down at the station." He pushed Hughie up against the car and opened the back door. "You have the right to an attorney. If you cannot afford an attorney, one will be provided for you at the public's expense. You can decide at any time to exercise these rights and not answer any questions or make any statements. Do you understand each of these rights that I have explained to you?"

"Unbelievable," Hughie said. "Actually, you know what? It's totally believable. This is so typical of you. Everything else always comes before us."

Bill forced Hughie into the back of the squad car. "I'll take that as a yes."

At the police station, Bill locked Hughie in the holding cell with the other offenders awaiting processing. He had never planned for it to go this far. He thought he would just threaten Hughie and that would be enough, but when Hughie was defiant, Bill escalated his actions. The more Hughie pushed back, the more Bill felt he needed to send a message. As he had the drugs measured and verified, he knew everything was spiraling out of control, but it was too late to pull back. He convinced himself it was for Hughie's own good.

When it was time to question Hughie, Bill requested another on-duty officer do it, along with one of the public defenders to advise Hughie. Bill just watched through the glass in the next room. Hughie's defiance had transformed to disinterest, staring off into space. The officer explained the fifty-six grams of marijuana was a fourth-degree offense, punishable with up to eighteen months in jail. He went on to advise that because MDMA was a schedule I drug and the amount, at fifteen grams, was between a half ounce and fifty grams, Hughie could face between five and ten years in prison.

Hughie looked at the glass to where he thought Bill was standing on the other side. "OK, I get it. You made your point."

Hughie's lawyer put his hand on his arm. "It's best if you don't say anything." He looked at the officer. "Could you leave us for a moment so I can confer with my client in private?"

Bill met the officer in the hall.

The officer said, "How far you want us to take this, Bill?"

"If he wants to play these games, treat him like any other criminal." Bill was strong on the outside, but twisted up inside. He really didn't know what to do, so he just followed protocol.

"I'm no lawyer," the officer said, "but you know how these things go. Technically, the drugs were not found in his possession."

"They were in his bag in his room," Bill said.

"In your house," the officer said. "I'm just saying, there's a lot of gray area here. He got the message. Let's just keep the drugs and call it a day."

No matter how much Bill wanted to, he wouldn't back down. He couldn't. He knew a lot was at risk, but he felt it would be much worse if he let Hughie slide. "Charge him for possession," he said. "Let the prosecutor decide what to do."

Bill left the station alone that night, at least content to let Hughie sit there all night and think about the looming consequences. But when Bill came home by himself, Darlene was as angry as Bill had ever seen her. They didn't fight often. Matter of fact, he couldn't even remember the last time they had even argued, but he never forgot this fight, and it only got worse when she returned home after bailing out Hughie.

Bill was reclined in his chair watching TV when Hughie barreled through the door and marched straight to his room. Bill didn't say a word.

Darlene came in next. Her eyes were red from all the crying. Her voice cracked. "Are you just going to sit there and let him do this?"

Bill's tone was flat, barely audible over the TV. "Do what?"

Darlene grabbed the remote and muted the sound. "He's leaving. I hope you're happy." She tore off to Hughie's room.

Bill could hear them talking, but couldn't make out what was being said. He pushed out of the chair and plodded to Hughie's room. Standing in the doorway, he watched Hughie stuffing clothes into the duffel bag. Bill said, "At least you figured out the proper use for that bag."

Hughie stopped packing just long enough to scowl in Bill's direction. "Well, it's not really any of your concern anymore. I'm leaving."

Darlene said, "Will you both just stop being so stubborn? Let's sit down and talk and figure out a solution."

Hughie peeled off his comforter and folded it into a rectangle. "It's too late for that."

"And where exactly will you go?" Bill asked.

"Anywhere I want," Hughie said. "I'm eighteen."

All Bill could think about was the time Hughie threatened to run away when he was seven because they wouldn't buy him a new bike. Back then Bill had helped him pack, and Darlene even prepared Hughie a lunch to take along. After Hughie left, he circled the block the block a few times, and came home. Bill was sure it would be the same this time. "Well, as long as you have a plan." Bill turned and retreated to his and Darlene's room. He was done with the foolishness.

Dow Jones Close: 5,498.27

Chapter Nine

Date: Wednesday, February 19, 2014

Dow Jones Open: 16,126.23

"**W**hat's that smell?" Penny asked, staring at her two fours against my five. "I mean, I've been trying to place it since my first time here. I know part of it is menthol cigarettes, but I can't quite nail down the rest." She drained her vodka and water, shaking the ice at the nearby waitress to signal she wanted another.

Penny was the hardest one of the five for me to figure out. Most people play blackjack for one of three things: money, challenge, or belonging. She never seemed to care about how much she won or lost, so financial gain wasn't a priority. She was slowly learning the game, but to be honest, she also seemed perfectly happy just to follow what others told her, so I didn't think she was in it for the thrill or strategy. That left belonging. But she didn't seem lonely. To be blunt, she was a drop-dead knockout. She could have gone anywhere she wanted and had men falling over themselves to hang out with her. On top of it all, her personality seemed pretty solid. She could talk to anyone about anything and was good at getting others to talk about themselves. Of course, she had the fake boobs and puffy lips, but, who with any bit of money didn't have some plastic surgery? I mean, was it even a red flag anymore? My go-to strategy in deciphering a person's code was to find the cracks. Everyone had them. Just some were better at hiding them. And so far, I hadn't been able to see hers…yet.

"It's old people—combination of cheap perfume and unchanged diapers," the twenty-five-year-old kid from Dallas sitting at third base said. He wore a ten-gallon hat and had the typical Texas drawl and boundless confidence to match. He motioned to Penny's two fours, rubbing the couple days of stubble on his chin. "What's your play, darlin'?"

I offered my advice. "The pair of fours is one of the most misplayed hands in blackjack because the play changes according to the rules of the game. If you can double off the split, you should against a five or six. If you can't, just hit, except in single-deck. Then you double."

"I guess I'll split then." Penny pushed two red chips into the center. She inhaled another deep breath through her nose. "This smell is driving me crazy. Worse yet, when I go home, it's in my hair, and it's all I can smell." The waitress brought her a fresh drink. Penny smiled, offering a glimpse of her perfect teeth, or rather veneers. The waitress hesitated, subtly shaking her serving tray speckled with chips and cash from tips. Penny gulped her drink and focused back on the table. The waitress sneered and walked away. She wouldn't be back for a while.

For the first four in front of Penny, I dealt her a seven of hearts. "Eleven," I said. "Now you want to double."

"The prettiest horse ain't necessarily the best to ride," Dallas said, sitting on a nineteen. "You're probably taking all his bust cards."

Penny ignored his warning and slid over two more red.

I flipped a king. "Twenty-one."

"Whoop whoop!" Penny stood from her chair and thrust her arms above her head in triumph. Dallas looked directly at her chest. She noticed his southward gaze. "Come on, cowboy, eyes up here and get up out of your chair. We have to do the twenty-one dance." With her arms still above her head, she waved them side to side and rotated in a circle. "Every twenty-one, we got to do a dance." The four vodkas were obviously kicking in. The filter on her voice and movements was disintegrating.

"You don't need a twenty-one to dance, baby," Dallas said. "You can shake it on a twelve for all I care."

I turned over the next card—a ten—for the other four. "Fourteen."

Penny frowned and slumped back into her chair. "Boo! That's not very good. I hate fourteens. I lost something important when I was fourteen." She covered her mouth. "Oopsie. TMI, Penny." She slugged more of her drink. "I should probably hit again, right?"

"Not against my five," I said. "Remember, always assume the down card is a ten. I probably have fifteen and should bust roughly forty percent of the time."

Penny waved her hand over the fourteen. "I'll stay then."

Dallas stood on his nineteen.

I flipped over my down card, a nine of diamonds. "Fourteen."

"Stupid fourteens," Penny said.

Next card was a six of spades. "Twenty," I said, collecting the green chip from Dallas.

"Story of my life. All smoke, no fire." he said. "We both would've won if you just would've doubled."

"The book says to split." I said, collecting the money from Penny's losing fourteen hand and paying her four red for the successful double. "You made ten dollars."

Dallas said, "The book. Shiiiiit. I bet the casino wrote that damn book."

"Did I do it right?" Penny asked. "Cuz you gotta tell me if I make a mistake." She leaned on the table and motioned Dallas over with her finger. "Come here. Want to know a little secret?" Dallas moved toward her. She said, "Don't tell anyone, but I don't know what I'm doing." She laughed loudly and shushed herself. "Sssshhhh! And I'm a little drunk." She sat back in her chair, giggling.

Dallas shook his head. "You did just fine, li'l lady." He evaluated his chip count. He was up about three hundred fifty. "If yer riding ahead of the herd, you can't be surprised if a bull sticks you in the rear from time to time."

"Carpet deodorizer," Penny exclaimed. "The other smell is carpet deodorizer. Menthol cigarettes, cheap perfume, and carpet deodorizer." She clapped her hands together repeatedly, more excited by her discovery than her win.

I dealt another hand. A blackjack—ace of clubs and queen of diamonds—for Penny and a sixteen for Dallas.

"Whoop, whoop!" Penny yelped and rose from the chair to do her dance. Despite his sixteen, Dallas joined her, becoming more interested in Penny than the cards.

Penny was officially loose. Now I'm not one to judge or discourage someone from having a good time, but I always get concerned when I see the Jekyll and Hyde, the 180-degree personality shifts when alcohol is added. Previously Penny had always kept things on the surface or gotten people to talk about themselves. Now she was center stage, swinging from the rafters.

I tried to ease her back with some conversation. "What do you do for work?"

Penny blinked a few times and smiled, taking another drink. "I'm not working right now."

Dallas said, "Well, what brought you to these parts?"

"A new job," Penny said.

Dallas and I exchanged confused looks. He said, "Hang on a sec. I know I'm from Texas, and we take life a little slower there, but didn't you just say you don't have a job?"

Penny sat up straight in her chair. "I said I wasn't working," She seemed annoyed that we weren't following her. "I have a job, silly. I just haven't started yet."

"Well, what is it?" Dallas looked at me. "Typical woman—speaks in riddles and expects you to understand."

Penny said, "I'm a TV reporter. I just don't start for a few months. I moved here early to get settled."

"Why don't we cash these in and grab some chow. You can tell me all about it." Dallas pushed his chips to the center of the table. "Like my granddad used to say, don't be at the table when you should be at the chuck wagon."

Penny squinted, scanning him up and down. "How old are you?"

"Old enough," Dallas said. "How old are you?"

"Older." She slammed the rest of her drink and picked up the sixty dollars in chips she had left. "Let's go, cowboy."

Now, I'm not sure if they ever did get anything to eat or not. I heard from my coworker Birdie that they paid him a visit at the Parlour Bar. He said they sat in front of him, drinking and carrying on until about eleven, then left together leaning on each other and heading toward the elevators. I didn't see Penny for a few days after that.

Dow Jones Close: 16,040.56

Chapter Ten

Date: Tuesday, October 23, 2012

Dow Jones Open: 13,344.90

Father Bennett sat across from Les at the rectangular conference table in Father Bennett's office. As senior priest, he had the additional space and area to accommodate meetings of this size, but Bishop Pence had also directed Father Bennett to mediate the allegations.

Father Bennett had come to Les's office a few weeks earlier. He said, "Father Banks, do you have a minute?"

"Absolutely, Father." Les scribbled a few more words on a yellow legal pad and closed the Bible on his desk. "Just making some notes for this weekend's homily. Please have a seat."

Father Bennett eased into one of the two chairs facing the desk. He removed his round, rimless eyeglasses and slid them into the pocket of his black blazer. Concern tightened his usually soft face. Smoothing his short gray hair, he said, "Some alarming news has been brought to my attention." He folded his hands in his lap. "I received calls from the parents of Lucas Silverton and Malcolm Vaughn."

Les leaned forward onto the desk. "I've been meaning to come talk to you about them. We had a bit of an incident after mass on Sunday."

"It sounds like you did," Father Bennett said. "The parents are quite upset and are threatening to go to the press if we don't take immediate action."

"The press?" Les asked, confused. "Why would they care? I talked to the boys. They were contrite and open to punishment. I thought we had agreed to keep it between us, but I guess the guilt got the best of them."

It was Father Bennett's turn to be confused. He shifted in the chair, tilting his head, searching for the meaning behind the words. "Wait a second. Why don't you tell me your side of what happened?"

Les walked out from behind the desk and sat in the chair next to Father Bennett. "I left the boys to close up after mass and returned to the rectory to get ready to leave for the Riveras' for dinner and to bless their new house. My holy water container was almost empty, so I went back to the sacristy to top it off." He hesitated, contemplating the best way to describe what he had seen. Father Bennett encouraged him to continue. Les said, "I heard the boys in the servers' room. They had gotten into the wine and seemed quite inebriated. They were stripped down to their underwear—well, Lucas was. Malcolm had his underwear around his ankles, and Lucas was kneeling between Malcolm's legs." Les didn't say any more. He didn't have to. The imagery conveyed enough for Father Bennett to understand what was going on.

Father Bennett rubbed his forehead and down the length of his face. "What did you say? What happened when they saw you?"

"Well they stopped immediately, of course," Les said. "They were both quite embarrassed and ashamed. I told them to get dressed and waited for them in the sacristy. I didn't think we needed to involve the parents and could just handle it through counseling and some additional work chores for the abuse of the wine. What do the parents think happened?"

Father Bennett closed his eyes and shook his head back and forth. He looked back at Les. "Well, according to Malcolm and Lucas, they were changing in the servers' room, and you came in and said you needed help finishing the wine. You then poured them each a cup and made them drink it. Afterward you had them take off their underwear and touch each other while you did the same to yourself."

Les leaned forward in his chair, both elbows resting on his knees. "Father, I can assure you that did not happen. You have known me since my Xavier days in New Orleans." Les had met Father Bennett at a conference at Louisiana's Institute for Black Catholic Studies, the main center for educating ministers for the black Catholic community. Les was still a student then, and Father Bennett was a guest lecturer. Les said, "You know I have always held myself to the highest of standards. I have never once given wine to an underage person and would never engage in such behavior."

Father Bennett raised his hand, lowering it slowly to encourage Les to relax. "That's what I told the parents and why I came immediately to talk to you."

Les recognized his aggressive posture and eased back into the chair. "What did the parents say when you challenged the story?"

"They backed their sons, of course," Father Bennett said. "Wondered why the boys would make up such a story if it wasn't true."

Les's agitation returned. "Well, it's obvious why. The boys were afraid I would go to their parents, so they decided to accuse me first."

"Here's what I suggest we do," Father Bennett said. "Let's all sit down in a room together and hopefully the boys will admit what really happened."

"What if they don't relent?" Les said. "What if they stick to the lie?"

Father Bennett rose from the chair and walked toward the door. "We'll deal with that when it happens. In the meantime, I'll inform the bishop, to get his input." He stopped in the doorway and faced Les. His eyes sagged, somewhat from stress but mostly with sadness. "I think it goes without saying that this couldn't come at a worse time. With the shifting demographics of the community, your ethnicity, and the boys' different ethnicities, this could get to be a real mess."

To call it a potential problem was an understatement. The congregation had always been diverse, since the county was a landing spot for refugees new to the country. But in the past ten years, the needle had moved even more dramatically. What was originally 20 percent of the population, made up of roughly four hundred families from a scattering of Caribbean islands, Latin America, and African countries had grown to 65 percent, with over thirteen hundred families representing over sixty countries. And not everyone in the community was happy about the rapidly changing demographics. There had been several racial-fueled flare-ups, and the tension was spilling over into the church. An accusation like this could further divide the congregation or, even worse, set off a chain of violence similar to other communities, when color became the issue more than what had actually transpired.

After Father Bennett left, Les reclined back in his chair staring at the ceiling, numb. The feeling itself wasn't new because most days as of late he felt detached, like he was drifting and just going through the motions. In that moment, though, the source of his stupor was shock and disbelief. He hadn't seen this coming at all. He had wanted more connection to the parishioners. At that moment he felt further away from ever.

Now seated across from Father Bennett in his office awaiting the Vaughns and Silvertons, he didn't know what to feel. Anger nipped at the edges of his usual compassionate countenance. He searched for meaning in the betrayal he felt from the boys. He understood their actions. He just couldn't understand why it was happening to him.

Sister Vera brought in a pitcher of water and glasses and placed them in the middle of the table.

"Thank you, Sister," Father Bennett said, waiting for her exit to continue the meeting. "Father Banks, after more thought I just don't think it's wise for you to be in the room for the initial meeting. Your presence may escalate the emotions and make the parents more aggressive."

But in Les's mind, there was no way he was not going to be in the room. He needed to sit face to face and hear the lie from their lips. He said, "With all due respect, Father," Les said. "I believe it will be much more difficult for the boys to perpetuate the lies with me in the room."

"It also might create friction and cause the parents to be more rigid in front of each other and more protective and defensive of their own children." Father Bennett stood and poured them each a glass of water. "But I understand why you would want to be here and be your own advocate."

Sister Vera returned with the Vaughns and the Silvertons. Lucas Silverton and his mother were seated to the right of Father Bennett and the left of Les, and Malcolm Vaughn sat between his mother and father on the other side. Both boys stared at the floor. Even though Father Bennett knew everyone in the room, he made the introductions. He said, "I appreciate your coming in to discuss this matter. I have talked to each of you individually, but I think it's important that before we take any action, we have all the facts."

Lucas was shaking his leg, causing the whole table to vibrate. Ms. Silverton reached over and put her hand on his thigh, rubbing it gently. There was no Mr. Silverton, or maybe there was. He just wasn't in the picture anymore. He had split when Lucas was two. Ms. Silverton hadn't heard from him since. The ten years as a single mother were visible in the lines on her face but not in her affection for Lucas. She said, "I really don't understand what there is to discuss. We told you what happened."

"Well, that's just it," Father Bennett said, "We have a discrepancy in the accounts. As you know, Father Banks performed mass that day. He was scheduled to go to the Riveras' for dinner, so he left the boys to clean up after. Before departing for the Riveras', Father Banks went back to the sacristy to refill his holy water for the blessing at the Riveras'. He didn't see the boys, so he had assumed they had finished and left. While filling the bottle, he heard noise in the servers' room. Upon investigating, he discovered the boys had gotten into the church wine and were engaged in sexual activity."

"With who?" Mrs. Vaughn said, leaning forward, ready to leap from her chair.

Father Bennett hesitated, knowing he needed to choose his words with care. "Well, with each other."

"With each other?" Mr. Vaughn gasped. "What does that mean?"

"I don't think we need to go into the details of what they were doing," Les said.

"Is this true?" Mrs. Vaughn glared at Malcolm. His eyes remained fixed on the floor. She grabbed his chin and directed his face toward her. "Look at me, boy, when I'm talking to you. Have you been lying to me?" Malcolm's eyes darted toward Lucas. She shook his chin. "Don't look to him. Tell me what happened."

Malcolm's voice cracked as he spoke. "I'm not lying, Mama."

Hearing Malcolm's words, the numbness returned to Les. But this time it had transformed to powerlessness. He knew he could dispute the allegations, but it wouldn't do any good. If the boys were going to stick to their story, the accusations alone would be damaging to him and the Church. In that moment he knew his only course of action was to leave, not just the parish, but the Church. He wasn't sure if his resignation to the consequences was just a further evolution of the debilitating dullness he had been feeling, but for the first time in a long while he opened up to the possibility of a new path.

Taking back control of the meeting, Father Bennett addressed Malcolm and Lucas directly. "Boys, I hope you understand the severity of this situation. What you have accused Father Banks of will hurt a lot of people and the Church. Are you sure what you say happened really happened?"

Both boys returned their eyes to the floor and sunk into their chairs.

Mr. Vaughn stood up. "Is that what this meeting is? An ambush? You trying to pressure the boys into changing their story?" He pointed at Les. "This man violated the trust this parish has placed in him and needs to be punished. Against my better judgment, we came to you first to provide the opportunity to deal with it and not cause the Church any embarrassment."

Father Bennett said, "And we appre—"

Mr. Vaughn had obviously heard enough. He stood and banged his fist on the table. "Now we know that's not going to happen, we'll be going to the police and file charges." He pulled Malcolm's chair back. "Let's go." Malcolm and Mrs. Vaughn followed him out of the room.

Ms. Silverton put her arm around Lucas. "Father, Lord knows my boy ain't perfect, and I haven't been the best mother, but he ain't ever lied to me." She stood and took Lucas by the hand. "I don't want to cause no fuss by going to the police, but we can no longer come here as long as Father Banks is here. I trust you to do the right thing." Ms. Silverton slid her arm down to Lucas' hand and stood, leading him out of the room.

Silence filled the room. Father Bennett and Les just looked at each other. Father Bennett had a look of apology and bewilderment about what the next step was. The blank look on Les's face was one of eerie contentment. He was not ready to reveal his next move, but he was at peace with it.

Dow Jones Close: 13,102.53

Chapter Eleven

Date: Friday, November 22, 2013

Dow Jones Open: 16,008.71

The valet plucked the ticket from Max's hand. "It'll be just a minute, Mr. Doler. We kept it close for you."

Max nodded and tilted his head back, wincing in the glow of the showering neon. He hated the strip, but it was a necessary evil for business. Downtown was coming back, but not quite there for the power dinner when he needed to close a deal. And business visitors didn't come to town to be carted off the strip. Maybe after a few trips, after they got tired of the gambling, celebrity chef restaurants, and brand-name shopping, the strip properties packaged into homogenized uniqueness. That's why he always chose Joe's Seafood & Steak at the Forum Shops for his business dinners. It was center strip, so easy for visitors to find, and since it was in the Forum Shops and not in the casino, there was a separate valet. He could zip in and out without having to set foot inside the casino. He loved to gamble, just not inside the shopping malls most of the strip casinos had become.

The valet pulled up in Max's bronze Maserati Quattroporte. He exited the car, holding the door open and extending the key fob to Max. "Have a good evening, Mr. Doler."

Max handed the valet the ticket with a ten-dollar bill. He slid behind the wheel and revved the turbo V6 engine, rumbling the twin oval tailpipes. Inside, the cool air blasting from the vents was a welcome change from the hot evening breeze blowing outside. Max emptied his lungs in relief, sinking into the body-hugging seat. The deal with McDonald's was done. Their initial order was for $4.5 million Lapkins at $1.50 each by the following June 30, and another million due for each of the following three months. That was an initial payment of $6.225 million and another $4.5 million over the next three. He had produced a total of ten million in three years. He had seven months. His production cost was two dollars in the downtown factory. For his typical orders in which he packaged four together for $9.99, his profit came from the shipping charges. Without that, he would have to figure out a way to trim at least another seventy-five cents off the per unit cost. He could always outsource overseas, but he liked having the operation local to keep an eye on everything.

As Max contemplated each challenge, he pressed the modified accelerator deeper toward the floor. He needed to go fast. The Stratosphere loomed in the near distance. Weaving in and out of the Las Vegas Boulevard traffic, he imagined each passed car would bring him closer to answering the questions flooding his mind. He had been working so long and hard on this deal that he hadn't considered what he would do if he actually got it. Anytime someone would bring up a risk or issue, he said, "That'll be a good opportunity to have." Now, on the other side of it, he wasn't ready to deal with those problems. There would be plenty of time for that tomorrow. For now, he knew only two things for sure: after all the alcohol at dinner, he shouldn't be driving, and he wasn't ready to go home yet. Fortunately, or maybe unfortunately, in Vegas, as long you have a pocket full of cash, there are always people willing to hang out with you.

He zoomed past the Stratosphere, glancing up at the top through the moon roof. The red flashing OG sign winked ahead. "I'll just go in for a drink and a quick drive-by motorboat," he said aloud, like voicing his plan gave it more credibility and legitimacy. He angled into the parking lot and sped past the valet. He didn't see the point in valeting at OG when he could park it himself and be in the club in thirty seconds. It wasn't like he had to go up five levels in a parking garage and walk ten minutes. Plus he liked the walk to the car when he left the club to gauge just how much of a lawbreaker he was about to be during his short drive home. It also eliminated the chance the valet would not surrender the keys if they thought he was too drunk to drive. He knew they really didn't care about him. They were just covering their own asses anyway.

Darius, the main host, immediately recognized him at the door. "Welcome back, Mr. Doler. It's been a while. You want a booth?"

"Nah, just in for a nightcap. I'll sit at the stage." Max peeled off a hundred and a twenty and gave them to Darius. "Can you get a hundred in fives and keep the twenty?"

"Absolutely, Mr. Doler. Have a seat at the stage. I'll send over a cocktail waitress and bring your change."

Max breezed by the swarm of girls milling by the front, a pack of predators waiting for fresh meat, for the right drunk tourist to stumble in so they could separate him from his credit card and rack up a few thousand in charges. He felt their eyes on him—through him—sizing him up to determine if he was worth their time or if they should wait for a bigger fish to come on the line.

A Latino girl in her mid-twenties walked up and put her arm around him. "Where you headed, papi? Why don't you take me in the back and show me what a big man you are."

The top of Max's head came up to the bottom of her breasts. He put his arm around her ass, resting his hand on her hip. "I'm just going to the stage to have a drink. Maybe later, babes."

She stopped and pulled him toward her. She leaned over and pushed her boobs in his face, holding the back of his head and shaking her shoulders. "I'll come find you, then you can come for me."

A brown-skinned Asian girl on stage, wearing only bikini bottoms and five-inch wedges, crawled around on all fours, collecting the bills littered across the stage. A blonde with pigtails and D cups wiped the pole down, waiting for her turn.

Perfect timing for Max. He had always been a breast man. The bigger, the better. He sat directly at the stage. Darius dropped off his change.

A cocktail waitress approached. "What can I get you, sweetie?"

"Gin and soda with a lemon," he said. He had told himself he was going to have only one drink, but he hadn't thought about what that drink would be. The gin and soda order just popped. Once he said it, though, he knew it wasn't going to be just one. Gin and soda was his drink when he had already had enough and was going to have a few more than a few more.

The DJ's voice, in the standard strip club tone and cadence, flowed through the speakers. "Gentlemen, we're still fifteen minutes away from two-for-one lap dances, but while you wait, turn your attention to the stage, where Jade is going to make you believe in a higher power."

The opening notes of Madonna's "Like a Virgin" played. The DJ talked over the intro. "Joy, you're on deck. Felicity is in the hole." The music escalated. Jade sauntered toward Max. His drink arrived. He paid and ordered another without taking his eyes off Jade. Peeling a five from the stack Darius had given him, he tossed it on the stage. Jade shimmied out of her plaid skirt and untied her white button-down, revealing a matching sequined bikini. Bending over, she picked up the bill by pushing her breasts together. Max put another five in front of him. She picked it up with her hands, creased it lengthwise and put it in his mouth. Bending over on all fours, she crawled toward him and put her breasts in his face on each side of the five. Without lifting her arms, she pushed her shoulders together, snagged the bill, and leaned back, letting the bill slide down her stomach and fall between her legs. He flopped back in his chair. It was going to be a long night.

After Jade's set, she joined him at the stage. She said, "Why don't we go somewhere I can dance just for you."

Max motioned for Darius. "Better get me a table after all." He slapped forty dollars into Darius's palm. "Make it a booth."

Jade said, "Can I bring my girlfriend? It's going to be two for one."

"I don't know if I can handle you," Max said.

Jade cupped her hand around his crotch. "I think you'll be just fine."

The brown-skinned Asian girl who had been on stage before Jade joined them in the booth. Jade kissed her on the cheek. "This is Faith."

The cocktail waitress arrived with another gin for Max. "Drinks, ladies?"

Jade said, "Let's do a shot." She turned to Max. "How about it?" She ran her fingers through his thick hair and down his neck, pushing the suit jacket off his shoulder. "Let's get this out of the way right now."

Max nodded to the waitress. "Bring us three fireballs."

Faith slid into the booth on the other side of Max. She loosened his tie and unbuttoned his shirt. "Why so dressed up? You trying to impress us?"

Max had his arm on Jade's shoulder, his hand resting on her right breast. They had to be fake. They were too big and too perfect. He said, "I had a business dinner on the strip."

Jade nuzzled closer to him. "How'd it go, baby?"

The waitress arrived with the shots and set one in front of each of them.

Max flipped a black Amex on the tray. "Keep it open." He picked up his shot. "Let's just say it's time to celebrate."

Five lap dances and two more shots followed. Max was getting Vegas drunk, the kind of buzz that tourists who weren't used to having alcohol available twenty-four hours a day got and locals tried to avoid altogether.

Faith straddled him, pulsing to Snoop Dogg's "Drop It Like It's Hot."

Jade kissed his neck and rubbed his chest. "Let's go in the back where we have more privacy."

"I don't think I can take much more." Max turned toward her. "I'd hate to disappoint you."

Jade kissed the end of his nose. "I got something to keep you going." She reached down into her bottoms and pulled out a baggie. Using her nail, she scooped some of the white powder and lifted it to his nose. He inhaled without hesitation. It was coke. Jade kissed the end of his nose again. "Good boy."

Max tilted his head back and sucked a deep breath through his nose. He stared up at Faith, who was still on his lap, wearing only a thong. The coke hit him fast. He wanted more…of everything. He reached around and put a hand on each of her cheeks. "You're coming, right?"

Faith shook her shoulders back and forth, her breasts bouncing in his face. "Of course. The celebration is just beginning."

Both girls put their clothes back on, and with Jade on the right and Faith on the left, they led Max back to the VIP area.

Darius was there to greet them. "Ready for some privacy? It's $350 per girl for a half hour and $600 each for an hour plus drinks."

Max said, "Let's start with an hour and how about a bottle of Veuve? I have a tab open with the cocktail waitress."

"Of course, Mr. Doler. If I could just get your driver's license. I'll get your credit card from the front," Darius said. "Girls, please escort the gentleman to booth one and make yourselves comfortable."

The VIP area was a large, dimly lit room with a smaller dance floor not currently being used in the center, a separate bar, and private wraparound high-backed booths around the perimeter. Each booth had walls that extended to the ceiling and black sheer curtains across the opening to at least create the illusion of privacy. Being in booth one, at least they would be farthest away from the flow of traffic.

Jade pulled open the curtain. "Paradise awaits." She removed his coat, which he had put back on out of habit, and hung it outside the booth.

Faith loosened the tie and lifted it over his head. "You won't be needing this anymore." She placed it on the hook on top of the jacket.

A waitress brought the champagne in a bucket with three glasses. Everything was moving fast for Max, too fast to think, but that was exactly what he wanted. He already had enough to think about. He didn't need any more.

Darius returned with Max's card and several papers to fill out. "OK, Mr. Doler. We just need you to sign this and close out your tab from the front. Here's the receipt for the girls with your card and driver's license, I just need to get a quick thumbprint next to your signature." He put an inkpad on the table next to the receipt.

Anyone who has spent any length of time in Vegas knows it's never a good sign when someone is asking for your thumbprint.

Max complied with all the requests. "You're really making me work for this."

Jade continued to stroke her fingers in a circle on the back of Max's head. "Almost finished, babe, then it's our time to have some fun."

Darius put another receipt down on the table. "This last one is for the champagne. Just need you to add the tip for the waitress and total. If you want to add time with the girls, just let me know and we can add it on. No more signatures required."

Max filled out the last receipt. "This is the hardest I've worked in a while."

"That should do it." Darius collected all the paperwork. "Take good care of him, ladies." He drew the curtain as he left.

Faith picked up a glass of champagne and handed one to Max and one to Jade. "Here's to a celebration to remember."

"Or maybe one to forget." Max said, clinking his glass to theirs and downing the entire thing.

Faith unbuttoned his shirt down to his belt. Jade climbed on top. She pulled the bag of coke out of her bottoms and poured some on her breast. Max bent down and snorted it off, growling in pleasure. Faith picked up the bottle of champagne and tilted his head back, pouring some in his mouth. She did the same to Jade then took a drink herself. She leaned over and licked Jade's breasts and kissed Max's chest.

Standing on the seat, Jade put her crotch in Max's face. "You want to taste this?" She slipped off her bikini bottoms, wearing only a thong underneath. She pulled the front to the side, revealing a smoothly shaved surface. She pushed it toward Max's face, then let the front of the thong snap back over the top. "Not yet, baby."

Faith loosened his belt, unbuttoned his pants, and pulled down his zipper in one smooth motion. She thrust her hand inside his silk boxers. Jade gave him another bump, then took a condom from her purse. Dropping his pants to his ankles, Faith pulled his boxers down. Jade ripped open the package and slid under the table between his legs. Faith poured more champagne down his throat.

Things got a bit fuzzy after that. All Max remembered was, $5,500, six hours, two bottles of champagne, and one and a half orgasms later, he was stepping out into the Vegas morning sunlight. He estimated the second orgasm as a half because he couldn't finish. Maybe it was closer to three quarters. He really didn't know. He did recall ordering another bottle of champagne and them getting him going again, but not much after that until it was time to pay. He didn't feel like racking up another hour just to finish, so he considered the second one a half. He could always round up and call it two when he retold the story. One thing he knew for sure, he shouldn't be driving. Staggering, he closed one eye to find his car in the parking lot. He didn't care though. He had driven in much worse condition when he had to actually go down to the parking garage the next day just to see if his car was there.

Dow Jones Close: 16,064.77

Chapter Twelve

Date: Sunday, August 26, 1990

Dow Jones Open: Closed

"My sweet Cai Yin."

That was Crystal's first memory, the first time she heard her mother say her real name. She was five years old. It was the night before her first day of kindergarten. Her mother, Valeria, was singing her a children's song in Chinese.

"月儿明，风儿静，树叶儿遮窗棂啊,

(Bright moon, quiet wind, leaves cover window frames,)

蛐蛐儿叫铮铮，好比那琴弦儿声啊,

(Crickets are chirping, like the sound of the strings,)

琴声儿轻，旋儿动听，摇篮轻摆动啊,

(Soft tweedle, melodious rhythm, cradle rocks gently,)

娘的宝宝你闭上眼睛，睡了那个睡在梦中.

(Mommy's baby closes her eyes, sleeps in a dream.)

报时钟, 响叮咚, 夜深人儿静啊.

(Clock tick-tack, ding-dong sound, in the quiet night.)

小宝宝快长大, 为祖国立功劳啊.

(My little baby grows up quickly, contributes to the country.)

月儿那个明, 风儿那个静, 摇蓝轻摆动啊.

(Bright moon, quiet wind, cradle rocks gently.)

娘的宝宝, 睡在梦中, 微微露了笑容

(Mommy's baby sleeps in the dream with a smile.)

Valeria leaned over Crystal to see if she was asleep. She wasn't, of course. The first day of school was the following day, and Crystal was way too excited. She faked it anyway.

Crystal loved the sound of her mother's voice. It was why she wanted to become a singer. Unfortunately she had only gotten to hear her mother perform live a few times. Clubs and bars were no place for a young girl, according to Valeria. By the time Crystal was old enough, Valeria had stopped doing live gigs. Crystal still had several cassette tapes, which she wore out from listening over and over, of live performances and audition recordings. And of course there were the countless one-on-one performances singing along with whatever music her mother had decided that Crystal should learn. Valeria would always be a star in Crystal's eyes.

Stroking Crystal's hair, her mother whispered, "My sweet Cai Yin. You're growing up into such a beautiful young girl. I've always loved the sound of your name. It means silver fortune. Maybe I shouldn't have changed it. I just thought it would be easier. There's so much I want to tell you. Someday maybe…when you're ready." She continued to hum the song.

Crystal knew a little bit about her past. How could she not? Her first look in the mirror, she knew she was different. Not in a bad way. Just no one she had seen looked like her. The Mexican features from her mom mixed with the Chinese from her dad creating quite an exotic beauty. The black hair from both seemed to compound and deepen the color, radiating a purplish hue. She had her mother's narrow face and angled jawline that rose to high, prominent cheekbones, creating a shelf to display the narrow, dark eyes of her father. Crystal had frequently questioned Valeria about her father, but over time, her mother's rigid body language and vagueness in response taught her to stop asking.

What Crystal didn't know until much later in her life was that she was actually born in China when her mom was teaching English and Spanish in Shanghai. Valeria had graduated from UC Berkeley with a music degree, and somehow decided the best way to grow artistically was to teach foreign languages in China, so she could travel and see the world. All Valeria initially told Crystal about her father was that he was Chinese and that things didn't work out. To further sever the ties, when Valeria applied for an American passport for Crystal she dropped Cai Yin completely and used the name Crystal, with Valeria's maiden name of Morales, which she later changed to Moore, de-ethnicizing to help her get acting and singing gigs. It also made it more difficult to find them if the father ever came looking after they had moved to Los Angeles just before Crystal's second birthday.

Fortunately, Valeria never had to find out that Crystal one day would use another name yet again to conceal her identity, this time for a completely different type of stage.

LA was the only place Crystal remembered living as a child, so she assumed they had always lived in the small studio apartment in Silver Lake. It wasn't much, but they didn't need much. It's probably also why she didn't feel any urgency to leave the shoebox studio at Siegel Suites. She was most comfortable in tight, cramped spaces. In the Silver Lake studio, they had a kitchen area with a table, a big closet for all their clothes, and a living area with a few chairs, cable TV, and a couch that folded out into a bed when it was time to sleep. Valeria always went to sleep when Crystal did unless she had picked up a gig singing backup for one of the local bands. In those cases, Crystal was always asleep when Valeria got home, so she never heard anything. Sometimes Crystal woke up early in a panic that her mom didn't make it home, but she would roll over and always find Valeria lying next to her. Snuggling closer, Crystal would instantly fall back asleep.

That night before Crystal's first day of kindergarten, when Crystal learned her real name was Cai Yin, Valeria, probably assuming Crystal had fallen asleep, stopped humming the lullaby. Crystal rolled over. Blinking several times and staring blankly at her mom, she pretended to be half asleep.

Valeria said, "I'm sorry, baby. Did I wake you?"

"No, mama. I was having a dream." She pressed her body closer to her mother's.

"A good one or a bad one?" Valeria asked.

"I don't know," Crystal said. "Just a dream. It was about my father. What was he like?"

Valeria leaned over and kissed her forehead. "That's not a discussion for tonight, baby. You got school in the morning—we both do. We'll talk about this another time." In addition to the singing gigs, Valeria taught music at a nearby preschool, the same one Crystal had graduated from the previous year. Crystal wished her mother was moving on with her and continued to wish that every year she advanced, going forward. She knew she would miss seeing her mother at school every day and hearing the other kids talk about how nice and beautiful Miss V, as they all called her at the school, was.

"You promise?" Crystal asked.

Valeria kissed her again. "Cross my heart." She traced an X on her chest and tapped Crystal on the end of the nose. "Now you get some sleep." She reached over, shut off the light, and curled up behind Crystal, wrapping her arms around and pulling Crystal to her chest. Crystal could feel her mother's heartbeat against her back. She listened to the sound of the traffic on the street below until she fell asleep. She was happy. She had everything.

Chapter Thirteen

Date: Monday, February 25, 2013

Dow Jones Open: 14,000.57

Bill and Darlene had been to Vegas enough over the years that he knew exactly what he was looking for when buying their retirement home: close to Fremont Street, no stairs, a westward view, and no upkeep. They had always felt more comfortable downtown. Of course, since he would be on a fixed income, the affordability was important, too, but it was more the history and the openness. They liked that while the area around the downtown casinos had changed, the places themselves were relatively the same since they first started coming, and they could easily move between casinos. On the strip, the long distance between properties made them feel like prisoners once they were inside. With the no-stairs criterion, he was just thinking ahead. While they were both still pretty spry and able to get around, he knew that would probably change at some point. The last thing he wanted was for either of them to have to trudge up and down stairs. The westward view was for Darlene. She adored the Vegas sunsets, watching the sun dip behind the Spring Mountains and Red Rock Canyon radiating the full spectrum of color across the valley. The no-upkeep stipulation was all him. He was retired after all. There was no way he was spending his days doing yard work or cleaning a pool, especially in the desert heat.

Their familiarity with the area allowed them to slip quickly into a comfortable routine. On Sundays, they would walk down to Du-par's at the Golden Gate and split the Vegas Stack, which was three pancakes. One each was not enough and two apiece too many, so splitting the stack of three was perfect. After breakfast, they would casino hop, but they rarely gambled together. Darlene liked to play the slots, while Bill was a video poker player and both had different styles. Darlene preferred to stick and move, never getting too comfortable at any particular machine. She would play a small fixed amount at one then move on to another until she hit a decent jackpot. Bill's strategy was to find a machine serviced by an attractive cocktail waitress and set up camp until he hit a royal flush, his money ran out, or Darlene was ready to move to a new casino. The breakfast was filling enough that they would skip lunch, and their dinner was determined by how their fortunes ran that day. If they both won, they would go to one of the nicer sit-down restaurants. If only one was the winner, it was the loser's choice of sandwich or pizza shop with the winner paying. If both lost, they went back home licking their wounds with their tails between their legs, and Darlene whipped up something from what they had in the fridge. They enjoyed their new life. It was predictable, comfortable, and most importantly for Darlene, Bill was with her all day and not out risking his life.

On this Sunday, Bill noticed he was almost finished with his half of the stack and Darlene had just been picking at hers. "Everything OK, hon?" Bill said. "You've barely made a dent."

Darlene forced a smile. "Just not hungry this morning."

"Well, there's a first. Usually I got to fight you off from my half. You sure you feel all right? Your color is looking a little off." Bill had noticed she wasn't herself the past week. Although small in stature, especially when next to him and Hughie, she had always been the engine of the family. Lately though, she had been quieter and seemed a bit down. He had asked about it several times, but she had insisted everything was fine. Bill assumed it had something to do with Hughie, and she just wasn't telling him. For the most part she had accepted the secret relationship she had to maintain with their son, but every so often it would well up inside her, and she and Bill would have to have the talk again about how it was Hughie's responsibility to apologize if the relationship were to be mended. Bill reached for her hand. "We can just go home and rest this afternoon if you want. All these places will be here tomorrow."

"Don't be silly," Darlene said, putting her hand in his. "Probably just need to move around a bit."

They paid the check and walked out to Fremont Street, deciding to stroll and get some fresh air first. A few steps into the closed-off and canopied street now known as the Fremont Street Experience, Darlene doubled over, clutching her upper abdomen. Bill eased her down to the sidewalk. "Here, just sit," he said. "Can I get you something? Maybe some water?"

"No, I'll be fine," she said. "Probably just something I ate."

Bill's voice trembled. "But you hardly ate anything, and what you ate, I ate too." Darlene looked up and smiled at Bill to quell the fear that he knew she could hear in his voice, but the look only magnified his worry. The pale shade he noticed at breakfast had transformed to yellow. He cupped his hand under her chin and studied her face. The jaundice color had spilled into her eyes as well. "Hon, I think we need to get you to a hospital."

"Don't be ridiculous." She got her feet underneath her and eased herself up with Bill's help, but she couldn't straighten her body. "Maybe we should just get a taxi and go home and rest."

"Nonsense. We're going to the emergency room." Bill flagged over a security officer, who was already moving in their direction. Bill's words exploded toward the officer. "We need to get her to a hospital."

The officer arrived and looked her over. "Do you know what's wrong?"

Panic seized Bill. "I have no idea. We need to call an ambulance." Even Darlene didn't argue with him this time. She remained doubled-over, holding her stomach, leaning into Bill's chest as he kneeled beside her, both arms wrapped around her. Her eyes, usually filled with purpose and understanding, floated, searching for focus. He twirled his index finger through her hair, which was still the same short, textured cut it had always been but was now gray instead of auburn. His finger followed the same pattern he had done every day when she would greet him at the door after work and they would walk back into the house together to talk about their days. This time it was as much to comfort him as her.

The officer reached up to activate the radio clipped to his shoulder, tilting his head to call for an ambulance to the corner of Fremont and Main. Bill was used to being on the other side of this interaction, being the one to diffuse the stress and tension. But in that moment everything was happening too fast, yet still not happening fast enough. He begged for the officer to hurry. He recognized the same deliberate questions and actions from the officer that he had performed countless times before. A faint siren moaned in the distance, increasing in magnitude as the seconds passed.

Upon arrival, the paramedics checked Darlene's vitals and immediately lifted her on a gurney and into the ambulance. Bill climbed in the back and rode with her, never letting go of her hand until arriving at the urgent care facility, where the nurses made him sit in the waiting area while they ran tests on Darlene. Not too happy about it, but realizing his protests were merely holding up the procedure, Bill reluctantly followed their instructions, flipping through magazines, standing, pacing, anything to make the time pass after Darlene disappeared into the back. After his fifth trip to the reception to ask for an update, the doctor, a male in his late thirties with red curly hair, came out and asked him back to the examination area.

Bill felt a sharp pain in his own stomach when he stepped behind the curtain and saw Darlene reclined in the bed with an IV hooked up to her skinny forearm. He couldn't imagine his life without Darlene in it. Everything good he ever had was because of her. He rushed to her side and took hold of her hand. She opened her eyes and smiled. He said, "You gave me quite a scare."

The doctor stood at the foot of the bed, a folder tucked under his freckled arm. "We put her on an IV. She was pretty dehydrated and her weight is significantly low."

Bill stroked Darlene's hair. "Her color looks better."

"We also gave her something for the pain." The doctor removed two X-rays from the folder and put them on the backlit display next to the bed. "Based on the pictures we took of the abdomen, there's some abnormal activity in the pancreas and liver area."

Bill said, "What do you mean abnormal?"

"Some more sophisticated imaging tests will need to be done," the doctor said. "Depending on those, perhaps a biopsy."

"Biopsy?" Bill moved closer to the screen as if he could tell what he was looking at. "So you think it might be cancer?"

Darlene was quiet the whole time. She had obviously heard all of it already or maybe the drugs had just taken over.

The doctor said, "I'm going to refer you to an oncologist." He scribbled a name and address on a pad. "Here is a good one in the area." He ripped off the paper and handed it to Bill. "Once the IV treatment is completed, she'll be OK to go home, but get in to see the oncologist as soon as possible. It's never good to put these things off."

Bill said, "We'll go first thing in the morning. You sure it's OK for her to go home tonight?"

"She'll be fine." The doctor handed him a small envelope of pills. "These will help with the pain and keep her resting comfortably."

Dow Jones Close: 13,784.17

Chapter Fourteen

Date: Monday, August 8, 2011

Dow Jones Open: 11,433.93

Penny often woke up in the middle of the night to an empty bed. She and Alec still slept in the same room and went to bed at the same time, but they weren't together. They hadn't been together in a long time. They were just sharing space. Each one just a reminder to the other, like all the other objects in the house, of the life they used to have.

Tonight was no different. She awoke and reached over to the opposite side of the bed, feeling for his warm body. Instead her hand rested in the impression in the sheets where he had been sleeping. She rubbed the vacated space, gauging the warmth to determine how long he had been gone. Ice cold. It had been a while. She rolled over and attempted sleep, but just like other nights and most things as of late, she failed. The room was black. Sunrise was still hours away. She got out of bed and treaded in the dark to the basement steps where Alec's office was, stopping at the top and listening for the TV, some music, anything to indicate that he was still in the house and hadn't left. She couldn't bring herself to go down the stairway and find out for sure. She wanted to pad down the steps, crawl next to him on the couch, and lie between his legs with her back resting on his chest like she used to. Closing her eyes, she could still feel the warmth on her back and hear the sound of his slow, controlled breathing. This is how she wanted to fall back asleep. She just couldn't. She wasn't sure he would let her, and it was better not to know than be rejected.

Instead Penny retreated to the baby's room, or what was supposed to be the baby's room. A crib, dresser, and rocking chair, all a glossy white color, still occupied the room even though a baby never did, or, as it appeared, never would. The walls were also white, but it was just an eggshell primer. They had been waiting to finish once the baby was born and they knew the gender. The white furniture on the freshly treated hardwood floors with the soft, velvety enamel from the walls put her at ease. It was empty, just like her. But that was OK. At least nothing could hurt her in there.

She sat in the rocking chair and tottered back and forth. The sound of the rails rising and falling on the floor filled the space in her mind. Nothing could fill the void in her heart. She heard a creak, a slow groan. She stopped rocking, unsure whether it came from the house or somewhere inside her. She listened for another sound, an indication someone or something was there with her.

She thought Alec might be in the hallway. She pictured him standing with his hands and forehead resting on the door, frozen like she had been at the top of the basement steps. Rising from the chair, she walked over to the door and placed her hands and forehead where she thought his might be. She wanted to reach down, turn the handle and open the door. But she couldn't. All she could do was turn and quietly shuffle back to the chair and rock herself to sleep.

When she awoke hours later, she crept back to the bedroom. Alec was facing away from the door with his back to the middle of the bed. She slid in next to him, careful not to wake him or cause him to roll over. He didn't stir, but she knew he wasn't asleep. They both just lay there, back to back, never touching or uttering a sound. As daylight slipped through the blinds and filled the room, she lay still, not wanting to be the first one up. She was like an adolescent in a stare-off, determined not be the first to blink. She waited for him to rise, and once she could hear him in the shower, she got up and made coffee, pretending like none of it ever happened.

During this sad time Alec communicated to her only by announcing his movements. *I'm leaving for practice. I'm running to the store. I'm going golfing.* And the last one he did a lot. First thing pretty much every morning. Just once she would've liked for him to ask her if she wanted to go, or really, just ask her to do anything. Her job had always been her hobby. She had tried to go back to work early, but the station had brought someone in on a six-month contract to cover for her while she was on maternity leave, and they didn't want to break it. She had doubts about whether that was true or if they just weren't sure she was ready to come back. That's what they implied, at least, when she first approached them about returning early. The contract excuse came later when she pressed them.

Losing the baby had created a hole in her heart, and each time she heard Alec give another excuse for running away, it was like another spoonful was scooped out. She already felt empty, but she was learning that emptiness, like everything else, had varying degrees and levels, and she obviously wasn't at the bottom yet. She needed something to fill her back up before she got there, or at least numb the pain. That was how the drinking started.

She always waited until Alec was gone. Not because she thought he would be upset; because by waiting, it felt like retaliating. The drinking was something she could do to counter his leaving and make the pain go away. By doing something, she wasn't a victim anymore. She was taking action. She was fighting back.

Through the window she would watch him back out of the driveway, pouring straight vodka over ice into her coffee mug. Every time she pressed the mug to her lips, she swallowed in spite; she swallowed in anger. She liked the contrast of the cold and burning feeling filling her mouth. She liked having to force it down. She liked how even before he was out of sight, the warming sensation swelled in her stomach and spread through the rest of her body. He was nowhere close to his destination, but she was already at hers.

Although the drinking helped, it wasn't enough, and she learned quickly that more was not better. Passing out and waking up late in the afternoon only made for a rough evening and a long night. Making it all worse, he didn't even seem to notice, or maybe he just didn't care. Whether she was awake or asleep, he glided around like she wasn't there, never once asking why her moods fluctuated so significantly or she slept so much during the day. She was losing. She had to raise the stakes.

That opportunity came later that afternoon. In a deck chair by their pool, Penny reclined topless, well into her third vodka. The summer sun on her bare skin along with the alcohol warmed and comforted her. She drifted in and out of sleep.

The bell for the front door rang through the intercom. She assumed it was a package delivery. Trying to ignore it, she gulped the rest of her drink and sunk back into the chair. The ringing persisted. Needing another drink anyway, she put on her top and threw on her black long-sleeve see-through cover-up and went inside. A Lamborghini Aventador sat in the driveway. *Definitely not UPS,* she thought.

On the other side of the door stood Fritjof Stridh, the young Swedish star center for the Blues, holding a yellow binder. She didn't know him well other than brief interactions at various team functions and some postgame interviews. Last season he had led the team in scoring and was third overall in the league, and the rumor was he was equally as productive off the ice as on. She checked her appearance in the window, tousling her hair and adjusting her breasts under the cover-up.

Opening the door, she leaned up against it to steady herself, feeling the vodka. "Fritjof. What a nice surprise."

Fritjof removed his Cartier sunglasses. His assailing blue eyes flashed hope and possibility as he scanned the full length of her body. He had textured, spiked blonde hair criss-crossed and bunched into an inviting, messy display like an unmade bed. "Sorry to interrupt your pool time. Alec told me it would be OK to stop by. Did he mention it to you?"

"He's golfing." She turned and walked down the hallway. "Come on in. I was just going to fix myself a drink if you're thirsty."

Fritjof followed. "No, I'll just be a minute. We got our playbooks mixed up. Just need to do a quick switch."

"One drink won't hurt. It's the off-season. Live a little." Penny continued on to the kitchen. The Absolut was still on the counter from earlier. She held up the bottle. "You'll be helping your country's economy."

"Why not?" His eyes traveled down and back up the length of her body again. "But only if you're having one."

Penny retrieved another glass from the cabinet and filled both with ice. Neither person spoke. The ice cracked and shifted as she poured the vodka. She could feel his eyes on her, but she wasn't uncomfortable. She was enjoying the tension. Remaining silent, she didn't want conversation to distract from the feeling. Still offering only a smile, she handed him the drink.

Fritjof wrapped his long muscular fingers around the glass and extended it toward her. "Skål."

Penny reciprocated with "Cheers." They exchanged small talk about his new car, his success last season, and the expectations for the upcoming season, skillfully dancing around anything of substance and meaning. As the level of vodka dropped in their glasses, the awkwardness in the room and on their faces diminished. Genuine laughter replaced their previously painted-on polite smiles. After Penny sipped the last of her drink, she rattled the ice in the glass. "Twist your arm for one more? I can't tell you how long it's been since I laughed like this."

Fritjof put his glass to his lips, even though it was empty. He took one of the ice cubes into his mouth. "I don't know if it's my place, or if you prefer not to talk about it, but I'm so sorry about the baby, Penny. I know how much you and Alec were looking forward to being parents."

Penny focused on making the drinks. She had been avoiding the topic and was hoping Fritjof didn't say anything at all, but now that he had, she was relieved. It felt good to get it out of the way. It felt good for someone to acknowledge it out loud. She was tired of sidestepping the pain and carrying the burden all by herself. She handed him the glass, this time filled up to the top. "Thank you. It has been hard, but I'm getting better by the day. Will be good when I can get back to work. Going a bit crazy in this house every day."

Fritjof said, "Take your time. We have a saying in Swedish, *Tiden läker alla sår.* It means time heals all wounds."

"Same as the English phrase." She touched her glass to his, holding her gaze upon him. "Skål."

Fritjof shifted his eyes from hers to the binder. "Before I forget why I came in the first place, can you tell me where Alec's office is? He said my playbook is on his desk."

"Follow me." She turned and breezed out of the kitchen, her cover-up flowing side to side from the movement. She could feel his eyes on her ass. She crossed one foot over the other as she walked to accentuate her hips. Her mind was swimming from all the alcohol, but more than that, for the first time in a long while, she felt appreciated and wanted.

Penny headed down the basement steps to Alec's office, which was more of a man cave than a place to do work. He paid other people to do any real administrative tasks. The desk in the corner with the printer was the only thing that resembled an actual office. Other than that, it looked like a little boy's room: framed jerseys on the wall, shelves lined with trophies and awards, two leather recliners and a sofa facing a large flat-screen TV mounted on the wall with wires extending to a video game console, and stacks of video games.

Fritjof angled immediately to the Gretzky jersey on the wall. "I didn't know Alec played with the Great One."

"It was just one year. The Blues traded with the Kings. Gretzky was here only for a short time. Played in like twenty games or so I think." Penny gulped from her glass and set it on the desk, exchanging it for the binder. "Here's your playbook." She turned around and Fritjof was standing in front of her. He leaned toward her and reached around to set the other binder on the desk. His perfect angular face glided by inches away from hers. She threw the playbook on the floor and pulled him in for a passionate kiss.

Fritjof pressed his body against hers then pulled back. "We can't do this. He's my teammate. This is his house."

Penny removed her cover-up and untied her top. "It's my house, too, and he's my husband. I think I have more of a say in what we can and can't do." She lifted his shirt, running her hands down his sculpted core, unbuttoned his pants and pulled them down to his ankles. Taking him in her mouth, she listened to his objections fade into fevered moaning. She ripped down her bottoms and spun around, planting her left hand on the desk and reaching between her legs with her right to guide him. She pushed back into him. The emptiness was gone.

Dow Jones Close: 10,809.85

Chapter Fifteen

Date: Wednesday, October 31, 2012

Dow Jones Open: 13,107.44

In his office at the church, Les sat at his desk with his back to the door, staring at the floor-to-ceiling bookshelf. His eyes flashing from book to book, he attempted to recall when and where he finished each one. A knock sounded at the door. "Come," he said, and spun around in his chair.

Sister Vera entered. "Bishop Pence and Father Bennett will see you now."

Les followed Sister Vera to Father Bennett's office. Bishop Pence and Father Bennett stood when they entered. Les first shook hands with Bishop Pence, a short, stout man in his early sixties with large, round eyes and a bald head with tufts of gray hair on the sides that ran above and behind his ears and connected in the back, forming a U-shape. "Nice to see you again, Your Excellency."

"I wish it were under better circumstances, Father Banks," Bishop Pence said. Les nodded, then exchanged greetings with Father Bennett.

Sister Vera said, "Can I get anyone anything?"

Bishop Pence answered for everyone. "No, thank you, Sister. That will be all." He waved his arm toward the table, directing the others to sit. The room fell quiet. Les knew it was not his place to speak. Bishop Pence folded his hands and turned toward him. "Father Bennett has informed me about the unfortunate events that have transpired. First, I want you to know that we believe you, and you have the full backing of the Church." He paused, inhaling and releasing a long breath. "But we are in a difficult position here. With the multicultural makeup of this parish, the differing racial component of the boys, and the precarious financial position of this parish and the Archdiocese of Atlanta in general, litigation, regardless of the outcome, could be devastating."

"I understand, Your Excellency," Les said. "I appreciate the support of the Church. It really means a great deal to me. But after a great deal of reflection and prayer, that's why I feel it is best if I leave the Church and request laicization."

Father Bennett was not happy when Les first informed him of the decision. He had probably hoped hearing Bishop Pence might change Les's mind. Forgetting protocol and decorum, Father Bennett spoke out of turn. He said, "I don't think you understand what His Excellency is saying. The Church is not going to suspend you or deliver any penance."

The Bishop lifted his hand to silence Father Bennett and spoke directly to Les. "Let's not be rash. You are a valued member of this clergy, and we believe that the boys have fabricated these charges to protect themselves. That is why no penance, loss of benefits or remuneration, or expiatory penalty will be levied. We do believe, however, based on the circumstances, a transfer is in order. I have spoken to Bishop Sellers of the Archdiocese of New Orleans, and he has a position open for you there."

Les understood exactly what they were saying. They had responded just as he expected them to because he was telling the truth. What they didn't realize was that he was already a few moves ahead. The boys had used him to avoid a potentially embarrassing situation with their parents. He was using the boys as a way out of the Church. It wasn't clear to him exactly how much he wanted to leave until the door was opened for him. He said, "Thank you for your support and understanding. I have given this a great deal of thought. Regardless of where I go, these allegations will follow me. While you have given me your support and trust, most will not. They will assume guilt, and this will ultimately reflect negatively upon the Church."

Bishop Pence asked, "Why so little faith, Father?"

"With all due respect, Your Excellency," Les said, "my faith has never been stronger. I believe this has happened for a reason. It is God's way of telling me to go in a new direction and spread His Word to a wider audience."

"But why this extreme measure of laicization?" Father Bennett asked. "Why not a temporary leave of absence and allow the opportunity to come back to the Church?"

Les knew it was the only way. He said, "In order to embark on this new path, I must commit to it with the same will as the one that brought me here. In order to do that, I must relinquish my title, but that does not mean my beliefs will change. The hand of God will still be guiding me as strongly as ever."

Bishop Pence stared at Les, contemplating his words. Silence again filled the room, but this time fueled by disappointment and not uncertainty. He finally spoke.

"I can see that you have given this a great deal of consideration, and I respect the decision you have made, but perhaps we should take some more time to decide. Go to New Orleans. Meet with Bishop Sellers. Hear what he has planned for you. Perhaps there are aspects to this that have not been revealed yet."

"Your divine advice is appreciated, Your Excellency," Les said, "but I believe the best course for all parties is for me to leave the Church." He glanced at Father Bennett and back to Bishop Pence. "If it is acceptable to both of you, I'd like to just go ahead and sign the settlement agreement that we discussed."

Bishop Pence nodded to Father Bennett, who opened a folder and removed a document. Taking a pen from his pocket, Father Bennett placed it on top of the document and slid both across the table to Les. "I think you'll find everything as we agreed to. Would you like a moment to review it?"

Les glanced at the first page and immediately flipped to the last. "I'm sure it's fine." He removed the cap from the pen and signed on the line above his typed name. In one fluid motion of the pen, he felt the burden he had been carrying for much longer than the weeks following the incident disappear. He knew he had made the right decision, or maybe it had been determined long before, and he hadn't realized it. Although in that moment, a new path had opened, but the destination remained the same. By leaving the Church, he was not moving away from God, but actually moving closer to Him.

SETTLEMENT AGREEMENT AND MUTUAL RELEASE

This Settlement Agreement and Mutual Release (hereafter "Agreement") is made by and between Lester Banks and the Roman Catholic Archdiocese of Atlanta (hereafter "Archdiocese"), and all of its affiliated entities.

WHEREAS, Lester Banks has determined to voluntarily leave the priesthood of the Roman Catholic Church under certain conditions, as more specifically set out below; and

WHEREAS, the Archdiocese is willing to accept Lester Banks's resignation from the priesthood of the Roman Catholic Church, and in reliance on that resignation is willing to agree to the terms set out below; and

WHEREAS, Lester Banks and the Archdiocese wish to settle and compromise all claims that either of them may have against the other, and wish to accomplish the complete and total separation of Lester Banks from the priesthood of the Roman Catholic Church;

NOW, THEREFORE, in consideration of the mutual promises herein provided and other valuable consideration, receipt of which is hereby acknowledged, the parties to this agreement hereby agree as follows:

1. The Archdiocese agrees to pay to Lester Banks the sum of $50,000, receipt of which is hereby acknowledged. All parties will bear their own costs and attorneys fees associated with this settlement.

2. Lester Banks presently is entitled to a severance reimbursement from the Archdiocese priests' pension fund. This reimbursement will be paid to Lester Banks pursuant to a letter from Lester Banks directing how these funds are to be paid, so long as consistent with the rules of the plan.

3. Lester Banks agrees to sign a letter of resignation in the form attached as Exhibit A to this Agreement.

4. The Archdiocese agrees to pay for six months of medical insurance for Lester Banks, commencing on the date that he signs this Agreement and letter of resignation. Following that six-month period, Lester Banks shall inform the Archdiocese if he elects, pursuant to law, to continue that coverage at his own expense for eighteen more months. The Archdiocese shall have no obligation to pay any amount toward medical insurance following the six-month period referred to above.

5. In return for the payments set out above and for the mutual promises contained herein, and for other good and valuable consideration, receipt of which is hereby acknowledged, Lester Banks agrees to release and forever discharge the Archdiocese, and all of the Archdiocese's employees, agents, officers, directors, and assigns, including, without limitation, all members of the Roman Catholic clergy, and all parishes and with the Roman Catholic Church in the territory of the Archdiocese from, and covenants not to sue them for, all schools and any person- or entity-affiliated claims, causes of actions, charges, and demands, whether in tort, contract, or otherwise, of any nature that he may have had at any time, up to and including the date of signing of this Agreement, including without limitation any claim of any nature arising from any entitlements he could assert from having been a priest in the Roman Catholic Church. By signing this Agreement and attached letter, Lester Banks hereby resigns from the priesthood of the Roman Catholic Church, and agrees never to function in any capacity

as a priest, nor to seek reinstatement to the priesthood of the Roman Catholic Church at any time. He further agrees to give up any claim or entitlement that he may have to any benefit compensation support, or other attribute of the Roman Catholic priesthood, other than as specifically set out in the Agreement. He further agrees not to perform any of the functions of the priesthood, including, without limitation, administering the sacraments and the celebration of mass, and in no respect will hold himself out to be a priest of the Roman Catholic Church in the future.

6. The Archdiocese, and all of its affiliated entities, hereby release and forever discharge Lester Banks from all claims, demands, and causes of action of any nature that they may have had, up to and including the date of the signing of this Agreement.

7. The parties agree that this Agreement is not an admission of liability on the part of any party.

8. The parties agree not to disclose to any third party, including, without limitation, any newspaper, any electronic media, or any reporters, or to release for publicity any of the provisions of this Agreement.

9. In witness of this Agreement, we have signed below on the dates indicated.

Lester Banks

Date: 10/31/2012

Archdiocese of Atlanta

Date: 10/31/2012

_____

Witness

Date: 10/31/2012

Dow Jones Close: 13,096.46

Chapter Sixteen

Date: Monday, February 3, 2014

Dow Jones Open: 15,697.69

Max, on top of the comforter, still fully clothed with his shoes on, rolled over in his king-sized sleigh bed. His head throbbed from the cognac the night before. The sunlight blazed through the floor-to-ceiling windows of his penthouse apartment on the twentieth floor of the Ogden. He pulled a pillow over his head, squeezing it against his temples to contain the pulsing. The dull thud persisted. He lifted the pillow. The pounding boomed from outside his head. He lunged forward, scanning the room. A two-foot vomit stain soaked one side of the bed. His phone lay facedown in the center with chunks from the upheaval stuck to the back. The relentless banging was radiating from the front door. He wiped the phone on his pants. Five missed calls. Two from an unknown number, three from the door person. Thick black wool filled his head. He rubbed his forehead. Nothing. Not a single memory after the El Cortez. He shuffled toward the door. "All right. All right. Coming." He reached into his pocket. Black, green, and red chips filled his hand. He opened the door. Two officers, an Asian female in her early thirties and a black male in his mid-twenties, stood on the other side.

The female officer said, "Max Doler?"

Max just turned and waved for them to follow. His head didn't throb as much if he kept moving. Both officers hesitated, looking at each other, surprised by his indifference.

Max walked to the kitchen and retrieved a bottle of water from the fridge. He waved his hand at the stools tucked under the breakfast counter. "Please have a seat." The officers walked to the counter but didn't sit down. He opened the water and gulped.

The male officer said, "Mr. Doler, do you own a Maserati Quattroporte S Q4?"

Max lowered the bottle from his lips. "Ahh, I'm sorry. A bit parched. Would either of you like something to drink, water, coffee, anything?"

The two officers again looked at each other, growing impatient. The female officer said, "Mr. Doler, about the car."

"So nothing to drink? Suit yourself." He sipped from the bottle. "Yeah, I have that car."

"Do you know where it is?" the male officer asked.

"Should be in the garage. Why?"

The female officer removed her phone and pulled up a photo. "Your car was found crashed into the old Western Hotel on East Fremont early this morning." She showed a photo on her phone to Max.

Max studied the image, draining the rest of the water. He walked to the fridge for another bottle. "Sure I can't get you two something? So thirsty. It's like we live in a desert or something."

"So the last time you saw your car was in the garage?" Impatience tightened the male officer's words. "You think it was stolen?"

"No, the last time I remember seeing the car was at the El Cortez valet last night around ten o'clock. I probably walked home."

The female officer said, "You don't remember?"

Max took his phone out of his pocket. Both officers looked at the smeared puke on the front and back. Max walked back into the kitchen. "I think I've said enough and should probably call my lawyer to help straighten this out." He fetched a paper towel, doused it with some of the water from the bottle, and wiped off the front and back of the phone. "Should I have her come here or meet us at the site?"

The male officer said, "Have her come here. We'll go down and review the security tapes here and at the El Cortez to see what happened."

Max pulled up his lawyer Amanda in his contacts and held the phone to his ear. "Hey, Amanda. Have a bit of a situation here. Somebody crashed my car into the Western last night...No, I didn't do it...Yeah, the cops are here now. Can you come over?...OK. See you then." Max lowered the phone. "She'll be here in thirty minutes."

The officers left to view the footage. Max used the time to shower and piece together the evening, but it was all a blank once he started playing blackjack. He didn't believe that, even as drunk as he had been, it could've been him who wrecked his car though. The El Cortez was right across the street from the Ogden. He usually walked home and got his car the next day when he was that drunk. The Western was four blocks away in the opposite direction.

Max was on his third bottle of water when the door guy called to announce Amanda's arrival. The water wasn't working. He was going to need something stronger. While the espresso maker was warming up, he filled a coffee mug one-third of the way with Jameson. Once the green light came on, he brewed two shots and added them to the Jameson.

Amanda knocked but didn't wait for a response before she entered. "So I called a contact at the El Cortez. They said according to the security tape, you left the casino at 1:30, got your car from valet, and went left on Sixth Street to the light, then took another left onto Fremont. Where the hell were you going?"

Max sipped from the coffee mug. "Good morning to you too. Coffee?"

She walked over and smelled the contents. "Jameson? Really? Isn't it a bit early for brown liquor?" She swirled the mixture in the mug and slugged the rest. "Come on, we don't have much time. The cops have probably seen the video by now and will be back."

Max looked into the empty mug and went back to the Jameson and the espresso machine to make another. "So how do we play this?"

"Well it occurred on private property, so unless the owner presses charges, that should keep the cops out of it." She took another empty mug from the rack and set it next to his on the counter. "But it might get expensive."

"Whatever it takes." Max added Jameson to her mug. "I can't afford any bad press right now with this McDonald's deal happening."

"You said you needed additional space downtown, right? How would you like to be the proud owner of prime, ready-to-be developed commercial space? Been empty for several years."

"That place is huge. Probably way more than I need." Max dumped the two shots of espresso into Amanda's mug and handed it to her.

"I'm sure you'll come up with something. "

He sipped from his mug, and the wheels started to spin. "I guess we could set up the production lines on the old gaming floor."

Amanda clinked her mug with his. "There you go. Now you've got your thinking cap on."

"Powered by Jameson." Max took another drink. "We'll just have to figure out what to do with all those rooms."

Dow Jones Close: 15,372.80

Chapter Seventeen

Date: Thursday, February 13, 2014

Dow Jones Open: 15,946.99

Not long after Max relayed his version of meeting Crystal at Olympic Gardens, she came into the El Cortez and shared her side of the story as well. Of course she had no clue, or at least no conscious one, that Max had told me, and I never gave her reason to think otherwise. Dealer-player confidentiality, of course. Most likely the same mysterious force that caused him to reveal what happened that night, also pushed her to my table to tell me what "really happened." Long ago I stopped trying to figure out this never-ending cycle of cause and effect, what triggers people to say the things they say, what directs them in and out of our lives in a seemingly random yet far too coincidental pattern. Anymore I just watch the dominos fall and see where they land.

It was a Tuesday night—pretty much the refresh and reload night in Vegas. The long weekenders had cleared out, and the Wednesday-to-Saturday and Thursday-to-Sunday warriors hadn't arrived yet. Crystal was alone at my table. Only three shoes in, and she was already up $275. Definitely on her way to a good night. She rarely said much, and that night was no different. The cards, not the conversation, were usually her focus. But as she accumulated chips, she relaxed, and the number of words she offered also increased. Another example of how winning has a friendly effect on people.

Not too long into Crystal's run, Penny sauntered in and sat down to play. The two immediately struck up a conversation, or rather Penny talked and Crystal responded, mostly about the last time they saw each other at the juice place up the street and went to the Container Park together. Based on the awkward and one-sided flow of the conversation, I wouldn't say they were friends but they seemed to be heading in that direction.

After a successful double-down on an eleven with a fifty-dollar bet, Crystal raked in the hundred-dollar profit, saying, "You know, I knew him from way before that one night."

"Who's that?" Penny said. Now, I think she knew exactly whom Crystal was referring to, but she saw an opportunity to get Crystal talking so she played dumb.

"That asshole Max," Crystal said. "I know the casino here probably loves him because he spends a lot of money and is a big tipper, but I can't stand guys like that. Thinks that just because he's handicapped with his height and has a lot of cash, he can say and do whatever he wants."

Penny encouraged her. "There's never a good reason to be a jerk."

"He used to come in all the time," Crystal said, collecting the winnings from another fifty-dollar hand. "I usually just avoided him because he's so fucking handsy. And not just a rub here and there. He grabs and squeezes. The night he was talking about, it was right before Thanksgiving, the start of the slow time of the year, and I was broke. My girlfriend owed me for pulling her in with another guy earlier in the week, so I went along with it."

"A girl's got to do what she's got to do," Penny said, and that was all Crystal needed to hear. She immediately went into a blow-by-blow account of what transpired. Where she lacked detail, Penny interjected and asked for clarification, which Crystal, with her consistent winning, aided by the flow of alcohol, was more than happy to provide.

That night organ music was playing over the strip-club speakers. With one hand on the pole and her body angled out, Crystal rotated in a circle like a schoolgirl around a street sign waiting for the bus. When the soothing intro music shifted to the distinctive guitar strums, finger clicks, handclaps, tambourine, and hi-hat lead-in, Crystal bounced into her signature routine for "Faith" by George Michael. The song might have been over twenty years old, but everyone still knew that riff and remembered the video, with George Michael in a leather jacket, ripped jeans, and sunglasses, playing an acoustic guitar and jumping around that old Wurlitzer jukebox.

One of the reasons Crystal liked the song was that it had been released the year she was born. The other was it had been one of her mom's favorites. She remembered listening to the album with her, both of them singing and dancing, imitating George Michael in their small apartment. Her mom had told her that she liked the album so much, she almost named her Faith instead of Crystal. The only reason her mom changed her mind was because she thought Faith would be too common due to the popularity of the album. When it came time for Crystal to pick a stripper name, Faith seemed like a good choice. Although she knew her mom would not have approved of her occupational choice, the name was a reminder to Crystal of when life was simpler and happier.

At least Faith was a better name than the standard formula others suggested: taking the name of her first pet and the street she grew up on. While Valeria and Crystal hadn't had enough space or money in that studio on Lucile Avenue to have a real pet, like a dog or a cat, Crystal was able to convince her mom to allow her to have a hamster, which she named Meatball. Although Meatball Lucile might be an accurate description for many of the girls working at the club, it was hardly a good one for attracting customers.

The night Max came in, it was dead. A single patron sat at the stage while Crystal wrapped up her set with "Faith." She usually used slow nights to work on her routine and experiment with new moves. That night she was just going through the motions, preoccupied with generating a new excuse for why her rent was going to be late again that week. She saw the host, Darius, leading Max to the stage. She recognized him from other visits. He always tipped well, usually giving fives rather than ones. She knew she could squeeze money from him in the time she had left, and probably several lap dances after, but she enjoyed ignoring him more than pandering to him. Something about him just made her uneasy. It wasn't like he was the most disgusting guy that walked through the doors. He was clean and decent looking, and his size didn't bother her. She actually thought that was the most attractive thing about him. It was just his attitude. His sense of entitlement, like it was OK for him to be a dick.

Crystal collected the few dollars scattered around the stage, avoiding eye contact with Max. Her girlfriend Jade wiped down the pole in preparation for her set. The one other guy who had been at the stage was waiting by the steps for Crystal to finish. She smiled at him, thinking to herself, *Sixty bucks.*

Descending from the stage, Crystal extended her hand toward her chubby suitor. She actually preferred dancing for the fat guys mainly because they were soft and comfortable to move around on. So much better than the skinny guys, who would dry-hump and grind with their narrow, bony crotches, rubbing her thighs raw, or the muscular guys, who, regardless of where she would touch them, felt the need to flex.

This particular guy waiting for her at the steps, she learned, worked for a large dairy farm in Wisconsin, and was in town for a conference. She tried selling him right away on a trip to the VIP room, but he only wanted a few lap dances. She led him to a dark corner. Seated in the chair, waiting for the first song to begin, he said, "Want to see how we say hello in Wisconsin?" He held up his hands with his fingers interlocked and thumbs pointing down, instructing her to do the same. When Crystal complied, he took hold of her thumbs in a milking motion. "Nice to meet you."

Crystal laughed like she did at all the stupid jokes she heard. Straddling him, she removed her top and pulled his head between her breasts. She said, "This is how we say hello in Vegas." One song became two, and halfway through the third song, beneath the extra cushioning, she felt his body shuddering, then go slack. Apologizing profusely for stopping prematurely, he tipped her an extra twenty. Prematurely wasn't his word, but as Crystal watched him pad straight to the restroom afterward, she knew he was another satisfied customer and would be leaving soon after cleaning up. The men's room attendant had told her that he would always find pairs of underwear in the stalls or in the trash because men didn't want to go the rest of the night with creamed drawers or explain the crusty stains to a significant other.

After her brief session with the milkman, Crystal roamed the floor, contemplating just taking the rest of the night off. She was still short on her rent and needed to stay, but looking around at the dismal prospects on the floor, it didn't look like she would make enough anyway. She might as well just get a bag of coke. Her girlfriend Jade, who had taken the stage after her, rationalized buying coke as a business investment, that the bag would provide a return ten times over if sharing a few bumps of it got a guy into the VIP room. But for Crystal, as of late, it had become a straight cost and merely decreased her profits because she did more than she ever shared. She decided instead to go play video poker at the bar and try to turn the hundred she had into four hundred.

Jade stopped her on the way to her favorite machine. "Hey, I think I got a live one over there." She motioned to a booth where Max was talking to a cocktail waitress. "We can definitely get him back to VIP."

"Take him by yourself," Crystal said. "I can't stand that guy."

Jade stroked the back of Crystal's arm. "Don't be like that. Come play with me. I owe you from the last time. You said you needed rent money anyway. It'll be fun. I promise."

Max was wasted already when Jade introduced him to Crystal. So much that he didn't even remember the other times they had met, or maybe he just didn't care. She pegged him as the kind of guy who remembered you only if you could help him. In the booth, Crystal and Jade took turns dancing for Max. Five songs and three shots later, Jade pulled out her bag and served Max several bumps while

Crystal straddled his lap, providing cover. Knowing it was the perfect time with the alcohol, cocaine, and testosterone mixing together, Jade suggested all three go back to the VIP room. Crystal was still undecided if she was going to go, but when Max sunk both his hands into her ass cheeks and implored her to join, she suddenly looked forward to it. She knew she would enjoy fleecing the obnoxious asshole for all she could. The look in his eye communicated that he felt special, that their time together would mean something. All it meant to Crystal was that she would make her rent payment on time for several weeks.

Sometimes Crystal felt bad for guys in the VIP room. It was true that a lot of strippers waited for them to have impaired judgment, or even orchestrated it. They would whisk them back to a quiet, comfortable environment, have attractive women bringing them more drinks with one or more topless girls seated next to them to keep their guards lowered as the host shoved paper after paper to sign, including a thumbprint. Any of these things independently should be enough to communicate the hustle was on, but most guys were already blacked out or too far gone to pull back. If their credit cards weren't declined, the charges would keep mounting until the guys were spent physically. But this time, with Max, she didn't feel bad at all, not one single bit.

Letting Jade take the lead, Crystal just sat next to Max and drank champagne. She occasionally served him some when his glass got low and rubbed on him if his eyes ever wandered from Jade, which they rarely did. Jade continued to bump him up, and since they were the only ones in the VIP room, Jade even let him snort the coke off her chest. All guys fell for the same tricks, thinking they were so unique and special but hooked by the same clichéd stuff.

Sitting next to him, Crystal unbuttoned his pants and lowered his fly. Jade stood over him on the seat and teased him with her crotch, lowering it to his face, then rising up as he stretched his lips and tongue toward her, clamping his head between her thighs if he got too close. Crystal put her hands around his waist and pulled his pants down. Sliding down between his legs, Jade took a condom out of her purse and put it on him. Max leaned his head back. As Jade worked harder below, Max became more aggressive above, and Crystal pushed him away with more force, which seemed only to add to his pleasure. As his body gyrated and tightened from Jade's determination below, Crystal poured champagne between her breasts. It ran down her stomach, into her crotch, soaking through her thong, only making Max want to lean over and lick it off her that much more. Crystal put her palm in the middle of his forehead to keep him at bay.

Jade emerged from under the table with the used condom pinched between her fingers. "I'm going to go freshen up."

Max smacked her ass as she scurried away. His words slurred. "Don't be long. I'm almost ready for round two." He refastened his pants, not even bothering to zip them up.

Crystal sat back in the booth next to Max, using the napkins on the table to dry the champagne off her chest.

Max leaned over, pushing his head toward her chest. "Here, let me lick that up."

"Easy, tiger." Crystal pushed him back into the booth. "Give me a minute." She expected him to come back stronger, but he slid lower into the booth. As she finished drying herself off, she heard a low snore from his direction.

Jade came back, shaking her shoulders. "So who's ready for more?"

Crystal pressed her finger to her lips, speaking in a whisper. "Passed out."

"What should we do?" Jade asked.

Crystal, said, "Fuck it. Let the baby sleep."

And so for the next several hours they did just that. Each hour, Jade just went to Darius and told him that Max wanted to extend for another hour. Since it was an Amex black card, there was no chance it would be declined, and since the club had his thumbprint, there was no way he could dispute the charge. After the champagne was gone, they ordered another bottle and just tipped the waitress extra to not say anything. They ended up having quite a fun evening with him, or rather on him, much more than if he had been awake. They took turns posing for pictures with him, like he was a doll at some sort of twisted tea party.

At around six in the morning, with the bill over five thousand dollars, both of them pretty drunk and tired themselves and completely out of coke, they decided enough was enough and carefully woke him up. He was so out of it, he didn't realize he had even passed out.

Dow Jones Close: 16,027.59

Chapter Eighteen

Date: Friday, December 16, 2011

Dow Jones Open: 11,825.29

Darlene had tried to reconcile Bill and Hughie many times—sometimes subtly and sometimes not so subtly—in the first few years after Hughie moved out. But each attempt was met with the same stubborn resistance from both sides. Neither was willing to admit he was the wrong one. Bill couldn't forgive Hughie for jeopardizing his and Darlene's future, putting his career at risk, and embarrassing him in front of his friends and colleagues. Hughie argued Bill was always a police officer first and a father second.

Even though Hughie ended up getting off with a fine, twelve months of probation, drug counseling, and periodic drug screening—all of which he completed with no problems—he refused to acknowledge that Bill's service record and relationships had anything to do with the lighter sentencing. Instead Hughie dwelled on how he never would have been in that position if Bill would've handled it as a family matter.

And in the middle of all the rationalization, resentment, and good intentions was Darlene, always trying to negotiate the peace. At first she seemed to think both just needed more time, that the wounds would eventually scab and heal and they could be a family again. She would remind Bill of Hughie's birthday, reminisce about the past, and even let details slip about Hughie's life to Bill, like the high marks he was receiving at Rutgers, when he got a girlfriend, and how he got accepted to law school. Bill assumed Darlene did the same with Hughie about him. But despite her persistent and well-meaning efforts, none of it softened Bill. It just made him more certain that he had done the right thing, that by turning Hughie in, he had taught his son a valuable lesson that shaped his character and put him on a path for success. Over the years Bill had watched countless people parade through the station blaming others for their misfortune rather than taking personal responsibility. They never accepted that being arrested might have actually prevented future unfortunate outcomes. Instead they chose to focus on what happened as a result of the action instead of the worse events that were avoided. Bill was OK with the criticism for how he handled Hughie's situation. Anytime he had doubts about what he had done, he looked at all the good that happened in Hughie's life afterward. In Bill's eyes, he saved Hughie. There was no way he was ever going to apologize for that. He had forgiven Hughie for making bad choices, but if there was an apology to be made, Bill was going to be on the receiving end.

This was how so many years passed with nothing changing. Bill's and Hughie's paths neither converged nor diverged. They just ran parallel. Regardless of how much Darlene tried to get the two to intersect, they remained a safe distance from each other. Bill had his life in New Jersey, and Hughie had his as a lawyer in New York City. After a while, Darlene stopped trying to force a reconciliation. She became content with being in the middle and having one hand in each of their lives. That's at least what she told Bill when he recognized she hadn't been pushing for them to get together any longer. She said she was happy with her life with Bill and pleased to see Hughie's life taking a positive direction.

That wasn't to say Bill ever thought Darlene gave up all hope. She was just being more discreet. Bill had noticed that, despite not talking about it, she still liked to leave reminders around the house, like the article Hughie wrote for the school paper, his graduation announcement from Rutgers, his acceptance to University of Virginia law school, and his wedding announcement. All of them Bill read with great pride and satisfaction, but he never said anything, and neither did Darlene.

As any of the important dates approached, Darlene would just make arrangements to go alone. What no one else knew was once she was gone, Bill would go too and stay just far enough away that no one would know he was there, but he was close enough to feel a part of it. As a policeman, he knew how to keep a safe distance. He watched Hughie walk across the commencement stages and receive his diplomas at Rutgers and UVA; he saw countless meals with Darlene and Hughie and his girlfriend and eventual fiancée, Grace; and he watched Hughie and Grace exit the church for the first time as husband and wife.

When the event was about Bill—when he made police captain, when he won officer of the year, and on his sixtieth birthday—he often scanned the perimeter to catch a glimpse of Hughie. Bill liked to think Hughie was out there somewhere, too, watching from a distance like Bill had done so many times before.

When Bill decided to retire, it was no different. On the way to the retirement party, Bill came right out and asked Darlene. "Did you tell Hughie and Grace about the party?"

Darlene feigned surprise. "Now, why on earth would I do that? If you wanted him to know, you should've told him yourself."

"Come on, Darlene," Bill said. "I know all those notes and articles over the years I've found about him were left intentionally."

"Did you want me to invite him?" Darlene asked. "'Cause I can call him right now—or better yet, you call him." She extended her mobile phone toward him.

Bill kept both hands on the wheel and eyes on the road. "No, I was just wondering."

"William Price, I have put up with this baloney for too many years," Darlene said, still holding out the phone. "I'm tired of being in the middle. If you want him there, call him and say so for yourself."

Bill shook his head. "That's OK. I just wanted to prepare myself in case he was going to be there."

Despite Darlene's denial, all night Bill watched the door of the Fraternal Order of Police hall where the party was held. Regardless of the conversation or activity he was engaged in, if someone entered, Bill's eyes flashed in that direction. His preoccupation did not go unnoticed by Darlene. At one point she took his hand and said, "I told you, if you wanted him here so badly, you should've had me invite him." Bill did not respond to her comment, but when the next person appeared in the doorway, Bill's eyes were the first to greet that person.

The retirement party had been all Darlene's idea. If it were up to Bill, he would've skipped the whole thing and just gone out to dinner with Darlene. He had told her as much, and it was her insistence on having the party that made him think she had bigger plans. Bill never liked being the center of attention. He was more comfortable hanging back, observing, ready to act only as a last resort. That was probably what made him such a good police officer. He let the situation dictate what response was necessary, and was more interested in diffusing than initiating action. That's also probably why he had such a hard time letting go of what happened between him and Hughie. Bill knew that, by taking Hughie down to the police station, he had completely left his comfort zone and overreacted, but he couldn't bring himself to undo any of it.

Watching Darlene at the party and seeing how happy she was, Bill recognized that the celebration was about more than the divide between Bill and Hughie or giving Bill the send-off he so rightly deserved. The party was actually for Darlene.

It was the milestone she had been looking forward to more than any other. The end of Bill's career as a police officer was the end of her worry. No longer would she have to stiffen at the sound of every siren, wondering if it was Bill rushing to danger; or avoid all news reports until Bill returned safely home each night; or crease the carpet, pacing, if he wasn't home when he was supposed to be. The party officially signified that those days were behind her, and the part of her life—the one she had always dreamed of, where it would be just the two of them—was beginning.

So while each of Bill's friends and colleagues delivered toast after toast in his honor, and while each one got longer and more sentimental as the alcohol took over, Bill just smiled and gazed upon the remarkable woman seated next to him and promised himself that every moment going forward would be about her and making up for everything he had put her through.

As the chief spoke about Bill's career and prepared to present him with a plaque for his thirty-seven years of service, Bill knew everyone would be expecting him to say a few words. Darlene, aware how much he hated public speaking, had coached him on the moment. She had said, "Now, you don't have to talk long. Just thank everybody for coming and for their friendship and support over the years. You can talk as long or as little as you like, but you have to say something."

But the thing was, in that moment, as the chief said his final words and extended the plaque toward Bill amongst all the applause and jeers for a speech, Bill knew exactly what he was going to say and what he was going to do. He had planned to wait until they got home, but seeing how happy Darlene was, he knew there was no use in waiting any longer. She had waited long enough.

Bill shook the chief's hand with the right while receiving the plaque with the left, holding the pose so the photographer Darlene had hired for the party could capture the moment. As Bill lowered the plaque to his side, the chief retained hold of his right hand and pulled him in for a hug with the left, eliciting cheers of "Get a room!" from the well-lubricated attendees. Darlene told Bill later that she had never seen him so red.

As the chief returned to his table and the hoots and gibes faded, Bill read the plaque, and then looked out at all the men and women that had been such a big part of his life.

"Well, you know I'm not one for speeches. If a person strings ten words together in a sentence, in my opinion they probably used four too many—of course, excluding you, Chief." He nodded toward the chief, eliciting laughter from the audience.

"You don't have to kiss his ass anymore," someone yelled, causing more crowing from the crowd.

"No, I suppose I don't," Bill said. "In all seriousness, I'd like to thank the chief and all the officers and staff for the support over the years." He looked at the plaque again. "Thirty-seven years. To me it seems like yesterday I was just getting out of the academy. But I know one person who doesn't feel that way. For her, the time has not flown by at all. She has lived every second of these past thirty-seven years, probably many times over. You see, the life of a police officer is toughest on the spouse. When we're not home, they worry about if we're coming home, and then when we are home, they have to deal with what we went through while we were away. There's very little off-the-clock time for our spouses.

"As many of you know, Darlene and I have been going to Vegas every summer for as long as I can remember. Now, we're not big gamblers. We just like getting lost in the shuffle out there. The last few years we've been talking about what we're going to do after I retired, and during the last trip to Vegas, we even went as far as to look at a place." Bill removed a paper from the breast pocket of his jacket and looked toward Darlene. "Well, honey, I bought that place." He held out the plaque in one hand and the paper in the other. "I'd like to dedicate tonight to all of our families and especially to my sweet Darlene. Thanks for the past thirty-seven, and here's to thirty-seven more in Vegas."

As much as Darlene had planned everything for the party, judging by the look on her face, she hadn't anticipated this. Tears streamed down, but her smile had never been wider. She blew a kiss toward Bill. Forgetting all the other people in the room, he walked over, set the plaque and paper on the table, and lifted her up into his arms. He said, "You don't ever have to worry about me leaving you again."

Dow Jones Close: 11,868.81

Chapter Nineteen

Date: Wednesday, September 15, 2010

Dow Jones Open: 10,526.42

In a Midwestern sports town like St. Louis, when the starting goalie of the NHL team starts dating and eventually marries the most popular local TV sports reporter, it's more than news. It's a downright modern fairy tale. It harkened the public back to a simpler time, when the quarterback dated the prom queen, and people weren't consumed with jealousy and resentment and actually wanted them to make it. Penny and Alec were local royalty. St. Louis was not known for having a lot of paparazzi, but when Penny and Alec were in public, a crowd formed and flashes popped. People could not get enough of their storybook romance. Unfortunately the security the fans felt in the mob fostered brashness and invaded Penny and Alec's privacy. The more public the setting and the more that people gathered around them, the more personal the questions became. First it was, *How did you meet?* then, *Was it serious? Whose house do you sleep at? When are you getting married?* and almost immediately after the ceremony, *When are you starting a family?*

None of the other questions bothered Penny because she knew the answer and just chose not to share. But when it came to the family question, she wasn't sure. The whole courtship had been such a whirlwind that they had never really discussed it. Both were so busy with their careers and the wedding, what little time they did have was focused on more pressing needs, not looking into the future.

Penny had always had a strict no-kids policy. Maybe it was because her mom deserted her dad and her when she was only three. Maybe it was because her dad died when she was a junior in college and she was left all alone. Whatever the reason, she knew she never wanted to be responsible for another human being. If a guy she was dating asked her about children or even looked with that goofy smile and fond "someday" resolution at a child, she broke up with him, or at least demoted him from boyfriend to occasional booty call. After one scare in college, she never had even a single close call. Her birth control had control. It was like a safe locked inside a vault in the secret room of an impenetrable fortress, surrounded by a wall with a moat. Nothing was ever going to make it through again. It wasn't the children she ultimately was afraid of; it was the impact on her career. If she was going to give something up, it was kids. Even if she didn't have to relinquish her job completely, she knew the whole kid thing would at least slow her down. She wouldn't be as mobile, and her life would no longer be as simple. Regardless of what others told her, with all other characteristics being equal, if a promotion came down to a person with baggage and one without, the person with kids in tow would lose every single time.

What bothered Penny so much when they questioned her and Alec about children was the sudden shift the question triggered. It was no longer just about what she wanted. The path on the map she had been following had suddenly merged with another. For the first time in as long as she could remember, how, when, and in which direction the new path would continue was unknown. After the wedding she knew her life was going to change and that she would need to compromise on some things, but she had never realized she would have to chart an entire new course.

Later that night at home, Penny walked into their bedroom in her robe, toweling her hair. Alec was in bed, watching the sports highlights on the flat-screen TV hanging on the wall in front of the bed. She said, "I still get shocked by what complete strangers will ask us. Just because we both work in the public eye, our entire lives are on display."

"To tell you the truth, I don't even hear them anymore." Alec aimed the remote and turned off the TV. "You referring to something specific or just in general?"

"I don't know." She walked over and sat on the edge of the bed. "Just in general, I guess. They get so personal, like they actually know us."

"Can you blame them?" Alec leaned forward and kissed her. "They fall in love with you the same way I did."

Penny pushed him away playfully. "Like they're really interested in me. There are a lot more hockey fans than news fans." She rose from the bed and ambled over to the mirrored closet doors, wrapping the towel around her head and flipping the end back like a turban. "You know, we never really did talk much about a family."

"What's there to talk about? I just assumed you never wanted kids."

Even though that was true, Penny took offense to the remark. "Why would you say that? You don't think I'd make a good mother?"

"It's not that at all. I just can't see you staying home wiping noses and asses." Alec got up from the bed and walked up behind her. "You'd be an incredible mother." He wrapped his arms around her and kissed her exposed neck.

She dropped her head forward. "But what do you want?"

"I think we should practice as much as possible." He loosened the belt on her robe, which fell open. Penny turned toward him. He said, "Practice makes perfect, you know."

She pushed him back onto the bed. "I guess there's not much to really worry about anyway. You goaltenders have never been known as great scorers."

"Don't underestimate us." He rolled her over on her back. On top of her, his gaze burned through and melted her, just like the first night they met. "We know where the defense is most vulnerable and weak." With her guiding him, he thrust inside her. "And can slip one by anytime we want."

Fear shot through Penny, not because she believed he could and would, but because she wanted him to.

Dow Jones Close: 10,572.73

Chapter Twenty

Date: Saturday, December 15, 2012

Dow Jones Open: Closed

After Les decided to leave the Church, for the first time in his adult life he was on the outside looking in. His first call was to the one person he knew who shared his passion and belief but had chosen to practice and share his benevolence outside the structure of religion: Martin Samuels, an old friend and classmate from his time at the Institute for Black Catholic Studies. Whereas Les opted to go into the ministry, Martin hadn't agreed with the direction and support provided by the Church for lower-income urban areas, so he went a more general philanthropic route and opened the Oasis, a homeless shelter in Vegas, about twenty years ago.

Les and Martin initially became friends over long and often late into the night debates over the balance of power in the Church. Martin believed in more collaborative governing, allowing the bishops freedom to fix their positions on public issues. Les was more willing to acquiesce and trust the decisions made at higher levels for a more aligned and unified Church. While as the years progressed their discussions didn't happen as frequently, Les and Martin had always remained connected, first by letter then by email. They never fully agreed, but with the appointment of Pope Francis and his guidance toward a more synodal practice, they were as aligned as they had ever been.

It had been six weeks since their last email exchange, just before the incident and accusations surfaced. For as deep as their conversations usually delved, Les started his phone call as simply as he could. "Martin, it's Les."

Martin's voice escalated, infused with energy. "Well, Father Banks, so nice to hear from you. Tired of the delayed gratification of our correspondence and finally call to argue with me in person?"

Les said, "I was actually hoping to do it face-to-face. Thinking about coming for a visit."

"Don't I feel special?" Martin said. "Twenty years and you're finally willing to spend some of that abundant vacation time on an old friend."

"It's not really a vacation." Les paused, still not comfortable with the words he was about to say. They jumbled in the back of his throat then just tumbled out. "I've chosen to leave the Church."

The enthusiasm emptied from Martin. "What? Where is this coming from? None of your last e-mails even mentioned this. What happened?"

"There will be plenty of time for questions," Les said. "I'd rather not get into it on the phone. Consider this more of a spiritual pilgrimage for counsel from a trusted advisor. That is, if you'll have me."

"Of course. We have plenty of space and could always use another set of hands and a heart like yours. Actually, your timing couldn't be more perfect. I could use some of that pragmatic Banks perspective as well. When should I expect you?"

Les said, "Sooner rather than later. I have a few things to wrap up here but should be finished by the end of the week. I'll book a flight for Saturday and email the details."

The excitement returned to Martin. "Wonderful. Indeed a blessing. I'll come pick you up at the airport."

As a priest, Les was used to being looked after. He knew that would all stop, and thought it best to start fending for himself. "Thank you, but that's not necessary. I'll take a taxi. I'm sure you have plenty of better things to do."

Martin said, "Don't thank me yet. You haven't seen the old beater of a truck I have. Mostly just a grocery wagon, but it can make it to McCarran and back. You might want to pack your rosary in your carry-on though and say a few prayers."

From their years of debate, Les knew he wasn't going to change Martin's mind. Only God could do that. Martin didn't leave the Church because of his lack of faith and commitment. He left because of it. The Church just happened to be on the wrong side of his beliefs. Martin trusted that if God had wanted him to stay in the Church, he never would've been able to leave. Of all the cardinals, bishops, and priests Les had known, Martin was the most spiritual, and that was why Les knew Martin was the right person to seek out. Even something as trivial as a ride from the airport, if Martin had it in his head he was going to fetch Les, Martin would be there, whether Les accepted or not. "OK, my friend," Les said. "I'll send you the arrival details and you tell me where to meet you."

Seventy-two hours later, Les's plane touched down at McCarran. Martin had said he would come inside and wait at the bottom of the escalators by the baggage claim to ensure he wouldn't miss Les. Both had taken care of themselves, so despite some wear and tear from the years and the loss and graying of their hair, they easily recognized each other. As with all dear friends, the time apart faded in a blink, and the two picked up right where they had left off.

Neither had ever been one for small talk, so it wasn't surprising that before they had even turned off Russell Road, leaving the airport, Martin was grilling Les about the events leading up to his departure. Les had expected Martin to be supportive and approve of the move if for no other reason than as a vindication of Martin's own actions so many years ago. Instead, with the changing attitudes in Rome and the years Les had put in, Martin challenged and questioned Les's decisions for almost the entire ride. It wasn't until Les explained the details of his exit and the choices he would have had, or the lack thereof, if he had stayed that Martin conceded. It actually might have been the only time Les bested Martin in a discussion. Most ended in a draw. This one went to Les for the simple reason he turned Martin's own thinking on him. "If God had wanted me to stay," Les said, "He probably wouldn't have let me leave."

"I can't argue with that." Martin smiled, acknowledging his defeat as he pulled up in front of the Oasis in the Arts District. There was only one other car on the street, and most of the other surrounding buildings were boarded up, with the exception of a locksmith on the opposite corner from the Oasis. A sold sign and picture of the future development stood in the vacant lot across California. Les surveyed the desolation of the surrounding area. "Looks like your neighbors don't give you much trouble."

"Not yet at least," Martin said. "This whole neighborhood is changing over though. Everyone else has been forced out by rising rents. Good thing I had the foresight to sign a ten-year lease. People said I was crazy and that I overpaid, and maybe I did the first few years, but now I'm one of the few left."

Outside the door, a line or rather organized encampment had already formed in search of dinner and a bed for the night. Fortunately, in late September there were always plenty of both. Most days the temperatures hovered in the low to mid eighties during the day and sixties at night, so many of the regulars were happy to fend for themselves and sleep outside. It was the June to August and December to January periods when food and space were both tight. Martin grabbed Les's suitcase out of the back of the truck. "Here we are. What she lacks in personality, she makes up for in character, or maybe it's the other way around."

"Are we talking about you or the building?" Les said.

With dinner only ninety minutes away, Martin immediately put Les to work. He explained how the volunteers usually showed up about an hour before, but since he never knew how many would come, he liked to get an early start in case he was on his own. Saturday was spaghetti night, so he put Les in charge of boiling the pasta, showing him how to transfer it to the silver serving trays to keep it warm in the oven while making another batch. As Les churned out the pasta, Martin tended to the sauce.

While they worked, Martin filled Les in on the operation. Thirty to fifty people usually showed for dinner, so all the recipes were made to feed forty. Martin directed the volunteers to serve smaller portion sizes until he was sure they had enough to accommodate everyone. After that, he made seconds available for those still hungry. In all the years Martin had been serving dinner at the Oasis, he had never run out and never had leftovers. Sometimes twenty ate for forty and others, the same amount served sixty. Most important was that everyone who came to the Oasis received a hot meal.

After dinner was served, anyone who wanted to stay for the night could choose a bed in the billet, which was simply a five-thousand-square-foot rectangular space with four rows of ten single cots. Any remaining beds after dinner were made available on a first come, first serve basis to late arrivers. The doors stayed open from six to ten p.m. If the beds filled before that, Martin locked up for the night. For liability and safety reasons, following several altercations a few years back, Martin had installed video cameras and hired a security person to work through the night from ten to six in the morning, when he got up to prepare breakfast.

Anyone who spent the night got breakfast the next day, which was more continental than traditional, consisting of a banana, a yogurt, a bagel, and an orange juice. When they first opened, Martin had tried doing two hot meals a day, but it was just too much work. Anything left after the overnighters ate was made available to the public. Unlike dinner, they almost always ran out due to the prepackaged portions. Everyone had to be out by eight o'clock, when he locked up again and reset for the evening.

Seeing it for the first time, it seemed like a lot of work to Les, and it surely was. But for Martin, he had been doing it so long that it had become an efficient operation, and he did get a lot of help from volunteers. The cleaning and prep work were usually done by ten or eleven in the morning, so he had his afternoons pretty much free other than shopping a few days a week. Since Martin didn't require more than five to six hours of sleep, he also always had a few hours of free time after closing each night.

On the night Les arrived, Martin took him up to the roof, where he liked to spend most of his evenings, after the work was done. The building was only two stories, but in the Arts District, hardly any of buildings were more than two, so he had a 360-degree view of all the twinkling lights from the strip to downtown and all around the surrounding valley. For being in the middle of a city, it was surprisingly peaceful and quiet. The occasional squeaking bus brakes, a car horn, or an accelerating motorcycle were the only sounds.

Martin walked to the edge and lit a cigarette. Les shook his head. As long as he had known him, Martin had been a smoker. "All these years, and you still got that bad habit?" Les said. "You always said you would quit."

"Well there's a lot I always said I would do." Martin filled his lungs and exhaled slowly. "I've cut back a lot...at least on the smoking. Down to just one a day. I still talk more than I should."

"Seems like you're doing a lot here." Les walked up beside him, standing shoulder-to-shoulder and looking southward toward the strip. "Almost twenty years of forty people a day. That's roughly fourteen thousand a year times twenty... uh, two hundred eighty thousand people. Pretty impressive."

Martin laughed. "Still good with numbers, I see. You could be dangerous in this town. Remember that time after our college graduation before seminary school when we went out on that riverboat and you won over three grand playing blackjack? They banned you from the table. Said you were counting cards."

"I was counting." Les said in a matter-of-fact tone.

Martin coughed a cloud of smoke. "What? You never told me that. We all gave that pit boss such a hard time. Even pulled the religious card on him. If we hadn't been out on the water, they would've thrown us out."

"I'm pretty sure they were thinking about it anyway," Les said. "In my defense though, I donated that money to the Church."

"All of it?" Martin asked.

"Well most of it. How do you think I supported myself back then?"

Martin pointed his cigarette at Les, the red tip bobbing in the darkness. "Lester Banks, you dog. All those late nights I thought you were studying, you were actually out cruising the Mississippi, fleecing the casinos. Maybe you coming here is meant to be."

The last comment piqued Les's interest. His voice rose, filled with curiosity. "What do you mean by that?"

Martin dropped his cigarette and snuffed it out with the bottom of his shoe, picking up the butt and dropping it in his breast pocket. "Nothing really. Just for about the past year I've been thinking about a change. Just feel like I need to do something different. Been reading a lot about missionary trips in Africa, but every time it comes to taking action, I think about this place and what would happen to the people who need it. When you called and told me about your situation and wanting to come for a visit, I thought we might be able to help each other. The Lord doesn't always work in such mysterious ways. Sometimes they're quite simple and right in front of us."

Les said, "I'll admit, the timing is curious. But I don't know anything about running a mission or these people or this area. I mean, you're a part of this community. They trust you. I'd be an outsider."

"Trust me, you'd have it down in no time," Martin said, his cadence increasing as he started to sell Les on the idea. "Every day is the same. And it's not like I'm just going to run out on you. I'd stay a month or so until you were comfortable with everything and everyone knew you. It's amazing how quickly people accept you when you're doling out food and lodging to forty souls a day."

Les stared at the blinking lights on top of the Stratosphere. "I guess it's not something that needs to be decided tonight. How about I just stay for a few weeks and pitch in and help and we see where we are? God has brought us here. Let's see where He intends for us to go."

Dow Jones Close: Closed

Chapter Twenty-One

Date: Monday, November 5, 1990

Dow Jones Open: 2,490.84

Max boarded the school bus. His morning ride to Raisinville Elementary was the worst fifteen minutes of his day. If he was lucky, he'd find an empty seat at the front and avoid the runway of ridicule he faced going to the back. He didn't need an entire seat for himself. He would gladly share one. But the unoccupied seats always seemed to have books or backpacks shoved over when Max came down the aisle. If he stopped and asked the people to clear the seats, they either didn't acknowledge him or conveyed that the seats were saved. He didn't even try anymore. It just drew more attention to how no one wanted to be next to him, and they teased him even more. On this day, his seat was two-thirds of the way back on the right.

Max never expected to be at Raisinville as long as he had been. He started in first grade and now was in fifth. Being a foster kid, he just expected to move around. One move was good. It probably meant the child landed with an adopting family for permanent placement or possibly back with his or her original family, as long as whatever issue that put the child in foster care in the first place had been resolved to the state's liking. More than one move almost always was bad. It surely didn't mean the child was in demand. Most likely it signaled problems between him or her and the parents or with the other kids in the home. But never moving at all was even worse. It suggested no one wanted the child, and probably no one would. At least when a child moved, he or she was hopeful things would be better or that the new move would lead to a final move.

Max had pretty much given up on all the options. His biological mother had surrendered him at birth because she was young and single and he had achondroplasia. Since Max's dwarfism wasn't going to change, Max didn't expect his mother's perspective on a special-needs child to change either. He actually had been fortunate, being adopted just after his first birthday by a young couple, which was how he ended up in Monroe. The young couple had been trying to have a baby for three years with no success. Eventually learning it was due to the husband's sterility, they turned to adoption and chose Max.

Unfortunately, when Max's adoptive mother became pregnant four years later and it wasn't by his adoptive father, they divorced. Sadly, neither wanted custody of Max. She was excited to start her new life with her new husband and baby. To his adoptive father, Max was a reminder of the infidelity and his own inability to father children. Optimistic that one of the adoptive parents might change their mind, the foster care review board decided to keep Max in a foster home in Monroe.

Max, too, had been hopeful for a permanent placement the first few years. Once he started kindergarten and moved on to first grade, he gained confidence and thought for sure someone, either new or old, would come along and claim him. But that never happened, so nothing changed. Well, nothing for him at least. The other foster children in the home where Max lived had changed twice. The first time a girl reunited with her birth mother after the mom finally kicked her drug habit. The other, a three-year-old boy, was adopted by a family from Toledo. Max's foster parents also had another baby, a girl this time, to go with the two-year-old boy they already had. With the household filling with actual offspring, Max thought for sure he would be moving. But it never happened.

The only thing that did change for Max was that each year the physical differences between him and his classmates became more noticeable. The confidence Max felt from the first few years of school eroded. He never thought of himself as disabled or different, but the other students did and treated him accordingly, so he never saw a reason to advertise it. He let them figure it out on their own. By fifth grade, with pretty much all of the boys over a foot taller than him, and his arms disproportionately short for the size of his torso, he knew pretty much everyone was wise to his condition. The ones who weren't got there pretty quickly due to his nicknames: Maxie Smurf, Maxkin, Mini-Max, Minimum, and of course all the other standards like Oompa-Loompa, Fun-Size, Niblet—whatever cruel names kids could come up with to keep the focus off of them.

Not everyone was mean to him though. Some of the kids tried to be his friend. The problem was that Max didn't want to be friends with them. They were all the socially awkward kids, in his view, the dorks. Max didn't see himself that way. He didn't make fun of these other kids, but he definitely didn't consider himself one of them. Aligning with the dorks would only bring more teasing. He was much happier on his own.

Heading down the bus aisle, three punches in the arm and one ear-flick later, Max poured himself into the vacant seat. It was actually a pretty easy day compared to usual. He hadn't been knocked over and didn't lose anything on the way. He slid to the window. The hot, stuffy air inside the bus had fogged the glass due to the chilly November air outside. He wiped the condensation with his sleeve so he could see out. The bus accelerated. He counted the mailboxes lining the side of the road. It was part of the game he created to help pass the time. He knew there were thirty-two on this side and thirty-seven on the other between his stop and school. Each mailbox counted one point if the flag was down, two if it was up. The previous record on this side was fifty-three. He thought with the holidays ahead, that record could be in jeopardy due to all the outgoing letters and packages. Focusing on the outside world was much more interesting, and safer.

Max leaned his head against the window. The cold, wet surface soothed his throbbing temples. His stomach groaned. He looked around. Fortunately no one else heard it. He didn't need to give them any more ammunition. Another growl erupted. His body was staging an obvious protest about his oversleeping and missing breakfast. Unzipping his backpack, he took out his sack lunch, which was already smashed into a ball. He hated stuffing it in with his books, but if he didn't, someone would just pluck it from him on his way down the aisle. A wadded-up sandwich and crushed potato chips were better than nothing at all.

Peeling open the brown paper sack, he removed the sandwich and flattened it on his leg. The strawberry jelly oozed out against the side of the plastic wrap. Too hungry to wait, he unwrapped the plastic. What he would eat for lunch would be a problem for later. Much hungrier than he realized, he took large bites, each bigger than the previous one. When he bit into the center, a glob of jelly dropped into his lap, directly on his crotch. Of course he hadn't put a napkin down. The jelly absorbed instantly into his khaki pants. Max fished out the napkin from his lunch sack, attempting to soak up the stain. He blotted; he pressed; he rubbed. But between the bumps and the shifting speed of the bus, all he managed to do was smear the stain across and deeper into his pants.

The student across the aisle noticed Max rubbing his crotch. "Having fun, Maxie? Hey look everybody, Max is playing with himself."

"No I'm not." Max lifted the napkin. "I just dropped some food."

The two students in the seat in front of him turned around. "Ooh," the boy against the window said. "Maxkin had an accident."

"Maxident, Maxident!" the one on the aisle chimed in.

"It's just jelly," Max said, shoving the jelly-stained plastic wrap toward their faces.

Students two and three rows away joined in. Row by row, heads popped up and rotated toward Max. One of the sixth-grade girls in the seat behind him said, "Gross! Max had his period."

Max wadded up the plastic and threw it at her. The bus driver's eyes appeared in the overhead mirror, searching for the source of the commotion. All the students were kneeling on their seats and turned toward Max. "Butts down everyone, or I'm pulling this bus over, and everyone is getting assigned seats."

The students dropped down, but the jeering didn't stop.

"Max is on the rag."

"Congratulations, Max. You're finally a woman."

"Somebody give him a Maxipad!"

A roar of laughter rolled across the bus. Seat by seat, the chant grew. Even the ones who didn't know what was going on joined the chant. "Max-i-pad. Max-i-pad. Max-i-pad. Max-i-pad. Max-i-pad."

Max didn't bother refuting them. He had learned that lesson long ago. Fighting back only added fuel to the ridicule. Ignoring it was the best way to let the fire burn itself out. Hearing the strength and cadence of this chant, he knew it was going to stick longer than just the bus ride to school. He took his Walkman out of the backpack, put the headphones on, and turned up the Genesis tape as loud as it would go. He could still hear the derisive melody around him, but they didn't know that. He focused back on the outside world, counting the remaining mailboxes amidst Phil Collins cooing in his ears about some kind of misunderstanding, some kind of mistake. The bus pulled up in front of the school. With the backpack in his lap, he waited until all the other students filed off.

On Max's way down the aisle, the bus driver stopped him. "What happened this time, Max?"

Max swung the backpack over his right shoulder and lifted up his puffy jacket that extended to mid-thigh. The three-inch round stain was in the worst possible position, dead center on his crotch. "Today's going to be a long day," he said.

"Don't let them get to you," she said. "What if you sit up by me from now on? I can save a seat right behind me just for you."

As much as Max wanted that, he knew it would only make things worse. They would just use it to make fun of him even more. He said, "Thanks, Shirley, but I'll be OK. Short on size, long on character." He looped his left arm through the other strap and shrugged on the backpack, adjusting the front of his coat down to cover the stain.

Max went straight to his classroom. He bypassed the coatroom and sat at his desk. At least with the coat on, the stain was hidden. Better to be hot and uncomfortable than show off a bull's-eye on your crotch. He dug out his unfinished homework and started working. Only a few of his classmates rode his bus. He just needed to stay under the radar long enough for everyone to find something else to mock.

The bell rang. The other students scurried to their seats. Max kept his head down, working on his homework. When Mrs. Peters entered, she said, "Good morning, class. Will everyone take out their math assignment from last night while we wait for the morning announcements?" She walked down the aisle, stopping at a desk and waiting until the student had followed her instructions. Principal Andrews's voice radiated from the speaker box with the typical daily nonevents.

Max could hear and smell Mrs. Peters coming up behind him. She always wore too much perfume. She stopped behind him, a blast of the flowery, powdery scent continuing down the aisle. He scribbled down the final answer. She bent over, speaking in a whisper, her breath smelling of coffee and nicotine. He preferred the perfume. She said, "Max, you know we don't allow jackets in the classroom. Please take yours to the coatroom."

Pushing his finished homework toward her as a bargaining chip, Max tilted his head, pleading softly. "Can't I keep mine? Just for today. I promise."

Mrs. Peters had red, bushy hair and deep-set green eyes—or maybe her eyes weren't that deep. Her cheeks were just that round. She waddled back a few steps to give him space to get out of his desk. "If I let you, then others will want theirs." She put her hands on her hips, which stuck out like two shelves. "It would be an absolute mess."

"But—"

"No buts, mister. Hustle up." She lifted her left arm from her hip, extending it toward the coatroom. "We have a lot to do today."

Max trudged to the coatroom, regretting his decision to keep the coat in the first place. If he had dumped it right away, he might have gotten to the first restroom break before anyone noticed his pants. Now he was going to be on full display on the way back to his seat.

Mrs. Peters was on her way down the next aisle with her back to Max when he emerged from the coatroom. He hurried to his seat. One of the students looked up and snickered. Others followed. A student from the bus roused the refrain from the ride to school. "Look at Maxi-pad!"

The class erupted.

Mrs. Peters spun around. "That's enough." Her eyes flashed to Max and down to his crotch. "Settle down, everyone. Just a little accident."

The student from the bus chimed in. "A Maxident!"

"Evander! Hallway, now," Mrs. Peters pointed to the door and followed him amongst a chorus of "Ooohs." She turned back toward the class. "If I so much as hear a peep from anyone, you'll be in for recess for a week."

Under the stern watch of Mrs. Peters, the rest of the morning was uneventful, but everything started again at lunch. Since Max's lunch had caused the whole problem, he didn't have much to eat to distract him from all the staring and sneering in the cafeteria. Like most days, he sat at a table with third graders. Under normal circumstances, the lunchroom monitors probably wouldn't have allowed someone in fifth grade sitting with third graders, but physically Max blended in, and there were never any problems. The third graders never said anything to him, and he never spoke to them. Listening to his Walkman, he quickly devoured his remaining chips and the bruised, mostly brown banana and got a head start on his homework until the bell signaled it was time to line up to go back to class.

The second half of the day wasn't as bad as the first. Mrs. Peters allowed Max to stay in for recess and helped him clean his pants. Well, actually she did it for him. She had gotten a pair of shorts from the gym teacher and had Max change once all the kids were out at recess. Max waited in the nurse's office while she cleaned his pants in the teachers' lounge. All that was left was a faint outline around the edge of the stain. Unless somebody knew what they were looking for, they'd never see it. *Good ol' Mrs. Peters.* She really saved the day. He'd never make fun of her perfume or shape again.

On the bus ride home, even though earlier Max had discouraged a special seat, Shirley had saved one for him. She said, "Just for today. All this will blow over by tomorrow."

Exhausted from all the stress and drama, Max gladly accepted the charity. He ducked into the seat behind Shirley and stared out the window to count the mailboxes home, knowing exactly what he was going to do first thing he got there. What had happened that day was never going to happen again.

Shuffling off the bus amidst fading cheers of "Maxipad," Max headed straight to the garage, which was open, with his foster mom's car on the left and a vacant spot on the right, since his foster dad was still at work. Max dropped his backpack on the floor in the middle of the vacant space and started rummaging through all the leftover supplies from when they remodeled the basement. He examined pieces of carpet, paneling, and curtains, but none of them were quite right.

Max's foster mom came out from the house, his baby foster sister tucked under her arm. "I thought I heard you out here. Good day at school? Whatcha looking for?"

Max didn't bother telling her about school. She would just worry, or worse, go to the school and complain. He said, "Remember that roll of the fake leather stuff we used to cover those cushions for the bench in the basement? It's called neatherhyde or something like that."

"You mean Naugahyde?" She walked over, bouncing the baby on her hip. "I think it's in the cabinet over there." She motioned with her head to the standing cabinet to Max's left. "What on earth do you need that for?"

"It's for a project at school. Do you care if I use it?"

"Use it all," she said. "I've been trying to get Jim to throw it away for a year. You know how he is though. Hates wasting stuff. Always thinks he'll use it later."

"Thanks, Gwen." Max opened up the cabinet. The roll was leaning in the corner behind a few rakes and shovels. "There it is. This should work perfectly." He moved the tools and pulled out the roll, dropping it with a thump onto the garage floor.

"Be careful," Gwen said. "The princess and I are going to head back in and finish dinner. Pot roast tonight." She turned but hesitated. "Do me a favor though? Don't tell Jim you needed it. I'll never hear the end of it."

"No problem. It'll be our secret." Max unrolled a large section of the Naugahyde. Gwen went back in the house. He dug out a pair of lawn shears from the cabinet and cut the material in different sizes and shapes, positioning them in front of him on the concrete. Sitting cross-legged, he picked up each one and stretched it across his lap. Deciding on the square piece eighteen inches by eighteen, he collected the others and threw them in the garbage, piling other trash on so Jim wouldn't see them. A used wooden paint stirrer rested on top. "Handles," he said. "This thing is going to need handles."

Dow Jones Close: 2,519.06

Chapter Twenty-Two

Date: Wednesday, March 11, 2009

Dow Jones Open: 6,923.13

Crystal's mobile phone vibrated, belting out the Destiny Child's ringtone assigned to her agent: *Say my name, say my name. When no one is around you, say baby I love you. If you ain't runnin' game, say my name, say my name.*

She yanked the phone out of the back pocket of her stretchy capri jeans. Calls from her agent never got screened. Whether she was expecting a callback or just hoping for another audition, she was always happy to hear that ringtone. The real problem was when the phone didn't ring. No news was ever good news when it came to Maura.

Maura had known Crystal since she put on her first pair of ballet shoes and angled into her first turnout. Maura had been Valeria's agent, and over the years had booked her for gigs from television commercials to studio work to live performances all throughout Los Angeles. Maura probably could've landed a lot more for Valeria, but Valeria was never willing to travel because she didn't want to be away from Crystal.

Valeria didn't just turn away work for herself. Maura always seemed to find ample opportunities for Crystal as well: *Leggy seven-year-old with dance background, Fresh-faced nine-year-old with strong pipes, Tall, graceful ten-year-old with piercing eyes.* Crystal qualified for them all, but Valeria was firm. She didn't want Crystal starting until she was fourteen and had a strong vocal and dance foundation. That way Valeria would be sure Crystal was in it for the right reasons. She knew from her own experience that the only thing that got a person through all the rejection was the passion.

Not only did Crystal stick with it until she was fourteen, she excelled at every recital and performance opportunity she had. Regardless of the show, everyone always wanted to know afterward, *Who was that exotic gazelle with the golden voice?*

Even though she knew the answer when she called Valeria with opportunities for Crystal, Maura made Valeria decline every one, hoping she might relent. But Valeria never did. She didn't want to be one of those showbiz moms who forced her own failed dreams on her daughter. And Crystal was never to know about any of it. That was the agreement, and Valeria was adamant that if Maura ever broke the agreement, she would never book anything for Crystal even after her fourteenth birthday. So it became a game they played: Maura would pitch an opportunity, Valeria would decline, and Crystal was oblivious, always thinking Maura was calling to talk to Valeria about her career. When Crystal knew her mom was talking to Maura, she would get excited, jumping up and down, screaming, "Did you get it? Did you get it?" Valeria would just tell her it wasn't the right part and say nothing more.

Once Crystal turned fourteen and her beauty and talents blossomed, taking on a momentum all their own, the opportunities also increased. But there were still rules. Crystal could not work on school nights, and either Valeria or Maura had to accompany her. If Crystal ever broke either rule, Valeria vowed to void the contract with Maura and not let Crystal work until she was eighteen. Like all teenagers, Crystal pushed the limits and crossed the line a few times, and somehow every time Maura would find out, but Maura never told Valeria, so it was like the pre-fourteen auditioning game, only this time Valeria was the oblivious one.

Even with the working restrictions, Crystal worked steadily through high school and made enough money that she never had to take a normal job like other high schoolers and was able to contribute to their living expenses so they could move out of their studio apartment into a two bedroom. Valeria wanted Crystal to save the money for college, but she also knew Crystal was too old to be sleeping in the same bed as her mother (even though one of them always seemed to find her way into the other's bed after they moved at least three or four times per week). So despite her reservations, Valeria accepted the money but still found a way to stuff half of what Crystal gave her into a savings account, and, if Valeria ever was short during the month, she scraped together what she needed by sacrificing her own needs. Everything Valeria ever bought for herself was second- or maybe even third- or fourthhand. Who knows how many times the thrift store items exchanged hands before they landed in hers? She didn't care though. Her baby girl was worth it.

Crystal pressed the phone to her ear, launching into the conversation. "Whatcha got for me, Maura?"

"Well hello to you, too," Maura said. "I'm great. Thanks for asking."

Crystal regressed to her little girl voice. "Awww, you know I love you, Aunt Maura. I just get excited when you call."

"If you love me now," Maura said, "wait until you hear what I found for you. This could be the one, kid. It's for a show opening in Vegas called *Beached*."

Crystal immediately thought of what it might do to her mother if she left LA, but she also knew she was probably projecting some of her own fear because she had never been away from her mother much more than a night or two. "But what about Mom?" Crystal asked. "I can't leave her. I'm all she's got."

"Slow down, kid. Just give it a shot before you talk yourself out of it," Maura said. "I'm telling you, this could be huge for you. If the show is successful, they plan to take it to Broadway. This could be your ticket. Your mom can move with you."

Crystal had heard enough. She was hooked. "What's the part?"

"I mean, it sounds like it was created just for you; 'Rangy dancer and singer with exotic/Polynesian/Hawaiian features.' With your eyes and skin, you're a natural. It's a love story about a shipwreck on an island in the Pacific and how the captain falls in love with the daughter of the chief of the island natives. The captain feels obligated to get his crew and passengers off the island, but he doesn't want to leave the girl. She wants to help him get discovered, but doesn't want to betray her father and the rest of her tribe, so it's all about people being stuck in situations and having to choose between what is best for them and for the greater good."

"Sounds like it might have potential," Crystal said, already downplaying the opportunity to limit her expectations. "All right, I guess I'll go. What are the details?"

"Auditions are next Tuesday at the 3rd Street Dance Studio in West Hollywood. Check in at eight a.m. for makeup and hair with your resume and headshot. Callbacks are in the afternoon, so if they like you, you'll just stay. I'm telling you, I got a good feeling about this one, kid."

"You always have a good feeling, Maura," Crystal said. One of the first things Crystal learned was never to get her hopes up. It just hurt that much more when things didn't work out. Her mother taught her, *Feelings are cruel traitors. Never get too high or too low. Focus on the process, and the return will always exceed what you put in.*

Dow Jones Close: 6,930.40

Chapter Twenty-Three

Date: Thursday, June, 2013

Dow Jones Open: 14,992.54

Darlene sat on the edge of their bed with her withered arms raised above her head. Bill slipped the dress over and let it fall to her waist. Helping her get dressed was just one of the many things she hated but had to accept. She wasn't sure which was worse, the cancer or the treatment. She rocked back and forth for momentum, and with assistance from Bill, she stood, allowing the hem of the dress to drop to her shins. When she had bought the dress for his retirement party only seven months before, it had hung just below her knees. Now with all the weight that she had lost following the surgery, radiation, and chemotherapy treatments, the dress draped over her bony shoulders as if it were dangling from a wire hanger.

Bill reached behind her and zipped the dress. "I've always loved this color on you."

She looked in the mirror and frowned, grabbing handfuls of the excess fabric around her waist and hips. "I look ridiculous," she said. "I might as well cut a hole in a sheet and wear that."

"Nonsense," he said and kissed her forehead. "You look as beautiful ever."

"You're as blind as you are crazy," she said.

Bill held out his arm. "May I escort you to your table, my lady?"

After the last visit to the doctor, when they discovered the chemotherapy had failed, and the cancer had spread from the pancreas to the liver and into the lungs, Darlene had plummeted into deep depression. She rarely got out of bed, barely touched her food, and hardly even spoke to Bill. All she wanted to do was lie in bed with the TV on. Her spirit was shutting down like her organs. The doctor had told them she could have a month or six. While they knew she didn't have much time left, Bill wasn't ready to let go—but she was.

In an attempt to bolster her spirits, Bill had planned a special surprise, some of which he had told her because he really didn't have a choice. She asked too many questions for him to slip everything by her. The best part of the surprise, though, he would wait until the actual day. As part of the preparation, he had her wedding ring resized, which she couldn't wear any longer because it circled her finger like a hula-hoop due to the weight loss. He might have been able to sneak it out of the apartment without her knowing, but if she did look, and it wasn't there, he didn't want to cause any additional stress.

For Bill, preparing a meal had never involved more than two slices of bread, some cold cuts, and potato chips. Despite his limited skills and imagination, he managed to prepare, with the help of the young neighbor girl next door, Darlene's special meatloaf and mashed potatoes from the recipe cards he found in the cupboard. All day he banged around in the kitchen as the neighbor girl came in and out to help. Bill had made Darlene promise not to come out. He didn't think she would have anyway, but he knew telling her not to would provoke curiosity, which would get her out of bed and seated at the candlelit table later that night even if hunger didn't.

As they ate, Darlene peppered him with questions, saying more during the meal than she had in the previous days combined. Enjoying the teasing and using suspense as motivation, Bill refused to reveal the surprise he had planned unless she cleaned her plate, which she surprisingly did, in between suggestions, of course, on how he could improve the dish next time. Bill was toying with her, and she wasn't going to let him be the only one who was having fun.

For dessert, Bill served her favorite, strawberry ice cream, which he admitted he cheated on by buying at the store. Afterward he knelt down and took her hand. He said, "You have given me more joy in this lifetime than I ever could've dreamed of."

She pulled her hand back. "What are you doing, you old fool? Get up before you hurt yourself."

Bill remained kneeling and took her hand again. "You have always said life will bring people together, but it is up to us to stay together." He removed the ring from his pocket. "The day we married was the most important day of my life. I want to experience that day again." He slipped the ring, which now fit snuggly, on her finger. "Will you marry me again?"

Darlene looked at the ring, then at Bill kneeling awkwardly before her. The candlelight softened the creases in her face. She said, "You don't have to do this. You know I love you more than anything." Her eyes filled with tears.

Bill reached up and caressed her cheek, wiping the stream that had broken free with his thumb. "You have always stood behind me, regardless of how stubborn and foolish I've been. I want you to know that I will be there for you. It doesn't matter whether we have weeks, months, or years left together. My love and commitment will never change."

Darlene slid his hand from her cheek to her lips and kissed the back of his fingers. She said, "Of course I'll marry you again. I'm so sorry for how things have been. I know I haven't been the easiest person to be around lately."

"Not another word about that." Bill pulled himself up, needing the side of the table for leverage after kneeling for so long. "Somehow I remember that being easier the first time around." He smiled, needing a few moments to straighten his legs and back. "So there's only one more decision I need for the wedding: Elvis or no Elvis?"

Darlene said, "No Elvis. I can only handle one king at a time."

Dow Jones Close: 15,176.08

Chapter Twenty-Four

Date: Monday, May 16, 2011

Dow Jones Open: 12,594.77

Penny and Alec and his twin brother René sat in the waiting room before Penny's twenty-four-week prenatal checkup. Alec had insisted René, who was visiting from Vancouver, come along since they had a tee time right after the appointment. Penny probably would've let Alec skip all together, but he had missed the previous two appointments for what she thought were questionable excuses: a meeting with his agent and another golf outing. Both of which could've been rescheduled. She wasn't about to let it happen again. She hated the feeling after the doctor finished the ultrasound when, filled with good news, she had no one to share it with.

A male nurse with a round face and body to match opened the door leading to the examination rooms. He had a receding hairline but what hair he did have was long enough to be pulled back into a three-inch ponytail. "Mrs. Baudin?"

Penny and Alec rose from their chairs and walked toward the nurse.

René looked up from his magazine and wished them luck.

"Come back with us," Alec said without checking with Penny or the nurse if it was acceptable. "You can see your nephew…or niece."

René looked at Penny. "You sure it's OK?"

She knew how close Alec and René were and how little time they got to spend together. She had always felt insecure about Alec and René's relationship. They had such a special bond that, no matter how much time she spent with Alec, she would always be the second closest person to him. But on that day, she had already won by getting Alec to the appointment. René was family after all. If she had a sibling, she would want him or her to come back as well. "Sure. You can see what you put your poor mother through with both of you crammed into such a small space."

The nurse led the three of them into the examination room and directed Penny to the chair. "Please have a seat. The doctor will be in to see you shortly." He smiled and left, closing the door behind her.

Alec gestured to René, holding out his pinky. "The ponytail should at least be longer than the…" His words trailed off as he wiggled his finger.

Penny shook her head and reclined in the chair. "You two will never grow up."

"I hope not." Alec said. He walked over and fiddled with the stirrups. "The doctor's not going to use these, is he?"

"He sure does." Penny laid back, lifted her legs, and picked up the ultrasound wand. "He stands down there and puts this in."

Alec contorted his face and turned to René. "Maybe you should wait outside."

"She's joking with you, idiot." René punched him in the arm. "You always were the gullible one."

Penny laughed, shaking her head. "No, silly. The doc just puts some lotion on my belly and moves this around, and we watch the screen." She loved pushing his buttons. It was another way to feel more in control in the relationship and keep her own insecurities buried.

The doctor, a bespeckled Indian female with streaks of gray running through her shoulder-length black hair, entered with the male nurse who had brought them to the room. The doctor reviewed a chart on a clipboard. "Well, Mrs. Baudin." She looked up and noticed Alec and René. "And Mr. Baudin, or rather Baudins." She moved her finger back and forth between the two, noticing their identical appearance, unsure who was whom.

Alec stepped forward. "Nice to meet you, doc. This is my younger brother René, or rather, 'the placenta that lived,' as he was known growing up."

René simultaneously reached out to shake the doctor's hand with his left and smacked Alec in the back of the head with his right. "The better-looking, smarter brother as I'm known now."

The doctor shook hands then pulled a stool next to Penny. "So how have you been feeling lately?"

"Physically I feel really good, better than last month actually," Penny said. "But I haven't been feeling any movement for the past week or so."

"Periods of inactivity are common, so probably nothing to worry about there." The doctor looked again at Penny's chart. "Your blood pressure is a bit higher than last time."

Alec walked over and stood at the head of the bed with a hand on Penny's shoulder. "Is that bad?"

"Not necessarily," the doctor said. "At this stage, I would expect it to stay consistent or maybe go down until a few weeks before birth." She picked up the wand and a tube of coupling gel. "Let's have a look." She held the tube over her belly. "You know the drill. This is going to be a little cold." She squirted the gel and spread it around with the transducer. Penny winced then relaxed. The doctor said, "Never get used to that, do you?" She flipped on the ultrasound machine and applied the transducer to Penny's belly. All their eyes flashed to the screen, even though most of them didn't know what they were looking at. The shape of a fetus formed on the screen. The doctor moved the transducer around.

Penny shifted her eyes from the screen to the doctor. Panic seized her. "There's a problem, isn't there? I knew it. I should've come in last week."

The doctor handed the nurse the transducer. She removed her gloves. Her soft, dark eyes drooped. "I'm sorry. There's really no good way to say this. I wish I could tell you what happened or why, but sometimes these things just happen."

"Please no. Don't say it." Penny fought to hold back the tears. "This can't be happening."

The doctor placed her hand on Penny's. "I'm so sorry."

Alec said, "What happened? What do you mean? We could see the baby on the screen."

"The baby is still there," the doctor said. "The heart has just stopped."

Penny clutched her stomach. "When? How?" She had known right away something was different. She could just tell. She hadn't been as tired or emotional. She was actually feeling normal. She had wanted to call the doctor right away, but Alec thought she was overreacting, that her feeling better was a positive sign. Penny closed her eyes and looked away. René drifted toward the door, trying to be invisible. The nurse wiped the gel from Penny's stomach and lowered her shirt to cover her belly.

The doctor said, "I'm so terribly sorry. I wish I could tell you more. The good news is there is no reason why you can't try again." The doctor stood up. Penny still couldn't look at her. She couldn't look at anyone. Her head remained turned away from Alec, eyes closed. The doctor said, "I'll give you some privacy and come back in a few minutes to discuss the options."

Penny heard shuffling noises as the doctor stood and left. The sound of the door latching echoed through the room. The emotion she had been restraining and allowing to escape as gentle whimpering burst into full sobbing. She expected to feel Alec's hand stroke her hair or his lips on her cheek, or at least hear his comforting voice, but there was nothing. She rolled over and scanned the room. "Alec?"

The room was empty. He had exited with the doctor, nurse, and René. Later he explained that he thought he was supposed to, that when the doctor said, "I'll give *you* some privacy," it meant everyone should leave. But in that moment, lying there completely alone in the sterile examination room, she couldn't fathom a single reasonable explanation as to why he would leave her. All she could hear was the sound of her sobbing bouncing off the white walls, which only made her cry that much more.

A knock sounded at the door. Penny stifled her sobbing and sat up, wiping the tears away with her hands. She plucked a tissue from the box on the stand next to her.

The doctor stuck her head into the room. "Is it all right to come in or do you need more time?"

Penny didn't want to spend another second alone in that room. "No, please come in," she said in a nasal tone due to the crying. She blew her nose into the tissue. "I'm sorry for being such a mess."

The doctor entered, carrying pamphlets and literature. "That's OK. I understand." She looked around the room. "Should we wait for your husband?"

Penny fought the urge to cry again. "No, he is getting some air," she said. "He doesn't like hospitals too much."

The doctor handed the papers to her. "First, I want to reiterate that you didn't do anything wrong. Some babies are just not strong enough to make it through the pregnancy. The important thing is that we keep you healthy so you can try again when the time is right."

"Oh no," she said. "I'm not putting myself through this again."

"No need to make that decision now," the doctor said. "But what we do need to decide is how we are going to resolve this. Based on the ultrasound, no membranes have ruptured or signs of infection are apparent so we can wait for natural labor to commence, or we can schedule an induction."

Penny didn't hesitate. "How soon can we do the induction?"

The doctor said, "The materials I gave you go over the options, so take some time and discuss with your husband and get back to me. There's no rush. The most important thing to remember is that you are not at risk."

"No, the sooner, the better," Penny said.

The doctor scribbled notations on her chart. "OK, I understand your urgency. My assistant will come by with available times and we'll get that scheduled right away."

"Doc, can I ask you something?" The emotion flooded back into her voice. "Was it a boy or girl?"

The doctor put her hand on Penny's knee to comfort her and soften the impact. "You were having a girl."

Dow Jones Close: 12,548.77

Chapter Twenty-Five

Date: Friday, March 21, 2014

Dow Jones Open: 16,332.69

Two different people from two different worlds, living very different lives. That's what I was thinking while watching Les and Crystal play together at my table. There wasn't very much interaction between them other than the occasional acknowledgement of one another's smart play. Both knew the game and recognized that in each other. Beyond that there just wasn't much common ground between them.

I asked Les. "Where'd you learn to play?"

"Church," he said, waving off a hit to stand on his fourteen against my three. He had become quite the regular, often playing twice a day, once in the afternoon from about three to five and again in the evening from nine to eleven or so depending on his luck.

Crystal looked up from her sixteen. "That's my kind of church." She played every night without fail, always sitting at first base if she could, wearing her green cap and some baggy casual outfit similar to the navy plaid flannel with oversized white V-neck and black wide leg poplin pants she was wearing on this occasion.

Les nodded encouragingly at her comment and the sight of the ten under my three and the following nine from the shoe for a twenty-two. He said, "Actually, I perfected it at church. Learned it in college on the riverboats in New Orleans. At the church we used to have an annual casino night every year as a fundraiser, and I was the blackjack dealer."

I paid them both for their wins. "Ah so you been on my side of the table. Not as glamorous as it seems, is it?"

"To be honest, it was one of my favorite nights of the year," Les said. "I enjoyed interacting with parishioners in a casual setting when they let their guards down. Wish there had been more opportunities like that." Wistfulness replaced his usual reticent demeanor. "There was one little old lady, Mrs. Simmons. Eighty-seven, I believe she was. Her husband had passed many years before. She came to mass every day. On casino night, she would sit at my table the entire time and tell stories about being a child during the depression, working in the factories during WWII, meeting her husband when she hit him on his bicycle with her car, just all kinds of rich, slice-of-life stuff. The woman could really spin a yarn. I think I learned more in one night than I would seeing her every other day of the year."

"Those old birds do love their gambling," I said, dealing Crystal an ace-seven and Les two fives against my six. "We get a few bus loads a week from various senior centers. Gets quite lively."

"Maybe I need to start hanging out during the day more," Crystal said. Staring at her hand and her bet of fifty dollars, she tapped one of the three stacks of eight green chips in front of her. She peered up from the table. "How would you guys play this? I always get a bit confused on these soft hands. I feel like I should double, but eighteen is a good hand."

I offered my opinion. "This is one of those hands that separate the serious players from the recreational. Easiest way to remember what to do on the soft hands is never soft double against a deuce, always soft double eighteen or less against a five or six, and when the dealer has a three or four, add the dealer card to your non-ace. If they total nine or more, double. Only exception is always double A-4 against a dealer four. That's it."

Les went even deeper. "Against a six on soft eighteen, you profit about twenty-eight cents on every dollar bet for standing, nineteen cents for hitting, and thirty-eight cents for doubling. When you're feeling weak with a fifty bet in front you, just ask yourself, would you rather net fourteen, nine-point-five, or nineteen dollars over the long haul?"

Crystal stacked two green chips next to her bet. "Let's gamble."

Next card was another ace. "Nineteen," I said. "Improved by one." Les already had three red pushed into the circle for his two fives. "Split or double?" I asked. Again demonstrating his prowess, he extended a single finger. "Doubling fives," I said, pulling a seven from the shoe for him.

Crystal groaned. "Ooh, sorry. You would've had twenty-one if I hadn't hit."

"Still in good shape," Les said. "Dealer busts forty two percent of the time with a six showing."

I turn over my downcard and reveal a queen. "Sixteen."

Crystal, still not convinced in her play, said, "Dealer would've busted with that seven." She held her hand over her eyes. "I can't watch."

Next card was another ace. "Seventeen," I said. "Player wins on the double with nineteen." I combined her four green in a single stack and awarded four green from the house tray, then replaced both stacks with two black chips. "Two black going out," I called out to the pit boss. Crystal scraped the $200 toward her. I moved over to Les, bouncing my fist twice in front of his hand. "Seventeen's a push." Les pulled back his double bet, leaving the other three red in the circle for the next hand.

"See, I cost you money," Crystal said. "My bad."

"Not like I lost," Les said, wrapping his hand around his chin and stroking his beard. "Better for you to win a hundred than me thirty."

"How about you?" I said to Crystal. "How'd this godforsaken game get its hooks into you?"

"Pretty much out of boredom," Crystal said, pushing three green into the bet circle. "Started playing video blackjack at work to kill time and realized odds were probably better playing at the tables than on a computer that shuffles every hand. Also it's something I can do by myself to get out of the house without people harassing me like in a bar."

Penny plodded down the aisle stopping upon seeing Crystal and Les. She wore a baggy gray cashmere tunic that extended down to mid-thigh of her tight, black leather pants. The neckline had slid down her left arm exposing her shoulder and a thin, black bra strap. On her head, cocked slightly to the right, rested a black stovepipe baseball cap with "Life Is Beautiful" printed on the front in white, block lettering. A lean, twenty-something guy with a steel blue eight-pointed star tattooed on his neck and a man bun knotted on his head trailed behind her. She leaned on the table in the open spot between Les and Crystal. "Well hellooooo." Her eyes were glassy and her speech loud and slurred.

Not in much better shape, Neck Tattoo stumbled behind her, speaking with an Australian accent. "Babe, I thought we were doing shots."

Penny plopped her black leather tote on the chair and opened it. A mixture of fives, tens, twenties, and a few hundreds covered everything underneath. She swiped one of the hundreds, sending a twenty and five to the carpet without her noticing. Giving him the hundred, she said, "Go to the bar and order us drinks. I'll be there in a second." Neck Tattoo snagged the hundred and charged off without saying anything. Penny watched him walk away. "Doesn't he have the cutest bum? That's what he calls it: a bum."

"Nice hat," Crystal said. "Let me guess, that's his, too?"

Penny adjusted the hat. "Isn't it great? Met him over at Commonwealth. He said I should wear it since I'm so beautiful." She giggled. "Don't you just love these young guys? So cheesy and predictable, and best of all, they do whatever I tell them."

Les pointed to the ground. "You dropped some money."

"Oopsie," Penny said, giggling again. "Guess I need to watch what I'm doing." She picked up the money and threw it on the table. "Deal me in." Moving her tote to the open chair next to Crystal, she sat down beside Les.

"You all right tonight?" Crystal pushed the money down in Penny's purse and fastened the clasp.

"Red or green?" I asked, flattening her bills on the table.

"Never better," Penny said, swaying side to side as she focused on the table. "Green, please." I slid one green chip to her. She pushed it toward the circle, leaving it on the edge. I moved it to the center. She closed one eye, touching her bet with her finger. "Sorry, my aim is a little off."

Around the horn I went: ten for Crystal, ace for Penny, nine for Les.

Penny chanted, "Come on, ten, ten, ten, ten, ten."

Next cards off the top were eight for Crystal, another ace for Penny, a king for Les, and two on top for me. Crystal stayed on her eighteen. I moved to Penny. "You got two or twelve or you can split."

She scrunched her perfect nose and pushed out her lips. "Ugh, too many choices. What should I do?"

In unison, Crystal and Max said, "Split."

Penny dug down in her tote and pulled out forty more dollars. "I guess I'm splitting 'em."

I changed the cash for a green and three red and separated the two aces, putting her original twenty-five-dollar bet behind one and the new green chip behind the other and sliding the remaining red to her. First card was a jack. "Twenty-one," I said. Penny thrust her arms in the air and cheered, knocking her hat off. I dropped the next card. A queen. "Twenty-one again. Can't get any better than that."

Penny stretched her arms toward me, palms up, flapping her fingers toward her. "Gimmee, gimmee, gimmee."

"Doesn't count as blackjack when splitting aces. Got to wait to see what I get." Les stayed with his nineteen. I turned over a four underneath my two. "Power six for the house," I said. Next card was a five. Eleven. "Six or less," I said, pulling the next card from the shoe. A five. "Reverse that. Need a six or higher now." I peeled the next card off the top. It was an eight. I said, "Twenty-four. Too many. Everybody wins."

Penny pumped her fist in the air, barking. "Woo woo woo."

"Aren't you supposed to go meet your friend?" Crystal reminded her.

"He'll wait, or he'll come back. Either way, don't care."

Crystal, always the eternal pessimist about people, said, "Or he left out the back with your money."

Max walked up and hung his blue blazer on the back of the chair at third base. Removing his wallet from the jacket, he climbed up in the chair and counted out ten one hundred dollar bills. "This table looks hot. Mind if I jump in?"

Penny squinted at him. "Hey, we know you."

The previous light and friendly energy dissipated. Crystal rolled her eyes, pushing her chips to the center of the table. "Well that's it for me."

"Don't leave on my account," Max said. "Let's make some money."

Crystal glared at Max. "Don't flatter yourself. I wouldn't do anything because of you. I'm just tired of playing. Going to take my winnings and walk."

Les counted through his money, up ninety-five. "Yeah, I think I've had enough, too."

Penny cupped her hands around her mouth and spoke in a loud whisper toward Max. "I don't think they like you too much."

Max looked at Crystal. "Come on, you're not still mad about that one night, are you?" he said, picking up his money. "I don't want to break up the party. I'll go to another table."

"Too late for that," Crystal said. "I'm done. I work too hard for my money to piss it away." Picking up the $625 in chips I colored up for her, she pushed back from the table and walked toward the cage.

Les said, "I got to get back and close up shop anyway. Catch you all later. Penny, you good to get home?"

Neck Tattoo strolled up holding a drink in each hand. Penny said, "Think I'll be just fine." She held up two of the green chips she had won in each hand and pressed them against her eyes, turning toward Neck Tattoo. "Look, babe. I only have eyes for you."

Dow Jones Close: 16,302.77

Chapter Twenty-Six

Date: Tuesday, January 18, 2011

Dow Jones Open: 11,783.82

Max stared at the job description. He had done tough jobs before, ones in which he didn't have any training or experience, that he had lied about his qualifications to get. But this was the first time an employer had sought him out and offered him more, and that made him uncomfortable. He was used to being on the hunt, seeing what he wanted, devising a plan, and going after it. This time it wasn't like he felt pressured to accept. He knew he could always say no. His boss made that very clear to him. She didn't even use the word promotion. She told him to consider it "a change of pace, a growth opportunity that could lead to much more."

His eyes just kept scanning the words, attempting to pull the answer of what he should do from the words on the page.

A casino marketing specialist plans and manages customer events by performing the following duties:

1. Develops, prioritizes, and implements tactical project plans, including customer promotion programs and event meetings.

2. Compiles estimated cost models, submits final budget, and tracks budget statistics.

3. Assists in theme, demo, and exhibit space layout development for events.

4. Sets up sales-meeting and press-event schedules, organizes materials, reviews transportation itineraries, and reserves venues and services.

5. Coordinates registration and payment procedures, promotional advertising and mailings, and corporate sponsorship activities.

It sounded important, and also really hard. Maybe that was his apprehension. He wasn't completely convinced he could do it. He didn't consider himself the corporate type, never even worked in an office before, let alone in a job that required prioritizing project plans, compiling cost models, and coordinating corporate activities.

His boss had sensed his reluctance. She had told him, "Don't let the words intimidate you. All job descriptions sound that way. They're meant to scare away the people afraid to work and to entice those with big enough egos not smart enough to run away to apply."

Max came clean. "But I haven't done any of these things."

She said, "Don't worry about what you have done. Focus on what you're willing to do."

That made it easy for Max, because the answer to that was always: *whatever it takes*. From his arrival in Vegas ten years ago, he had always done whatever it took. When that meant dressing like a leprechaun and working as a barker in front of O'Sheas in 110-degree heat, he did it. When it meant painting himself green and flinging himself down a slicked-up alley in a game of human bowling on St. Patrick's Day, he did it. And when he got the opportunity to dress in a tuxedo on New Year's Eve and masquerade as Agent 003½ to run the Big Six Wheel, he did that, too. While pretty much all of the marketing promotions Max was involved with were popular, which meant profitable for the casino, it was the last one that really got him noticed by the upper management.

Max had learned early in his time in Vegas that while egos drove the casino business, there really was no room for ego either. It was all about profit. Pride and vanity might be the fuel, but profitability was the destination. That was probably why he excelled. He had never had the luxury of having a big ego. For as long as he could remember, he had just been surviving. If sacrificing some of his dignity triggered a few laughs, then at least he was in control of what was happening. Better to hold the hose than have to sidestep the stream.

Another early lesson Max learned was that the Big Six, also known as the Wheel of Fortune or Money Wheel, was a total sucker's bet. While one could argue, since the house always had the advantage, all bets in a casino were sucker's bets, The Big Six was more *suckerish* than any others. It stood by the front entrance of pretty much all casinos—red flag number one—and the dealer, usually an attractive, well-endowed female—red flag number two—spun a vertical wheel with a limited number of easy to understand bets—red flag number three. The more enticing and accessible the game and the easier to understand and bet, the deeper the casino already had its hand in your pocket. The spaces on the wheel were associated with one, two, five, ten, twenty dollars, or two special symbols, typically a joker and the casino logo. The number of spaces with each symbol determined the probability of winning and the odds. All of which were heavily slanted in the house favor ranging from 44 percent for the one dollar bet with only a one to one payout all the down to less than 2 percent for the casino logo with a forty to one return, and the house edge for those same bets starting at 11 percent and skyrocketing up to 24 percent. Just an absolute scam. Hence the positioning by the front and the babe doing the spinning. Blind them with beauty and beat them before they knew what hit them.

But on New Year's Eve, with Max at the wheel, no one seemed to care. They were lining up five-deep. And for what? They could've walked another fifty feet and thrown their money down on red or black on roulette for close to one-to-one odds and increased their probability by almost two percent. But it didn't matter. They waited; they pushed; they shoved. Just for a chance to throw their money down and let Agent 003½ decide their fate.

Max had lobbied his boss for a month to give him the opportunity to run the Big Six on New Year's Eve. She refused, saying people expected to see a beautiful woman running the wheel, and they weren't about to break tradition on New Year's Eve. Max easily shot that one down, citing example after example of how New Year's was all about breaking tradition to gain an advantage over their competition. Every excuse she had, Max had convincing counters. In situations such as these, he could be very persuasive, because he knew just how far to push people without backing them into a corner. Just at the breaking point, he would back away and wait for the next opportunity to make another run.

The conversation about New Year's Eve with his boss went on for weeks. Max could sense her position shifting. He decided to press. He just needed to wait for his chance. It had to be perfect. It had to be a situation where they would be alone, so others wouldn't view the boss as soft. He would need to have enough time to make his case; yet the meeting had to seem casual and not orchestrated. Any miscalculation or misstep could sabotage the ultimate goal.

Max got his opportunity two weeks before New Year's. He was in the break room by himself with ten minutes to go on his break when his boss came in. Max pretended to be distracted and not see her. She waved her hand in his line of sight. "Earth to Max, come in Max. Everything OK?"

"Oh, hey. Sorry. Just thinking about New Year's."

"Not this again. We've been over this."

Max stood up to make his final pitch. "Just hear me out. If you don't like this, then I'll never mention it again."

"OK. I'll give you five minutes but that's it. No more." She sat down at the table.

Max walked in front of her. He had been practicing the pitch for the past week. She had given him five minutes. He knew he needed only two. He said, "On New Year's Eve, people wear nicer clothes, they go to fancier restaurants, they're willing to spend more money. Overall, they want formal. They want the casinos of old, the ones they have seen in movies. And who do people think of? James Bond. Agent 007. The suave, tuxedo-clad gambler. So imagine me dressed in a tux, but not as 007, as Agent 003½." Max paused, waiting for the expected laugh, received it, and continued. "I'll be running the Big Six Wheel with two beautiful Bond-type girls as my assistants. Maybe we call them Bondage girls and have them scantily dressed in leather. That could draw some attention. I'll leave that for you to decide. On the side we set up a martini bar that we could probably get one of the liquor companies to sponsor so it wouldn't even cost us. How great would that be? People coming off the street would immediately get a martini—not a beer from a tub like other places—and the first game to play is the Big Six, the best odds for the house. Even if they didn't play, they would have one stiff drink in them before they even attempted to play another game." Max sat down at the table across from his boss. Now he just had to be quiet. He knew in any negotiation the person who talked first always lost.

She remained silent with her eyes fixed on Max. A smile widened across her face. "Agent 003½, huh? I'm not so sure about the Bondage girls, but I think you might have something here. I'll run it up the flagpole and see what they say."

Max banged on the table. "That's great. No pride of authorship here either. Feel free to change it as you see fit and take all the credit if they like it. If not, blame me."

Of course the bosses liked it. Something new and different to stand out on New Year's Eve, with the costs absorbed by a liquor company, which Grey Goose vodka so willingly did, was a no-brainer—exactly as Max had calculated. Just as he had known his boss would have no problem taking the credit. His suggestion to do so was just his subtle way to let her know he knew the game and was willing to play by the rules.

On New Year's Eve, the "Double Your Money With Agent 003½" promotion— with the exception of the Bondage girls, which were replaced with Grey Goose girls at the request of the liquor company—was launched exactly as Max had pitched and was an instant success. People were immediately drawn to Max in a tux, spinning the wheel and working the crowd with the Grey Goose girls passing out martinis. Of course they were plastic martini cups to keep the speed of service up and costs down. Sure the plastic made it trashy, but no one said it had to actually be classy. It was the front of the casino. Nothing in the front of a casino was really classy. It only had to look classy to attract people and get them to stop. The high-end stuff was in the back for the people the casinos knew would spend money.

As midnight approached, the promotion was working too well. The crowd swelled, congesting the entrance. Lines backed up onto the sidewalk, while seats sat empty at tables inside. Seeing the crowd out front, new guests passed on to other casinos. Management had to position security by the front to keep the crowd flowing. They pushed gamblers to games with better player odds to make sure everyone could get in the door. It was better to pay out a few extra dollars than have the money walk down the street. After all it wasn't like they were giving it away. The odds were still stacked in the house's favor. The stack just wasn't as high.

Spin after spin, Max, standing on a black wooden box so everyone could see him, fine-tuned his feel for the wheel. He surveyed the board, calculating the symbol that would cost the house the least amount of money based on the bets played. He didn't hit the target every time, but as the night went on, he was averaging about three out of four. And when he didn't, he was only a space forward or back. Once the bets were frozen, he would even call out the number to add to the excitement. If he got hot and hit four or five in a row or noticed someone picked up on his pattern, he missed a few on purpose. If there were attractive women, soldiers, or newlyweds in the crowd, he pulled them into the act and let them spin the wheel. If dealers could be in a zone, Max was in one. He fist-bumped; he high-fived; he even head-butted one overexcited reveler.

As the time crept toward two, he noticed bettors were staying away from the O'Sheas casino symbol—a forty to one payout—so he aimed right for it. As he waved his hand to freeze the bets, he said, "No one wants that forty to one, huh?"

A guest threw a twenty down on the emblem on the board. "I'll take that action."

Max pushed the money back. "Sorry. Too late. You'll have to wait until next time."

The wheel rotated, the pointer rubbing against the pins separating the spaces. Players' eyes followed the casino emblem, each time taking longer to make the journey around. As it passed the bottom and circled back toward the top, the pointer grabbed each pin, holding it, then releasing it before moving on to the next. Eyes widened as the O'Sheas emblem approached. The pointer rubbed passed the front side pin and grabbed the backside one, but just before it moved to the next space, it settled back on the O'Sheas emblem, bouncing between the two pins.

A collective groan for the missed opportunity shuddered through the crowd. Max said, "I told you it was going to hit. Who thinks I can do two in a row?" The crowd cheered, following with a rush of money on the O'Sheas emblem. Needless to say, Max came up one space short that time. The crowd didn't care about losing.

They just loved the action and increased their bets on the next spin to make up for it.

At the end of the night, when Max clocked out around seven in the morning, he had not only grossed the highest revenue for any shift of the Big Six Wheel all year but also the highest for any year. Even better than that, his control of the wheel yielded the highest profitability of money taken in versus paid out. When someone produced success like that, it didn't take long for the news to travel through the management ranks. Spreading equally as fast was the rumor, which Max vehemently denied, that the promotion was his idea all along. No matter how much people prodded him to admit to them the truth or winked at him, saying they knew the real story already, he remained committed to his boss. He knew nothing good would come out of making his boss look bad. That was the short play. Max was always about the long play.

Max reminded himself of that as he read the job description. He thought about what the best long-term play was. His seek-and-conquer mentality had served him well, but he knew what got him here, wouldn't always get him there, to the next thing, whatever that might be. Perhaps it was time for a change in strategy. He liked his boss. She had always been good to him. Why not trust her a little further? He figured it would take a lot more time and energy to climb the ladder on his own than to make his boss look good by working hard and letting her pull him up to the next level. If she thought he could do the casino marketing specialist job, then he knew he could do it. It didn't matter how or why the opportunity arose. He would surpass expectations, just like he did with everything else: by doing whatever it took.

Dow Jones Close: 11,837.93

Chapter Twenty-Seven

Date: Tuesday, March 17, 2009

Dow Jones Open: 7,218.00

Only in West Hollywood would a dance studio be sandwiched between a dry cleaner and a patisserie—and be painted magenta. Crystal stood before the bright pink façade, closing her eyes, breathing slowly and deliberately to calm her nerves. No matter how many times she went through the process, her anxiety always skyrocketed before auditions—and as much if not more when she got the part. It actually was much easier if she didn't get it. That way she could just tell herself she tried, that she was still putting herself out there and doing her best, and wait for the next opportunity. She was comfortable with that part of the process. It was all the questions that flooded in after she got a part that she really struggled with. All were some version of *What if I'm not good enough?*—even though she always was. But still, it didn't ever seem to help quiet the doubt, just as it wasn't calming her nerves that day. One more deep breath, and she grabbed the wrought-iron handle, pulled open the wooden door, and charged up the steps.

She checked in with her résumé and headshot and reported to makeup and hair. Because of Crystal's natural skin color and features, not much work was required. For once everything was progressing as Maura had advised. Not that Maura ever directly lied, but she did have a tendency to oversell. Today Crystal filed away the fortunate developments as conveniences rather than positive signs of an impending successful outcome. No matter how many good things appeared, she knew the room would be filled with her type, some taller, some thinner, some something.

The casting agent summoned all the girls into the studio and directed them into four lines of ten facing the mirror to learn the dance number. Crystal was first in the third row, but she wasn't worried. She knew they would be subdivided again when it was time to perform. The casting agent joined the producer, the director, and the choreographer at a table in front of the mirror.

After the people at the table introduced themselves and provided more background info than was necessary, the choreographer, a mid-forties male with narrow shoulders and hips to match, walked in front of the table and faced the mirror in the same direction as the girls. He spoke in a high-pitched, nasal tone. "We're going to break you up into groups of four and have you perform with two in the front and two in the back. We'll do the number twice, then switch the front and back and do it twice more. OK?" He scanned the group in the mirror, checking for questions in a way that suggested he didn't expect anyone to really ask anything. He gathered himself, focusing on his reflection in the mirror. "Five, six, seven, eight." He moved forward to initiate the number then mimicked his instructions. "To the side, two, three, four, and back for two, forward for two, spin right, three, four, and back to the center, two, three, four." He stopped and addressed the group in the mirror in the same dismissive manner as before. "Any questions? No? Good. Let's go through it together."

He counted off and led the group through several repetitions. With each rendition, they became more synchronized. Comfortable with their progress, he stopped dancing but kept instructing their movements, counting and providing the same verbal cues. Moving back and forth, around, and through the lines, he offered coaching instead of the directional advice in between the number counts. The others seated at the table pointed and gestured at the group, whispering amongst themselves.

After several minutes, the choreographer clapped his hands. "OK, OK. That should do it." He pointed at Crystal and the other girls at the beginning of their rows. "You four in first position are group one, second position, group two, and so on."

Crystal would've liked to have had more time to practice off to the side. There was no advantage to going first. When you were done first, it just meant you had more time to wait and think about what you wished you would've done differently.

Crystal lined up in the back row of her foursome. The choreographer counted off. "Five, six, seven, eight." They went through the number twice. Crystal tried to focus straight ahead in the mirror and block everything else out, but she could see the four at the table doing more of the leaning and whispering, and now shuffling the headshots into piles. The choreographer directed them to switch the front and back rows, and Crystal was face-to-face with the ones controlling her fate. This was her moment, the time to channel the years of hard work and preparation into only thirty seconds. She looked in the mirror, sharpening her stare. The reflection of the windows behind her faded. All she saw was herself, and for once she wasn't nervous. The sounds around her dampened. As the choreographer counted them down, his voice trailed off as if it were disappearing into a tunnel. She launched into the number. All she heard were the patter and shuffling of her feet on the floor and her voice counting in her head. When she landed on the last eight count, the room came back into focus, and the surrounding noise registered in her ears like waking from a dream.

"Very nice, very nice," the choreographer said. The other three at the table murmured to one another while organizing three of the headshots into one pile and one in the other. It was obvious which was the keep pile and which was the cut, just not who the chosen one was. The choreographer motioned toward the girls on the side. "Come on. Come on. Let's have the next group."

And so the process repeated nine more times. After the last group, the choreographer thanked everyone, picked up the keep pile, and announced the list of who would get to stay for the afternoon. Crystal's name was, surprisingly, first. Maybe there was some advantage leading off. After the final name was announced, the choreographer said, "Let's break for lunch and start getting your sixteen bars ready. We'll begin at one o'clock in the same order as the names were read."

Eat lunch? No way Crystal could eat after that. The stress of the morning had her stomach feeling like a wad of overly kneaded dough. She just sat off to the side, flipping through her binder of sixteen-bar auditions: *Phantom*'s "My True Love," *Oklahoma*'s "Out of My Dreams," and "What Is a Woman" from *I Do! I Do!* Since it was a love story set on an island, something from *South Pacific* might be appropriate. Eventually she decided on "A Cockeyed Optimist." Rethinking her position on going first, she thought at least she didn't have to worry about someone using her piece before her.

Crystal remained in the studio and sat against the wall, quietly humming the sixteen bars. Just like her mom had taught her, she closed her eyes and visualized singing to the four people from the morning. She even did the breathing and relaxation techniques, the ones that she always thought were stupid and a waste of time. She used to complain to her mom, *We breathe all day, every day. How can focusing on breathing help?* But in that moment she was open to anything that might help. She had tried to keep her expectations low, but after the dance performance that morning, she knew she had nailed it and admitted to herself that she really wanted the part.

The musical director and a pianist joined the director, producer, casting agent, and choreographer for the afternoon callbacks. The musical director, a short, chubby woman with a white headband around her black hair-sprayed flip hairstyle took over from the choreographer as the one directing the auditions. Her glasses hung around her neck on a silver chain. She put them on, then removed them, alternating as she looked at the girls and her notes. She said, "Congratulations, ladies, on making the callbacks. For the afternoon, each of the twelve of you will come up, provide your music to the pianist, tell the panel your name and song, and sing the sixteen bars. Please stick around after you finish. At the end, we may ask some of you to sing again or sing another piece. Any questions?" Again, like the choreographer, she scanned the room but was looking past the group, ready to move on. She looked down at the stack of headshots in her hand underneath her notes. "Great. First up is Crystal Moore."

Crystal walked over to the pianist and presented her sheet music. They discussed the piece quietly for a few seconds, then Crystal returned to the front and presented herself to the panel. "Hello, my name is Crystal Moore. Today I'll be singing, 'A Cockeyed Optimist' from *South Pacific*." She smiled and nodded to the pianist. He played the introduction. On cue, Crystal sang, "When the sky is a bright canary yellow, I forget ev'ry cloud I've ever seen, so they called me a cockeyed optimist, immature and incurably green." The pianist played the final notes. Crystal smiled, studying the faces of the panel for some indication of how she did. But it was just more whispering, scribbling, and shuffling of papers.

The musical director called up the next singer. Crystal faded into the background with the other girls. She listened to each performance, losing more confidence with each one. She was always so impressed with everyone else's talent at the auditions and thought that the fact she even got in the door was more a testament to Maura's abilities than her own. By the time the last girl finished, Crystal was sure she would not be amongst those who would be going to the first rehearsal.

As advised at the beginning, the musical director requested that several girls sing again and asked a few girls to sing some other pieces. Crystal was not one of these girls. She prepared herself for the inevitable disappointment. The musical director picked up a pile of headshots and walked in front of the panel. "Well, you girls are not making this easy on us. Even if your name is not called, we may still call you for other roles in the production. We ask that these four girls please stay."

Crystal braced herself, remembering what her mother had taught her: *Each rejection is one step closer to your big break.*

The musical director looked down at the first headshot. "Crystal Moore." He shuffled to the next headshot, but Crystal didn't hear the name. She didn't hear anything, or see, or feel anything for that matter. She was numb. Tears pooled in her eyes. It wasn't until another girl came over and hugged her that she fully realized it was really happening. Her first thought: *I need to call Mom. She is going to be so proud.*

Dow Jones Close: 7,395.70

Chapter Twenty-Eight

Date: Friday, July 19, 2013

Dow Jones Open: 15,524.17

Following his proposal to renew their vows, an immediate change surfaced in Darlene. She was still limited in what she could do, and often had to stop halfway through to rest, but whether it was getting dressed, going down with him to get the mail, or eating her meals at the table, she was trying. But more than anything, she was filled with questions. "Where are you going?" "What are you doing?" "Do you need any help?"

At first he tried to do everything himself because he didn't want to burden her, but he slowly realized the more she was involved, the better...for both of them. He brought back the brochures and packets from each of the chapels in the surrounding area, which was more of a chore than he anticipated, since there were at least ten within a few blocks. While he might have to drive a few miles to find a grocery store, he could throw a rock and hit plenty of choices for chapels, lawyers, and bail bondsmen. The Vegas Wedding Chapel right across the street from their building with its chablis stone exterior, authentic stained glass, and white steeple would've been perfect if it wasn't for its neon-lit "Fast Lane" for drive-through and walk-up weddings. No way Darlene was going to get married at a church with a drive-through. After days of deliberation, she decided on A Special Memory Wedding Chapel on the corner of Fourth and Gass. She liked that one the best because it had a New England-style façade with white wooden paneling, gabled stained glass windows, and a three-tiered steeple entrance, actually resembling a traditional church. There was also a plush yard with a gazebo and a fountain where they could have pictures taken, and it was only a block away, so Bill could easily wheel her there without being drenched with sweat by the time they arrived.

The most difficult task Bill had to do in preparing for the wedding was the call he knew he had to make for Darlene but kept putting off. Every day it started at the top of the list but moved down as he pulled ahead less important items. The first time he purposely called Hughie's office number, which he had obtained from Darlene's address book, after normal business hours. He didn't expect him to be there, but at least he could tell himself he had tried. The next day Hughie was in court. Bill declined to leave a message. No way he wanted to be in the position that anytime the phone rang, it could be Hughie on the other end calling him back. He wanted to remain in control of the situation and have the conversation on his terms. By the fourth attempt Hughie's secretary already knew his voice. She told him exactly when to call so Bill was sure to reach him. Bill had run out of excuses.

Hughie was stern and businesslike when Bill called back later that day. "This is Hugh Price."

Bill froze at the sound of his son's adult voice. He contemplated hanging up. Hughie repeated himself. Bill said, "It's me—your dad."

Hughie said, "Is everything OK?" The words expressed concern but the tone was still composed and distant.

"Yes, well no. I'm not sure if you're mother told you—"

"I know. She has cancer. Did something happen?"

"No. Everything is the same. Well, actually she's doing better." Bill paused. He had been so focused on making the call that he wasn't sure what he would say once Hughie was on the other end. Hearing Hughie's voice after so many years full of such poise and confidence was comforting but unnerving at the same time.

"Hello?" Hughie said. "You still there?"

"Uhm, yes, I'm here. Just surprised how grown up you sound."

"Yeah, well, that's what happens," Hughie said. "So you called me. If everything is fine with mom, what did you want then?"

"Yes, of course." Bill cleared his throat, mustering the strength to continue. "Your mom and I have decided to renew our vows at a chapel in Vegas." Bill hesitated again, not expecting a reaction, just searching for the right words. "It's really lifted her spirits, which the doctor has advised is the best possible medicine. I know it would mean the world to her if you were there to walk her down the aisle. It's still not for a couple weeks, so—"

"I'll be there," Hughie said. Then it was his turn to be silent for a moment. "But I'm not bringing Grace or the kids to the ceremony. I don't want to involve them in our drama. They can wait at the hotel, and Mom and I can go back there after."

"Of course. Whatever you think is best."

"Anything else?" Hughie said, not waiting for Bill to answer. "I have to be in court in twenty minutes. I'll transfer you to my secretary so you can give her the details to book the travel."

"OK, sure. Your mom will be—" Soft cello music played over the line, ending abruptly when the secretary came back on. In taking down all the relevant details, she was pleasant and friendly, which only stung more. Bill wondered if she knew the whole story or maybe she was just good at handling awkward phone calls for Hughie. He hung up the phone, hurting that he didn't know the answer.

On the morning of the ceremony Darlene complained nonstop—about the dress, her hair, all the same stuff she worried about the first time. Bill thought it was cute that so many years later, she was the same fretting bride he had married. When they left the Juhl—her in the wheel chair and him pushing behind—he could tell she was excited. She tilted her head back, looking up at Bill leaning over her with the clear sky as the backdrop. Not a single cloud floated above, a fresh coat of indigo painted across the entire canvas. It wasn't even eleven o'clock and already north of a hundred degrees, but she seemed to be enjoying the hot, dry air on her skin. Other than investigating the chapels, it was the first time she had been out of the building for a nonmedical reason in months. He watched her face light up as he wheeled her down Fourth and the chapel came into view. He knew it was only the beginning of her excitement once she learned what else he had planned.

In the weeks following Bill's proposal, Darlene's mind had flooded with memories from their original wedding. She made him dig out the photo album from storage to clarify some of the details that they remembered differently. Most of which, when they verified, she had been right about. Her pancreas might be failing, but her mind was as sharp as ever.

At the chapel, Darlene asked, "Do you think we can leave the chair outside and you help me down the aisle? If we go slow, I should be OK."

Bill said, "Now since when does the groom walk the bride down the aisle?" He looked over his shoulder, out into the parking lot, recognizing a face very much resembling his own through the windshield of a car. He hadn't seen it in many years, and it was much older than he remembered, but still much younger than his. He nodded toward the person, prompting him to exit the car.

"Well, I can't make it on my own," Darlene said. "And I don't want to be hanging on some stranger."

Hughie's voice floated in from behind them. "I guess it's true, women are the most beautiful on their wedding day." Bill offered a tight-lipped smile and stepped back. Hughie walked in front of the wheelchair. "Hi, Mom."

Darlene shook her head and just stared at Hughie. She had tried so many times to bring the two of them together, and now they were standing right in front of her. She said, "What? How? Where's Grace and the kids?"

"They're at the hotel," Hughie said. "Dad and I thought it best for me to come alone so we don't confuse the kids. We'll catch up with them later. They're excited to see you."

Darlene looked at Hughie, then at Bill. The emotional weight of the moment was sinking in. "So you two talked? Things are OK?"

"Dad called and invited me to come. Said you needed someone to walk you down the aisle." He extended both hands to her. "What do you say?"

"That sounds aces to me." She grabbed his hands, climbing into his arms. The emotion that had been building behind the shock of seeing him washed over her face. "I don't know what I'm going to do with you two," she said, sobbing.

"I'll give you guys a moment," Bill said. "I should go inside and make sure everything is set. Come in whenever you're ready."

Inside the chapel, when it was time to begin, Bill stood with the officiant at the front. The trumpets sounded over the speakers, playing "The Prince of Denmark's March," which Darlene insisted be used for the processional exactly like the first time. Darlene and Hughie ambled down the red-carpeted aisle under the vaulted ceiling. Bill could tell by the look on Darlene's face that she didn't care that the pews were empty. With Hughie on her arm and Bill waiting for her, she had all she needed. When they got to the end, Hughie handed Darlene off to Bill and turned to walk to the first row. Darlene took his hand and positioned him on her left. She wanted to make the moment last as long as she could.

Darlene cried from start to finish. Bill removed his handkerchief and blotted the tears to preserve the work she had put into her makeup. When it was his turn to confirm the vows, he said, "I do—even in fits of crying and laughter." Afterward they went outside for pictures, some with just Darlene and Bill, some with Hughie, and some with all three. The temperature was pushing 110 degrees, according to the thermometer on the side of the chapel, but no one complained. All just dutifully posed and smiled until Darlene had every last picture she and the photographer could imagine.

Afterward Darlene wasn't showing any signs of slowing down. She said, "Where to next?"

Hughie and Bill exchanged an awkward look. Hughie said, "Well, I thought we could go back to the hotel and meet up with Grace and the kids."

Bill softened the awkwardness with a joke. "After all that crying and this heat, you're probably dehydrated." He took out the handkerchief again and wiped the beads of sweat from his own forehead. "I know I'm probably running a quart low."

They walked over to the wheelchair. Bill showed Hughie how to collapse and expand the chair for storage. Darlene looked at Bill. Disappointment replaced the happiness that had filled her face since Hughie had walked up. She said, "Why are you showing him? You're not coming?"

"Today is for you," Bill said. "I haven't met Grace or the kids yet. I would just be a distraction there."

"Not for me," Darlene said. "I want you there."

Hughie said, "You're welcome to come if you want."

Bill took hold of Darlene's hands. Despite Hughie's invitation, Bill knew he didn't want him there. Hughie had made that clear on the phone. He just didn't want to disappoint his mother seeing how happy she was. Bill decided he would let Hughie off and take the blame on this one. "Nothing has changed," he said. "We did this for you, but I don't want it affecting others. Can we have it stop here? I'll come pick you up and we'll stop at that frozen custard place you love on the way home."

Darlene reluctantly nodded. Bill could tell she wasn't happy about it and was just agreeing not to push the issue. Of course there was a reason to press him, and Bill probably would've caved if she had, but it had been a big step, and that apparently was enough. She said, "OK, we'll save that for next time. Something to look forward to."

Dow Jones Close: 15,543.74

Chapter Twenty-Nine

Date: Thursday, December 8, 2011

Dow Jones Open: 12,195.91

After their initial time together, Fritjof refused to meet Penny at her house. He said there were too many reminders of Alec, and the guilt was too much. But it wasn't so much that Fritjof stopped seeing her completely. They just met elsewhere. At first they convened only at his place and hotels. The rule was they could never be seen together. Eventually the meeting places escalated to parking lots, quiet neighborhoods, parks, anywhere they could slip in and out, steal twenty to thirty minutes, and not be noticed. And Fritjof's flashy Lamborghini made that pretty difficult. So when they met in public, Fritjof stashed his car in one location and walked to another, where she picked him up. When she did, she made him sit in the back. With the tinted windows on her Range Rover, the only risk then was getting in and out of the car. But no one ever would suspect a Range Rover. If people did see him, they would just assume it was a driver picking him up. Fritjof complained about all the stealth maneuvering, how nervous it made him, how he wanted her to leave Alec so they could be together. She appeased his grumbling, but she had no desire to leave Alec. That would just create more stress and perhaps ruin what she had with Fritjof. She was not about to change the one thing that was bringing her some joy and made her feel in control of her life again, even if they were only occasional stolen moments.

Penny loved the secrecy of the affair. She enjoyed texting Fritjof, making plans for when and where they would meet, with Alec right in the room; she relished the feeling of leaving her house, which had become a museum of sadness; she delighted in the possibility of being discovered meeting or leaving the scene with him; and most of all, she reveled in returning home with another man's sweat on her skin and lying next to Alec like nothing ever happened. She knew it was wrong, but she didn't feel bad. After the way Alec had abandoned her when she needed him most, she could've done a lot worse.

Once Penny went back to work, meeting Fritjof got even easier. She didn't have to make up excuses for leaving or coming home late. Work provided that for her. Whether it was editing in the studio or researching a story in the field, she had a reason to be anywhere at any time.

What wasn't so easy was quitting the drinking. She thought once work started, she would be able to just stop and go back to her old routine. And so she tried to quit, making it a whole day and a half without anything. But she didn't feel like herself, or rather her new self, without it. She thought way too much about everything, and her anxiety skyrocketed. So much so, that on more than one occasion doing run-throughs prior to broadcasts, her cameraman stopped filming to ask if she was OK because the microphone was tremoring in her hand. It got to the point that he would just say, "You're doing it again." She always attributed it to nerves from the long layoff or stress and made sure to start including a few shots as part of her prep. She called it maintenance drinking. The shakiness disappeared.

Penny hated that Alec and Fritjof were on the same team. Not for the obvious reasons. She was fine with all that. It was just because when Alec was out of town on a road trip, so was Fritjof, and she got bored. The other distractions she found to fill her time were never quite as enjoyable as Fritjof.

That all changed the night Penny discovered Alec sitting in the dark at the kitchen table when she got home from work. She had just aired the final segment in her series on the most eligible bachelors in St. Louis sports. The premise was she interviewed the top five single players or coaches from the three professional sports teams. She came up with the idea as an excuse to spend more time with Fritjof, because he was surely one of the five. After all the interviews aired, fans voted via the station website on who they deemed the best catch. The winner then came in for a live interview on the evening news to accept a check for $10,000, donated by the station to the charity of the winner's choice.

For each of the individual segments, Penny spent three to four hours with each of the bachelors, doing the things they enjoyed to escape the pressure and stress of their sports. The interview with Fritjof was the last of the five to air. For Fritjof, the half-day expanded to a full day, since he took her to the Heartland Lodge in Illinois, about two hours north of St. Louis, to go bird hunting.

During the segment, Fritjof talked about how the drive was just far enough to feel like he was escaping, and how being in the country reminded him of home in Sweden. His family would go to their cabin in the fall and winter there, and he would hunt with his father and brothers. For the piece, he showed her how to shoot, and they actually went hunting. Even with a cameraman shadowing their every move and the fact she hated guns, it was the best day she had in a long while.

The voting was close between Fritjof and one of the Cardinal pitchers, but in the end Fritjof's accent and the stories about his family secured the victory. That evening Fritjof came into the studio to accept the donation and present it to the Boys and Girls Club of Greater St. Louis. Regardless of her motivation in creating the story and the indecent circumstances surrounding it, she was happy when she got home that night, like she had turned a corner and some good was coming from all the pain.

When Penny got home that night, she parked in the driveway rather than pull into the garage like she usually did. No lights were on in the house. She assumed no one was home, which was fine with her. She wanted the peaceful feeling inside her to last. She tossed her purse on the counter and went for one of her bottle stashes under the sink. Crouching in the dark, she groped around. Only the coarse plastic of cleaning solutions met her fingertips. She stood and flipped on the light.

"Looking for this?" Alec's voice boomed from behind her.

She whipped around. Alec was sitting at the table in the dining room connected to the kitchen. She said, "Geez, you scared me. Why are you sitting in the dark?" She noticed an empty glass and the bottle that she was looking for, along with two others, perched on the table in front of him. She could tell just looking at him that he was drunk.

"Grab a glass. I'm buying." He poured some vodka into his glass and slammed it back. "You know, the drinking I was willing to overlook. I figured, 'She's grieving and who am I to judge how a person deals with pain.' God knows I haven't been the best example."

"Alec, I'm fine now. Those bottles were from before." She really wanted a drink, but not enough to approach him. She didn't know exactly how much he knew. The kitchen island between them protected her while she figured it out. She said, "The drinking just helped me relax until I got back to work."

Alec wasn't looking at her. He just stared straight ahead speaking in a low, flat tone. "That's what I told myself. I said, 'Once she gets back to work, she'll be better. Just give her time and space.'" Alec slugged his drink in a single gulp. "Then I started finding bottles hidden in cabinets and drawers, and every day the levels were lower."

"I know it's silly to hide them," Penny said. "I just didn't want you to worry."

Alec threw his glass, shattering it against the dining room wall. Penny screamed. He said, "Don't you dare say you did this for me."

Getting the hell out of there was her first thought. She had never seen him like this. But she knew the fight was long overdue. She composed herself. "OK, so I've been drinking more than usual. Big deal. I'm going to work every day."

"Ah yes, work," Alec said, his eyes still avoiding her. "I saw the results of the bachelor's contest on your show tonight."

"Pretty great, huh? Can't believe he pulled it out."

"I don't know." Alec said, finally turning toward her, glowering. "Seems like he has been doing a lot of that lately, or maybe you just let him leave it in."

"What are you talking about?" She walked toward him. "I'm surprised you even noticed. You're never home, and if you are, you're just hiding down in your office in the basement."

Alec rose from the chair, intercepting her in the kitchen. "So how long has it been going on?"

Penny still didn't know how much Alec knew. She thought he could just be fishing for confirmation. She said, "The drinking? Since we lost the baby." Alec recoiled and walked past her. With his back to Penny, he extended his arms and leaned on the counter, staring out the window. She didn't relent. "See, you can't even hear the words without running away."

"I'm going to ask you once." His voice was low and strained. He was fighting to hold back the emotion. "Was it even my baby, or were you fucking him before?"

The comment enraged Penny. She wasn't going to stand there and be the victim. She had been through enough. "My God, who? You keep mentioning someone. Who do you think I'm fucking?"

"Fritjof." Alec spun around and faced her. Tears streamed. "After everything you and I have been through, I can't believe it. I don't want to believe it. But I saw you two on TV, and it all came together: the drinking, the mysterious errands, the extended work hours." He slid down to the floor against the kitchen cabinet and buried his face in his hands, sobbing. "And it had to be a teammate."

Penny didn't know what Alec had actually seen, or how he had found out. Maybe he got suspicious and followed her, or maybe Fritjof told someone and it got back to Alec. It didn't matter. She was done lying. Dropping to the floor, she leaned back against the cabinet across from him. "Of course she was your baby. I wanted her more than anything."

Alec looked up. "She? We had a girl?"

"Yeah, and I had to carry her inside me for two whole days after that ultrasound before they could do the induction. The doctor told me the day of the ultrasound the baby was a girl. Remember that? When you left me alone in the examination room? You never asked after that, so I never told you. You barely even talked to me. I felt like you blamed me for what happened. Do you know how alone I felt?"

"That's why you started drinking?"

"That's why I started everything."

Dow Jones Close: 12,548.37

Chapter Thirty

Date: Monday, September 30, 2013

Dow Jones Open: 15,249.82

In his office at the Oasis, Les sat at his desk, scrutinizing the budget on the dated computer. The primrose walls were barren except for a single wooden cross in the center of the wall facing him. The edge of the desk was pushed against the wall to the right, two-thirds of the way up. An empty inbox and full outbox in the upper left were the only other objects on the desk. A single chair stood in front against the wall, and a filing cabinet filled the corner. A cot and dresser were against the wall behind him, making the office his bedroom as well.

The fading color and flickering of the monitor made the screen difficult to read. But it, like most things in the building, had been donated, so he couldn't really complain. His choices were simple: use what he had and wait for a better donation, buy a new one using the Oasis funds, or dip into his personal account for an upgrade. Money was tight on the last two so he opted for the first. He was already subsidizing the operation out of the settlement money he had received from the Church, which was pretty much all the money he had. Unsure how long that would last, he thought it best to hold on to as much cash as he could.

Martin had been right about one thing. It didn't take Les long to learn the ropes after taking over. Martin had set up everything on routines, more for the visitors he claimed. The fact it made managing the operation easier was just an added bonus. When Martin first opened the Oasis, he had recognized that the lives of the guests were so unstructured, having a place where they knew what to expect and when it was happening gave them at least some normalcy in their lives. It also cut down on the complaining. Martin even went as far as to make the first letters of the meals match the days of the week. There was Meatloaf Monday, Tuna Tuesday, Wiener Wednesday, Turkey Thursday, Fish Friday, Spaghetti Saturday, and Sloppy Joe Sundays.

From the start Les really enjoyed the new work. He liked being outside of the pretense of the Church and simply to be helping people on the most fundamental level: with food and shelter. There were no titles, no confessions, no discussions of heaven and hell. Just good, solid, hard work. Each day he had a list of tasks to complete and each night he had tangible output to show for his effort. He understood right away why Martin had dedicated himself to the place, and why it was tough for him to leave. After the second week through the cycle with Martin, Les knew there really wasn't a decision to be made. The path had already been determined. He was meant to stay and assume management of the Oasis.

Although religious discourse rarely found its way into their workday, Les and Martin still had their fair share of debates, usually up on the roof at the end of the day, when the body was tired and the mind was feeding off the energy from the accomplishments of the day. It was here that Les, in his usual obtuse yet eloquent style, told Martin of his willingness to stay. "Like a pond after a storm, the more time I spend here, the more the water clears. I was meant to continue the great work you have been doing and allow you to embark on a new mission."

"Well, that's great news," Martin said. "I knew once you got here, it was more than two old friends catching up. It just took you a little bit longer to realize. You always were a slower learner than me."

"I think you mean more cautious," Les said, smiling. "When do you think you'll leave? Hopefully not for at least a few more weeks."

"You're not getting rid of me that easily. I'll stick around at least another month. The humanitarian group I plan to join meets in Washington, DC, during early December to prepare for the trip just after the first of the year. That will give us plenty of time to get you acquainted with all the regular donors and transfer everything into your name."

Les said, "Wait a second, transfer?" He was fine with filling in, but taking over financial responsibility sounded too sudden and too permanent. "Why do you have to transfer anything? You're coming back at some point, right?"

"Who knows what will happen? Better to be safe than sorry. Besides it's not like the Oasis is worth much. We lease the space for $2,500 per month, which includes all the kitchen appliances. Pretty much all the other stuff was donated or isn't worth much. The rent and all the other costs like utilities, food, insurance, the security guard, are covered by donations. If something happens, I just want you to be in a position to make a decision and not have to wait while you try to contact me halfway across the world. I may not just be a phone call away."

"No, I guess it makes sense," Les said. "I just thought I'd be filling in until you came back. I never thought of it as being my place."

"Well, since it's not really worth anything, it's not really anyone's, or maybe it's everyone's, depending on your perspective. Some months there's a surplus, and some months a deficit, but one way or the other, the place always seems to break even over the long haul. You'll just be in charge, which you would've been anyway, so it's really just a formality. The only thing I ask is that you find a way to keep the doors open and make sure those in need get a meal and a bed."

Just as the days became a set of tasks for Les as he learned the routines and built the relationships, the weeks became a schedule of days. As Martin's departure approached, Les grew confident in his ability to operate the Oasis. He was more concerned about losing the companionship of his friend. Once Martin was gone, Les would be on his own, something he had not been in a very long time. In fact, after dropping off Martin at the airport, following the route that only months before he had taken for the first time, he suddenly realized that he had never been completely on his own. With the Church, he had had Father Bennett and the other priests and nuns who he had worked with over the years. Before that, he had been with his classmates all the way back to when he first started parochial school, and he had lived with his parents even before that.

The ease and comfort Les had felt with the operation were instantly gone, and stayed that way for a while. It had been much easier following directions than giving them. To manage the chaos, he clung to the routines Martin had set, including the nightly visit to the rooftop, although usually he didn't stay long. The stark solitude had a way of closing in around him and causing him to think too much. Instead he would retire early and opt for bedside prayer to clear his head. As time passed, however, the stress and struggles dispelled, and he started making the routines more his own. He kept the day-to-day operations of the Oasis the same, but he tinkered with how he spent his free time. He used the days to explore the strip and downtown, walking through every casino, and on a few occasions he returned to tune up his blackjack skills if he saw a table that presented advantageous rules. The more he made the place his own rather than following Martin's plan, the more comfortable and less lonely he felt.

As so often happens in life, when one area becomes more balanced, another falls into disarray. It was this way with the operation of the Oasis. Not the actual physical operation. That continued to run smoothly exactly as it had been. It was the financial side of things where Les had growing concern. Reviewing the budget and the actuals, he just couldn't understand how Martin had stayed open as long as he had. In the nine months Les had been running the Oasis after Martin's departure, he had already put in $15,000 of his own money, and according to his estimates, they were short another $1,800 for the month. He knew Martin didn't have a lot of money, so he couldn't have been pouring much capital into the place.

Reviewing previous years' records, it appeared the main reason was that the donations were significantly down from other years. Martin had said the neighborhood was gentrifying, and most of the previous neighbors and regular donors had sold or been forced out by the rising rents. The new neighbors were supposed to pick up the slack, but that wasn't the case. They viewed the Oasis as more of a problem than a solution, and wanted to see it go. Although they never said as much, it was quite clear by their limited charity. Each time Les went on a fundraising campaign, he came back with fewer contributions.

With the current donation level and the thirty grand Les had remaining in his account, he estimated he could keep the doors open for another year, maybe eighteen months at the most unless something changed. He didn't have the time or energy to take on another job. He thought about increasing his fundraising efforts, but he was already seeing a pattern of diminishing returns. The current course would probably produce less, not more. Instead he went back to the same solution he used when he was in school and he had limited time and needed maximum return for his investment: he turned to gambling.

Dow Jones Close: 15,129.67

Chapter Thirty-One

Date: Tuesday, January 10, 2012

Dow Jones Open: 12,394.51

Max had worried the job as the casino marketing specialist would be too challenging, and it was pretty difficult at first. But not for the reasons he had expected. He thought he wouldn't be able to fulfill the responsibilities, but the actual work was the easiest part. It was learning the new language and the way people spoke and interacted with each other in the office that took some getting used to. He was used to being in a fast-paced operational environment where everyone told each other exactly what they thought and needed, bawdy humor and sexual innuendos kept things interesting, and the shifts went by quickly. In the new job, it was quite the opposite. The days crawled by, which was actually OK because it gave him time to sift through all the passive-aggressive comments and vague subtext that represented how everyone spoke to each other. He also had to upgrade the filter on his speech, because the slightest inappropriateness could land a person in human resources. This would've served Max well in his younger years, when he was often the butt of most insensitive comments, but now he could give as good as he got, so he actually enjoyed a more lively banter instead of the boring, diluted exchanges that he was forced to participate in.

But like most things, once Max learned the rules of the game, he used them to his advantage and flourished. Even though he was on salary and no longer had to punch an actual time clock, he figured out it was even more important to come early and stay late. Busybody coworkers were always watching and recording who was present, who was not, who was at their desk, and who was outside smoking or in the cafeteria. It didn't matter what he was working on. As long as his body was visible and active, either at his desk or in a meeting room, he was excelling. The corporate world was just like school. Keep quiet, stay in your seat, and don't cause trouble, and you'll advance.

At first Max was disciplined and only worked on company business when he was at the office, but as time went on and he became more skilled in his job, he learned his efficiency and effectiveness worked against him. The more quickly he got the work done and the more he did, the more it got scrutinized, and the more his coworkers resented him. Instead he made sure to stay within, what he liked to call, the occupational sweet spot. He did enough quality work to exceed the results expected of him, but not so much that he drew attention to himself. This took him about five hours a day, which left him about four or so, depending on how long he took for lunch, and he usually brought that from home and ate at his desk, except on Fridays when he went out with coworkers to at least appear social. It didn't matter if it was sincere; as long as he put in some time, the gossip and snarkiness seemed to be directed elsewhere.

All the things that Max thought he would hate became why he loved the new job. For the first time in his life, he had safety and security and felt like he didn't have to continually prove himself. Of course at first this was uncomfortable and not an easy adjustment. After clawing and scratching for so many years, it took him some time to just slow down and accept that he deserved all the good things that were happening. But once he did, the pace and lower expectations really agreed with him. He used the extra time in his day to research and explore ideas he had. The extra money he was making, he stuffed into a special account. Initially it was for a house, but as the ideas took shape, he realized they were his true assets and that was what he would use the money for.

The first idea on the list and the one that always seemed to stay on top when he would prioritize and decide what to work on was the Lapkin. Max prided himself on being analytical and able to separate his head from his heart. He didn't want to show favoritism toward the Lapkin just because it was his first invention and had ties to his childhood. The fact that the Lapkin stayed at the top of the list was a testament to the strength of the idea, one that the public would later substantiate.

Max could do all the research, design and development, planning, and purchasing of materials while at the office, but for the production, that had to be done elsewhere of course. The base of his operation was in the living room of his one-bedroom apartment in Henderson. He replaced the Naugahyde material he had used in the original Lapkin with a lighter weight Gortex fabric. The wooden paint stirrers he had fitted for the sides, he swapped for thin, flexible plastic rods. Each morning he made two before going to work and eight when he got home. On the weekends he made $25 each day for a total of $100 a week and $450 the first month. Learning a few shortcuts and improving his sewing skills allowed him to hit five hundred fifty the second month to bring his total inventory to a thousand. It was time to go to market.

Another unexpected takeaway from his day job was he learned the power of digital marketing and all the various channels available to sell a product. Max had always had an innate street sense of marketing. He knew how to recognize an opportunity, develop a solution, create the demand, and deliver the result, but it was always service-oriented, and he was the one providing the service. For the Lapkin, that would never work. Of course he could've quit his job, walked the strip every day, and sold his Lapkin face-to-face. No doubt with enough time and effort, he could've supported himself and created enough demand after a while to set up a booth or popup store, but who would've been making them while he was selling? And what about his other ideas? How could he develop new ideas if he was so busy making and selling Lapkins? No, he knew in the short term that might work, but in the long run he'd just be another hamster on a wheel.

Instead Max organized his whole life as a company. He used his job as his main revenue stream. He made sure the quality of work at his job was above the expected threshold to maintain the security of the flow. He used his surplus work time in the office to develop the sales and marketing plan, which was a combination of internet ads and social media campaigns, all directing traffic to the Lapkin website. He steered clear of traditional print media because it was just too expensive. For the web and ad content, he recruited Jake, a UNLV student living upstairs, and Felicia, a cocktail server at Tao nightclub, to pose with various stains and mishaps with and without a Lapkin for before and after pictures. Many of the pictures were silly, but that was the point. The genius of the Lapkin was its whimsy. It was so simple people would feel foolish that they didn't think of it.

Max priced the Lapkin at $9.99, with additional orders available for $6. It cost him just over four dollars to make, not including his labor or any of the sales and marketing costs, which would've turned it all upside down. He knew he couldn't get more than $9.99 for one anyway, so he decided to worry about driving the costs down later.

With a thousand Lapkins in inventory, the sales and marketing plan set, the website and ordering and payment system live, he launched on the first Monday in December to capitalize on the holiday buying season. He got his first order after three days. Two more orders came in the following day and five the day after. He still tried to meet his production goal of ten per day but the packaging and shipping cut into his time. After a week, the hundred he had been making reduced to fifty, and that was how many he sold. The following week, a TV morning show featured the Lapkin on a segment dedicated to novelty Christmas gifts. Orders spiked to over four hundred. He had to stop making the Lapkins and just focus on shipping. The TV spot also triggered a wave of inquiries and requests for interviews. Hits to the website increased tenfold, eventually crashing the site until he could configure more bandwidth and server capacity. Other shows and best-of lists featured the Lapkin. The week before Christmas, orders surpassed seven hundred, about a hundred and fifty more than he had in inventory. Max had to shut down the ordering system and put up a "Sold out! Please stop back after New Year's!" message, but that didn't stop the inquiries. The Lapkin had gone viral.

To help get the existing orders out and the backorders filled, Max hired Jake and Felicia, who had helped with the photos. When it still looked like he might miss the Christmas shipping deadline, he asked Jake and Felicia to reach out to friends, relatives, anyone they knew that might want some part-time work. He was hesitant to tap into the network he had built, since most of his friends were casino colleagues as well. He had been very careful to keep the news of his side business quiet. At the office, work-life balance was encouraged, but it was one thing when the life part was family and leisure activities, and another when it was an additional full-time job. Fortunately for him, during the holidays, while there might be enough cheer, there was never enough cash, so there were ample people looking for a quick, easy buck. He was able to get all the orders produced, shipped, and delivered by the promised date.

When Max tallied the final numbers, he had sold 1,247 Lapkins in just over three weeks. With the regular price and the reduced fee for additional orders, he had grossed a few pennies shy of $10,790. Less the $4,988 for materials and another $1100 in part-time labor, he was left with $4,702 in profit. While he was happy to make any money at all, and things had gone way better than he ever anticipated, it wasn't enough to quit his job. After all, it was Christmas. He might not sell another thousand over the next six months. Even if they did sell a thousand a month, meeting that quota in December had almost killed him. He knew he was going to need help, and the operation had to be running while he was at work. So during the holiday break, he set up two six-hour shifts from ten to four and four to ten. Felicia would run the first shift and Jake the second. Max handled all the sales and marketing, logistics, and back office administrative work. Even if the demand wasn't strong in January, he planned to just focus on building inventory. Once the stock was replenished and high enough to withstand a significant spike in demand, he could scale back.

When Max turned the shopping cart on the website back on after the holidays, he had expected the orders to trickle in. But within a week, he set a new daily record for orders, and that week he had over eight hundred total orders, surpassing his best week in December. With the additional staff and shift, they were able to produce a thousand a week, but with another increase in orders, they would be right back to the December problem.

One evening while Max was reviewing the order report on his laptop at the kitchen table, the evening crew worked in the living room. The chucking of the sewing machines accelerated into buzzing as the needles picked up speed, plunging through the fabric.

Jake walked over. "Looks like we might hit three hundred today. How are the orders?"

Max rubbed his forehead to alleviate the mounting tension. "Too good. If things continue as they are, we won't be able to keep up."

"Have you thought about outsourcing overseas?" Jake asked. "They can probably make these in China for a fraction of the cost."

"I'm sure they can. I just want to keep things local."

Jake said, "Well there's got to be a factory in the US that could make these."

"But that would probably require a minimum-order commitment and take months to get them up and running. The novelty of this could wear off tomorrow. I'd feel a lot better with six months of order history under our belts before we made a commitment." Max closed the laptop. He was getting tired. He could always tell because he was growing negative, noticing more of the problem than the solution.

"So let's expand locally," Jake said. "There's all kinds of available space in downtown Vegas. They're practically giving it away for anyone who wants to open a business, and since you're creating jobs, they might even subsidize you."

Max sat back in his chair, interlocking his fingers and putting his hands behind his head. "I don't know. That just makes it so official. It's one thing to be running this out of my living room. We're under the radar. I mean, opening a shop downtown really puts us out there. What will they say at work?"

"As long as it's not interfering with your job, who cares what they say? It's none of their business what you do during your off time."

"I'd agree if they used logic," Max said. "It's rarely the determining factor in corporate decisions. If they get even the slightest whiff that I have other interests or commitments, they'll sacrifice me, if for no other reason than to set an example to others."

"Let's do this then." Jake started sketching on a yellow legal pad on the table. "Let's cap orders at fifteen hundred per week. We'll put a counter on the website so people can see how many orders are still available. When those orders are sold, people need to wait until next week."

Max jotted some calculations on the notepad underneath Jake's markings. "That could work. Kind of like a line outside of a club. People see the line and think it's crowded inside, which makes them want to go in even more. We'll increase the demand by limiting the supply."

Dow Jones Close: 12,462.47

Chapter Thirty-Two

Date: Wednesday, April 30, 2014

Dow Jones Open: 16,534.86

Crystal picked up the flute of champagne and gulped her last swallow, her left hand never leaving the video poker machine. The screen was a blur of changing images amidst the rapid slapping of the buttons. Even with just one hand, she worked the machine with the speed and efficiency of a courtroom stenographer.

The bartender, Birdie, immediately replaced her empty flute with a fresh one. We called him Birdie because of his short-cropped hair, the slight bump on his long nose making it resemble a beak, and his long wingspan. He was six-foot three but had the reach of someone much taller. He could stand in the middle of the bar and cover all the stools and the service well while hardly moving. Usually two bartenders were needed. Birdie could do it alone. Another bartender just got in the way, which also meant he didn't have to split tips with anyone.

Champagne Thursdays, with five-dollar glasses of French champagne, not prosecco or cava or other sparking wine often passed off as champagne, combined with karaoke, brought a mixed crowd into the Parlour Lounge. The sheer fact it had to be advertised with the redundancy of French and champagne said all you needed to know about the customers it attracted.

When Crystal came in, Birdie always made sure to take care of her because he knew she tipped. The ones who tipped never had to wait; the others who didn't, waited until they figured out it was actually a six-dollar glass, with one dollar going to Birdie. Since Crystal was playing video poker, the drinks were comped, but she still slid Birdie a five every time.

The karaoke DJ took the mic back from the last person, who had butchered a Hank Williams Jr. song. She said, "Let's give it up for Marshall and his heartfelt version of 'Family Tradition'…I think. That was 'Family Tradition,' right?" The crowd groaned, then laughed. She said, "Come on y'all. Moneta just kids. We're all friends here. Just having a little fun. It don't matter what you sound like, only that you're having fun. That's right, it's Champagne Thursdays at the Parlour. You got me, Moneta, controlling the mic, and Birdie with the power of the pour. Both of us work the same way. The more you tip, the quicker you get served. Keep those requests coming. Up next, we got Angie singing 'Like A Virgin.'" A skinny woman in her midforties with a cropped halter top and cutoff faded jeans stepped behind the mic stand in the center of the stage. As the music started, Moneta said to the crowd, "Looking at Angie, I think we need to pretend it's twenty-five years ago." Angie snarled and stuck her tongue out at Moneta while waiting for the first verse to start.

Birdie walked over in front of Crystal and looked down at the video poker screen. "Any luck?"

Hearing that Angie's voice was fairly decent, Crystal stopped playing to listen. She picked up her champagne and rotated her chair ninety degrees so she could watch Angie and still talk to Birdie. "Up and down," she said. "I started with forty bucks and now have, what?" She looked down at the screen. "A hundred eighty-five credits, so I'm up a little over six bucks."

"This machine hasn't hit in a while, so you might get lucky," Birdie said. "You going to treat us to a song tonight?"

Crystal sipped some champagne. "I think I'll do one. Any requests?"

Birdie didn't hesitate. "I love when you do Whitney. Anything by her—or no, I know the one I want. How about "I Will Always Love You?" Love that song. You're one of the few people who can pull it off."

On stage, Angie finished her song. Crystal downed the rest of her champagne, put the glass on the bar, and clapped for the performance. She turned back to the machine and started playing. Birdie refilled her glass. She pushed another five toward him.

He pushed the money back to her. "Give this to Moneta when you sing."

Crystal nodded, directing her eyes to the screen. "Did you know that song was originally written and recorded by Dolly Parton in the early seventies, and it's not about romantic love at all? Dolly recorded it for Porter Wagoner as a way to express her appreciation for him and what he had done for her professionally when she decided to leave his television show. That song reached the top of the charts three times. Twice by Dolly. Once with the original, the second time in the eighties on the soundtrack of *The Best Little Whorehouse in Texas*, then again in the nineties with Whitney for *The Bodyguard* soundtrack."

Crystal could talk music for hours. This was all her mom's doing. Valeria used to play all different types of music, from folk to country to pop to rock to R&B and even rap, despite disapproving of the messaging and violence. Her mom believed all music was connected and that to appreciate any type, one had to study all the types. So when Crystal as a young girl had taken a liking to the Whitney version, her mom made her go back and listen to the original and also to the second release for the movie, which of course Crystal wasn't allowed to watch because of the adult content. Instead her mom had Crystal study up on Dolly's life and her impact on music, since she was such a unique and influential figure.

Moneta's voice radiated through the speakers. "Keep those requests coming, y'all. If you don't, Moneta is going to have to sing. I work hard enough. Don't make me sing too. Tonight is for you to shine."

Crystal looked up from the screen at Birdie. He smiled and nodded toward the stage. She said, "Watch this for me?" He opened up a bar napkin and covered the machine. Crystal stood up, gulped another mouthful of champagne, and bounded toward the stage.

Moneta saw Crystal heading in her direction. "Look out, folks. You're in for a special treat tonight. She can sing, she can dance, and, as you can see, she is also pretty easy on the eyes: the lovely and talented Crystal." She covered the mic so only Crystal could hear her. "What's it going to be, luv?" Crystal told her Birdie's request. Moneta said, "Brilliant. No one ever does that song." Moneta spoke back into the mic. "So fill up your drinks, sit back and relax, and enjoy this sure-to-be-stunning rendition of Whitney Houston's 'I Will Always Love You.'"

Crystal waited for the text prompt on the karaoke screen to start the a cappella beginning so the timing would be right when the music kicked in. The first words flowed in perfect pitch. All conversations stopped. Any eyes that weren't on the stage snapped to Crystal, and any that were, stayed there. "If I should stay…Well, I would only be in your way…"

As she continued, outside the Parlour several passersby stopped to listen, which only drew more people to see what the attraction was. The bar area filled three and four people deep. Birdie was at his post behind the bar, but he didn't bother asking anyone if they wanted anything, because no one cared. Everyone was transfixed by the siren on stage.

With her eyes closed, Crystal lost herself in the music, never missing a note. She blended the final lines expertly with the light musical accompaniment. Her voice rose, hitting the final notes perfectly. "You, darling, I love you…ooh, I'll always, I'll always lovvve yooooou." When she stopped and the last of the sound had drifted out into the room, seconds of silence passed. Everyone remained still, basking in the beauty of what they had just heard. Crystal put the mic back in the stand and walked toward her seat at the bar.

Moneta spoke into her mic in a soft voice. "That was Crystal, ladies and gentleman. Let's show her our appreciation." The crowd roared, clapping and whistling. Moneta said, "That's right. Maybe we can get her up here to do another song." The crowd timed their clap to be in unison, urging Crystal for an encore. Ignoring the attention, Crystal sat down and focused back on the machine. Moneta, recognizing Crystal was done, at least for a while, didn't push her. She said, "OK, well, after that, you deserve a break. We all do. No one wants to follow that. Let's all take a pause for the cause, refresh our drinks with one of those five-dollar champagnes on special all night, and keep those requests coming." She dimmed the lights and flipped on a recorded mix to fill the silence and keep the crowd entertained. "Dancing Queen," by ABBA, flowed through the speakers.

Crystal, her adrenaline racing following the performance, ignored the compliments and accolades being thrown at her. Fortunately everybody kept their distance. One of the reasons she didn't like to sing, or waited until right before she was ready to go home, was people always wanted to come talk to her afterward. And it was always the same questions: "Where'd you learn to sing like that?" "Why don't you sing professionally?" "What is your favorite song to sing?" They meant well, and Crystal knew if she didn't want the attention, she shouldn't get up and sing. But for Crystal, singing was more about keeping that part of herself alive and staying connected to her mom, which made it special and also painful at the same time.

She was vaguely aware that the person two seats down was sitting quietly and watching. Head down, Crystal continued to bang away at the machine. When she drew three aces, then followed with another ace and a three for a $2,000-credit win, she took her hands from the keys and sat back in her chair, satisfied to just admire the picture she had worked so hard to create.

The woman who had been watching her slid down one seat, right next to Crystal. "I guess tonight is your night in more ways than one."

Crystal glanced to her right, ready to brush off a stranger. Seeing it was Penny, she said, "Oh, hey, I didn't see you. After I sing, I put blinders on."

Birdie walked down, seeing the big score on the machine. "Did it finally hit? I told you it was due." He noticed the two of them talking. "You two know each other? Man, this town is so frickin' small."

Crystal said, "From the tables. We've played together a few times."

"And the juice place," Penny corrected her. "We also met there and hung out at Container Park. We go way back."

Birdie lifted a bottle from the well and angled it toward Penny. "Ketel and soda?"

Penny pointed at the bottle. "I'll take the Ketel and the ice with a lemon. No soda." She turned to Crystal. "Can I buy you one?"

Crystal looked at her glass, which was getting low again. Birdie grabbed a bottle of champagne and extended it toward the glass. Crystal waved him off. "I'm good on the champagne. I'll have the same thing as her, and take it out of this." She tapped the pile of money on the bar from the original hundred she had cashed in. "I got this round."

Birdie put the bubbly back and iced two rocks glasses. "Ooh, girls after my own heart. Drinking straight booze, buying each other drinks. You two strip down to your bra and panties and get in a pillow fight, and I might think I've died and gone to heaven."

Penny looked around. "I don't see any pillows."

Birdie said, "Let me call housekeeping." He set the drinks down in front of them. "These are on the house."

Crystal balled up a napkin and threw it at Birdie as he served other customers. "Such a perv." She took one more look at her big win on the screen and pressed the button to deal a fresh hand.

"Wait. Shouldn't you quit?" Penny said. She looked at the payout table on the machine in front of her. "I mean, that's like the second-best hand you can get, right? The chances of doing better are pretty slim. You should quit while you're ahead."

Crystal ignored the conservative warning and kept banging at the keys. "Number one, you never leave the machine on a winning hand. You always play at least one more. Second, these machines are streaky. The winning hands come in bunches. Another good hand, and I don't have to go into work tonight."

Penny touched her glass to Crystal's. "I'll drink to that. I could use a night out."

Crystal picked up her drink, forced a smile at Penny, and took a sip, still continuing to play the machine with her left. After five glasses of champagne, the stiff taste and watery texture of the vodka were a welcome change. She wasn't 100 percent sold on Penny, but outside of the club, she didn't really have any friends, and she didn't exactly consider the girls at the club friends. She couldn't. Because if she did, it meant she was one of them. She still liked to tell herself that it was only temporary, even though she didn't really have a plan for what was next. Her castmates from *Beached* were long gone. They had either moved away for a job, were traveling with a show, or had landed a new gig in town, which meant they had a new set of friends. People tried to stay in touch with Crystal, but she thought it was just a waste of time.

Friendship to her was usually about one of two things: convenience or guilt. People stayed connected because it was easy or because they felt bad if they didn't. Even as a young girl in school, Crystal didn't have many long-standing friendships. She was popular and friendly in class, but she knew at the end of the year she was going to move to the next grade and would make new friends. Another big part of the reason she didn't get too attached to her school friends was that her mom was her best friend. She didn't need anyone else. After her mom passed, Crystal had sealed up that part of herself. She didn't want to let go of her mom, and she didn't want to share that space with anyone else.

Penny sat quietly, trying to follow the blur of images on the screen. She finally asked, "Why do you go so fast? How do you even enjoy it?"

Crystal said, "It's not sex. I'm playing to win. The sooner I plow through the losing hands, the sooner I'll get to the winning ones. It's nice to just get into a rhythm. Everything else fades away. It's just you and the machine."

"But look," Penny said, pointing at the number of credits. "You're already down to almost twelve hundred from over two thousand. That's like two hundred and fifty bucks. You could have had a lot of fun with that."

"Like I said, things run in streaks. Most people play right into the casino's hands. They get conservative when they're up and aggressive when they're down. I'm not here to grind out a fifty to a hundred profit every night. I want to win big or lose and move on." As she spoke, three threes, a king, and an ace popped up on the screen. Crystal slowed down so Penny could follow. She kept the threes. "Need another three and an ace through four to win eight hundred."

Penny pointed at the screen. "But you have an ace there. Why not keep that one?"

"Getting another three is most important," Crystal said. "Discarding both cards gives me better odds because I'm drawing two, not just one. Getting an ace through four with the threes is just a kicker that doubles the winnings. Nice to have but not absolutely necessary." She moved her hand toward the button then hesitated. "Go ahead, you push it."

Penny shakes her head. "No, I'm not very lucky. I'll lose for sure."

"Luck has nothing to do with it." Crystal sat back in her chair and slugged her drink. "It's either going to hit or it isn't. Go ahead."

Penny reached over, put her hand on the button, and closed her eyes. She mumbled something and pushed down. Crystal saw the new cards come up but didn't say anything. Penny opened her left eye and peeked down at the screen, which showed four threes and a four. Her right eye popped open. "That's good, right? We won?"

"I don't know about we," Crystal said. "But that's two hundred bucks. Back up to almost two thousand credits."

Penny scooted her stool over closer. For the next several hours, Birdie kept the vodkas coming, Moneta had the karaoke flowing again, and the two of them played video poker, with Crystal teaching Penny the strategy of what hands to go for, what to hold, and what to discard. Together, they ran the total to over three thousand credits.

Drawing two sixes, two eights, and a four, Crystal quizzed Penny on what the next move should be. There was no answer. Crystal repeated the question, looking over at Penny, who was gazing pensively back at her. Crystal said, "You OK? What's wrong with you?"

Penny reached over and took off Crystal's usual green cap. "You're so beautiful." She touched the side of Crystal's face. "And with that voice, why are you hiding it?"

Crystal snatched her hat back and put it on, pulling the brim low. "You're drunk. Maybe it's time to cash out."

"No, I'm serious," Penny said. "You have a gift. You should be sharing it…and I don't mean at a strip club or karaoke. People should be paying to hear you sing."

Any bit of openness and warmth fostered in Crystal throughout the night disappeared in an instant. She pressed the cash out button and motioned to Birdie to close her tab while she waited for the machine to print her ticket. "Those days are behind me. I had my shot. It didn't work out. Now I sing for me."

"It doesn't have to be that way," Penny said. "My agent is based in LA. Let me introduce you. I'm sure he can get you auditions."

"I already have an agent. I'm done with LA," Crystal said. "There's nothing for me there."

Birdie came over. "You ladies are good. You played the whole time so all the drinks are comped." Crystal took two twenties from her pile of money and set them on the edge of the bar for Birdie. Birdie snagged the money and dropped it in his tip jar. "Not necessary but appreciated. So what's next on the agenda? You off to work?"

Not comfortable with Penny and the direction of their conversation, Crystal stuffed the remaining money from the bar in her pocket and just spoke to Birdie. "Nah, I'll probably cash this ticket, play some blackjack or just grab some food and call it a night."

Penny didn't give up, never taking her eyes off Crystal. "It doesn't have to be LA. He has connections all over." Birdie recognized they were in the middle of something and diverted his attention to washing glasses. Penny said, "My agent is coming here in a few weeks. You don't even have to meet him. Just let him come hear you sing. You won't even know he's there. If you want to meet him after, you can. What's the harm in that?"

"Why do you care so much?" Crystal eyed the exit, planning her escape. "Just leave me alone and mind your own damn business. If I wanted to perform somewhere, I would. You're so busy poking your nose in my life; focus on your own."

Penny reached for Crystal's hand. "Don't be like that. You can't compare your talent to mine. I read news and interview jocks. Nothing too special there. There's about a five-year window in my business for women. It lasts from your mid-twenties to your early thirties. If you don't make it national by then, you might as well just give up and settle on a local job or raise a family, because every year there's a whole new group younger and more determined. I screwed up my chance, but you don't have to. Let me help."

Crystal pulled her hand from Penny's. "You want to help someone, help yourself. If this agent is so great, why aren't you working?"

Penny scowled, her compassion and understanding disappearing. "I'm not working because I don't have to. Thank you very much. I might've struck out with my job and my marriage, but I got paid for both, so now I have options. I'm just waiting for the right opportunity."

"Good for you. It sounds like you really earned that money." Crystal tucked her purse under her arm and stormed off.

Penny trailed after her, out of the Parlour and across the casino floor, winding through the maze of slot machines toward the door. She hurried up alongside Crystal. "Will you just hang on a sec and talk to me?"

"Just drop it. I don't need your charity. I can take care of myself." Crystal slowed, waiting for the sliding door to open, and walked out onto the sidewalk toward her bicycle chained to a parking sign.

Penny stood next to her, while Crystal fiddled with the lock. Slightly out of breath from the chase, Penny said, "It's not charity. I know talent when I see it. I'd be helping my agent as much as you. Will you at least consider it?"

Crystal freed the bike and tossed the lock in the basket. "If I say yes, will you leave me alone and not pester me about it?"

"Yes, I swear." Penny traced an x on her chest with her finger. "Cross my heart."

Crystal hesitated, staring at the brief imprint left on Penny's chest, remembering that her mom used to make promises to her the same way. She softened. "OK, I'll think about it. But no guarantees."

Dow Jones Close: 16,580.84

Chapter Thirty-Three

Date: Tuesday, August 27, 2013

Dow Jones Open: 14,939.25

While neither Bill nor Hughie were prepared for Bill's first call inviting Hughie to the wedding, Hughie was ready for the second call. There were still the breaks in speech, but they were filled with sadness rather than resentment. Darlene had just called Hughie the day before. She was barely strong enough to speak except to express her love and say good-bye. Hughie had offered to fly out to be with her, but she told him that she wanted him to remember her as she was the day of the wedding. The real reason was that there wasn't enough time.

After the ceremony, Darlene's condition improved, encouraging them all. Her appetite came back, and she wanted to get out of their apartment more and more. On the past Sunday, she and Bill had even been able to continue their Fremont Street ritual with breakfast at Du-Par's and an afternoon of gambling, during which she won sixteen hundred quarters with three sevens on an old Red, White, and Blue slot machine in the Vintage Vegas section upstairs at the D Casino on Fremont. She loved going there because the machines still accepted and paid out actual quarters. It reminded her of when they used to visit before everything went digital and before her insides started turning to mush. Over the years she had always worried about something happening to Bill at work, that she would be left alone. After the diagnosis she worried about him, because it was her that would actually be leaving first, and he would be all by himself. She pressured Bill about this on several occasions and no longer hid her desires and intentions for him and Hughie to reconcile. If she was going to be gone, she wanted to know the two most important people to her would have each other. Bill wasn't ready to deal with that though. Twisted by grief and guilt, he believed taking action on the latter would bring the former even sooner. Besides, after the ceremony, everything seemed to be looking up. Even her doctor shared the optimism and thought that she might make it closer to the six-month mark or maybe even longer.

But that all changed when Bill woke up in the middle of the night and found her on the bathroom floor. He rushed her to the hospital, but all the doctor could do was manage the pain. Darlene drifted in and out of consciousness. The doctor ran the imaging tests again. The cancer had spread further into the lungs. He changed his prognosis to days. Bill stayed by her bedside, surrounding her with pictures of their life together. He put some on the stand next to the bed and on the traystand over the bed where they served her meals, the ones she was never able to eat. He wanted them all around her so that if she awoke even for a second, she would see a reason to hang on and keep fighting.

Later that first day in the hospital, Bill was sleeping in the chair. He heard Darlene's voice. Thinking it was a dream, he searched for a face to go with the sound. He couldn't find one. He realized it was actually her. He jarred himself from sleep. Her head was tilted in his direction on the pillow. The smile that had been missing since he found her in the bathroom stretched across her face. She said, "Boy, you were really zonked out. Sorry to wake you."

Bill sprang up. "That's OK. Do you need something?"

"I'm just so thirsty. Can you get me some water?"

Bill filled her water cup from the pitcher on the traystand. Elevating her bed with the remote, he handed her the cup with the straw angled for easy access. "Here you go. Remember, the doctor said to just sip."

She pulled water slowly through the straw, scanning the pictures around her. "When did these get here?"

"I ran home earlier," Bill said. "I thought it would be nicer to wake up to these memories rather than just my ugly mug."

Her mouth, still tight-lipped around the straw, flattened and curved upward. She picked up the picture of her, Bill, and Hughie at the chapel. She stared at it in silence until the slurping noise from the cup indicated she needed more water. Handing Bill the cup, she said, "Did you call Hughie?"

Bill had thought about calling him. He even picked up the phone several times and pulled the number up on the screen, but he couldn't bring himself to make the call. Bill knew Hughie would have a lot of the same questions that Bill had asked the doctor. The answers were tough enough to hear the first time. To tell another would make it all that more real. "I was going to," Bill said, "but I thought it best to wait until you woke up. Do you feel up to it now?" Bill extended the phone toward her.

She traded him the water cup for the phone. "Probably best to do it while I have the strength." She dialed the number. On the call, they followed the usual script of conversation about Grace, the kids, Hughie's job, the heat in Vegas, everything except the obvious question: How are you feeling? The longer the conversation danced around the topic, the more apparent it was that the answer would not be a favorable one. Darlene finally said, "I'm in the hospital again... Since last night... No, it's not necessary for you to come out... Who knows with these things? Probably a few days, maybe more, maybe less... There's nothing that can be done... But I don't want you to see me like this... Remember me how I was when we last saw each other... OK, put her on." She went on to have a similar call with Grace, then with the children, who, Bill could tell based on Darlene's remarks, didn't understand what was going on. They were talking about school and what was happening in their lives. All Bill could do was listen and watch as each sentence depleted Darlene a little more than the previous one. It was one of those conversations that you want desperately to end but keep finding ways to prolong. The phone finally made its way back to Hughie. Tears flowed from Darlene's bloodshot and swollen eyes. Bill remained next to her bed the entire time, holding her hand while she finished the call. "You know I love you more than anything," she said. "I'm so proud of everything you have achieved and the family you have. I'll be with you always...I love you too. Good-bye, son." She lowered the phone, her eyes focused on Bill, filled with sadness and pleading.

Bill said, "Do you need anything? Want me to get the doctor?"

She squeezed his hand, which consisted of several pulses more than prolonged tension due to her weakened state. "Are you finally ready to talk about it?"

"Why don't you get some rest? We'll talk about this later."

"No. We need to talk about what happens after–"

"Let me go get you another pillow." Bill let go of her hand and poked at her pillow. "Looks like you could use a fresh one."

"After I'm gone." She lifted her withered arm and patted his hand, which was still fidgeting with the pillow. "We can't put it off any longer."

Bill sat in the chair next to the bed and stared at the floor to hide his tears. She had seen him cry only twice in their lives. The first, when they got married, and the second, when Hughie was born. "Of course. Just let me know what you want me to do." Bill knew what she would want—the same she had wanted for so many years. He just didn't know if he could follow through. So many years had passed and so much had happened. He wouldn't even know where to start and he didn't want his last oath to her to be a broken one. He flexed his hand in hers. "I'll do my best."

Darlene said, "It's more about what I don't want." Bill looked up surprised. She said, "I don't want a funeral. I just want to be cremated and stay with you. Hughie and Grace and the kids should remember me as I was the last time we were together."

Bill's surprise transformed to confusion. "Are you sure that's it?

"Of course that's not it." Bill braced himself. She said, "I want you to hold onto my ashes and have both of ours disposed of together on one of those cliffs we used to hike to in Red Rock in our younger days."

Bill stood and leaned over, kissing her forehead. "We'll be together forever. I promise."

Dow Jones Close: 14,776.13

Chapter Thirty-Four

Date: Saturday, April 28, 2012

Dow Jones Open: Closed

As a reporter, Penny had learned how to compartmentalize. Once the camera turned on, she could become whatever the story required her to be. And it didn't stop there. Until Alec confronted her back in December in their kitchen, she had been managing her personal life the same way. She had been the empty housewife with Alec at home, the clandestine cheat sneaking around town with Fritjof, and the on-air sweetheart of the St. Louis sports scene in the public eye. Each role had complemented the other and created a balanced whole. As long as she kept the worlds separate, all coexisted quite nicely, and she had a sense of balance in her life.

After the interview with Fritjof for the bachelor charity contest had aired, however, and Alec had confronted her about the affair, she knew she had gotten greedy. It was one thing to meet with Fritjof privately but to do an extended segment with him for all to see, and more specifically for Alec, was too much. With Alec knowing both of them independently, she should've known that he would be able to tell something more was going on. Maybe that was her point all along; she wanted to get caught. She wanted to hurt Alec as much as he hurt her when he left her alone in the examination room and subsequently withdrew from their relationship.

In the weeks following the night in their kitchen, she contemplated these intentions on more than one occasion. She expected things to get worse and that surely chaos would ensue with Alec retaliating at her in some way or confronting Fritjof. But everything actually became easier. The holidays were of course awkward, but once they got through those, somehow her life recalibrated, and a new order and balance resumed. Things were actually better than before. There was a feeling of relief. Everything was out in the open. Both Alec and Fritjof knew what was going on with the other. Of course being the empty housewife at home didn't change, but at least she didn't have to pretend any longer. She could finally move forward.

Unfortunately, Alec didn't want to. Getting everything out in the open for him was a wake-up call. He finally became present. There was no more running away. He wanted to just forget what happened and go back to how things had been in the beginning of their relationship, before the baby. The acknowledgement of the affair had opened him up to change. Not ready to let go, he recognized his mistakes and wanted to work on the relationship. He was ready and willing to compete for her affections, but it was too little, too late. Penny no longer wanted to play that game. She was ready to move on. And it wasn't because of Fritjof, whom Alec seemed to be obsessed with. If Penny went to the store or to yoga, Alec asked her question after question, all of which ended with the accusation that she was going to meet Fritjof. On many occasions she even saw Alec's car pass by the location she had told him or he would be parked down the street or several rows away checking up on her. But the truth of the matter was she never slept with Fritjof again after Alec found out about the affair. Once Alec and Fritjof merged into a shared reality, she had no interest in either of them. They had become a single world from which she wanted to withdraw completely.

Fritjof reacted to her lack of interest in their relationship much the same way Alec did, like Penny was a prize in a competition. She wondered how much of their tireless pursuit was really to have her and how much was just not to lose to the other. The worst part of it all, they both became blubbering blobs of sensitivity. When Fritjof contacted her saying "he needed to talk" the night the Blues got back from a long East Coast road trip in February, she complied. He was waiting for her in his Lamborghini at their usual meeting spot by the Boathouse in Forest Park. She broke their typical protocol and parked, going to his car instead of him coming to her. She wanted to be able to make a fast exit if needed.

The scissor door rose as she approached his car. Not exactly inconspicuous, but it didn't matter anymore. A blast of heat radiated from inside, creating steam when meeting the ten-degree air outside. She slid into the heated leather bucket seat rubbing her hands on the leather to soak up the warmth. The door closed as effortlessly as it had opened, sealing her inside. It would be the only easy part of the evening.

"Thanks for meeting me," Fritjof said, reaching over and putting his hand on hers.

Penny didn't reciprocate. Instead, her whole body tightened. Fritjof retracted his hand. She said, "So what's up? You said it was important."

"It's just, I'm not doing so well with all this. You're all I can think about," Fritjof said. "It's affecting me on the ice. Not sure if you noticed, but I didn't exactly have the best road trip."

"Come on, don't you dare put that on me. I got enough shit to deal with."

"No, no, no, I didn't mean it that way. What I meant to say is that I just miss you. I need you." He turned toward her, leaning over on the console.

Penny looked over at him, pulling back and resting against the door. His angular features seemed to be melting right before her. She said, "I thought we agreed it's over. It's not fair to you or Alec. There's just too much at stake with the team."

"Fuck Alec. Fuck the team. What do you want? That's all that's important. If you want me, you can have me. They'll just have to deal with it." Tears filled Fritjof's eyes.

Penny looked away, staring at the fogged-covered windshield. "Don't do this. Please, just let it go."

"No, I want to hear it from you." Penny wouldn't look at him, but she knew he was crying. She could hear it in his staggered speech. He said, "Just say it. God damn it. You owe me that much."

The last statement lit a fire in Penny. She looked directly at him, the tears fully flowing as she expected. It didn't affect her. She narrowed her stare, leaning toward him. "I don't want you. It was fun, but now it's over."

Fritjof was the one who looked away this time. He clenched the leather steering wheel with both hands, trying to fight the tears, but they only increased. "No, you're just saying that because you're afraid. You're afraid of caring, of what people might say."

None of it fazed Penny. This was the part of relationships that she had the most experience in: the break-up. And guys always took the news the same way. The instant they were rejected by females, they decided they needed to open up and show their softer side. She had heard enough. She cinched up her coat and adjusted her wool stocking cap down to cover her ears. "Look, I'm sorry you're hurting. I know this hasn't been easy, but you have to accept that it's over. You're only making it harder on yourself. Just let it go and turn your focus to the ice." She hit the button to open the door and escape into the cold night air. She felt his hand on her back as she climbed out of the car and heard him calling for her until she was safely inside her Land Rover.

Starting the vehicle, she looked back at the fog-covered Lamborghini, which was still not moving. She shook her head. To be sitting in the passenger seat of a $400,000 sports car watching such a strong and beautiful man who made

$6 million a year cry like a baby was a pathetic sight. No one wanted to see that. How could she respect him now? Worse yet, Alec was acting the same way. She was able to keep her emotions bottled up. She expected the same from both of them. The last thing she needed was to be force-fed a steaming bowl of sentimental soup every time she saw either of them.

After the incident with Fritjof in Forest Park, things quieted down for about a week, then the text messages from him started again and the incessant questioning from Alec commenced. Penny decided she needed to clarify things once and for all. Since she viewed them as two parts of the same dysfunctional whole, she treated them as one, delivering the same speech to both on separate occasions. She said, "I think for everyone's best interest, we should put all the drama on hold until after the season. I'll stay at home to avoid causing speculation but will sleep in a separate bedroom. In public, we'll all play the appropriate roles of husband, wife, and teammate and friend. The most important thing is for the Blues go as far as possible in the playoffs." She appealed to their competitive sides while allowing their egos an easy way out. Both begrudgingly conceded. A draw was never a satisfying outcome but seemed to be acceptable in this situation.

With the Blues winning the Central Division for the first time in over ten years, the city rallied behind the team and had high expectations for the playoffs. As so often is the case, the communal success quelled their individual personal dissatisfaction. Regardless how toxic the situation was, all three recognized it was working and nobody wanted to be the one to blow it up. Once they got to that point, the rest became an easy rationalization. They all became martyrs, sacrificing their happiness for the benefit of the team and city. Subjugating three enormous egos was not an easy feat, but when the stakes were as high as they were, it somehow seemed to work.

The fever heightened as the Blues, who were the second seed in the conference, breezed through the conference quarterfinals with a four to one series victory over San Jose, and were to face the Los Angeles Kings, the eighth seed who had upset the top-seeded Vancouver Canucks, in the next round. With the upset of Vancouver, the Blues were the top seed and would have home ice advantage all the way through to the Stanley Cup finals.

In the opening game of the series in St. Louis, the Blues and Kings were locked in a one to one tie late in the third period. Alec had been masterful in allowing only one goal in twenty-four shots. Fritjof had scored St. Louis' lone goal on a one on two breakaway. Penny was in the press box, readying herself for the probability that she might have to interview both players at the same time. Despite all the team success and the drama moratorium they had been enjoying, she had never had to deal with both men at once. Even though in her mind she had merged them into one situation, she had been able to keep them separate physically.

With just over two minutes to go, the Kings fired a shot from the left wing, and it was redirected by a Kings player in front of the net. At the last second, Alec was able to adjust and knock away the puck before it crossed the line into the goal. The puck bounced around in front of the net. Alec dove on the puck. Kings players pushed Blues players; Blues pushed Kings. A pile of bodies ensued. "Sandman" by Metallica blared through the speakers. As the referees peeled away the bodies, a fight broke out at the bottom of the pile. The fans cheered. A penalty on the Kings would give the Blues a huge advantage and almost-certain victory. But as the referees cleared the melee, it was clear that the two involved participants wore the same-colored jersey. It was Alec and Fritjof. Penny watched, horrified. On top of Alec, Fritjof delivered two punches, both glancing off Alec's helmet. With the other bodies cleared away, Alec was able to roll Fritjof off him and counter. The music stopped. A lull fell over the crowd. The Kings players skated back. The Blues looked at one another, unsure what to do. Even the referees froze. Everyone just watched in disbelief as the two teammates rolled around on the ice, trading punches. Finally a referee blew his whistle. The other officials descended to break up the fight, which they had to thwart three more times once both men were back on their feet. Several Blues players intervened to separate the two, eventually removing Fritjof from the ice.

A lengthy discussion between the referees followed. The press box buzzed with confusion. No one had ever seen two members of the same team fight each other. They turned to Penny for answers as to what could trigger Alec to fight with his own teammate. Penny sunk in her chair, pretending to be as shocked as everyone else. Other reporters crowded around, peppering her with questions. She reached for her phone in her pocket, faking an incoming call to escape to the hallway, which was equally abuzz. People rushed in both directions to get back to their seats to see what would happen. Once they recognized Penny, a frenzied crowd of strangers swelled around her. At least the press box was confined and she knew everyone there. She slid back inside.

On the ice, the referees assessed both players with major penalties. Since there was less than five minutes in the game, the Blues had to finish regulation three against five. If the game went to overtime, they would begin with three players until the penalties expired. Since Alec was goaltender, the Blues were allowed to keep him in and remove another player in his place.

When play finally resumed, the once-raucous crowd was reduced to a murmuring, confused mob. The Kings needed less than a minute of the power-play to score a goal and go ahead two to one. The crowd booed. Whether it was more out of disappointment or embarrassment was unclear. They had seen the Blues give away some games over the years, but this was unprecedented for any team. The Kings easily added another goal in the final thirty seconds when the Blues pulled Alec for an additional skater, to end the game three to one.

Penny had been dreading a possible collision of the Alec and Fritjof worlds in an interview after the game. She never imagined it would happen before. For her postgame recap, she stood in front of the net where the fight had occurred. "Blues fans have been treated to several firsts this year. First division title and playoff series win in over ten years, but no one expected what transpired on the ice tonight. For the first time in NHL history, two players from the same team were penalized for fighting…with each other. It happened with a minute fifty-one left in regulation with the score tied one to one. After a save by Alec Baudin, a pileup occurred in front of the Blues net. As the referees cleared away the bodies, a fight broke out at the bottom of the pile between Baudin and Blues star center Fritjof Stridh, leaving both teams, the referees, and this capacity crowd of nearly twenty thousand in shock. It took several attempts and intervention from many of the Blues players to quiet the fracas. In the end the Blues were left at a three-to-five disadvantage for the remainder of the game, resulting in a three-to-one loss in this crucial game one of the conference semifinals. We'll have to wait and see if the NHL levies further penalties and how this will affect the team for the rest of the series. When I asked Blues coach Ken Hitchcock if he knew what caused the fight, he said, 'Your guess is as good as mine. I'm just as stunned and embarrassed as the fans. I'd hate to see all the good we accomplished this year be overshadowed by one unfortunate incident.' So there you have it. I'm Penny Market, reporting live from the Scottrade Center, where a Blues team squabble has left everyone red-faced."

Unfortunately the fallout from the fight didn't stop with that one game. The clip made its way on every national sports show and went viral on the Internet. The Blues became the punchline to a myriad of sports jokes. To avoid another incident, the League levied a full game misconduct and suspended both players for game two, which the Blues lost five to two. Just when things were dying down and everyone was hoping to move on in game three, someone leaked the story about the affair. What had been a sports blooper became a full-on celebrity gossip frenzy. All the tabloids descended. The Blues lost game three, four to two. The love triangle was fodder for all the TV late show monologues. Penny was nicknamed the Bluesy

Floozy. The station put her on administrative leave to dampen the hysteria. But it didn't matter. The story became a storm. Nothing could slow or stop it. It just had to run its course. The Blues lost game four, three to one. The season was over. Alec escaped to Vancouver to visit René. Fritjof fled to Sweden. Penny didn't leave the house for two weeks. The station informed her they would be terminating her contract based on a morality clause. Her worlds had not only collided; they had exploded. She knew that she also needed to get out of St. Louis—for good.

To decide where to go, she taped a map of the US on the wall. With a red marker she crossed out all the cities with hockey teams. The less the locals knew about hockey, the less likely it was that they would recognize the Bluesy Floozy. She also wanted to eliminate any possibility that, when she got a job, she would ever have to cover either of them coming to town as well as the chance of them getting traded. The choice was an easy one. Go to the one city in the middle of a desert with zero professional sports teams: Las Vegas.

Dow Jones Close: Closed

Chapter Thirty-Five

Date: Saturday, October 12, 2013

Dow Jones Open: Closed

L es was counting cards and had been for quite some time. I just didn't see any reason to alert the pit bosses. It was their responsibility to identify and deal with the counters. Besides, even though Les was steadily winning, it wasn't like he was backing up a truck to cart away his haul every time he sat down. And contrary to popular belief, counting cards isn't illegal or cheating. It'll never land you in the pokey, but it might get you banned or flat bet at the blackjack tables. The casinos, similar to a bar or restaurant, can refuse service to anyone, whether it be because a patron is rude or too drunk (which is usually the goal, so that rarely happens), or if the casino feels the patron has an unfair advantage over the house.

It's usually easy to spot counters by how hard they concentrate and watch all the cards that are played, how they vary their bets, and when they diverge from the basic strategy. To count cards, most use a high-low method, where they count every two through six with a value of positive one and ten through ace as negative one. Seven through nine has no value. The theory is that the more cards between two and six that are played, the higher the count will be and the greater the odds of getting tens and above. Of course the house has the same increased chances of getting the high cards, but because blackjacks pay three to two, and players can split and double down for twice their initial bet, the players have a greater advantage. There are other considerations, but no point in boring you with those details here.

I've flipped so many cards over the years, I don't even have to add up the totals anymore. It just happens naturally. One look at the table and I instantly know the count. It's more visual than linear. It's like when people are amazed by how quickly I can add up the player hands. The thing is, there's no math involved at all. After seeing the combinations over and over, I remember the results for clusters of cards rather than adding up the individual ones. One look at a 4-K-A-A-5, I know that it's twenty-one and negative one on the count. So when I see people not speaking to anyone, staring intently at each card, often with their lips moving as they adjust the count, and increasing their bets as the count ticks up, I know they're counting. Occasionally pressing the bet when the count is high might just be a lucky coincidence. But doing so every time is a dead giveaway, and when players are formulaic about the increase, like betting two units at a count of two, four units at three, six units at four, and eight units at a count of five or more, or just raising their bets one unit for each increase in the count, I want to reach across the table and smack them upside the head. The best counters, you'll never know, and they will even intentionally tank hands and not be so obvious about how much they raise their bet.

The order and rules of counting are what attract most people to it. There really is no thinking or feeling involved at all. The cards tell you everything you need to know. Counters just have to memorize the rules and follow the math. The pit bosses only get involved when the players go against conventional logic, like splitting tens or doubling on a hard twelve, because I have to call out those hands. If the players weren't on the pit boss' radar before, they are from that point on. Whether they'll be asked to leave or not all depends on how much they win.

For Les, his average win was between seventy-five and a hundred bucks. He would buy in for $200 and play for two hours or until he won a hundred, whichever came first. If he sat down and won the hundred quickly, he would walk with his profits. If he was close to the two-hour mark and the count was negative, he would cash in early. If the count was positive, he would ride it out. And on the rare occasion that he burned through his initial $200 before it was time to go, he would buy in for another hundred, but he was disciplined and never went deeper than that into his bankroll in any single session. No matter how bad the beat was he'd always push back from the table. What made Les such a good gambler and so many others merely casino contributors was that he had no ego. He was dispassionate and approached it like a job, and he never varied from his mission.

On this fall Saturday, in addition to blackjack, Les was preoccupied with the USC–Notre Dame football game on one of the pit TVs. So much that I could tell he kept losing the count at the table. His eyes would drift to the game and he would watch a play, then attempt to total up the count before I cleared the cards. After a Notre Dame fumble on their own forty-one yard line in the fourth quarter, leading fourteen to ten, I knew he had missed the end of the last hand and had no idea what had transpired. I said, "Plus three."

He said, "No, ND is up four."

I glanced around to make sure the pit boss wasn't behind me. "No, I mean the count is plus three."

Les smiled and shook his head. "Is it that obvious?"

"As long as you stay conservative, you should be all right." I dealt another hand. Ten and a two for Les. A two up for me. Count was now plus four.

Les studied the cards. The normal statistical play was to hit a twelve against a dealer two. Les said, "I'll stay." He knew at a count of plus three or higher, the better play was to stay because there was a greater probability a ten could come. His eyes went back to the TV.

I flipped my down card to reveal a ten. "Dealer has twelve." Next card out of the shoe was a jack of hearts. "Name of the game is twenty-one not twenty-two. Dealer busts." I paid Les twenty dollars by giving him a green chip and taking away one of the red. Les cringed as USC got a first down on the Notre Dame twenty-one. I said, "You got ND, huh?"

"Minus three." With the count down to plus two, he pushed two red chips into the circle.

"Still looking good." I dealt another hand. Five and a four to Les. A three for me. Count was plus five.

Les didn't need me to tell him to double that hand. He put two red chips next to his bet. "Unfortunately I also have the over. Past two weeks they've been putting up all kinds of points. An ND win with no points does me no good."

"You need to root for overtime. An SC touchdown here followed by an Irish field goal will get you to thirty-four. Once you get to overtime, anything can happen. Overtime is a friend to the over in college football."

After rooting for ND all day Les now had to cheer on USC. I love watching sports bettors. An outsider would think they are psychotic. One moment they are celebrating one team and cursing it the next, trying to will the outcome that secures their bets.

Unfortunately, as we mapped out the scenario Les needed, a penalty pushed SC back to the thirty-three. After a short gain to the twenty-six, it was fourth and fifteen. With only about three minutes to go, SC opted to bypass the field goal and go for it, failing and turning the ball over on downs.

Les flopped back in is chair. "Well, that should do it." He turned his attention back to the table and counted his chips. In addition to the $200 he started with, he was up ninety-five. "So looks like I'm breaking even today. Should've just bet them straight up."

"Ah, the lure of the parlay," I said. "Smaller investment for greater return. The sportsbooks love them. So many people have good bets, but add legs to get those better odds. Why make two straight bets up for less than even money odds when you can make one for 2.6-to-one?"

Les said, "I'm just shocked that game went under. Didn't see that coming. Their defense gave up ninety-three points combined the past two games. I thought the game would be a shoot-out."

The count was down to minus one. Les stayed with the minimum five-dollar bet. His first card was a queen of diamonds. Second card was an ace of clubs. "Ace from space," I said. "Player has blackjack." My upcard was a nine of hearts. I paid him the one and a half times his bet for the blackjack. "Player wins seven-fifty."

He shook his head. "Of course I get the blackjack with the minimum bet."

"That's Blackjack Universal Law number one," I said. "Blackjacks have the greatest probability of happening when you lower your bet to the minimum."

"Ain't that the truth?" He counted his chips. The win put him at $102.50, just over his quit threshold. Not to mention with the jack I had under, that meant three high cards had played, dropping the count to minus four. "Probably time to quit, huh?" He said and tossed me the $2.50 as a tip.

I nodded in appreciation, combining the chips with the others he had given me throughout the afternoon. "Thanks for the tips." I stacked the four one-dollar chips and the two fifty-cent pieces with the other four red chips and colored up for a green, tapping the $25 chip on the table twice and dropping it in the tip slot. "Your goal is to win a hundred, right?"

"But technically I'm even after the parlay loss." Les put his four green together and had the remaining red in four fifty-dollar stacks. Combining two of the red stacks, he pushed them to the center with the green.

I counted the two hundred for the cameras to see. "Two black going out."

Les slid another of the red stack of fifty to the center. "This, too."

I divided it into two stacks of twenty-five and took two green from the house. "Two-fifty going out."

Les dropped the $250 in black and green in his shirt pocket and put the remaining stack of ten red five-dollar chips into the bet circle. I had never seen him vary from his strategy and never this aggressive, especially with the count against him. He had been playing more often lately and was also much more focused, but I had assumed it was because he was working on his counting. Seeing this move, I wasn't so sure. He was playing like he needed the money, like he couldn't afford to break even. I checked one last time before I dealt. "You sure about this?"

He nodded and stood from his chair. "Come on, one time." First card was a five of spades. He said, "Well, that's not a good start." I slid my downcard in front of me and reached for his second card. He said, "How about a six?"

I gave him a five of diamonds. He released a deep breath, his shoulders relaxing. "That should work."

My upcard was an eight of hearts. His two fives were a double-down hand, but it's much harder to double with fifty dollars bet than it is with five. Also he didn't have any more money on the table. He would have to dig into his winnings to fund the hand. I said, "Universal Blackjack Law number two: Double downs and splits have the greatest probability of happening when you're playing your last hand and have to dig back into your pocket."

He grimaced, rubbing his face, the tension returning. Looking at his cards, then at mine, and back at his, he reached into his pocket and put down the two green next to the stack of red. Holding out one finger, he said, "One card, up, please. No sense dragging it out."

"Doubling down. Good luck." I reached for the next card and slid it facedown, turning it over at the last second. "Eight of clubs. Player has eighteen. Let's hope I have a nine or less to go with my eight."

Les was quiet, just leaning forward with both hands on the rail, eyes burning a hole through my downcard.

I flipped it over. "Seven of diamonds. House has fifteen." I pull another card from the shoe. A four of hearts. "Fifteen and four is nineteen. House wins. " I collected his hundred in chips. "Tough break. Thought you had it when I had fifteen."

Les was quiet, just staring at the empty circle where his hundred dollars used to be. He reached into his pocket and pulled out one of the black chips and placed it on the table. "Let's go again."

"You sure you don't want change?" I asked. In the last hand, an ace and two fives and a four had been played. The two eights and the seven didn't affect the count. It was now plus one. Not high enough to justify such a big bet.

Still standing, Les pointed to the table. "Please just deal."

I called out to the pit boss notifying her of the increase in bet. "Checks play." She gave her approval. First card was a queen of spades. Second was a six of clubs against my ten of diamonds. Surrendering wasn't an option, so in basic strategy sixteen versus a ten is a hit, but with a count of plus one, player should stay.

Les said, "Hit me." Next card was a three of hearts. Nineteen. He waved his hand over his cards. "I'll stay."

I nodded at his hand. "Nice hit." Turning over my down card, I revealed a jack of spades. "Dealer has twenty. House wins." I cleared his cards and collected his black chip. "Cards seemed to have turned on you."

Count was now zero. I expected him to walk away, but he dipped his fingers into his breast pocket for the remaining black chip and plopped it down on the table. Winning would make him even with the $200 he started with. A loss, and he'd be down two hundred. Again I called out and received approval from the pit boss. With it being two times in a row, she walked down to observe.

Les's gaze didn't lift from the table. He was clutching the rail with both hands and subtly rocking back and forth. His first card was a king of clubs and second, a queen of diamonds for a total of twenty. He exhaled in relief. I turned over a ten of spades for my up card. Rare frustration spilled from Les. "Come on, you got to be kidding me. Can I catch a break just one time?"

I slid the corner of my down card over the mirror to check for a blackjack. Shaking my head, I looked up at Les and flipped over the ace of diamonds. "Dealer has twenty-one." I scooped up his last black chip.

Les dug into his pants pocket and peeled off two hundred dollar bills from his money clip. "Two black, please." He was now chasing his losses. His body was rigid, his face tight, pupils constricted. Even when he was looking at me, he wasn't seeing me. He was staring right through me. Probably furious with himself for not walking away, all he could see were chips and cards. The only thing that would lift the haze was to get back to even. No doubt about it, Les was on tilt.

I gave him two black. He pushed both to the bet circle. The count was minus four, and there was less than a half of a deck remaining in the shoe, making it a true count of minus eight. He should be decreasing his bet to the minimum, not increasing it. He pressed his finger into the felt. "Let her rip."

His first card was an eight of clubs, his second, an eight of hearts. I had a four showing. He reached back into his pocket and counted out his final two hundred dollars to split the eights. I exchanged the cash for two more black chips, stacking them next to his bet and separating the eights into two hands. The pit boss moved closer to the table to watch the hand. If Les won, he'd have all his money back plus $200. A loss would put him down six, seven if including the hundred he could've walked away with. I said, "Here we go. Splitting snowmen."

First card was a nine for a seventeen. He waved over the hand to stand. On the second eight, he got a two for a total of ten. He shook his head to decline the double opportunity. "Figures. Just hit me."

"Sure you don't want to double?" I asked.

Les said, "Don't have any more money." He nodded his head toward the hand, again signaling a hit. It was a five.

"Fifteen." I looked to him for direction. Against my four, he should stay, but as bad things were going, I wasn't so sure.

He just waved his hand through the air in frustration. "I'm done. Hopefully you'll bust."

Underneath I had a four for a total of eight. Next card in the shoe was a six. "Fourteen," I said. "Still got a chance."

"Come on, eight or higher," Les said. "Just bust one time."

I slid over the next card, a seven of diamonds. Les just stared at the cards, not saying anything. I called out the total. "Twenty-one." Still no reaction. I collected the cards and the four black chips. "That got ugly fast."

Shaking his head, Les finally acknowledged the outcome. "Unreal." He buried his hands in his pockets and slunk toward the exit.

I could tell he was just sick. I was, and it wasn't even my money. It's probably a good thing he didn't have any more cash because he probably would've gone again. It was all so out of character for him. What I didn't realize at the time was why he was taking the chance in the first place.

Dow Jones Close: Closed

Chapter Thirty-Six

Date: Friday, February 14, 2014

Dow Jones Open: 16,018.08

Max hurried up the sidewalk toward the Western Hotel. His lawyer, Amanda, his real estate agent, and his lead contractor stood in front of the boarded-up entrance where Max had crashed into the building.

Amanda glared at her watch. "You're twenty minutes late."

Max didn't acknowledge the comment. He gestured toward the plywood covering the entrance. "Boy, somebody did a number on this place. Guess we're going to have to use the back door."

His real estate agent said, "Max, I don't have to go inside to tell you this place is overpriced for what you want to use it for. They're asking five million for the eight thousand nine hundred twenty-five square feet. That's five hundred sixty dollars per square foot. I can find you just as much space three to four blocks from here. Won't be as nice, but it'll be a third of the cost."

Max said, "Cost isn't my only motivation."

Amanda chimed in. "I'm sure if we agreed to pay to have the damage repaired and an inconvenience fee, the building owners would be willing to drop any potential litigation."

"That might be the smartest play," the contractor said. "You're going to have to pay to fix the front anyway. Why overpay for the inside?"

Max kept his face emotionless, staring in silence at each of them, rotating his gaze. It looked like he was listening, but he was just waiting for them to stop talking. They had assumed he was only interested in keeping himself out of legal trouble, but his main concern was how he was going to fulfill the McDonald's order. He knew there was no way he could do it at the other location. He shook his head. "You know the best part about unsolicited opinions is that they are as easily forgotten as they were requested."

The annoyance returned to Amanda's tone. "If you don't want to listen to us, then why did you ask us here?" She had the longest and closest relationship with Max. She knew—or at least she thought—she could stand up to him with no repercussions. The other two recognized their jobs could be chopped in an instant. With a potential $400,000 commission on the line for the real estate agent, and a few hundred thousand in buildout costs and a potential fat ongoing maintenance agreement for the contractor, both hired hands kept their mouths shut and their eyes fixed on the ground.

Max said, "I asked you here to use your expertise to get the best deal, not to talk me out of it. So if there aren't any other objections, shall we?" He motioned to the right and walked in that direction.

The real estate agent reluctantly spoke up. "Um, Max, it's best to go around the other way."

Max spun around. "Very well then. Now you're proving to be of some value."

The group walked down Fremont toward Ninth Street. The real estate agent switched into sales mode. She pointed at the bus stops in front of the hotel on each side of Fremont. "You have the Boulder City Express North- and Southbound bus lines right out front, very convenient for work commuters." As they rounded the corner to Ninth Street, she pointed to the vacant lot on the opposite corner to the northeast, the site of the old Ambassador Motel with their neon sign advertising, "Llamas Stay for Free," still standing as an homage to the old Vegas. She said, "Ample parking on the Ambassador lot for any of those driving workers." They walked down Ninth Street; the red words, "Viva Lost Vegas," painted along the side of the white building were another shout-out to the past. She waved her arm at the message. "Of course any of the old signage can be removed, or these murals painted over."

"I don't know," Max said. "I like keeping it as it is. I want to stay connected to the past. I don't want to replace it."

The contractor pointed up to second-level terrace lined with white doors. "Assume those are the rooms up there. What are the plans for those?"

"There's a total of one hundred and sixteen rooms," the real estate agent said. "All are stripped down but still have functioning plumbing."

The contractor said, "We could easily convert them to offices or knock some walls down to open up space."

They came upon the first of the side-door entrances about a third of the way back. The real estate agent put her key in the industrial gray door. She said, "Just prepare yourself. The inside is pretty rough. Not much has been done since they closed the place two years ago." She pulled the door open with several tugs. The bottom scraped across the concrete. Holding the door with her hip, she cleared away spiderwebs with one hand while removing a flashlight from her purse with the other. "Just wait by the door when we get inside while I turn on the lights." She ventured inside with Max following, then the contractor, and finally Amanda, who straddled the threshold, holding the door. The air was stale and humid, smelling of cigarette smoke and mold. They watched the beam of light bounce across the floor toward the front. With the exception of the daylight from the open side door and the streams sneaking through the cracks in the plywood covering the front, the room was pitch-black.

Max took a few more steps inside and inhaled through his nose. "Whoa, that's pretty ripe. Hopefully we don't find any bodies."

The contractor, still trying to make up for earlier, kicked his foot against the carpeting. "We can rip up all this old stuff and disinfect and power wash the floor. That should take care of the smell."

Max roamed further toward the center, his eyes adjusting to the darkness. Amanda, still holding the door, called out. "Max, be careful. Who knows what was left behind? You could trip and hurt yourself."

As the warning flowed from Amanda's lips, the real estate agent flipped the breaker. The lights above buzzed and crackled. Faint light drifted down, increasing in intensity with the passing seconds. Except for some overturned tables and chairs, a pile of empty cardboard boxes, and several large rolls of bubble wrap, the floor was open space.

Max stood in the middle of the room. Head back, eyes closed, arms outstretched at his side, he rotated in a circle as if he were basking in sunlight. "I think this place will do just fine."

The lights radiated at full capacity. What moments ago had looked eerie and ominous became shoddy and dilapidated. From the pile of boxes, two rats ran in opposite directions.

The real estate agent walked toward Max in the center of the room. "The place has been empty for two years, so it's going to have some unwanted guests."

The contractor joined them. "Nothing an exterminator can't take care of." He opened his notebook and scribbled down some text.

Amanda looked down at the open-toed sandals she was wearing. "Maybe I should wait outside. I didn't exactly wear rat-friendly footwear."

"Nonsense," Max said. "They're more afraid of you than you are of them." Another rat shot out from the pile of boxes, this time running right at them. Max charged in its direction. The rat diverted course and ran toward the back. "See, what I'd tell you?" He turned and walked toward the front. The others filed in behind him. Amanda hurried alongside, her eyes fixated on the floor, scanning the surrounding region. Max stopped in front of the boarded-up entrance. "I liked the tinted glass that was here before, but make sure it's stronger or partitioned so that if some other drunken idiot crashes through, it doesn't destroy the whole front." The contractor recorded every word, or at least he translated it into the language he would understand later. Max turned and faced the open room. "We'll set up three production lines, right, left, and center. Shipping and receiving will be in back. Add two truck bays onto the back of the building. One for incoming and one for outgoing." Max walked to the left, where the bar was still pretty much intact, including the stools, tables and chairs.

The contractor said, "We can rip this out, no problem."

"No, I kind of like it," Max said. "We can use it as a lunch and break area."

The real estate agent said, "A bar in the office? Where do I sign up?"

Amanda, as legal counsel, stated the obvious: "No alcohol of course."

"Of course not," Max said. "Well at least not out here. Can't say the same for my office."

They proceeded through the tour in that fashion. Max barked out ideas of what he wanted, the others offered their opinions, Max made a decision, and the contractor wrote it down to include in his estimate. For two and a half hours they covered the entire property from the kitchen to the restrooms to every single one of the hotel rooms. At the end, the contractor had over five pages of notes. They had seen fourteen rats, although some of them could've been the same ones, two bats, and one dead animal carcass, which looked to be a rabbit at one point or maybe a cat. It was too decayed to tell. In the rooms they found everything from used needles and condoms to stuffed animals and an empty shopping cart with no wheels. No one was really sure what had come before and what had come after the hotel closed.

At the end they reconvened on the sidewalk under the mostly cloudy skies of the seventy-degree winter day. Max, with minimal trepidation, made one of his most significant business decisions, definitely the largest purchase at least, with relative ease. Normally extremely impatient and in a hurry to finish one thing to get to the next, he was strangely at peace. He stepped back to the edge of the curb and scanned the building from back to front and top to bottom, waiting for the real estate agent to lock up. The contractor flipped through the pages of notes, reviewing what he had written and making his final marks. Amanda removed a wipe from her purse and cleaned the dust and dirt from her face first, then her arms and hands and any other exposed skin, using six of the formulated cloths in the process.

The real estate agent twisted the handle to ensure it was locked, and spun around. "So what do you want me to do?"

"Make an offer," Max said, his voice calm and confident.

"Full asking price?" she asked.

"Full price. I want to close within a week. Construction estimate within two days. Amanda, make sure all the i's are dotted and t's are crossed." Everyone looked at each other and just nodded. Max nodded back. "Good work today, people." He turned, put his hands in his pockets, and walked down the sidewalk like a third grader on his way to his bicycle after a good day at school—that is if the new Tesla he bought to replace the Maserati was a bicycle and a good day at school was the same as spending $5 million.

Dow Jones Close: 16,154.39

Chapter Thirty-Seven

Date: Wednesday, September 23, 2009

Dow Jones Open: 9,830.63

Crystal stood next to the hospital bed, clutching her mother's hand. The respirator pushed air in and out of her mother's scarred lungs in a soothing, yet menacing rhythm. Each gentle whoosh signaled one more breath she was alive, but also another one that could be her last. It also mirrored Crystal's ire. One second it would swell as Crystal questioned how her mother never revealed how sick she really was. But in the next instant, as the anger heightened, compassion and the fear of what Crystal would do without her seeped in. She blamed herself. If she had never left, her mother could've never hid this from her.

Crystal had just finished rehearsal when Maura called. Since landing the part and moving to Vegas, Crystal hadn't talked much to Maura. Hearing the familiar ringtone triggered a smile. She lifted the phone to her ear. "Checking up on me?"

"Hey, kid." Maura's voice was low and deliberate. "How are things?"

Crystal recognized Maura's bad news voice. This was the tone she always used when things didn't go as they had hoped with an audition or performance. But Crystal knew rehearsals were going well. The choreographer and musical director had both just told her how pleased they were with her. She attempted to lighten the mood. "You know me, making the world a better place, one plié at a time."

"I'm afraid I have some unfortunate news," Maura said. "Your mom's in the hospital."

"What do you mean? I just talked to her yesterday. Everything was fine." Crystal said, recalling the conversation, scanning her memory for any indications to the contrary.

"That's the thing." Maura said, hesitating. "I guess things haven't been fine for a while."

"But I don't understand. Why didn't she say anything? Why didn't you say anything?"

"Honestly, kid," Maura said, "I didn't know. I hadn't seen her in a while. She turned down the last few gigs I had for her, but all she told me was that she was tired and couldn't go like she used to. Nothing more. I guess she just didn't want to worry us. You know how your mother is. She knew you would come home if you had the slightest inkling there was something wrong with her."

Crystal steadied herself. "Maura, how bad is it?"

"Well, they have her resting comfortably now, but you need to come home, kid…today."

Crystal didn't have to hear any more. The fact that her mother had hid it from her and that Maura was telling her to leave a paying job was all she needed. Things couldn't get much worse. Without even telling anyone the reason or getting permission, she left directly for the airport from the theater. Nothing mattered more than her mother. She didn't pack a bag and didn't even arrange a ticket. She just went to the airline that had the first available flight to LAX and bought a one-way, which wasn't an easy feat. With all the increased security measures, a person wanting a ticket with such short notice and no luggage created all sorts of warning signals.

Maura picked her up at the airport. She explained on the way to the hospital that it was an autoimmune disease called sarcoidosis. "The good news is that it's not cancer or contagious." Crystal flooded her with follow-up questions, most of which Maura couldn't answer. But she did warn her, "I have to tell you, kid. She doesn't look good. She has these small, purple patches on her face and arms, and her left eye droops something terrible."

Tears streamed down Crystal's face. The panic followed by the adrenaline to get home had kept all other emotions buried. But in the car with Maura, Crystal released them all—sadness, regret, guilt—they all came pouring out. She knew once she got to the hospital, she would have to push them back down again and be strong for her mother's sake.

"I should've been home with her," Crystal said to Maura, walking to the elevator in the hospital parking garage. "How did you find out?"

"The hospital called me," Maura said. "I guess she has me listed as her emergency contact with her doctor. Apparently she collapsed with a respiratory failure at the market."

Crystal shook her head, miffed that her own mother was still so protective of her that she didn't have her listed as the contact. She knew her anger was misguided and thin, but it was easier to latch onto than all the other feelings bubbling to the surface. She asked the question that she had been avoiding. "Is she going to be OK?"

Maura said, "The doctor said the percentages are in her favor, but she's been ignoring the symptoms for so long, it's spread from the lungs to the skin and nervous system and potentially other organs. They're doing more tests, and in the meantime, they're treating her with a combination of sedatives, antibiotics, and anti-inflammatories. We'll know more in the next seventy-two hours, depending on how she responds to the treatment."

Aside from using words like "alveoli," which Crystal learned were the tiny sac-like air spaces in the lungs where carbon dioxide and oxygen were exchanged, "granulomas," microscopic lumps of a specific form of inflammation that can form there, and "fibrotic," when the tissue becomes scarred, the young male resident attending to Valeria repeated what Maura had told Crystal as they stood over her mother, who was still sleeping due to the sedatives. Crystal's main question was, "What caused it?"

The doctor said, "The cause is unknown. Symptoms can come and go with or without treatment. Based on the pervasive symptoms with your mother, the disease has been affecting her for many years."

"But how could she hide this?" Crystal motioned toward the rashes on her mother's face. "I would've noticed."

"Unless a chest X-ray, CT scan, or biopsy is performed, sarcoidosis can be really difficult to diagnose. The early symptoms, like fatigue, dry cough, shortness of breath, red or teary eyes, and swollen or painful joints, are fairly common and can be attributed to other things."

As the doctor listed the warning signs and symptoms, Crystal was thinking, *Check, check, check.* Her mother had complained about all of them, but she had always attributed whatever was bothering her to picking up some bug from one of the kids at the preschool where she was still teaching music. Anytime Crystal urged her to go to the doctor, she just said, "I'll be fine," and Crystal never heard anything else on the matter.

Since there was nothing more to be done until the tests results came back and the doctor could evaluate the efficacy of the treatment, she encouraged Crystal to go home and rest. But there was no way Crystal was leaving the room. She had left her mother once. She was going to be there in case her mother woke up or the doctor had any additional news. Eventually relenting, the doctor permitted Crystal to stay in the room. The nurse even brought in a cot so Crystal would be more comfortable than in the chair.

So all there was to do was wait. Crystal just stood over her mother, watching her chest rise and fall. She thought about what she would say when her mother woke up, promising herself she wouldn't scold her for not going to the doctor sooner, for not telling her she wasn't feeling well, for not having her as the emergency contact…much, she wouldn't scold her much. But for now, she just wanted her mother to open her eyes.

Crystal glanced at the cot, feeling the emotion of the day giving way to sleepiness. She squeezed her mother's hand, not wanting to let go. Locating the remote control with her other hand, she shut off the light, climbed into the bed and curled up next to her mother. If she couldn't talk to her, she wanted to at least feel her body next to hers like she used to every night.

Dow Jones Close: 9,748.55

Chapter Thirty-Eight

Date: Sunday, September 1, 2013

Dow Jones Open: Closed

When Bill called, Hughie answered the phone sounding hopeful. "Mom?"
"No, it's your dad."

The line was silent. Both men knew the next words to be spoken, but neither wanted to be the one to say them. Hughie finally spoke. "When did it happen?"

"This morning. They had just brought her breakfast, but she sent it away because she didn't want to move all the pictures of her and me and you and Grace and the kids. She picked up the frame with the pictures of the three of us from the wedding day and with you all at the hotel. She just stared at it for the longest time. I asked her if she needed anything. All she wanted me to do was read to her. You know how she loved those *People* magazines. As I was reading, she pulled the picture to her chest and closed her eyes, saying she thought she would take a nap. A few seconds later she was gone." Bill fought to hold in the emotion, to be strong like he knew he should, but saying it to Hughie was too much. He wept into the phone.

Hughie said, "I'll catch the next flight out."

"That's not necessary," Bill tightened, swallowing the emotion. "Your mother left very specific instructions on how things should be handled. She wanted the last time you saw each other to be how you remembered her."

"But what about the funeral? You have to at least be having some type of ceremony."

"She didn't want one. Last rites were performed at the hospital, and she will be cremated. Her ashes will be stored until I die, then our ashes will be disposed of together."

Hughie's tone sharpened. "You sure this isn't just what you want?"

Bill fired back. "What's that supposed to mean?"

"I find it a rather big coincidence and very convenient for you that her wish completely cuts me out of everything. I guess you finally got your way. Congratulations."

Bill said, "I know you're upset about your mother, so I'll ignore that."

"Of course you will," Hughie said. "You've been doing it for years. Well, if you think this is going to get me to apologize, you're crazy. I'm not sorry for what I did. I was a kid who needed a father. But you know what? I got used to not having one, and my life is just fine. Let's see how you deal with having no one."

The line went silent. Bill knew Hughie wasn't there anymore, but he still held the receiver to his ear. His voice cracked as he spoke. "I'm sorry." Hughie's anger and his words weren't what hurt. Bill had beaten himself up far worse over the years. Besides they weren't accurate. No doubt that facing Hughie would've been tough for Bill because he would be forced to feel the full pain of the loss and also guilt for all the lost years and the memories he had deprived Darlene of by never reconciling with Hughie. But even though he wouldn't go back to the hotel with her and Hughie on the day of their wedding, he would've made amends with Hughie if Darlene had wanted him to. All she would've had to do was ask. For whatever reason, she just didn't. Bill figured she was just looking out for him and making things easy just like every other day of their life together. What ripped Bill apart on the inside in that moment was that he couldn't bring himself to say the words to Hughie before, and that he wasn't willing to call him back now.

Dow Jones Close: Closed

Chapter Thirty-Nine

Date: Thursday, May 1, 2014

Dow Jones Open: 16,580.26

Penny awoke, naked and wrapped in a beige bed sheet, stretched across a queen-sized mattress on the floor in a garage studio. It had to be around noon. The sun baked through the fiberglass panel garage door at the opposite end and blasted light through the domed skylights on the twenty-foot ceilings above. Canvases of various sizes and degrees of completion were scattered throughout the humid, rectangular room, smelling of paint and turpentine. Murals of pastel flowers and mushrooms sprouted on the windowless cinderblock walls with cartoonish butterflies and snails moving throughout the garden landscape. She hated waking up here.

Flinging off the sheet, she rolled toward the middle of the bed facing the long, lean body of Neck Tattoo, uncovered and naked on the mattress. The star tattooed on his neck was the beginning of a trail of stars that curved around and extended down along his spine, decreasing in size and disappearing into the crack of his ass. She couldn't deny, he was a beautiful and sexy man. He was just too young. She didn't really remember where she ran into him the previous night, but she knew it was probably her doing. She always called him when she got drunk and didn't want to go home to her empty house.

Massaging her temples to alleviate the tension from all the alcohol, it slowly came back to her. She remembered hearing Crystal sing and playing video blackjack with her at the Parlour Bar at the El Cortez. She thought they may have gone out together but recalled Crystal storming off because Penny offered to help her get legitimate singing jobs. *What is her problem?* she thought. *Why won't she accept any help? She obviously needs it.*

Penny traced the stars down Neck Tattoo's back. He moaned, wiggling his shoulders and burrowing further into his pillow. She stopped, not wanting to wake him. She'd sneak out just like the other mornings she had stayed.

Slinking off the mattress, Penny scanned the room locating her purse, clothes, and shoes scattered across the floor. She reassembled her outfit, stuffing the panties into her purse and carrying her shoes to not make noise on the concrete floor. She eased open the door, noticing the red five-gallon bucket next to it. No amount of alcohol would allow her to forget that. Since there was no restroom in the studio, her choice had been simple: pee in the bucket or out in the alley. The only other option was walking to the ampm on Charleston, and there was no way that was happening. The bucket and the alley were both probably cleaner. She remembered opting for the bucket and him, not surprisingly, wanting to watch.

Outside she slipped on her shoes and walked down the alley to one of the parked cars awaiting service in front of the garage for the used car lot on the corner. The high-seventies temperature with a slight breeze was a relief from the sticky, stale air inside of the studio. Bending down, she angled the side mirror in her direction to survey the damage. Not bad, she thought. Just some smeared makeup and matted hair. Nothing a tissue, some lip gloss, a hairband, and sunglasses won't fix. Digging the items out of her purse, she did a quick makeover and used her reflection in the car window to adjust her outfit. When she turned around, two mechanics were standing, snickering to one another, in one of the open garage bays. With a wave of the hand, she put her head down and trudged down the alley to Main.

Not seeing her car on the street where she usually parked, her first reaction was panic quickly followed by relief. At least she didn't drive. Sifting back through the haze, she recalled them walking along Las Vegas Boulevard, or rather him giving her a piggyback ride because she refused to walk. She concluded her car must still be in the parking garage. She'd have to get a cab to retrieve it. If she wouldn't walk last night, she sure wasn't going to do it in broad daylight, hungover.

Planning to get a coffee anyway, Penny crossed over Main to Makers & Finders, the coffee bar and restaurant she usually went to on her way home after staying with Neck Tattoo. Makers had the best lavender latte. It was smooth and creamy with just the right amount of floral and sweetness, both of which she always seemed to need to lift her up after a late night with Neck Tattoo.

Inside, the open, brightly lit space with positive affirmations written on the open duct work and urban art scattered throughout immediately made her feel better. The rectangular room was set up with a continuous bench along the full length of the right wall with individual tables for two. In the middle was a row of four-top tables that could be rearranged for larger groups. To the left was the coffee bar, which was similar to one in a tavern with high-back chairs for patrons to belly-up, and a long social table filled with local creatives and home office workers looking to escape their own four walls. Regardless of attire, they all assumed the same posture, leaning over laptops, banging away at the keys, with headphones buried into their ears.

Penny maneuvered to the bar, leaving her brown Tom Ford cat eye sunglasses on. After ordering she sat down in one of the chairs lined up, facing inside, along the front window for people waiting for takeaway items. Covertly scanning from behind the tinted lenses, she recognized Les seated on the bench against the right wall by himself at the last table. She looked away pretending not to see him and watched the barista prepare drinks. Without turning her head, she let her eyes drift back in his direction. He was looking directly at her, and waving. Feigning surprise, she jerked her head in his direction and threw her arms in the air. He motioned her over.

Turning to the barista, Penny said, "Better make mine for here," and pointed to Les's table as the destination for the drink. Still keeping the sunglasses on to hide her tired eyes, she forced a smile and weaved her way through the dining room to Les. "What are you doing? I didn't know you came here."

Les scooted the table back to squeeze out and gave her a hug. "I love this place. The Oasis is just around the corner. I come here three-four times a week. Get tired of my own cooking and not many places you can find good Colombian food. Bill usually comes with me after we finish the morning duties at the mission, but he had some errands to run today."

"Sorry I missed him." Standing close to Les, Penny was conscious of what she must smell like after a night out in the bars, and, well, a night in the studio with Neck Tattoo. Guilt for never stopping by the Oasis also nipped at her shaky confidence. Les motioned for her to sit and returned to his seat on the bench. Settling into the chair, she said, "How's the food? I've only gotten the coffee here. Can't get enough of their lavender latte."

A light-skinned male Latino, sporting a pompadour haircut with the sides and back clipped short, delivered a plate of food for Les and the lavender latte for Penny. Les said, "Judge for yourself. I have more than enough." He looked to the server. "Can we get another plate?"

Penny said, "No really, that's OK. You eat. I can't stay long anyway."

The server had already disappeared and was on the way back with the plate. Les took the plate and, despite Penny's objection, scooped one of the poached egg concoctions onto the other plate. "This is their Arepas Benny. It's like an eggs benedict but with an arepa instead of English muffin, coffee rubbed beef in place of the Canadian bacon, and a salsa verde hollandaise. So good."

"It looks delicious, but I'm really not even hungry," Penny said, even though she was. Her stomach was gurgling from drinking her dinner the night before. "I don't even know what an arepa is anyway."

Les immediately dug into his. "Just try a bite. They're thin corn pancakes used in Colombian and Venezuelan cooking. Actually the guy who brought our food is one of the owners. His family is from Colombia. He refers to the menu as Latin comfort food. We had some Colombians in the congregation, who would invite me over to dinner. Mexican food is everywhere, but it's so tough to find other Latin cuisine."

Feeling conspicuous with the sunglasses on since she obviously wasn't going anywhere anytime soon, Penny finally removed them. She could feel Les examining her appearance, more with curiosity than with judgment. Picking up a fork, she separated the egg, beef and arepa into three piles.

Les said, "Oh no. You have to make sure you get a little bit of everything on that first taste."

Penny cut into the poached egg oozing yolk onto the plate. "I know it's weird, but I can't. Have to have my food separated. Been that way since I was a kid." She took a forkful of beef for her next bite, nodding in approval.

"To each their own I guess," Les said. "So what are you doing in these parts at this time of day?"

Penny sipped her latte. "I got a house over in the Scotch 80's not too far from here."

Les said, "Surprised I haven't seen you here before."

Penny delved back into the food. It really was good, or maybe she was just that hungry. Regardless, she felt better with each bite. She said, "I'm usually in and out, just picking up a latte on my way home from a friend's. Actually you met him a few weeks back when I ran into you and Crystal at the El Cortez."

"Oh yeah, young, good-looking guy, had an eight-pointed star tattooed on his neck."

"Wow, good memory," Penny said. "Not sure I realized there were eight points."

Les said, "I just remember it because stars with eight points symbolize fulfillment and regeneration. But he probably already told you that."

Penny scoffed, "To be honest, I'm not sure he even knows that. He probably got it because of how it looks." The food, the environment, the conversation with Les, all helped relax her. "I'd just assume we forget that night. Not my finest hour."

"Ah, don't worry about it," Les said. "You were just having fun."

"Seems like it is happening too much lately though," Penny said. "Obviously not much of a future for the two of us."

His plate clean, Les crossed his knife and fork in the center. "You two do seem quite different."

"It started as a fun distraction. Now I don't know what it is. I tried hanging out with Crystal earlier in the night, but you know how she is. If you get twenty minutes of conversation from her, fifteen of it is probably her thinking how she can get away. He's just always around and open to meeting up." Penny scraped up her last bite, wishing there was more. She noticed how careful she was being to collect every bit. Looking up at Les, she laughed. "Guess I was a little more hungry than I thought."

Les leaned back against the wall. "You talking about the food or the other situation?"

"Good point," Penny said, washing down the food with a drink of her latte. "Guess it applies to both."

"I worry about myself in a similar fashion," Les said.

Penny snorted, shocked by his remark, steamed milk almost coming through her nose. "You do?

Les must've seen the surprise in her face. He said, "Well, not exactly in that arena. I was thinking more of gambling."

"No way. I can't believe that. You know the game so well and are always so under control."

"I should know it," Les said. "Been playing since I was kid. Believe me though. I've lost control on more than one occasion. One of the reasons I went into the clergy to begin with. Was worried what I might become. I was so fascinated by the numbers and the action. Could feel it getting its hooks in me."

Penny said, "I don't know. You're the last person I'd think had a gambling problem."

Les put his elbow on the table, propping up his chin with his closed fist. "I don't think I do either. But every so often I'm reminded that while I may not be an addict, I do have addictive tendencies. One night, not too long ago, I went completely off the rails and lost everything I had in my pockets. Would've kept going, too, if I had more."

Penny thought about what he was saying. He was talking about himself, but it easily could apply to her as well. She worried about her drinking and the recent rash of sleepovers, but she never considered herself an alcoholic, or promiscuous for that matter. She said, "How do you know you don't have a problem? Maybe you're in denial."

"I guess I don't if I'm being completely honest. But I quit for over twenty years. Only blackjack I played was as the dealer at the annual church fundraiser. Lately when I've gone too far, it was never only about the gambling. There was always something else out of balance triggering it. The gambling was just a symptom. If I don't address the cause, it will just come out another time. We try to hide or eliminate our demons when we really have to make friends and coexist."

"I definitely get that," Penny said. "For me, I always had my career. Now that I don't, I'm just not myself."

Les said, "Just go back to work. Seems like an easy fix."

Penny didn't like admitting to people why she wasn't working. People were so obsessed with money, there was just no good way to say it without sounding spoiled. She thought since Les came from a more pious world that he might understand. "I know this sounds terrible, and, believe me, I'm not complaining. It's just, I really don't have to. I've done well in life and really don't need the money."

Les said, "Just because you don't need money, doesn't mean you don't need work. Money is just one of the reasons people work."

The owner of the restaurant came to the table, asking if they wanted anything else. They declined, and he left the check on the table. Penny slid it toward her, resting her hand on the top. She asked, "So why do you gamble?"

Les nodded in gratitude for her picking up the check. He said, "For the money of course."

Dow Jones Close: 16,558.87

Chapter Forty

Date: Thursday, April 10, 2014

Dow Jones Open: 16,437.24

Max advanced across the Western floor, down the aisle between the center and right production lines, which were the only two running; the other sat ominously quiet. His purposeful stride forced workers' heads down to focus on their tasks and avoid becoming targets. Max had a reputation for shooting first and asking questions second when he patrolled the floor. With the way things had been going, he was locked and loaded and ready to fire. He watched the workers tracking his progress with darting glances, relaxing as he passed. Occasionally he shot a glare at one, hoping the person was stupid enough to make eye contact. While a public execution might not be good for morale, it would probably boost production, at least in the short term, which was all he cared about at the moment.

Max stopped at the end of the production lines. Sealed boxes containing a hundred Lapkins rolled off each line. Workers collected and stacked the boxes three wide, five deep, and five high onto pallets. A forklift picked up a full pallet and drove it to the loading cross-dock in the back of the facility. Max turned around and looked back across the operation, which barely covered half of the open space that for nearly forty years had buzzed with gaming activity.

Although Max ended up with the Western after his drunken mishap, he thought of it as a happy accident. Of course no one, least of all him, knew where he had been going that night or what had prompted him to turn straight into the front doors of the old hotel. All he could come up with was that maybe after leaving the El Cortez he had decided on a nightcap down the street at Atomic. Somewhere along the way he got turned around, saw the big white Western building, mistook it for the Ogden, and drove through the front doors, thinking it was the entrance to his parking garage.

The Western had closed for good by the time Max had moved his enterprise from his apartment to downtown, but he was quite familiar with the property. Every day he drove by it on the way to his offices and factory at Eleventh and Maryland. Although he had never considered it as a potential new location, with all the open space on the old gaming floor, a full kitchen and dining facilities, and rooms that could easily be converted to offices, it ended up working pretty well for the much-needed expansion to meet the spike in demand from the McDonald's deal. The extra space allowed him to add two more production lines, which he needed if he was going to make the McDonald's deadline by June 30.

Moving to the new location had been a seamless transition. He kept the old line going while working to get the Western up to code and set up two new production lines there. Once they were up and running, he moved the equipment from Eleventh Street to the Western to add a third line, and planned to hire additional workers and add shifts as needed, intending to make up any dip in production during the transition once all three lines were operational at the Western. Just like in the Western's heyday, Max was prepared to run it twenty-four seven if need be.

According to the forecast models, the company had the space, machines, and materials to meet the 4.5-million-unit deadline. What they didn't have was people. They were able to fill the first shift for all three lines no problem, and two of three for the second shift, but they couldn't find a complete crew for the third line during that shift or any of the lines during the third shift. They tried everything: unlimited overtime, free employee meals, referral bonuses for new hires, and even refurbishing some of the hotel rooms for employees to live free of charge, but they couldn't find reliable workers. There were plenty of people looking for paychecks, but not many interested in steady employment. Usually what happened was that people worked long enough to get a paycheck or two, then they would disappear for a week and show up again when the money ran out.

That day on the production floor, as Max searched for a sacrificial lamb, Ed, the operations supervisor, stood beside him, offering excuses on why the third line was not operating. Ed had on a blue button-down with an orange and brown striped tie, jeans, and scuffed-up brown leather work boots. Max never expected Ed to wear a tie, which, on that day, was four inches too short and resting on his protruding belly, but he always did, and they were never tied right. Ed nervously ran his hand through his curly black hair, continuing to gesture at the dormant line. Max didn't care to hear Ed's explanation and physically couldn't above the noise. Holding up his hand to shut down the fawning behavior, Max pointed toward the conference room and stormed off in that direction. Ed trailed like a scolded child even though Max hadn't said a word to him, at least not verbally. Max didn't have to. His body language communicated everything he was thinking. Jules, the head of human resources, and his CFO, Belinda, sat at the table, ready for their monthly management meeting to review the March numbers, overall first quarter results, and second quarter forecasts.

Max forced a smile. "Good afternoon, ladies. I hope your day is going better than mine." They nodded, smiling uncomfortably. Everyone seemed to know the meeting was not going to be a pleasant one. Max took his seat at the head of the table. Ed pulled a chair out to join them. Max stopped him. "What are you doing? No point in sitting down." He motioned toward the projection screen. "Might as well get to the bad news."

Ed walked to the front of the room, shuffling through the papers in the folder he'd had tucked under his arm. He opened the laptop connected to the projector and clicked on the keys until a spreadsheet appeared on the screen. Removing a laser pointer from his pocket, he directed the beam to the lower right of the screen. The light shook back and forth over the cells due to Ed's tremoring hand. "You can see even with ceasing production at the Eleventh Street facility and moving to the Western, we managed to surpass the one million mark. Now, with all three lines fully functional for the first shift and two lines running second shift, we're able to produce about twenty thousand per day." He moved the beam to another column on the spreadsheet. "And we've lowered our per-unit cost within the one-fifty target."

Max did some quick estimation in his head. "At twenty thousand a day, that's six hundred thousand per month and 1.8 million for the quarter, which puts us at a total of 2.8 million by the deadline. That's not going to cut it. We need 4.5 million by the end of June or they can cancel the contract."

"I'm doing the best I can with what I got." Ed switched to another slide in the presentation. "Look at these projections. If we can get more people and operate the other shifts, we can boost production to thirty-six thousand units, which will put us in the neighborhood of 4.5 million. With some other efficiencies and improvements, I think we can get there."

Max drew aim on Jules. Ed sunk quietly into a chair. Max said, "So Jules, where are we with the recruitment efforts?"

Jules stood and walked toward the laptop, taking the pointer from Ed. Composed and poised, she put on her red rectangular frame glasses and switched the presentation on the laptop. Directing the pointer to the screen, she said, "The increase you see the past two weeks is from relaxing the drug testing. The problem is we're getting quantity but not quality. I'm afraid our turnover rate will go through the roof, and we'll keep having to train new people, since a lot don't stick around more than a week or two." She flashed the beam on another bar. "We are attracting some good applicants with the advertising for part-time four-hour shifts, but we need twice as many people to fill an eight-hour shift."

Ed jumped back into the conversation. "And with the additional shift change, two four-hour crews will produce less than one eight-hour crew."

Jules dimmed the beam and slid the pointer in her pocket. "Also all the recruitment, employee incentives, and additional training due to excessive turnover have tripled our estimated onboarding costs."

"Enough!" Max banged his fist on the table. "You guys are coming to me with only problems. I want solutions. I don't care what it takes or costs. If you two spent half as much time working together as you did covering your own asses, we might actually be able to hit the target." He turned to Belinda, his CFO. "So how bad is it?"

Belinda stood from the table. She was a tall, confident black woman who Max had hired away from one of the strip casino groups with a big salary and a promise of more authority. Her short brown hair had layered bangs, adding length around her narrow face. She said, "It really comes down to whether or not you meet the deadline." She removed four stapled decks from a manila folder and slid one to each of them, keeping the last one for herself. "I did two income statement projections. With the purchase of the Western, the investment in the new production equipment, additional headcount, and other fixed cost increases with the expanded operation, both show losses in the first half of this year. If you compare the two, the difference is in the second half. The first assumes meeting the deadline and receiving the payments from McDonald's. The second shows the outcome if those payments are not made."

Max focused on the second page. "Wait a second. Without the McDonald's deal, we're bankrupt? How can that be? We had ten million in cash in the bank at the end of twenty thirteen."

"Go to page three," Belinda said. "The domestic orders are down sixty percent from first quarter last year, and the international orders are down seventy three percent. We had projected minimal growth in the first half of the year, with a significant spike in the second half, triggered by the McDonald's output." She flipped back to page two. "With the payment due for the four and a half million units on July 1, and the subsequent payments on the first of the following months for each additional million units, we are on track to exceed the twenty thirteen revenue."

"And without it?" Max turned back to page one. 'We're bust?"

"I wouldn't go to that extreme," Belinda said, choosing her words carefully. "But we would have to revert to some pretty severe austerity measures and sell some of the assets you have accumulated or seek help from external sources."

He threw the financial report in the middle of the table. "Max Doler doesn't do austerity."

Dow Jones Close: 16,170.22

Chapter Forty-One

Date: Wednesday, March 31, 2010

Dow Jones Open: 10,907.34

Crystal's brisk walk quickened to a jog. She glanced at her watch. Two minutes. She had missed the employee shuttle and couldn't afford to be late…again. The director had started locking the door promptly at six. Anyone late had to enter through the front and face his wrath. With the mood he had been in lately, she didn't want to land in his crosshairs.

She rounded the back of the theater into the alley, ready to sprint the final hundred yards. A group congregating around the stage door slowed her pace. She looked again at the watch. Still a minute to go. The door couldn't be locked already. She approached the group. Everyone was exchanging confused looks and mumbling. A handwritten note taped to the stage door read, "Today's rehearsal has been cancelled. Please report to the theater for a cast and crew meeting."

With the foul mood and disposition of the director, rumors had been swirling for weeks about the increasing tension between him, the producers, and the management at the Wynn. The show was on schedule to open on time but was significantly over budget, and the buzz and demand for tickets was not as high as expected. From the first rehearsal the director had been extremely demanding of the performers and the crew, causing significant turnover and rebuilding of sets, and the increased pressure lately was intensifying everything. Other than being late a few times, Crystal had gotten along well with him, but many of her castmates had not, choosing to leave the production rather than fight with him day after day.

As they all walked to the front of the theater, Crystal and the others posited the possibilities. No one had a clue what was going on, but the consensus was whatever the reason, it wasn't positive. Inside the theater, everyone was gathered in the first five rows with a clear division between the cast and crew. The performers filled the right side. The crew was on the left. A section of three empty chairs from front to back separated the groups. Everyone spoke in whispers. Crystal joined her people on the right, taking an open seat next to her girlfriend Janel, who was from Inglewood and had fluffy, corkscrew curls and a similar build and skillset to Crystal's. They had met during the first audition. While Crystal wasn't really friends with anyone in the show—or outside for that matter—Janel was as close as she got.

Crystal, like everyone else, spoke in a hushed voice. "So what's going on?"

"It can't be good," Janel said. "They don't pay us just to sit here."

"Maybe it's information about the previews." Crystal knew it was too sudden to be an informational meeting, but she was trying to counteract the pervading negativity. She didn't really have any other choice. She had just purchased and moved into a new condo two weeks earlier and was only four months into a three-year lease on a BMW. She had been in such a funk after her mom died, she had to do something to mix things up. As part of her own denial she had been reluctant to spend any of the insurance money. It just seemed wrong to benefit from her mom being gone forever. But with the opening night of the show rapidly approaching, she thought both moves were safe investments. More than anything, they would provide stability, something she desperately needed. Losing her mom had created a hole in her life because Valeria had been more than just a mom. She had been her only family, her best friend, her home. The only other person Crystal was remotely close to was Maura, and while she loved Maura, it was more business than personal. Without Valeria, Crystal had nothing waiting for her in LA if things didn't work out in Vegas. Putting down roots in Vegas seemed like the best solution.

The female lead, a rangy Hawaiian from Maui, turned around from the row in front of them. "No, this is bad news. They never bring the cast and crew together unless something really bad happens. The only question is how bad."

Crystal swallowed hard, her insides tightening by the second. She already had enough bad news for the year, for the decade for that matter.

The director walked out on the stage. His swollen face and fixed scowl did little to appease her growing sense of doom. He scanned the crowd once, twice, three times before speaking. "Apologies for the short notice on the meeting. I'm sure you're all wondering why we have brought you together today." His eyes skimmed across the crowd again, almost as if he were looking for someone specifically, but it became apparent he was just avoiding what he had to say. He dropped his eyes to his feet, taking a long pause. "I know I've been extremely tough on all of you over the past six months. I hope you understand it's because I see the potential in you and want you to come as close as you possibly can to achieving that potential.

It's because of this that I'm deeply saddened to inform you that the producers have decided to shut down the show and cease production immediately." He paused allowing the weight of the message to be absorbed.

Seconds of silence passed. Everyone exchanged looks of shock and disbelief. Pockets of murmuring percolated within the audience, escalating to audible questions yelled above the babel.

"How can this happen?"

"When is our last day?"

"Will we get severance?"

The director listened to all the questions. As the clamor quieted, he attempted to answer them all as completely and efficiently as possible. Now that he had disseminated the bad news, he clearly wanted to speed things up and get off stage and out of the line of fire as quickly as possible. He raised his hand to dampen the lingering discord. "So here's how we got here. Based on the sales forecasts and projections, the show is expected to lose money for much longer than was expected and would require additional and consistent investment to stay open. The producers, along with the Wynn, have decided not to seek additional money from current or new investors. As such, they feel the best course of action is to stop production immediately and cap the financial exposure to what has been spent and is owed to each of you according to your contracts. Today's announcement and the accompanying letter each of you will receive will serve as the official notification and explanation of your severance benefits. Details on your final pay are contained in the letters."

A male and female lower level assistant entered, each carrying a stack of envelopes. The guy walked over to address the crew; she took her position in front of the cast. They began reading names. Crew and cast members filed forward, picked up their letters, and returned to their seats, not sure if they were suppose to stay or go.

The director, usually brimming with confidence and certainty, seemed equally as confused about what should happen next. He filled the air with meaningless words and hollow sentiment. "Although this wasn't the end we had envisioned, we've all grown from this and will take the experience into our future endeavors and be better for it." With everyone more concerned about the content of their individual letters, there was really nothing more for him to say. He wrapped up his remarks. "I wish you all continued success and hope our paths cross again, and that we can build on what we have started."

Crystal studied her letter. "So wait. We're done as of today and they pay us for four more weeks and we don't have to do anything?"

"Hush money," one of the other girls said. "You don't have to go home, but you can't stay here."

Janel put her hand on Crystal's. "Don't talk about the details of your package. Not everyone gets the same. It's a very sensitive subject. Some have families and only get two weeks. Best to keep your mouth closed."

Crystal folded up her letter and tucked it in her purse. "So what do we do now?"

Janel stood, leading Crystal up by the hand. "We go get fucked up. That's what. We worry about the details and looking for a new job tomorrow."

One of the male performers jumped up. "Now you're talking. Casino crawl. Everyone throws in twenty dollars. We start here and move down the strip. One drink at each casino. Last one standing wins the pot."

And so a group of fifteen embarked: Wynn, the Palazzo, the Venetian, Casino Royale, Harrah's, O'Shea's, Flamingo. Eight drinks in, four people had already dropped out. Each stop took more time than the previous one, and the conversations became louder and more random. Crystal had hung out with the cast before, but not like this.

Crossing Flamingo Road to Bally's, Crystal's head was swimming from the alcohol and her uncertain future. Without the job, her only ties to Vegas were a hefty mortgage and car payment. She had thought she needed them to feel connected and to move forward. Instead they would wrap around her and pull her to the bottom. She could already feel herself sinking. She clutched Janel's arm. "I'm not sure I can take much more of this."

"Nonsense," Janel said. "We're just getting started." The drunken group stormed through the Bally's valet area toward the front entrance. All traffic stopped. With the group's determination and obliviousness, the drivers really didn't have a choice.

Inside the sliding glass doors of the main entrance, the group headed straight for the center bar. Janel pulled Crystal toward the restroom. "Come with me."

One of the guys who had been hitting on Janel for the past three stops saw them venturing off and followed after them. "Quitting already?"

Janel waived him off. "Just powdering our noses. Order us two Coronas. We'll be back in a sec." Janel giggled and squeezed Crystal's arm. "Looks like mama's getting lucky tonight."

In the restroom, Crystal went into a stall. She turned around, surprised to find Janel right behind her. The casino crawl had brought them closer but not pee-in-the-same-stall close. Crystal froze, unsure whether to sit down or let Janel go first.

She shifted from one foot to the other. She hadn't realized how badly she had to go, but being in the restroom next to the stall, the urge overtook her. She asked, "Um, did you want to go first?"

Janel rooted around in her purse. "Oh, you go ahead. I didn't come here for that." She removed her hand from her purse, holding up a vial of white powder between her index finger and thumb. "Here we go. This should keep us going."

Crystal dropped her panties around her ankles, hiked up her skirt, and sat down in one fluid motion. Uncomfortable with Janel being so close and what she was about to do, Crystal stared at the floor. She wasn't a complete prude. Her mom had always been open with her about, well, everything, and she had been around a lot of parties with drugs, but they were always in a back bedroom, bathroom, or behind some other locked door. Never this close. She felt trapped, but also a little curious. She looked up and watched Janel unscrew the cap and dump some of the powder on the stainless steel toilet paper dispenser. When Crystal stood, reapplying the layers as swiftly as she peeled them away, there were four lines of the powder.

Janel held a rolled-up twenty toward her. "Two for you; two for me."

"Oh I'm good." Crystal smoothed her skirt and fidgeted with her top, trying to sidestep Janel. "I don't really do that stuff."

Janel moved against the door. "Come on. A couple lines aren't going to hurt you, just like one cheeseburger isn't going to make you fat—which by the way we are totally getting later now that I don't have to care about what I look like in a bikini top and grass skirt in front of five hundred strangers."

Crystal bought herself more time. "You go first."

Janel pulled back her curls, bent down, and inhaled, once, then twice. She lifted her head. Only two lines remained. "See. Nothing to worry about. Trust me. You'll feel a lot better, and we'll be able to drink these other clowns under the table."

Crystal took the bill from Janel. She stared at the lines. Someone came into the restroom.

Janel sat down on the toilet, talking loudly and breaking into a made-up story. "So he said they were just friends, but I can tell he's lying." She released a slow, steady stream, further hiding their purpose. "I mean, I'm friends with a lot of guys, but I don't leave my earrings in their cars and lipstick on their collars." She nodded toward the lines.

Crystal played along. "What are you going to do?" She bent down and inhaled the first. The anxiety from being in the stall with Janel and trying coke for the first time instantly vanished. She relaxed. Confidence swelled inside her. The only way she could describe the feeling was that she felt taller and bulletproof, like she could handle anything. More importantly, for the first time in as long as she could remember, she didn't feel alone.

Janel smiled and motioned to do the other one, continuing with their charade of a conversation. "It's done. I kicked his ass to the curb. He can hang out with his friend."

Crystal finished the other line. She straightened her body and stared at the stall partition in silence.

Janel said, "I ain't got time for that shit. He thinks he can play me." Her words trailed off as she watched the feet of the person leave the restroom. She stood, grabbing the twenty and Crystal's hand, and charging out of the stall as the toilet flushed behind them.

From Bally's the group powered on to Paris, Planet Hollywood, MGM, and Tropicana, losing a person at each stop. With only six members remaining, and at the end of the east side of the strip, it was decision time. To continue they would have to cross over to the other side of the strip and resume at Mandalay Bay. Tracking back up the west side was another level of commitment, not just for the night, but the recovery time that would be required the following day as well. Crystal wasn't thinking about that, though. After two more trips to the ladies' room with Janel, she was ready and willing to keep going. She rarely even had two glasses of wine, and now was about to hit her twelfth casino in six hours. Of course that didn't mean twelve drinks. She and Janel had left several unfinished, split a few, and even subbed in a couple waters without the others knowing. Since they weighed about half to two-thirds as much as some of the other participants, they figured they were only responsible for drinking about the same ratio of alcohol.

From Mandalay Bay, they pressed on to Luxor, Excalibur, and New York–New York. The group was reduced to three: the two of them and the guy still hopeful he had a shot with Janel. Unfortunately he ended up sabotaging his own plan with his honesty and chivalry. He not only made sure he finished a beer or shot at every place, he often finished Janel's to prove himself a gentleman. A strategy he was no doubt regretting when doubled over the trashcan outside New York–New York.

Janel petted the back of his head gently. "You OK, babe?" Her action and tone were sincere, but her facial expression conveyed a different meaning. She stuck her tongue out, making fun of his barfing. "Looks like I should hold on to the prize money."

Crystal wasn't as nice. She did a victory dance a short distance away, singing "Another One Bites The Dust."

After another big heave and subsequent splash, he reached into his pocket and took out the wad of $300. With his head still hanging over the trash can, he extended the money back toward Janel. She stepped back, moving closer to Crystal, still feigning comfort for their fallen castmate. "You going to be OK? Can we get you anything, babe?" Not even listening to his response, she pulled Crystal toward the cab line in front of New York–New York. "OK then. Catch up when you're finished."

A few minutes later, after a short cab ride, arm and arm, Crystal and Janel stumbled into In-N-Out for their victory cheeseburgers. Even with their self-medication and subterfuge, they were both extremely drunk and ready to call it quits.

Over Double-Doubles, a mound of animal-style fries, and chocolate milkshakes, they laughed and joked about the day's events. But as their bellies filled and their energy diminished, the conversation also assumed a heavier weight.

Finally giving up on the cheeseburger like she had on so many of the drinks, Crystal dropped the burger on her tray and pushed back in her seat. "What in the fuck are we going to do? Do you think other shows are hiring?"

"Ugh, I don't even want to think about that." Janel took one more bite, then surrendered as well. "I just want to go home and sleep until I can't sleep no more."

"I don't even know if I can," Crystal said. "My mind is just racing. When will this stuff wear off?"

Janel reached into her purse again, this time pulling out a pill bottle. "I got just the thing. Take two of these. If you still can't sleep, take one more. That should knock you right out." She slid three pills across the table to Crystal.

Crystal examined them in the palm of her hand. "What are they?"

"Don't worry about it. Just a pain reliever. They'll relax you." Janel popped one in her mouth and washed it down with a gulp of the shake. "It's like a really strong Tylenol. You won't feel anything until you want to. If you need more, just let me know."

Dow Jones Close: 10,856.63

Chapter Forty-Two

Date: Friday, May 9, 2014

Dow Jones Open: 16,551.23

T he month of May is a gambler's paradise in Vegas. It's not as heralded as the Super Bowl or March Madness, but it's difficult to find a more action-packed month. With the baseball season in full swing, the Stanley Cup and NBA playoffs narrowing the fields, and the Kentucky Derby and Preakness filling up two of the Saturdays, no matter the time or the day of the week, somebody always seems to have action on something, preoccupying them with the TVs in the pit. With a single wager, they are no longer just spectators. They have a defined role in the drama unfolding on the screens. Every twist and turn is an affirmation of their choice or a conspiracy to rob them. Of course the money is a factor, but more than anything, most sports bettors just want to be right, to watch their chosen scenario come to fruition, so they can puff their chests out and say, "I told you so."

That's how it was for Bill and Les on the Saturday between the Kentucky Derby and the Preakness. They, like the majority of the West Coast bettors, had taken the favorite, California Chrome, and were rewarded for it. The Vegas sportsbooks took it on the chin with the favorite winning and also being a California-bred horse for the first time since 1962, but the losses were just a blip that all the action during the month would surely correct. Even when the sportsbooks lost, the casinos usually won. Winning only made people crave more action. Nothing spends easier than free money. For Bill and Les, that meant each betting a hundred on a parlay for game three of the NBA playoff series between the Pacers and Wizards in Washington. They both took the Pacers plus 5 points and under 183.5 to win $264.36.

Despite playing blackjack while they watched, they paid more attention to the basketball than the cards. Penny was also at the table, but didn't seem too interested in the basketball game. The first half was back and forth, with the scored tied at the end of the first quarter, and the Pacers up one at halftime, thirty-four to thirty-three, which meant they had six points to fade on the score and the pace was almost fifty under.

Bill was more nervous about the outcome than Les. A hundred dollars was a hefty single bet for him. That was a whole night of blackjack. He rarely bet more than twenty-five on a straight-up bet and ten to fifteen on a parlay. Even though he risked the same amount on the game as he would on blackjack, and the two-and-a-half-hour sporting event might last longer than the round of blackjack, he felt more in control betting the hundred at five a hand than plunking it down all at once. But playing with house money after the Derby win, he was open to taking a bigger risk and followed Les's bet.

Catching his breath at halftime, Bill sat back in his chair, rubbing the stubble of his flattop. "Halfway home. Two more quarters like that and we're cashing another ticket."

Les was calm and cool as usual. "No lead or total is ever safe in an NBA game. Either or both teams could come out and get hot and put up thirty to forty in a quarter and still push the game over. The only guarantee is that it'll be a sweat at some point."

Penny joined the conversation. "What was your bet?"

Bill fished the ticket from his pocket and set it on the table. It was wrinkled and already slightly faded, moist with sweat from his first-half nerves and excitement. He smoothed it out on the table, blowing to dry it out. "Maybe I should leave it up here for the second half."

Penny glanced at the ticket. "You'll be fine." Her tone was more than just polite reassurance. She was confident, like she knew something they didn't.

Les noticed it too. He said, "What makes you so sure?"

Penny never lifted her eyes off the table. "Pacers will pull away in the second half. Hibbert has stepped up his game since the series opener, and they're playing good team defense. Even though it's close now, Washington had to work hard for their shots in the first half. They're not going to be able to keep it up and will tire out. It'll be a low-scoring game somewhere in the one hundred fifty to sixty range, and the Pacers will win by at least ten. You won't even need the points. You should've taken the money line. The Wizards might win one more game in the series, but the Pacers will take it in at least six. No way it goes seven."

We all just stared at Penny, surprised by her detailed and concise prediction. I was trying to wrap my brain around how someone so beautiful and seemingly uninterested in sports knew so much. I had even stopped dealing, which she quickly corrected by repeatedly swiping for another card on her twelve against my ten. "I'd like a nine, please." She had to settle for an eight. Smiling contentedly, she said, "That'll work."

"Somebody is feeling it tonight." I flip over a nine to make a nineteen. "The lady wins with twenty." I pay her the fifteen she had bet and take Bill's and Les's bets for their losing eighteen and seventeen. "I don't know, gentlemen. I think you should listen to her. She seems like she knows what she's talking about."

Les asked, "You got money on this game?"

"Nah, I never bet on sports. Makes it too much like work." She upped her bet to twenty-five.

Bill said, "Well then, darling, if you don't mind me asking, how do you know so much about this game?"

"More than a pretty face, boys," she said. "I'm a sportscaster by trade. Actually I should give credit to my daddy. He was a coach back in Indiana. Bloomington High School South to be exact." She thrust her fist in the air. "Go Panthers. I used to watch game film with him. He taught me how to watch games and analyze the teams. Once you learn, it's something you never turn off."

Crystal walked up and sat on Penny's left. She said, "Sorry I'm late. Overslept."

"That's OK," Penny said. "You didn't miss much. Just me educating these male chauvinists on the evolving talents of women in modern society. I'm sure you could teach them a thing or two as well."

Crystal blushed. "Not sure the skills I have acquired would be of much interest to them."

Penny fanned her hand at Crystal. "I'm talking about your singing, which reminds me. I talked to my agent. He'll be here two weeks from tomorrow. We're going to dinner, then he wants to come hear you sing. Probably around eleven. Where should we meet you?"

The direct question unnerved Crystal. "So soon? Well, I mean, I, uh, have to work. Another night would be better."

"It has to be that Saturday," Penny said. "He's only here the one night. What about that place across the street from OGs that you said you go over to sometimes?"

"Dino's? I mean, yeah, they have karaoke, but—"

"Well, there you go. You never go to work before twelve anyway. Come there first, sing, and go to work afterward."

Crystal didn't say anything. She nodded like she was accepting, but the look on her face said, *Let's talk about this later.*

The second half of the game started. The Wizards took the lead early in the third quarter. Bill immediately turned negative. "Well, here we go. The beginning of the end."

Penny put her hand on his shoulder. "Relax. There's a lot of game left. You're going to be fine." Penny separated a hundred dollars in chips from her pile. "If I'm wrong, I'll reimburse you for the loss."

Les said, "Why don't you buy half the action so you got something to win."

"Yeah, do that," Bill said. "Give me fifty now, and I'll split the winnings if we win."

"When, not if," Penny said. "And I told you, I don't bet on sports."

As the third quarter progressed, the Pacers quickly erased the lead and took command by the end, leading by fifteen. The Wizards made a brief run in the fourth, almost cutting the deficit to single digits, but the Pacers surged ahead, winning by twenty-two: eighty-five to sixty-three, just as Penny had forecasted. Maybe it was luck. Too many variables in these things for it to be anything else. There was no way she could've known the Wizards would score the lowest total in franchise history, but her prediction was a hundred percent correct, so in everyone's eyes at the table she was a sports guru and would stay that way as long as she continued to be correct. That's the definition of an expert anyway. Someone who knows a sliver of information more and can maintain that gap.

When the final seconds ticked away, Bill stood and hugged Penny. "You nailed that one, sweetie."

Penny scooped the chips she had set aside to cover the bet and added them back to her stack, which was over $300 without it. She was having a good night all the way around. She said, "Basketball, football, and hockey are my specialties—especially during the play-offs. The public always gets enamored with offense and underestimates defense. The offensive stats are built over the course of the season against a lot of subpar defenses. When a good offensive team plays a good defensive team, the defensive team will usually win, and when they don't, they cover. You can probably win sixty to sixty five percent of the time just on that."

Les said, "Well, I guess we know who to come to for our sports tips from now on." He counted his chips, which totaled $285, just under his normal $100-profit hard stop. After he lost big that one night, he went back to his disciplined play and slowly won back what he had lost. Pushing his chips to the center, he said, "Think I'll take my winnings and run. I need to head back and close up. I was lucky to have enough volunteers tonight to be able to sneak down and watch the game."

"Come on, stay for a few more hands," Bill said. "We got a good group here."

Les shook his head. "If it was my money, I would. But I need this for the Oasis. With the sports ticket, I'm well over my quota for the week. I can't risk it."

Bill took fifty from his stack and slid it toward Les. "If you're struggling, just ask. I'm happy to help."

Les pushed the fifty back to Bill. "I appreciate it, but you're already doing too much."

"Nonsense," Bill said. "You made this money for me. I never would've bet this much. Just keep it. I'll stop by in the morning to help with breakfast." He turned to Penny and Crystal. "You ladies should come by, too. We can always use the help, and you'd sure brighten the place up."

Penny plucked a hundred from her stack and tossed it on Les's. "Let me add to that total as well."

Les became uncomfortable. "Don't feel any obligation to contribute. I shouldn't have said anything. This is not the time or place. Of course any donation, time or money, is appreciated. Feel free to stop by anytime. I'd love to give you the tour and discuss how you can get involved."

Crystal tossed fifty more his way. "Mornings are a little tough for me, but I only live around the corner, so maybe later in the day."

Penny got excited, drumming the table with both hands. "Oh, and you guys should come support Crystal next Saturday at Dino's. Have you heard her sing? Amazing. My agent is in town and wants to hear her."

Crystal glared at Penny, reaching over and grabbing Penny's hands, deadening the beat. Her arm tensed as she squeezed harder while she spoke. "It's just karaoke. Really no big deal."

Penny pulled her hands away, which were flushed with blood from the tight embrace. "She's just being modest. She has the voice of an angel. I know my agent's going to love her. It should be around eleven o'clock."

"A bit late for me," Bill said, "but I can make an exception."

Les looked at Bill. "Just help me close up that night, and we'll head over together."

"Super," Penny said. "And I'll come by soon for the grand tour."

Les picked up the black, green, and red I colored up for him, nodding at Penny. "And perhaps you can tip us off on any other games you like for the week."

Penny grinned back. "I'll see what I can come up with."

Bill didn't bother cashing in his chips. He just scooped them up, along with his winning sports ticket, which had completely dried and curled up around the edges. Dropping the chips in his pants pocket, he straightened the ticket on the edge of the rail. "I hope they still take this."

I said, "As long as they can read the ticket number, you're fine. Believe me, they've seen worse. I've heard of people going in with tickets taped back together or with food all over them after being dug out of the garbage after a miracle comeback. In some cases, they've gone in without the ticket at all and say what the bet was and when they made it, and the sportsbook was able to find it in the computer and match it to the person with the security tape."

Bill looked again at his ticket. "Well, I don't feel so bad then." He excused himself with a nod and followed Les to the sportsbook.

Penny and Crystal continued to play, mostly arguing about Penny's blabbing about the singing. Crystal said, "I told you I would think about it. I never said I would do it. Why are you making a big deal out of it and telling everyone? If I decide to do it, I just want to sing and not feel like I'm performing and have to entertain."

Penny snapped back. "You're the one making a big deal out of it. It's a public place. There will be other people there. Why not have them be friendly faces? The whole point is for you to start getting paid to entertain anyway."

"But that's my choice, not yours. I told you, I sing for me. I don't need you recruiting other people to support me."

They went back and forth like this for another twenty minutes. In the end, Penny agreed not to say anything to anyone else, but it was obvious that it was more to end the argument than because she believed it was the right thing to do. I just kept my mouth closed and dealt cards. I'm smart enough not to get in between two women having a difference of opinion. The only resolution that would come out of that would be them turning on me and agreeing I was the bad guy.

Bill turned up back at the table with a fresh beer and a crisp hundred-dollar bill to buy back in. "Mind if I jump in again?"

After their bickering, Crystal was happy to have another player at the table. She stood up and moved over to first base, where she preferred to play. It was also farther away from Penny. "Glad to have you back. It's a good time to shake things up."

"Thought you were going home," Penny said.

Bill held out his full beer. "It's still early, and I'm still thirsty. Let's gamble."

When my relief showed up for my next break, Crystal cashed in her chips. "I'll color up before you take off. I gotta be getting to work."

Penny put her arm around Bill. "How about you? You had enough, too?"

Bill counted his chips. He was up fifteen since he bought back in. "Yeah, I think I'll quit while I'm ahead."

Crystal stood from the table. "You guys going to the Oasis in the morning?"

"Planning on it," Bill said.

"I'll try to make it, but no promises. Depends how late I stay at work." She and Penny exchanged restrained good-byes, obviously still not over their disagreement.

Penny waited for Crystal to leave, then turned to Bill. "I got an idea. Let's play here a little while longer then go surprise Crystal at work. I've been wanting to go, but don't want to by myself."

"A strip club? I'm too old for that place," Bill said.

Penny clutched his arm. "Not with me. We'll sit off to the side. I'll make sure no one bothers you…unless you want them to."

Dow Jones Close: 16,583.34

Chapter Forty-Three

Date: Saturday, May 10, 2014

Dow Jones Open: Closed

When Penny and Bill left the El Cortez, it was obvious he didn't really want to go to OGs to visit Crystal. Penny's feminine wiles were pretty tough to resist, but the truth was, he just wanted to go home even less. At the club he thought he would feel out of place, like a dirty old man. But when he and Penny got there just after midnight, the place was actually full of men just like him, many sitting alone at tables, leering from the darkness, happy to pay for any bit of attention, which, on a weekend night, was plentiful for all ages, sizes, and tastes. Of course it wasn't the first time he had been to a strip club. There were several on his beat in New Jersey, and they would call the police routinely, usually for a fight or a patron refusing to pay his bill from an overextended stay in the VIP room. But he had never spent any length of time in one and just sat at a table and watched, continually having to fend off girls roaming the floor offering lap dances—and even more if they went to the back. And he certainly had never seen a girl he personally knew perform onstage, climbing and sliding down the pole, gyrating and thrusting across the stage, peeling off her clothes and pushing her breasts in a patron's face for a dollar or two at a time. It all made him extremely uncomfortable.

Penny, on the other hand, seemed quite at home. She knew to tip the door guy to get a good table, to ask the waitress for singles when she ordered drinks, and, as a female, the no-touching rule didn't apply to her. With her looks and build, she was a lightening rod of attention in the club.

A blond Eastern-European girl with pigtails named Candy was the first to set her sights on Penny. She sat down right on Penny's lap, twisting Penny's hair with her finger. "You look familiar to me. You come here before? You work at another club?"

Penny touched the end of Candy's nose. "Maybe it was just in your dreams."

"That might be it." Candy laughed, rocking back and forth in Penny's lap. "You want a private dance? I make a special offer for you, two for twenty."

"Not right now, honey," Penny said, and gave her the classic strip club brush-off, indicating she had definitely spent ample time in one before. "We just got here. Maybe after a drink or two."

Candy pushed out her bottom lip. "That's not how my dream goes." She stood, facing Penny and shimmying her shoulders with her breasts only a few inches away from Penny's face. "How about your uncle over there? Want to buy him one?"

Penny glanced over at Bill, who was shaking his head with widened eyes. Penny said, "Not just yet. We need to let our feet dangle in the water before we jump in. Do you know Crystal, er, I mean Faith? Is Faith here?"

Candy said, "Oh, so you like brown Asians? She's in the back, but she'll be out soon. Comes onstage after me." Candy turned and leaned toward Bill, offering him a similar shoulder shimmy while presenting her G-string-clad bottom to Penny. Looking back over her shoulder, she smacked her bare right cheek. "Let me know when you're ready to take a dip."

The waitress delivered a vodka on the rocks for Penny and a Miller Lite for Bill. Penny paid her in cash, adding an additional twenty for the banded stack of singles. She looked over at Bill, who still appeared more petrified than anything, and tossed another forty on the waitress's tray. "You better bring us two Patróns on the way back. We need to loosen up a bit." The waitress nodded and left. Penny scooted her chair next to Bill's. "You OK? It's a bit overwhelming, isn't it?"

"No, I mean," Bill dropped his head and laughed. "Yes, it's completely overwhelming. You seem to know your way around though."

Penny took the hairband off her wrist and pulled her hair back in a ponytail. "I worked around professional athletes with a lot of discretionary income. When you're out with the boys and they want to go to a strip club, you either go or call it an early night. It was a lot easier to get a scoop when they knew they could trust you." The waitress dropped off the Patrón shots and the sixteen dollars of change. Penny took the single and gave the waitress back fifteen for a tip. Tearing the band from the stack of singles, she added the lone single to the rest of the supply. "Rule number one: you can never have enough ones." She slid one of the Patróns in front of Bill. "Rule number two: strip clubs are a lot more fun with tequila."

Bill waved his hand over the shot. "Oh no, I'm good. I only drink beer."

She picked up the shot, holding it in front of Bill. "Rule number three: there are no rules."

Bill took the shot from her. She touched her glass to his and tossed it back. Bill followed a few seconds behind, after watching how she did it. He winced, forcing it down, then smacked his lips and tongue several times, relaxing his face. "That's not half bad." He smelled the empty glass. "Pretty good actually." He chased it with a long drink of beer, already feeling more at ease.

After Penny and Bill had been anchored for a while and their first round of drinks were gone, the sharks circled at a more frequent pace. Penny waved them off before they got close. "If you see one you like, let me know, and I'll bring her over."

"No, I think I'm fine right here," Bill said.

"Don't worry. I'll protect you." She scooted her chair even closer. She was clearly trying to distract him with other conversation. "So, what's the deal with Les? He used to be a minister or something, and now he runs this homeless shelter?"

"Catholic priest, actually," Bill said. "I'm actually kind of worried about him to be honest. I didn't know the Oasis was doing so bad."

"I thought you were helping out there."

"I do, every day. But he's never said anything."

Penny's eyes followed a forty-year-old man with an athletic build walk toward the VIP room holding hands with one of the young dancers. "Yeah, well, he probably appreciates your help and just doesn't want to bother you with his other issues. People do that, you know? They hold stuff back to not burden others."

The music faded as the song finished. The girl onstage collected the bills scattered around. The DJ's low voice filled the silence. "Ladies and gentleman, let's put our hands together for Scarlett. She's available for private dances, or if you ask really nicely, I'm sure she'll give you a private tour of the VIP room. Up next we have the sweet and lovely Candy, followed by Faith."

Penny whistled and clapped. She pumped her fist in the air, chanting, "Faith, Faith, Faith." The waitress came by. Penny ordered another round of drinks and shots. Bill issued no objections this time. Penny dropped her previous line of questioning on Les and focused on Candy. Bill had a hard time keeping up with Penny, but most people did. She switched gears so quickly. One second she was a girly girl with beauty pageant looks, and the next, one of the boys, banging back shots and talking sports. She could go from serious to bawdy in an instant.

The waitress dropped off the drinks. Bill didn't wait for Penny this time to do the shot. He touched his glass to hers and downed it right away. Penny banged hers back and slammed the shot glass upside down on the table. Snatching the stack of singles with one hand, she grabbed Bill's with the other. "Come on. Let's get a spot at the stage for Crystal's set."

Bill wasn't thrilled about being at the edge of the stage under the lights, but figured it was better than sitting alone at the table. At least at the stage he had Penny running interference. He trailed a few steps behind like a freighter being towed by a powerful tug.

At the stage, Penny split the stack, giving half to Bill. Not sure what to do with the money, he folded it and dropped his hands between his legs, out of sight. Penny stuffed two dollars in the neckline of her shirt. Candy sauntered over and dropped down to her knees. She covered her chest with one arm and reached around to the back with the other, untying the bikini top. She leaned toward Penny and let the top fall. Being so close made Bill even more uncomfortable. He looked away. Penny peeled off three singles and stuck them in the band of the G-string. Candy moved in and pulled the money out of Penny's neckline with her teeth and dropped it on the stage. Penny leaned toward her. Candy moved in and kissed her on the neck. Penny tossed more money on the stage. Candy moved up to Penny's jawline. Tilting her head back, Penny closed her eyes. Candy wrapped her arms around Penny, pulled her close, and put her lips on Penny's. The crowd cheered. Penny threw the rest of her money on the stage and put her arms around Candy, her eyes popping open momentarily when Candy slipped her tongue into Penny's mouth. But after the initial surprise, Penny just went with it. Afterward, she flopped back in her chair and fanned herself, playing to the delight of the crowd.

Candy said, "Hope the water was warm enough for you. I'll come find you later. Maybe we can go in the deep end of the pool."

Penny just smiled, still looking a little shocked about having Candy's tongue in her mouth. Bill, feeling like he had been drowned in the splash, handed Penny the money she had given him. It was damp and crumpled from him wringing it in his sweaty hands. "Here it looks like you need this more than me."

"Sorry, I didn't see that going that way at all. I guess the girls here are more aggressive than I'm used to." Penny took half and extended the other half back to Bill.

Bill waved it off, not wanting to find out what would happen if he gave the dancers money. "I'm just here for moral support."

Penny combined the two halves. "I guess that leaves all the immoral support up to me."

The DJ's voice boomed. "Let's hear it for Candy…and the lovely young lady who got a little extra taste of her sweetness." The crowd whistled and hollered. The kiss might have left Penny a little flushed, but it would take Candy well past flush in terms of money. Her dance card would be full for the rest of the night, based on the crowd's reaction and the number of guys lingering by the stage steps where

Crystal was also waiting to be announced. The DJ continued, "Now that everyone is warmed up, please welcome to the stage, Faaaaaaith." Her usual George Michael song kicked off.

Penny screamed and waved her arms. Crystal performed her routine, not even looking in their direction. Penny sprinkled singles on the stage. Crystal slid up and down the pole and finished her routine, still not giving them any recognition. The song transitioned to Rage Against the Machine's "Killing in the Name." The routine became more energetic and aggressive. All eyes in the room were on Crystal. The seats along the stage were all filled, and guys stood in the spaces in between. She didn't need to take her clothes off. Her moves and intensity commanded the room.

Bill was still in shock, but now for a different reason. He couldn't believe that underneath the hat that was always pulled low and the baggy clothes was a girl with so much charisma. He tried looking away, but his eyes always flashed back to her. Even Penny was quiet and just watched.

Showing her range and diversity, the next song was "Loca" by Shakira, during which Crystal worked the sides of the stage, giving attention to any of the patrons who were willing to part with a few dollars to have her sultry gaze directed on them. Any of the patrons, that is, except for Penny and Bill, the latter of whom was perfectly fine with the snub. Crystal worked to the right and left of them, but she never made eye contact. Penny tossed the remaining money on the stage. Crystal swept it toward the middle on her way by, never acknowledging their presence.

After the last song, Penny and Bill went back to the table. Bill said, "Wow, I had no idea she could dance like that."

"You should hear her sing. Even better," Penny said. "I don't think she was too happy to see us, though."

Across the room, Crystal reassembled her wardrobe and descended the stage amongst a gathering of eager suitors. She dispatched them and headed toward Penny and Bill. Glistening with sweat, she pulled up a chair with her back to the stage. "What are you guys doing? You don't belong here."

"First of all, holy shit! You're amazing," Penny said.

"Is this the part where you tell me I'm too good for this place?" Crystal picked up Penny's vodka and took a healthy drink.

Penny said, "No, I mean, yes that's true. I knew you could sing, but with moves like that, you have to get out of here."

"Find another project." She slammed the glass on the table and pushed back from the chair. "I don't know how many times or ways I need to say this, but I don't need your or anyone's help."

"Are you sure about that?" Penny stood, scanning the room. "Take a look around you."

Crystal's eyes burned with resentment. "I don't need to stand here and listen to this." She turned to walk away.

Penny grabbed her hand. "Just wait. I didn't mean that. I only came here to say I was sorry for blabbing about the singing earlier."

"So your way to apologize about getting into my business is by getting even more into my business?"

Bill intervened. "We just wanted to show our support."

Crystal spread her arms with her palms up. "As you already pointed out, all the years of hard work have paid off quite handsomely for me. I'm a lucky girl, what can I say? Just living the dream."

"Come on. Don't be like that," Penny said. "This is just a stop on a longer journey."

"Please save the pep talks. And tell your agent I appreciate the opportunity, but I'm not interested. Now, if you'll excuse me, I need to get back to work."

Penny started after her, but Bill stopped her. "Come on, we should go. She was right, we shouldn't have come here without her invitation."

Penny looked like she wanted to argue but didn't say anything. She offered to give Bill a ride home, but, worried about how much she had to drink, he declined, opting for a taxi.

In the cab, the driver angled off Las Vegas Boulevard to Fourth Street toward the Juhl, which was only spotted with lights at this late of an hour. The cab illuminated then went dark, alternating between the streetlights and the vacant buildings on the short ride back downtown. The drone of the tires on the road and low mumble of the driver talking through a cellphone headset soothed the ringing in his ears from the loud music at the club. The slightest of sounds registered: his pants sliding across the vinyl seat on the way out of the cab, the door slamming and echoing into the night, the key inserting into the building door, the tone of the arriving elevator. He was aware of it all.

In the hallway, Bill stood for a moment outside their apartment door. It would always be theirs, never just his. Some things he would never accept. He bought it for her. They lived there together. She would always be a part of it.

Bill hated this time of day, when he came home and had to face the emptiness. He unlocked the door and pushed it open.

The light from the hallway knifed into the dark interior. He didn't bother turning on the light. No need to see what was there. It would only remind him of what was missing. He kicked off his shoes and felt his way past the dining table toward the couch, where he slept every night. He had tried sleeping in their bedroom, but it never worked. He either couldn't fall asleep and just stared at the ceiling all night, or if he did drift off, he would wake up three hours later and never fall back to sleep. At least on the couch he got four to five hours.

Flopping down on the cushions, he pulled the afghan draped over the back on top of him. It was the one Darlene had knitted and given to him many Christmases ago. He adjusted the throw pillows under his head. He had tried using his pillow from their bed, but no matter how many times he washed the pillowcase, the smell was too much. He would still roll over and catch a faint whiff of their life and be up for hours.

Staring at the ceiling, he emptied his lungs in frustration. Streetlight crept around the blinds, which covered the sliding door to the terrace, forming a line across the floor, up the couch, and diagonally across his body to the wall. It was after two in the morning. He had been up this late many nights, but never out this late. The comfort and happiness he felt watching the game, playing blackjack and being around Les, Penny, and Crystal were gone. All he could think about was Penny and Crystal. Why does Penny get so drunk? He remembered Crystal's intensity on stage but the anger and shame that lingered behind it when she came over to the table. Rolling over, he buried his face in the corner of the cushions, trying to block everything out.

Unable to sleep, he sat up on the couch. Draping the afghan around his shoulders, he walked over and reached behind the vertical blinds to open the balcony door. He lifted back the blinds and stepped out onto the balcony. The cool concrete soothed his sweating feet, which were always hot when he drank too much. He cinched the afghan up around his neck to push away the cold. Laughter and loud talking radiated from a party several floors below. He walked to the edge of the terrace, wondering when things would get easier, when the pain would stop. He clutched the railing. Thoughts of Crystal drifted back. He knew they shouldn't have ambushed her, but maybe it was exactly what she needed, to see that there were others who cared about her, whether she liked it or not. Maybe she needed more of it and not less. It might be too late for him, but maybe not be for her. He let go of the railing, took a few steps back and dropped into one of the chairs. Wrapping the blanket around him, he closed his eyes and fell asleep.

Dow Jones Close: Closed

Chapter Forty-Four

Date: Sunday, May 11, 2014

Dow Jones Open: Closed

Predawn morning light soaked through the curtains. Summer was approaching. The days were starting earlier, which made getting up and, more importantly, waking everyone else up much easier. Les's first thought wasn't what day it was so he would know what to prepare for dinner. It was the other way around. Since last night was spaghetti, tonight was sloppy joes, which meant it was Sunday. Other than that, his days were all pretty much the same. He went down and showered in the men's locker room, which consisted of three stalls, two sinks, and four showers. A similar setup existed for the women, and surprisingly both got a lot of use. Most might think cleanliness isn't a high priority for the homeless when they're just going to be out schlepping in the sun all day. But it was one of the things the guests always said they appreciated most about the Oasis. Martin had told him that both locker rooms were added ten years ago, when the laundromat that had shared the building closed down. When that happened, Martin applied and was awarded a grant from the state to expand and do the renovations. It also allowed him to increase from twenty to forty people occupancy and upgrade the kitchen.

After his shower, Les relieved the security guard and proceeded to the kitchen to start putting out breakfast. He passed by the door to peek outside and check how many he might need to cover for breakfast in addition to the twenty-nine who had slept over. A shadow from the building across the street, which still concealed the sun, covered the five people camped out and sleeping on the sidewalk. He looked down the desolate street in both directions. A girl on a bike was riding in and out of the shadows from the south. As she got closer, he could see it was Crystal. Steering the bike onto the sidewalk, she wore the same baggy pink velour hoodie and sweatpants with the green cap he had seen her in at the El Cortez so many times with the addition of vintage bug-eyed sunglasses even though the sun was just coming up. He opened the door and spoke in a whisper. "Surprised to see you here so early."

She walked her bike up onto the sidewalk. "Actually late. I was on my way home from work and remembered you said you could always use volunteers. I just live around the corner, so it's on the way."

"Well, come on in." Les opened the door further so she and her bicycle could squeeze through. The man stretched out on the sidewalk at the front of the line stirred, then rolled over, pulling the black plastic that was covering his body over his head. In the hallway with the door closed, Les spoke in his usual tone. "I'm just about to start breakfast. It'll be nice having some company. Most volunteers don't show up until later."

She leaned the bike up against the windows and followed Les down the hallway. "Well that's good. It usually takes me a few hours to fall asleep anyway. Just tell me what you need done. I'm not much of a cook, but I can clean or whatever."

He led her to the kitchen. "Breakfast is easy. No cooking required. Just have to fill the tins with all the items and mix up the juice. Stripping, changing, and cleaning the bedding once everyone is up and out the door is where the help is really needed." He got the bag of bagels that were delivered earlier in the morning and showed her where the bananas and yogurt were. "Fill each one of the tins on the serving line with forty of each, bagels first, then bananas, followed by yogurt. I know, you're probably thinking, What does it matter? But a lot of the people have been coming here for a while. The slightest changes send them into a tizzy."

Crystal nodded, finally removing her sunglasses and putting them in her pocket. The florescent light from above reflected off the glitter makeup around her eyes. "Got it. Bagels, bananas, yogurt." She carried the bag of bagels over to the first tin. "So are Penny or Bill coming this morning?"

Les poured juice concentrate into a yellow five-gallon Igloo cooler. "Bill usually comes by around seven-thirty and helps me with the linens, and we grab breakfast afterward." He carried the cooler to the sink and turned on the cold water. "Penny said she was coming, but I never know who will show. I just always expect no one and am pleasantly surprised when anyone comes. Just like today. Never expected to see you when I looked out there this morning."

"Me either, to be honest," she said, arranging the bananas in rows of eight to keep count. "Ride by here all the time. Was thinking about what you said at the El Cortez and saw you so figured I'd pitch in this morning."

"Glad you followed your instincts," Les said. "Just let me know if any of our visitors give you any trouble. They're used to looking at me every day. Not sure how they'll respond to such an upgrade."

"I'm sure I'll be fine. Can't be any worse than what I deal with at work." She shifted back and forth, uncomfortable acknowledging to him what she did for a living.

Les fastened the lid on the cooler and carried it to the end of the serving line. "And how is work these days?"

"You do know what I do, right?" Crystal asked, rearranging the yogurts.

"I remember." Les walked over and inspected her work. "This looks good."

"I wasn't too good the other night though." Crystal looked down, recounting the items in the bin.

Les remained quiet, allowing her to proceed at her own pace. He could tell there was something she wanted to talk about. The timing of her visit was no coincidence. He was never a person to pry or push though. He let people reveal things on their own timetable.

"Penny and Bill came to my work Friday night after the El Cortez, and I didn't handle it very well."

He offered a comforting smile. "I'm sure their intentions were good."

"That's just it," Crystal said. "I'm not used to people helping me. I always expect them to want something in return."

Les poured two glasses of juice and handed one to Crystal, her hand shaking slightly as she reached for it. Les noticed but didn't say anything. Crystal steadied the cup with her other hand and lifted it to her mouth. Les said, "Accepting help from people is a sign of strength, not weakness. You're recognizing a need in them and allowing them to fill it. They cared enough about you to come see you in an environment that I'm guessing neither of them frequent very often."

Crystal sipped the juice, chewing on the rim of the plastic cup, considering his words. "I guess I can see that now, but at the time I just felt violated, like they were spying or checking up on me."

"I can see that being quite a surprise. They didn't tell you they were coming?"

Crystal shook her head. "Not at all. Can you believe that? At least give me a heads-up. I could've gotten them a booth or a round of drinks on the house."

"So it really wasn't that they were there? It was just coming without asking you?"

"I guess. I mean, I don't know." She looked down into the plastic cup while talking through her thoughts. "It is a public place. Anyone can come there, and Bill is so nice. I can't be mad at him. He doesn't have an evil bone in his body. It's more Penny. I know she means well, but come on. Just stop pushing so much." Crystal looked up from the cup. "I'm sorry. Don't know why I'm telling you all this. Should probably just talk to them."

"It's fine. I think you're all pretty terrific." Les looked at his watch. "But it is seven. Better get things rolling before the natives get restless. I'll wake everyone. You just stay here and make sure each person only takes one of each. After that we'll open up to the people outside."

Les left, and minutes later, still sleepy and scruffy, the overnighters trickled in from the billet to collect their breakfast. Crystal offered each a smile and a good morning wish, answering their questions about who she was and why she was there. Catching one person trying to palm two bagels at the same time, she said, "Ah, ah, ah, just one of each." He grinned playfully, as if he were testing her more than actually wanting the extra bagel. After everyone from inside was fed, they opened the door for those on the sidewalk, which had increased to ten, leaving one extra serving.

After everyone had been fed, Les said, "Why don't you take a break and have what's left before we start cleaning? Don't feel obligated to stay though. You've already helped so much. I'm sure a few others will come along."

Crystal glanced at the food and frowned. "Thanks, but I don't want to take food from someone who needs it. I have plenty at home."

"Don't be ridiculous. Everyone has been fed." Les walked over and tore the bagel in half. "How about we split it?" He took his half and refilled her juice. "Come on, let's sit down and take a break for a few minutes."

Crystal took the bagel and banana and left the yogurt, following him over to one of the long cafeteria tables. Voices blended with the shuffling of feet in the hallway. Les stood up. "Probably some late arrivals; I should probably lock the door." He had gotten halfway across the room when Bill and Penny breezed through the doorway. Both were laughing but looked extremely tired. The bags under Bill's eyes were swollen and extended the whole length of his eye with creases on the outer edge. Penny was wearing jeans, a red sweatshirt, and a St. Louis Cardinals baseball cap. For once, she appeared not to be wearing any makeup. The early wrinkles around her eyes and mouth, which she usually so expertly hid, were accented by the laughter.

Crystal looked at them, then down at the table, tearing the bagel piece in half and biting off a mouthful, chewing slowly. Penny and Bill stopped in the middle of the room, obviously surprised to see Crystal.

Les filled the awkwardness. "What a nice surprise. Perfect timing actually. We were just taking a break before we clean the billet. Sorry I can't offer you any food this morning. They wiped us out. We were actually splitting the last bagel and banana." He picked up the banana off the table. "You're welcome to this, though, to hold you over until after."

Bill held up his hand. "No, you guys have it. We haven't done any work yet."

"I wasn't sure I'd see you today," Les said. "I heard you had a late night Friday. Thought you might need the weekend to get back on schedule."

Penny walked toward the table. "That's what we were just laughing about. I woke up Saturday afternoon facedown on top of my bed with my clothes and shoes on. Didn't do a darn thing the rest of the day. Had to get out of the house today and do something productive. Was getting sick of myself."

"I won't even tell you where I slept," Bill said. "At my age, it takes a few days to recover from a night like that. I still don't feel right."

"This one over here," Les pointed to Crystal, "came right after work and has been helping me all morning." He peeled the banana and gave half to Crystal. Everyone just nodded and smiled. Les popped a bite of the banana in his mouth. He motioned toward the billet, speaking while he was chewing. "Sounds like the best thing for everybody is some work to get the blood flowing. Bill, you and Penny strip, and Crystal and I'll come behind you with fresh linens."

With four of them working, it took less than an hour to finish the twenty-nine beds. There was minimal talking, except for polite requests and thank-yous. Les always considered the simplicity and repetition of the work a meditation, even more so that morning. It redirected their focus from the trivial distractions to a unitary objective. No longer were they thinking about the other night or what should or shouldn't be said. They were all just there, helping each other.

Afterward, with all the morning work done, Les gave Crystal and Penny a full tour of the facility. Bill had seen it all before, but tagged along anyway. They ended on the roof. With it still only ten o'clock, the sun hung low in the eastern sky above Sunrise Mountain, keeping the temperatures in the mid-seventies. Wisps of clouds hovered above the ring of mountains surrounding the valley, fading into an azure sky that stretched from one side to the other in all directions.

Les said, "I mostly come up here at night, but you really get an appreciation for the desert beauty of Vegas in the daytime when all the lights are off. The whole picture changes as the light does throughout the day."

The others remained quiet, rotating to fully enjoy the majestic 360-degree view. They were in the middle of the city, but everything seemed to be happening away from them. There was the silent, constant flow of traffic on I-15, just a half mile to the west, the outline of the office and government buildings populating downtown, the Fremont Street casinos looming in the background to the north, and the seductive skyline of the Strip, the actual oasis most seek when coming here, to the south.

Crystal walked over to Penny and Bill. "I'm sorry for the other night. You guys surprised me, and I guess I overreacted."

Penny hugged Crystal, clearly taking her by surprise. Crystal's arms remained by her side. It didn't deter Penny, who pulled her closer. "No, it was our fault. We shouldn't come without letting you know."

"If it's any consolation," Bill said, "I was miserable the whole time."

Crystal finally lifted her arms, loosely patting and rubbing Penny on the back. "I think Penny had enough fun for the both of you." She put her hands on Penny's shoulders and pushed back from the hug. "You're not going to try to kiss me like you did Candy, are you?"

Penny closed her eyes and opened her mouth, pretending to move in for a kiss. Crystal put her hand on Penny's face and playfully pushed her away. Penny said, "You know, my agent is still coming a week from Saturday if you've also changed your mind about that."

Crystal thought for a moment. "Sure. That Saturday at Dino's. I'll be there." She turned to Bill and Les. "You guys can come if you want. A little extra support never hurts."

Dow Jones Close: Closed

Chapter Forty-Five

Date: Friday, May 16, 2014

Dow Jones Open: 16,447.32

Max weaved down the hallway, head down, reading emails on his phone. In the forty-five minutes he had been in the studio recording a new radio spot for the Lapkin, he had received eighty-seven new mails. Most of them he was just copied on, so he didn't need to respond. It was merely people covering their butts since most of the news lately was bad. While the hiring, production, and financial impact had all improved since the April meeting, the forecasts still projected falling short on the McDonald's deal. Max hadn't figured out how or when would be the best way and time to inform McDonald's.

Sensing a person in his path, Max veered to the right. The person moved with him. Still with his head down focused on his phone, he angled left. The person redirected toward him. He finally just stopped to stay out of the way. The person walked up and stopped directly in front of him. Max looked up from his phone, following the taupe Mary Jane pumps on her feet up to a white skirt to a simple navy button-up shirt with gold and maroon-striped colored cuffs. "Excuse me," he said, finally seeing the person's face. She looked familiar, but his mind was elsewhere, and he couldn't place the face. A brown leather portfolio and matching clutch were tucked under her left arm. She had full makeup on and her hair pulled back in a sleek, low updo. *Obviously a business contact*, Max thought.

The person giggled. "You have no idea who I am, do you?"

"Of course I do," Max said. "You work on my account here at Beasely." The Beasley Broadcast Group owned over fifty stations in twelve different markets in the United States and was the receiver of a large portion of Max's advertising budget.

"Not even close," she said, hesitating and waiting for another guess.

Max shook his head, dropping it forward to signal his surrender. "I'm sorry. I got nothing. My memory is not my strongest asset." He tucked his phone into the breast pocket of his chocolate suede jacket and focused his eyes on hers, narrowing his stare, almost as if drawing aim on her.

"Ah, now you're going to revert to charm, or is that your intimidation face? I can't really tell," she said. "Well I won't torture you any longer. It's Penny, from the El Cortez." She paused, allowing the reference to sink in. "We've played blackjack together on several occasions. Normally my hair is down." She turned her head to the side, showing the mound of hair tied in the back.

Max banged his palm on his forehead. "God damn it, that's it. I knew I recognized you. The different hair style and professional attire threw me off."

"So you're saying I normally look like shit, is that it?"

Max loved that she wasn't letting him off easy. He said, "Quite the opposite, actually. Just wasn't expecting to see you in this setting. What are you doing here?"

"Backpedal, backpedal, and change the subject. This must happen to you often," Penny said, still having fun with him. Holding up the leather portfolio, she finally backed off. "Had an interview. One of the morning radio shows is hiring a person to do the news. Figured it might be a nice change from TV and a good way to ease back into the workforce. Plus, I won't have to worry about makeup or what I wear."

"I didn't know you were a TV news person." Max tilted his head to the left and looked her up and down. "I guess I can see that. You definitely have the look." Max waved his arm back in the direction he came from. "I do a lot of business here, so let me know if you want me to put in a good word."

Penny said, "Nah, that's OK. To be honest, I'm not even sure I want it. Just dipping my toe in the water and tuning up my interviewing chops."

"Well the offer is on the table if you change your mind. I might as well get something out of my money. Not sure radio advertising is the smartest investment anymore." Max's gaze floated from Penny as his mind drifted to the business issues awaiting him in the emails.

Penny said, "Where you headed now? Have you had lunch?"

The questions pulled Max back to the conversation. Shaking his head, he said, "No, I was going to pick something up on the way back downtown. But if you're hungry, the Bagel Café is only one street over on Buffalo. Best corned beef and black and white cookies in Vegas. What do you say?"

Penny raised an eyebrow. "Black and white cookie, you say?"

"The absolute best." Max stepped around her. "Come on. You can ride with me. I'll drop you back here afterward."

Penny followed him to his Tesla parked right outside the door in one of the reserved spots. Inside the car she stared at the ultramodern dashboard display. "I haven't ridden in one of these yet. It's like a spaceship. What made you go electric?"

"I don't drive much. Put only like ten thousand miles on my Maserati in three years. Figured if I'm just banging around town, might as well be green." Max pulled out onto Durango, accelerating, weaving in and out of traffic. "As you can see, you don't sacrifice any of the power." He sped up and turned left on Charleston as the light changed to red.

Minutes later, they were pulling into the parking lot of the Bagel Café, a deli, bakery, and dining oasis for transplanted New Yorkers and all the workers who toiled in the surrounding cluster of medical offices. The smell of fresh baked marble rye greeted them as they approached the building. People filled the benches outside and lingered in the entrance way and around the hostess stand.

Penny said, "Looks like there's a wait."

Max waved Penny on, breezing by them all. "Follow me. I think they'll be able to squeeze us in." Max stopped next to the hostess stand and waited for the elderly lady with thick dark hair, who was also the owner, to return from seating a party of four. The bakery and deli cases were to the right. Signed photographs of famous diners adorned the wall to the left.

Penny pointed at his picture in the second row, third from the right. "I see you've been here before."

Max buried his hands in his pockets and shrugged his shoulders, attempting to look as humble as a guy who brought a girl to a restaurant with his picture on the wall could look.

In the middle of the floor on her way back to the hostess stand, the owner threw her hands in the air and excitedly approached Max. "Maxxie," she squealed in a heavy Long Island accent. "Where you been hiding?" Bending down, she wrapped her arms around him and squeezed, almost lifting him off the ground.

Max reciprocated the affection. "You know how it is, they only let me out on good behavior once a while anymore." He motions to Penny. "I brought a first-timer."

"Welcome." She grabbed two menus. "Come. I have a great booth for you in the back."

Max turned and smiled at Penny, proud of the VIP treatment they were receiving. Penny looked at the ground, carefully avoiding the sneers of the people who had been waiting.

In the booth, Max slid his menu to the edge without even picking it up. Upon direction from the owner, a waitress came over immediately. Max ordered a full corned beef with Swiss on marble rye and a black and white cookie. Much to his disapproval, Penny went the Greek salad route but copied him on the cookie.

After the waitress left, Max folded both hands in front of him on the table and wiggled anxiously in his seat. "So I have to ask you, do you hang out a lot with the people from that night we met?"

"All the time," Penny said. "Was just hanging out with them this past weekend. Really good people. Crystal, who you apparently know from her dancing, is also an amazing singer. Bill is an ex-cop who recently lost his wife. Just the sweetest guy you could ever meet. Les runs a homeless shelter in the Arts District. Why?"

Max said, "They just hate me, don't they? That one time I saw a few of you there, they left the second I sat down."

"Hate is a little strong, but you probably won't be receiving a Christmas card from any of them."

Max leaned forward, drinking his water through the straw, which was at the same level as his mouth. "In my defense, I was pretty drunk that first night."

"Is that supposed to be an excuse?"

"More of an explanation." The waitress dropped off their food and refilled their waters, retreating after both confirmed nothing else was needed. Max squirted brown mustard between the Swiss cheese and corned beef on his sandwich. "I just like to have fun when I'm gambling. People get so serious at the table. It's just a game, and it's only money."

"But it's their money, and a hundred or two for you is different to them."

His mouth full of corned beef, in between chews, Max said, "I tried reimbursing them."

"Not sure that made it better." Penny lifted her napkin to her cheek, indicating for Max to clean the mustard from his face.

Max wiped the spot with his free hand, not even putting down his sandwich. "Well if you see them, please pass on my sincere apologies. I'd do it myself, but, like I said, whenever I see them, they always play at other tables."

Penny studied him for a moment. She ate with precision, stabbing each item in the salad separately, careful to never combine two in the same bite, dipping each one in the dressing on its own. She said, "You really want to make it better?"

"I guess it depends on what that entails." Max put the half-eaten sandwich down on the plate and leaned back in the booth to provide his full attention.

Penny said, "You should go and volunteer at Les's shelter one day."

Max picked back up the sandwich, corned beef falling from the sides to the plate. "I wish I could. Unfortunately, I just don't have the time. How about I just make a hefty donation?"

"Normally, considering what happened the last time you tried giving them money, I'd say that's probably not the best idea." Penny leaned forward toward the middle of the table. "But, between you and me, I know Les is having some money issues at the Oasis. Not sure how much it will help with the others, but if they see you helping Les, it might gain favor with them. I don't know the whole story but from what I understand, the neighborhood is changing and donations are down."

"That whole area is the new hot spot," Max said. "Property values are skyrocketing. The other owners are probably trying to force him out. Does he have a long term lease?"

Penny said, "I don't know anything about that. I just know he puts his gambling profits right back into the place. Bill, the ex-cop probably knows. They're pretty close. I can probably find out if you want."

"Nah, I was just curious." The waitress came with two black and white cookies. Max pushed his plate with almost half of the sandwich remaining to the center of the table. "I don't know why I just don't get a half. I never finish it all." The waitress clears the plates. Max picks up his cookie and holds it so the black part is on the right and the white on the left. "I love the first bite when you get equal amounts of chocolate and vanilla."

Penny takes her cookie with the white part toward her. "Ooh, I don't like to mix them." She takes a bite of the white half. "I eat one side then the other."

Dow Jones Close: 16,491.31

Chapter Forty-Six

Date: Saturday, May 24, 2014

Dow Jones Open: Closed

Crystal rolled over on the couch. The news coverage, about a string of shootings in a Santa Barbara neighborhood, blared from the TV. She had tried to block out the noise and keep sleeping, but it just kept going on and on, repeating the same facts: seven people confirmed dead, including the lone gunman in a black BMW, and at least another seven wounded. Nothing new. Just the same information on an endless loop. She felt around blindly for the remote. No luck. She opened her eyes. Light filled the room. It was still daytime. She had hoped it would be dark by the time she woke up. Another shitty night of sleep. She had finally gone to bed, or rather passed out on the couch, only a few hours before, around two in the afternoon. With her alarm set for nine-thirty, she had had every intention of getting seven hours of sleep. But it was like the two nights before. Even though she needed more rest, she got less. Each time, her body woke her up, signaling it was time to feed her cravings.

She located the remote on the floor and switched off the TV. Her phone flashed on the coffee table. Messages were waiting. She rolled on her side, clamping the pillow over her head. The passing traffic outside on Charleston and voices, doors, and feet from neighboring apartments vibrated through. More sleep was not going to happen. The body had woken the mind, and there was no shutting that down.

Thinking back over the past week, Crystal wasn't quite sure how things fell apart so quickly. After being with the others on Sunday at the Oasis and agreeing to the informal audition, she was genuinely excited about the opportunity. She even promised herself she wasn't going to do drugs or drink the entire week to make sure she was in the best shape possible. But in the days that followed, her enthusiasm became stress followed by debilitating anxiety. She didn't leave her apartment the whole day on Tuesday. Thinking maybe she quit too much too fast, that first night of partying on Wednesday was just to take the edge off. But things escalated quickly. She woke up the next afternoon feeling worse than the day before. She knew her choice was either to shut down and suffer for two to three days while she detoxed, or keep going, feeding her body what it needed to function and get through the day. Based on the beginning of the week, she knew how the detox would go. No way she could perform like that.

The problem with the self-medication route she was on was that there were no directions for the prescription she was following. *As needed* might as well have been *As much as wanted*, because that's what she did. Once the hangover from the night before was gone and she was numb again, she kept going. Each day the drinking, the coke, and the pills started earlier and ended later. She promised herself, after the audition she would stop and get clean, this time for good.

Crystal got up off the couch and checked her phone. Three messages. All from Penny. One from last night and two from today. She walked over to the sink and fished a coffee cup out of the pile of dirty dishes, filled it with ice, and topped it off with bourbon. She needed a full drink for these messages.

Message one, 10:05 p.m. Friday: "Hey, it's Penny. Haven't seen you in a few days. Thought you might be at the El Cortez tonight before work. Wanted to confirm everything for tomorrow night. Give me a call when you have a chance. Hope everything is well. Call me. Bye."

Message two, 11:13 a.m. Saturday: "Hey, it's Penny again. Just was over at the Oasis with Bill and Les. Everyone is really excited for tonight. We were all going to grab breakfast. Wanted you to join. Call me when you get this. Talk to you later. Bye."

Message three, 2:35 p.m. Saturday: "Hey, it's your stalker Penny. Getting a little concerned since I haven't heard from you. Want to make sure you're OK and we're set for tonight. You probably worked late and are still sleeping. Just call me when you get up. I'm meeting my agent at Cosmo at seven, and we're going to STK for dinner. I don't know why I didn't think of it before, but you should totally join if you want. If not, no worries. We'll meet you at Dino's. Going to try to be there by ten. Just let me know what you want to do, OK? Can't wait for tonight. Call me. Bye."

Crystal took a long pull from the coffee mug and tossed her phone on the bed. A song or two she could pull off. No way could she entertain for an entire dinner. Deciding to shower first, she'd call Penny back later. While the water warmed, Crystal picked up clothes from the floor and arranged outfits on the bed, figuring out what to wear. Her wardrobe had really deteriorated over the past few years. She had sleazy clothes she wore in the club, and super casual ones she wore to and from. Neither were appropriate for a first impression.

She walked over to a stack of boxes in the corner, stuff she had moved from her condo but hadn't had any use for since. At the bottom, one was labeled, *Fancy Schmancy*. She pulled the box out, sending the others tumbling to the floor. Using her nail, she cut through the tape and opened the box. The floral, vanilla, and musky scent of the Narciso Rodriguez perfume she used to wear billowed out. It was just another one of the many things that had been part of her life that she had stuffed away. Her mom had always worn that perfume, so Crystal never used to leave the house without it on either. That way a part of her mom was always with her. She stopped soon after her mom passed, so she never had to think about her not being with her.

Crystal rummaged through the box. All the dresses that she no longer had the occasion or desire to wear were in there. She dumped them all out on the bed. Her high school graduation, the premieres and after-parties for the shows she had been in, the backup singing gigs she had done, some with her mom and some on her own, were lying tangled in a pile in front of her. Of course the dresses would all still fit. Except for her boobs being a little bigger, she was the exact same size as she had been in high school, making her the kind of girl other girls hated. She untangled the dresses on her bed. They should've been fond memories, things to cherish and to slip on and travel back in time. Instead they were reminders of what she had once had and now lost. She ran her hand along the black and bronze sequins of the Badgley Mischka she had worn to her first awards show. Not ready for a walk down memory's runway, she pushed it away and took another gulp from her mug. She would decide on the dress after calling Penny back.

In the shower, Crystal shifted to thinking about which songs she might sing. She knew she wouldn't be at her best, so she didn't want to sing anything too slow. She would need the music to help her keep the time and stay on key. But she still wanted to do something powerful, maybe something Motown or disco, possibly some Aretha or Gloria Gaynor. She hummed the melody to "I Will Survive," already feeling better. The steam cleared her stuffy sinuses, and the booze was kicking in. She just hoped it wasn't the best she would feel all night.

Toweling off, she walked backed to the bed and located her phone. Penny answered on the first ring. "Well, hey there, stranger. I was starting to worry about you. Where you been hiding?"

"Just working and sleeping really," Crystal lied. "You know how it is. Taking what they're giving because I'm working for a living." She sifted through the dresses, tossing the rejections back in the box. It was easier when she was on the phone. She didn't think so much. She was half-focused on the call and half on the dresses. Nothing left to dig up old memories.

"I can only imagine," Penny said. "Those hours have to be a killer." She sounded distracted, too, like she was putting on makeup or something. She said, "How are you feeling? You sound like you have a bit of a cold."

"No, I'm fine. Just waking up." She walked back into the bathroom and looked into the mirror, pressing and pulling under her eyes to see how much work she had to do on herself. "So you're meeting him at seven?"

"Yes, and I'm running soooo late. I should already be on my way. Are you going to join?"

Crystal hesitated like she was actually thinking about it. "I wanted to, but I wouldn't be there for at least another hour. I don't want to hold you guys up. I'll just meet you at Dino's."

"Are you sure?" Penny didn't push or seem too upset, which made Crystal think that it was no accident Penny had waited so long to invite her. "Well, I guess you'll have plenty of time to talk at Dino's."

"OK then. I'll let you go so you can finish getting ready." Crystal picked up a simple BCBG black spaghetti-strap dress that she used to wear when she was a backup singer for the R&B band Midnight Train in her early twenties. It would be perfect. Simple, not too fancy, and loose fitting. She definitely didn't want anything tight. She was feeling way too bloated for that. Free-flowing was the only option in her mind. She walked over to the full-length mirror propped against the wall and dangled the dress in front of her. Still on the phone with Penny, she said, "I'll see you there around eleven then. Enjoy your dinner."

Crystal hung up the phone and tossed it back on the bed. She slipped the dress over her head and let it fall along her body, turning, stretching and bending to check how much she might be revealing. Just because she pranced around on one stage didn't mean everyone was entitled to or wanted to see the show on another. Satisfied with the choice, she scooped up all the other dresses, stuffed them back in the box, and tossed the box back in the corner with the others.

She primped in front of the mirror. It felt good having a dress on again. The stretchy silk fabric blanketed and flowed with the contour of her body, caressing and comforting her skin. She looked closer at her face. The angle and lighting made the circles look worse. She moved into the bathroom for better light. Draining the rest of her drink, she set the mug on the back of the toilet. In front of the mirror, she pulled and stretched at the sides of her eyes again, watching the puffiness disappear and reappear with each movement. Most women would probably love to look as good as she did, even then at her worst, but all she saw were the imperfections. She layered on the under-eye concealer. It helped, but wasn't enough. She watched her shaking hand in the mirror as it moved closer to her eye to apply the mascara. She lifted her opposite hand to steady it. Applying quick touches rather than the usual slow, even strokes, she noticed even her head was tremoring slightly. She wasn't nervous; it was the excess.

Lowering her hands, she blinked her right eye, checking her work. It would have to do. She rested the wand on the edge of the sink and picked up the coffee mug, swirling the ice. She went to the kitchen to refill the mug and locate the tray with the Roxies she had crushed up to help her sleep. Scooping a nailful with her index finger, similar to applying the mascara, she guided her hand to her nose with her left, inhaling powerfully to get it through the congested passageway. She repeated the same for the other nostril and chased them both with a gulp of the bourbon. She hoped the booze and the Roxy would even her out for the moment, and a blast of coke before leaving would pick her back up. The rest of the night she planned to just drink and do bumps of coke to keep her going.

Ready to go by eight-thirty, she realized it was too early to go to Dino's and sit for two hours. She could've gone to OGs and bellied up to the bar to drink and play video poker, but she would've just gotten hassled by the girls wondering why she was dressed so nice and guys wanting her not to be dressed at all. No, she needed a place where no one knew her, and where those who didn't would be polite enough not to bother her. She was on foot too, since she couldn't ride her bike in the dress, so it had to be close. There were plenty of options between her and Dino's, but as she went down the list, she thought most were too smoky, too bright, too trashy, or too something. She opted for the Velveteen Rabbit, an upscale cocktail bar on Main in the Arts District, not too far from the Oasis. It was a few blocks out of her way, but worth the extra steps. A long, narrow, dark, artsy, nonsmoking lounge that poured stiff, tasty drinks was exactly what she was looking for.

When she arrived, it was still early in the evening, so she found a space at the bar on the far end in front of one of the three video poker machines. She fed a twenty into the slot. A bearded bartender wearing a denim vest and showing off a full sleeve of tattoos on each arm came over and set a drink menu mounted on a wooden board in front of her. "Here's our seasonal menu, and we also have all the drafts on the chalkboard above the bar. Or if you're feeling dangerous, I can whip up something special for you. What's your preferred poison?"

Crystal looked over the cocktail menu. "This all looks a bit too much for me. I was drinking bourbon earlier."

"Let's stay with something simple and brown. You ever had a Black Manhattan?" Crystal shook her head. He said, "It's the same two-one-two recipe, but instead of vermouth for the one, I use Amaro Averna, an Italian digestif. It's going to be a bit more spicy and herbal. I think you're going to dig it."

The first one was gone in three gulps. The next three lasted a bit longer, but not much. Her head was spinning from the alcohol. She walked back to the restroom. Her feet were heavy, and her movements, slow and deliberate. In the stall she bumped herself up to counteract the booze. She checked her phone. It was quarter to eleven. There was a text from Penny: *Just got to Dino's. At a table in the back. Les and Bill here too. See you when you get here.*

She hurried out of the restroom, stumbling on the way back to the bar. The bartender came over to clear the empty glass. He said, "Another? Or something else?"

"No, just the check," Crystal said. "I'm running late."

He looked her up and down. "You're not driving, are you?"

"No, I'm walking. Why?"

"As long as you're not driving, I was going to suggest we do a shot."

"OK, I'll do one, but then I have to run." She hit the cash out button on the machine to get the fifteen dollars in credits. "Put this toward the tab."

He put a leather check holder on the bar with two shot glasses. "I comped two drinks for your play, so you owe for two, or now just nine bucks with the credit." He poured two shots of Fernet.

Penny tossed two twenties on the bar. "Just keep it." They toasted, and she guzzled the bitter digestif and headed for the door.

On the street she looked for a cab, but there were never any in this neighborhood unless they had been called. She thought the fresh air and walk would do her good. Her gait was staggered and clumsy. She took off her heels and walked barefoot on the sidewalk. A few blocks before Dino's, she ducked between two buildings and served herself up two more keyfuls of coke. Her teeth and gums went numb. She put her shoes back on and hurried the rest of the way. The numbness spread to her face. She looked at her phone. It was eleven-fifteen. She had two messages. She didn't need to check to know who they were from. Cutting through the parking lot, she stopped at the door to adjust her dress and pull herself together as best she could.

Right across the street from OGs, on the corner of Las Vegas Boulevard and Wyoming, Dino's advertised itself as the last neighborhood bar in Vegas. Several of the polls that claimed to be qualified to make such distinctions had recognized it as one of the best dive bars in America. Dino's, like most places with any bit of history in Vegas, had mob ties going back to when Eddie Trascher owned and operated it as Ringside Liquors. Rinaldo Dean Bartolomucci, a.k.a. Dino, bought it from him in '62, and it had been in the family ever since, now being run by two of his granddaughters. But it wasn't the history or the atmosphere that Dino's was known for. It was the karaoke. Thursday to Saturday from ten until four, or even later if you tipped Danny G., the Vegas icon who had hosted karaoke there for over twenty years. Dino's was a melting pot of Vegas, drawing post-reception wedding parties, late-night revelers looking for another stop before home, motorcycle gangs, after-dinner dates needing an activity to fill the awkwardness while they decided if they were going to hook up, and the locals accustomed to the affordable beer and shot prices.

Crystal pushed through the swinging saloon doors. The L-shaped bar extended from just inside the door, along the right side, and wrapped around the back wall. The stage was next to the door on the left. All the tables were full, with most of the patrons huddled over thick songbooks, uninterested in the girl onstage singing—badly—Shania Twain's "Man! I Feel Like A Woman!" A group of men, which had to be a bachelor party, judging from the large baby bonnet and diaper on one of them, played beer pong in the game room to the far left by the restrooms.

Crystal spotted Penny and the others in the last row by the back bar. Not ready to deal with them yet, she went to the bar and bought a bottle of water. Penny saw her and stood on her stool, waving her arms. Crystal sipped the water, pretending not to see her, and watched the girl onstage.

Penny left the group and headed straight for Crystal. She started talking, pretty much yelling, halfway there. "Woo, look at you. Faaanceee." Penny took Crystal's hand and rotated her in a circle. "Let me get a look at you. What is that, BCBG?"

Crystal blinked several times and swallowed, staring blankly at Penny. "Uhm, yeah, I think it is." Sweat beaded on her forehead and streamed down her temples.

Penny grabbed a napkin from the bar. "You OK? You seem a little out of it."

Crystal took another drink of water. She could hear herself slurring her words. "No, I'm fine. I just walked here, so a bit winded."

"Well, just take a minute and go to the restroom and clean yourself up," Penny said. "We're in no rush. We got all night. Damon is really excited to meet you."

Crystal nodded. "OK. I'll be over in just a minute." She walked in front of the stage, stopping to talk to Danny G., who had just called up a duo called Matty and Stevie to sing "Hang On Sloopy."

Danny G., like most karaoke hosts who knew her, was excited about her singing. It gave him a chance to relax and also forced everybody else to step up their games. He covered the mic so only Crystal could hear. "Ah finally. Someone who can actually sing. Been a rough night."

"I don't know how good this is going to be, but I'll give it a shot." She filled out a slip for Aretha's "Respect" and put a twenty in his tip jar. "The sooner you can get me up, the better. Not sure how long I can stay."

Danny G looked over the sheet, smiling. "I got two other songs I have to do first, then I'll slide you in."

In the restroom, Crystal splashed cold water on her face and patted herself dry with a paper towel. She dug out the concealer, mascara, and eyeliner, but other than the concealer, it was useless. She was too drunk. The steady tremoring from earlier had become swaying and jerking.

On the way to the table, she forced a smile. The surprised look on Penny's face and the muted reception by others communicated she looked worse, not better, than when she had gone into the restroom. Penny recovered and effused more energy to compensate. "Here she is. Damon Withers, I would like to introduce you to the beautiful and talented Crystal Moore."

Damon stood to greet her. The first thing Crystal noticed was how tall and young he was. She had pictured a male version of Maura. Damon was quite the opposite. He was six foot five, with a shaved head and smooth ebony skin. He had on a gray three-piece suit with a white open-collar shirt that both concealed and accented his athletic build. He extended his hand, a stainless steel TAG Heuer watch fastened around his wrist. "So great to meet you. I've heard a lot about you. Penny usually only talks about herself." He winked at Penny. "So when she started raving about someone else, I knew I should make time to meet you."

Crystal shook his hand. "Nice to meet you as well. I hope I don't disappoint." She smiled, entranced by the way the light reflected off his smooth, shiny head.

Bill stood and hugged her. "Thanks for inviting me. Penny has been telling us about your last performance. Excited to hear you tonight." He hesitated as he moved to sit back down, then stepped away from the stool. "Here, take my seat. I prefer to stand anyway."

Les looked at her with his usual soft and kind expression. "You're looking especially lovely this evening, Crystal." She knew he was lying and just trying to be nice. She thanked him anyway.

Penny wasn't as subtle. She handed Crystal another bottle of water and a few more napkins. "I got you another water, like you asked."

Two of the bachelor party crew got up to sing "Radioactive" by Imagine Dragons, always a favorite, since the Dragons were from Vegas. Crystal sat on the stool, knowing she had to wait for only one more song before it was her turn. Their conversation consisted of Damon asking her where and with whom she had trained, what shows she had been in, what bands she had performed with, and what direction she wanted to go. Bill and Les remained quiet and just listened, both looking quite interested and impressed. Penny couldn't help herself and had to be part of the conversation. It wasn't really clear if she felt left out, or if she was just trying to help, since she felt responsible for bringing them together and could see Crystal struggling. But if there were any lulls in the conversation or Crystal fumbled through a response, Penny jumped in to clarify or share information about herself to fill the awkwardness.

After a woman in her fifties belted out a strong version of Nancy Sinatra's "These Boots Are Made for Walkin'," Danny G got on the mic. "Let's give a round of applause for Sandra as her and her boots are walking off the stage." Whistles and cheers radiated from the crowd. Danny G. picked up the next song slip. "You all should be happy you stopped in here tonight. Up next is one of my favorite performers. She doesn't come in that much, so when she does, it's always a special treat. Please welcome Crystal, as she reminds us about respect."

Crystal raised her eyebrows and flattened her mouth into a tight-lipped grin. "I guess this is me." Getting off the stool, she felt light-headed and had to steady herself with the edge of the table.

Bill put his hand on her lower back. "Easy now. You OK?"

Crystal shook her head and let out a deep breath. "Yeah, I'm fine. Just got up too fast." She angled toward the stage. She had hoped the fresh air, the water, and the time would help her pull it together, but it was getting worse as everything caught up with her. Her stomach was knotted, and her legs felt wobbly. She stepped behind the mic, removing it from the stand.

The music started. Crystal closed her eyes, trying to lose herself in the music like she had done so many times before.

Dow Jones Close: Closed

Chapter Forty-Seven

Date: Sunday, May 25, 2014

Dow Jones Open: Closed

The first line flowed from Crystal. "Ooh, what you want. Ooh, baby I got." Her voice was flat and slow. Bill hadn't heard her sing before, but based on Penny's descriptions, he knew something was wrong. At times Crystal hit the notes and would be good for a line or two, but she would slip at the next change. She didn't look like herself either. Sweat was streaming down her temples, and she had full black circles under her eyes. At the start of the second verse, she repeated the first. "I ain't gonna do wrong while you're gone." Then she mixed the words up between the two, sometimes stopping in the middle of the line to find her place. Danny G., the karaoke host, sang along over his mic when she fumbled the words, and he sang the backup vocals to help her. During the instrumental, she swayed clumsily, knocking over the mic stand. It was difficult to watch. Leading into the chorus, she fell completely apart, misspelling and mumbling through the words. "R-P-C-E-S-T. That is why you're mean to me. R-S-E—"

Crystal collapsed. The mic hit the ground with an amplified thud. She lay on the stage not moving. The wordless music with the backup track eerily continued. People stood on their stools to see what was happening. Bill arrived first to the stage. Penny and Les trailed right behind him. Danny G. cut the music and rushed over.

Bill sat Crystal up. Holding her face in his hand, he shook her gently. "Crystal! Can you hear me?" No response. He put his ear to her face. He could hear her breathing, snoring actually.

Penny took out her phone. "Should I call an ambulance?"

"I think she just passed out," Bill said. "Les, help me get her to her feet." Les got on her left and Bill on her right. Penny pulled down Crystal's dress, which had risen to her waist in the fall.

Crystal mumbled. "Just five more minutes. Please. Let me stay in five more—" She passed back out.

Les said, "Let's take her outside for some fresh air."

Outside they walked her over to Bill's car and put her in the passenger seat. Bill said, "What do you think we should do?"

Les said, "We need to get her to a hospital."

"Does she even have health insurance?" Penny said. "Maybe she has a card in her purse—oh, shit! Our purses." She turned to run back in, but her agent, Damon, was standing a few feet away with her and Crystal's purses.

Bill removed a penlight from his pocket and looked at Crystal's eyes. "Honestly, I think she just passed out." He checked her pulse, timing it with his watch. "I saw this on the job many times."

"We don't know exactly what she took though," Les said. "I think it's best to play it safe and go to the hospital."

Crystal sat forward in the seat, reacting to Les's last word. "I'm fine. No hopsital," she said, not even realizing her mispronunciation.

Bill stroked her head. "Shhhh, don't worry. Just sleep." He looked at the others. "Tell you what, I'll take her back to my place and keep an eye on her. If she gets worse, I'll take her straight to the hospital."

Les said, "I'll come with you and stay until I have to open the mission."

"Me too," Penny said. "We can take turns watching over her." She walked over to Damon, still just standing holding the purses. "Well, this didn't go as planned. I'm sure it was just nerves or something. I've never seen her like this."

He handed her the purses. "Penny, it's something a lot more than nerves. She's beautiful and has, from what I could hear from time to time, an amazing voice, but she's also damaged. I bet if we looked inside her purse, we'd find more than a bottle opener. I just can't afford to take on a project like that. You did a good thing in trying to help her out, but she has to help herself right now. I hope you understand. I'll call next week about the opportunities for you we talked about." He leaned down and kissed her cheek.

Penny hugged him. "Thanks for giving her a shot. Safe travels back to LA." She climbed in the backseat behind Crystal, leaning forward, stroking her hair. Bill started the car.

As they drove to Bill's, her snoring was loud and consistent, which they all agreed was a positive sign. When they arrived, Bill carried her in his arms into his room and put her to bed. She never stirred. The snoring throttled to heavy breathing. Bill sat on the edge and stretched a cold washcloth across her forehead.

Although he hadn't spent a single night in the room since Darlene passed, he did that night. He still wasn't able to sleep, but at least this time it was for a different reason. He left only to freshen the cloth with cold water. The rest of the time he sat on the floor next to the bed just in case she woke up. He wanted to make sure someone was there. Penny lay down in the guest room. Les was on the couch. They had offered to take turns, but Bill just let them sleep. He didn't see any reason why all three of them should be wrecked for the day. More than anything, it was his idea to bypass the hospital and come back to his place, so he felt responsible.

At five-thirty, Les crept in. Wiping the sleep from his eyes, he spoke in a whisper. "How's she doing?"

"Seems to be OK. Has hardly moved since we put her to bed. Just completely zonked." Bill touched the side of her check. "Feels a little warm, so I've been keeping a cold cloth on her forehead."

"You should've woken me," Les said. "You didn't have to stay up all night by yourself with her."

Bill stood and motioned toward the door for them to go to the other room to talk. He stopped in the doorway so he could still see—and more importantly be seen by—Crystal if she woke. He said, "It's not a big deal. You have to open the Oasis, and I thought you might need Penny's help today, so I let her sleep, too."

"I would've been fine." Les looked at his watch. "I do probably need to get going though. Just let Penny rest. I can manage. Usually get plenty of volunteers on Sundays."

"Yeah, Penny was pretty upset last night. I think she blames herself for pushing Crystal into something she wasn't ready for. She can probably use a little extra rest, too." Bill extended his hand. "Thanks for being here."

Les pulled Bill in for a hug. "You're a good man, Bill Price. Call me later and let me know how she's doing."

Bill agreed and returned to his bedside vigil as Les let himself out. Morning crept in through the blinds. Sitting on the floor with his back against the side of the bed, Bill scanned the room. He noticed details that couldn't be seen in the darkness. It reminded him of the nights he had sat in the same position, tending to Darlene. Maybe that was why it was so important for him to be there. He wasn't able to save Darlene, but maybe he could help Crystal. Or maybe it went back further. He never had to take care of Hughie when he was sick. Darlene always did that. She just let Bill sleep so he would be fresh for work. Maybe now it was Bill's turn to put in his time and look after others.

As his mind drifted to the past, his eyes lowered and his head slumped forward. When he woke, Penny was standing in the doorway. Her hair was pulled back in a ponytail, and she was wearing one of Bill's white T-shirts, which hung down just above her knees. She tugged at the excess fabric draped around her, accenting how much room she had. "Hope you don't mind I borrowed one of your shirts."

A tired smile stretched across his face. "How'd you sleep?"

"Apparently better than you." She walked over to look at Crystal. "How about her?"

Bill looked over at the clock, showing ten-fifteen on the bedside table. "Out cold for almost eight hours now." He stood up. "I'll make us some coffee."

Penny took his hand between hers, patting the top affectionately. "No, you just relax. Let me take care of it. I'm not much of a cook, but I can at least make a mean cup of coffee."

"That sounds great. Everything you need is on the counter in the kitchen." His eyes followed her out the door. He removed the washcloth from Crystal's forehead and walked into the bathroom to freshen the cloth. When he returned, he could hear the water percolating through the machine in the kitchen and smell the familiar burnt aroma that signaled the start of all his days, but something was different. There was also the scent of cinnamon. And even more noticeable than that was, for the first time since before Darlene got sick, life had returned to the apartment. Unfortunately the circumstances were not the best, but at least conversations were taking place and emotions other than loss and regret were being expressed. He stood over Crystal, watching her sleep.

Penny walked in with two mugs of coffee, handing one to him. Bill sniffed and took a sip. "Mmm, I thought I smelled cinnamon."

"I put it in right with the grounds," Penny said. "Reminds me of Christmas." She motioned for him to follow. "Come out with me for a second. I have something to show you." Bill trailed after her to the dining room. Crystal's purse was lying open on the table. Penny took out the small, resealable bag of coke and the container with the pills. "It looks like it wasn't just the alcohol."

"You went through her purse?" Bill looked away. It wasn't the drugs. He had seen his fair share on the job. It was the context. He flashed back to the last time drugs were discovered in his home.

Penny said, "I had to. I needed to see what we were dealing with."

"OK, so now we know." Bill walked back toward the bedroom. "Just put them back. It's her life. We can't force her to stop."

In the bedroom Crystal had rolled over on her side, facing away from the door. Bill walked to the side of the bed. She turned toward him, squinting and blinking, rubbing her forehead. "Where am I?"

"You're at my place." He picked up the glass of water on the bedside table and offered it to her. "Do you remember what happened?"

Crystal sat up grimacing and clutching her head. "Oww, um, not really." She took the water from him. "I, uh, remember I stopped at a bar between my place and Dino's for a few drinks. It gets kind of patchy after that though." She sipped some water. "I kind of remember being outside walking, but not much more than that. I guess being here means things didn't go too well."

Penny came in from the other room. She had changed into her dress from the night before. Crystal's purse was tucked under her arm. "I'll tell you what happened. You passed out on stage. You completely blew the opportunity and made me look like a fool in front of Damon, who, since you don't remember, is my agent. I wish I could forget it all."

"I'm so sorry," Crystal said, shaking her head. "Maybe somebody slipped something in my drink at the other bar." She forced down several more mouthfuls of water, wincing like even swallowing was causing pain.

"Or maybe you slipped yourself something." Penny tossed Crystal's purse on the bed. "I found the coke and the pills in your purse."

Crystal lunged forward and grabbed the purse, tucking it alongside of her, away from them. "Who said you could go through my stuff? Who asked you to do anything? You just push and push and push. Just leave me alone."

Bill sat on the side of the bed. "Hey, hey, hey, don't get angry. She was just worried about you. We all were. Les, too. He was here all night. We didn't know whether we should take you to the hospital or what. I was the one who suggested we bring you here."

"Lucky for you we did," Penny said. "Hospitals ask questions and have a tendency to share the answers with the police. You should be thanking us."

Crystal grabbed her purse and scrambled out from underneath the covers down to the end of the bed, still in the spaghetti-strap dress. She looked around on the floor. "Where are my shoes? I don't need to listen to this."

Penny picked up the shoes from next to the bedside table. "Here you go. Just run away. Seems like that's working really well so far."

"Look who's talking," Crystal said. "I bet they're still putting out the flames on your trail from St. Louis."

Bill stood from the bed. "Everyone, let's just calm down. We all had a long night and this is a lot to deal with." He knew the best thing to do was separate them. "Penny, why don't you go out in the other room and get some fresh air on the terrace?"

Penny pushed her hands out in disgust. "Fine. What's the point anyway?"

Bill waited for Penny to leave. He heard the terrace door slide open and close. Seated at the foot of the bed, Crystal dropped her head into her hands. Bill sat down next to her. He could hear her weeping. He put his arm around her. She leaned into him, letting go of the tears. He rubbed her back. "There, there. That's OK. You're both just upset."

Crystal looked up at him, her eyes full of tears. The makeup she had caked on the night before was smeared around her eyes forming dark circles. "I am grateful for you taking care of me. You didn't have to do that. You could've just left me or dumped me at a hospital."

Bill reached back and grabbed the wet washcloth and wiped around her eyes. "Nonsense. There was no way we were going to leave you anywhere, and you can stay here as long as you want. No questions asked."

Crystal looked up at the mirror above the dresser in front of her. She groaned at the image before her, releasing a frustrated laugh. She took the cloth from Bill and cleaned around her eyes. "I'm a mess."

"I'll tell you what." Bill rose and walked toward the bathroom. "I'll put out fresh towels, some Tylenol, and one of my T-shirts, which seem to be a popular item lately. You can take a hot shower and go back to bed for a few hours. When you wake, we'll get something to eat and figure out what to do next."

She opened the washcloth, stained with makeup, and stretched it across her lap. "I'm just screwing up everything lately."

"All this?" Bill said. "These are just bumps in the road. You want to hear about making a mess, I'll tell you about how I let my stubbornness screw up so much of my life."

Crystal got up from the bed, reaching down to steady herself. "Ooh, I am still feeling a little woozy. You sure it's no trouble for me to stay?"

Bill held out his hand. "Come on. Let me show you how the shower works."

While Crystal was showering and Penny was still on the terrace, Bill went back to the bedroom and located Crystal's purse. He took out the pills and the cocaine and walked to the kitchen sink. Turning on the water, he ripped open the bag of coke, washed the remnants down the drain, and threw the bag in the trash. He held up the pill bottle, reading the label. The prescription was for 30 mg tablets of Roxicodone for someone named Mildred Nickels. The dosage dictated one tablet every four to six hours as needed to manage pain and warned excess usage may cause sedation and depression of respiration. Bill cupped the pill container in his palm and went to his bedroom. In the closet, he opened his safe and locked the pills inside.

Dow Jones Close: Closed

Chapter Forty-Eight

Date: Monday, June 30, 2014

Dow Jones Open: 16,852.49

In the mirror in his office, Max cinched up his black tie and adjusted the white pocket square in his charcoal suit jacket. He thought about not even coming in that day. What was the point? He knew weeks ago they weren't going to meet the deadline.

His management team, Ed, Jules, and Belinda, were waiting for him in the meeting room. Ed sat in a chair pushed back from the conference table with his elbows on his knees, staring at the floor. Belinda banged away at the keys on her laptop. Jules scribbled notes on a yellow legal pad. They all glanced up at Max when he entered, then immediately lowered their eyes.

Seeing their deflation actually buoyed Max. He knew there was a time to scold and a time to encourage. He walked to the head of the table, mustering what little optimism he had. "First I want to say I'm proud of how everyone pulled together the past few months." The others raised their eyes in his direction. He said, "Come on, we all knew we weren't going to make it, but you still gave it your all and found a way to increase production. What was the final tally?"

Ed looked at his spreadsheet. "At the end of today, we'll be just over 3.3 million. At our current rate, we probably need another six weeks."

Jules said, "We have another group of workers starting third shift this week. We'll be able to have another line operating round the clock."

"Good job, both of you," Max said. "That's over five hundred thousand more than we thought we'd have and things look like they're only getting better."

Belinda said, "I don't mean to be a downer, but it really doesn't matter how close we are. The contract is pretty clear. Failure to meet the quota can void the deal. I don't think I need to go through again where we are without the payments from McDonald's."

Max said, "Has anyone informed them of our shortfall?"

Everyone looked at each other, shaking their heads. Ed said, "We have so much product in transit, it will probably take a week or so for them to tabulate the final inventory number."

Max said, "Good. Let's keep it that way. We'll continue operating all the lines and shipping product. That will give me some time to figure out a strategy." Max looked around at the dejection and worry hanging on their faces. "After work I want each of you to go out and treat yourself and your significant other or a friend to a nice meal on the company. We'll figure this out tomorrow. There's always a solution. We just can't see it right now." Max clapped his hands. "Come on. Heads up. Remember we set the example for everyone else in the company."

They filed out of the conference room. Max, Jules, and Belinda went to their offices. Ed returned to the production floor. In his office, Max flopped down in his chair and tilted back, staring at the ceiling. In front of the others, he had put on a brave front. Alone in his office, it was his turn to be disappointed. He had known failure. It had just been a while. Frustration and powerlessness set in. His mind raced but came up with nothing. He loosened his tie. The office suddenly seemed small. He stood and walked to the glass wall overlooking the production floor, watching all the people that were now dependent on him. His heart rate quickened. He struggled to catch his breath. Sweat soaked through his shirt. He had to get out of there. He needed to go somewhere to think.

Breezing right by his secretary without saying anything, he headed straight for the closest exit, the same one they had entered the first time visiting the Western. Outside, the queasiness that had been swirling in his stomach launched upward bursting through his mouth onto the side of the building. He braced both hands against the cinder block wall. Catching his breath, he wiped his mouth and angled down the sidewalk before anyone saw him. Afraid of having another episode while driving, he bypassed his car and just walked. He thought about going home, but he knew being by himself was the last thing he needed. Instead he went straight to the El Cortez where he knew he could be alone, yet still surrounded by people, and think, or more importantly, drink.

He was at my table when I started at six and didn't seem like he had any intention of going anywhere. His jacket and tie were draped over the chair next to him. The pit bosses informed me that he had been at the table most of the afternoon and was down around ten grand. Watching the way he was playing, it wasn't a surprise. He was really going for it. Every deal, he played three hands across at anywhere from $100 to $500 per hand. His play was erratic, too—even for him. He was doubling on anything seven or above and, of course, his favorite: splitting tens every chance he got.

Dark and brooding, he said more to the cocktail waitress when ordering his drinks than he did to me the rest of the time. His left elbow remained firmly on the table with his palm buried in his cheek or planted on his forehead holding up his head. All other actions—his betting, drinking, and decisions—were controlled by the right. People stopped to play at the other spots on the table, but his aggressive play, the stakes he was playing, and his disposition chased them away rather quickly.

When the money in front of him was gone, he called the pit boss over and requested a marker, which of course was granted, for $20,000. He upped his bet to $1,000. The twenty quickly became ten, then five, and down to two.

He reduced to one hand and bet $1,000. Got a twenty against my eight. He stayed. I had eighteen. Win.

He doubled his bet to $2,000. Fourteen against my ten. Hit. Got a five for nineteen. I had a six underneath. Hit. Eight. Twenty-four. Bust. Win.

He tripled the bet to $3,000. Seventeen against my eight. He went against the book and hit. Three. Twenty. I had eighteen. Win.

He put out five times his original bet for $5,000. Twelve against my seven. He should hit, but stayed. I had a nine underneath for sixteen. Hit. Ten. Twenty-six. Bust. Win.

I recognized the positive progression betting strategy he was using of one-two-three-five, each time going up a level with a win or back to one with a loss. It was a subset of the Fibonacci sequence that required a string of wins to profit. Each level up was the sum of the previous two bets. The next level after five was eight, and after that jumped up to thirteen. Most players using the progressive cycle got nervous after winning four in a row, and either stayed with five until they lost or took their profits and went back to one.

Max didn't hesitate. He pushed $8,000 into the circle. First card, eight. Second card, another eight. I had an ace showing. He declined insurance. I slid the card under the mirror to check for blackjack. Nobody home. He counted out the money in front of him. His remaining $1,000 with the four in profit he had from the progression left him three short. He got another marker for three and pushed another eight grand into the circle. Finally lifting his head from his hand, he straightened his body and leaned forward to watch the outcome. I separated the cards into two hands. First hand, he got a ten. Eighteen. He stayed. Second hand, a nine for a seventeen. He stayed. I turned over a six for a soft seventeen. Had to hit. Next card, a five. Twelve. Had to hit again. A three. Fifteen. Another card. A seven. Twenty-two. Bust. Win on both hands for him.

I counted out the $16,000 in winnings, for a total of $32,000 in front of him. He said, "Will you watch this?" I nodded. He got up and went toward the restroom.

When he came back, he looked over the stacks of brown, yellow, purple, and black chips. I said, "You're building quite a sundae there. You got chocolate, banana, grape, and some hot fudge."

"Not nearly enough." He reset the betting progression back to one thousand.

I dealt another hand. "What'd you start with, five grand?" He nodded, dropping his head back to his hand and resuming his morose posture. I said, "Well with the twenty-three in markers, that still puts you up four grand. Not a bad afternoon of work."

For someone who had been so quiet all day, Max really uncorked on my positive spin of his roller coaster ride. "Not so great when you mortgaged everything for a multimillion dollar deal with McDonald's, miss your deadline, are stuck with millions of branded units with nowhere to sell them, and have an eight-thousand-square-foot facility bleeding you dry." He flipped his hand, knocking his colorful stacks of chips over into a heaping pile. "This is nothing compared to what my company lost today."

"Forgive me," I said. "I was merely speaking to the accounting of today's play. My apologies."

Max dropped his eyes to his chips, again sorting and stacking them by color. "That's OK. I shouldn't take it out on you. You had no way of knowing. Don't know why I'm so down about it. Not like it was a surprise anyway. I've known for over a month we wouldn't make it. Just had to accept it today."

I remained silent and just dealt cards. He stayed with the progressive betting strategy, riding the waves up as high as forty-five and down as low as sixteen. He didn't win five straight again, but got to four in a row several times, and three many more.

On another upward trend, he had built his money back up to $42,000 and had just won a $5,000 hand with his fourth win in a row. If he played the $8,000 hand and won, he'd be at an even $50,000. A loss would reduce his profit to just $6,000. He counted out the $8,000 and placed it in the center of the bet circle. "Might as well go for it. I didn't come here to make friends or be sober."

The next cards out of the shoe gave him twenty against an ace for me. I asked if he wanted insurance. He declined. I checked for blackjack. Didn't have it. He waved off further cards. I flipped over another ace. "A pair of bullets. Dealer has two or twelve." I pulled the next card from the shoe and flipped it next to the two aces. It was a nine. "Uh-oh. nine-one-one means trouble. Dealer has twenty-one." I took the $8,000 in front of him and added it back to the house tray.

Max pushed back in his chair, puffing his lips in exasperation. "Figures. I can't even win with twenty. All I can do is sit and watch the madness unfold." He counted another $1,000 into the betting circle. "That's what's so frustrating about the other thing, too. There's always another play, and I just can't figure it out. I feel so powerless. Like everything is happening to me, and all I can do is sit back and take it. You ever feel that way?"

"Welcome to my life," I said. "Maybe it's like before though. You were playing three hands at a time, spreading yourself across so you had more chances to win. But you also had more opportunities to lose. When you got down to only a few units left, you consolidated and changed your strategy. You focused on one hand and pressed your bet when winning and reduced after a setback. You were always using house money to increase your bet rather than putting out more of your own. Just seems like a better way when you have limited funds."

Max became quiet again. I thought I might have overstepped my bounds and pissed him off, so I kept my mouth shut. I just flipped cards and relegated my comments to the table play. We went through a whole shoe and a half that way. Nothing spectacular, one way or the other. He would win a few then lose a few, slowly grinding upward due to the progressive bets and short streaks. His disposition had improved dramatically though. He was no longer slumped over to one side, sighing and mumbling at every outcome that didn't go his way. He was upright, leaning forward, eyes alert, following every move, aggressive without being reckless. After winning his second hand in a row to push his total to $43,000, he followed the progression and bet $3,000. I dealt him two fours against my eight. Neither a double down nor a split hand. Just a straight hit. He played the percentages and just hit. Got a ten for eighteen. I flipped over an ace for a nineteen. Loss. But it didn't derail him. He didn't chase. Just took the loss in stride. Comfortable at $40,000, he pushed the chips to the center.

"Had enough?" I said, counting out the chips, separating twenty-three for the markers, leaving him with seventeen.

"I've been looking at this all wrong." He tossed me one of the $1000 banana chips for a tip. "I've been so focused on not losing that I've gotten away from what got me here and what I have. I need to be more assertive. If I have extra space, I need to find a way to use it. If I have all this available inventory, I need to find someone else to take it. I need to create some leverage. When you paint yourself into the corner, you need to hold onto the brush and paint your way out."

Dow Jones Close: 16,826.60

Chapter Forty-Nine

Date: Wednesday, July 9, 2014

Dow Jones Open: 16,916.83

Les dropped the full laundry bag next to the others by the back door for pickup. Sweat was collecting in his graying beard, which was getting bushy and extended two inches below his chin. It's the longest it had ever been, and he was enjoying letting it grow. He wiped the sweat from his face with his shirt and wrung out his beard in a single swipe with his hand.

Temperatures had hit a hundred degrees every day of the month so far and hadn't been below eighty even at night. To save money, he set the air conditioning to keep the place at a tropical seventy-nine degrees. Sitting, doing nothing, it was bearable. Any bit of work like he was doing, or even standing, serving food, opened the sweat floodgates.

He walked back to the billet. Penny was making the last bed. Bill shoved the remaining dirty sheets in another bag. Crystal tied it off. Les, still out of breath from the last run, said, "Is that the last of it?"

Crystal grunted, picking up the bag. "Yep. I got this one."

Les noticed Bill watching admiringly as Crystal crossed the floor and disappeared into the other room. After her collapse at Dino's, she never spent another night at the Siegel Suites, taking Bill up on his offer to move into his spare bedroom. According to Bill, the first few weeks were rough—insomnia, puking, nightmares—from the detox, but she was steadily improving. The circles had faded from underneath her eyes, the shakiness was gone from her movement, her smile was more relaxed, her complexion was brighter, and most of all she wasn't so angry. She was still skeptical of anyone trying to help her, but she was getting better. Bill's rules were simple: no drugs, no working at the club, and she had to volunteer at the Oasis every day. In return, he provided a free room, meals, and a hundred dollars a week for spending money.

The buzzer at the front door sounded. Les looked at his watch, showing almost ten-thirty. He said, "Probably just someone checking for breakfast leftovers."

Penny said, "I'm finished over here. I'll get the door. You guys take a break."

Bill and Les went to the kitchen. Les filled a pitcher with water and grabbed four cups. Joining Bill at the table, he said, "Things still going well with Crystal?"

Bill beamed with pride. "So far so good—for me, too. I dropped ten pounds. I'm eating at home more, and she has me riding a bike with her. Can you believe it, me on a bicycle? I thought those days were behind me."

Crystal walked in on them in the kitchen. All eyes flashed in her direction. Bill just put the cup to his lips and drank. Les looked down at the table, pouring a glass of water for her. She sat down. "What are you two up to? You look so guilty. Were you talking about me?"

"Guilty as charged," Bill said. "Just was telling Les what a good influence you've been on me."

"Good thing you play blackjack and not poker," Crystal said. "You're a terrible liar."

Penny entered with the people who were at the door, but it wasn't whom everyone expected. Trailing behind her were Max and a woman in a business suit. Everyone at the table just stared, surprised to see all of them at the Oasis together.

Penny said, "Max, I think you know everyone here. Everyone, this is Max's lawyer Amanda." She had long, flowing black hair parted just off to the left, falling down on both sides of her shoulders. The four-inch heels she was wearing, which extended her to six-foot seemed like an odd choice considering she was with Max. One would think she would downplay the height differential, not accentuate it. But watching her eyes and mannerisms as Penny introduced her to the others, it was obvious she was all about power and control regardless of whom she was with. Penny said, "Les, Max says he has a business proposal to discuss."

Les slid his chair back to stand. Max pushed out his palm. "No, don't get up. Keep yourself comfortable. Apologies for coming unannounced, but I really wanted to present this in person. If another time is better, we can come back, or meet at my office if you prefer."

"Now is good. We just finished," Les said, feeling both curiosity and skepticism. "Please have a seat."

Max pointed at the stack of cups on the counter. "May I? With this weather lately, I need to remind myself to take in water any chance I get."

Les acquiesced with a wave of the hand. Max plucked two cups from the stack on the counter, and he and Amanda sat at the table. Amanda removed a legal pad and pen and manila folder with the label "Oasis Mission Proposal" across the tab.

Penny, Bill, and Crystal looked at each other, unsure whether to stay or go. Les answered the question for them. "These guys are part of the team here. I'd like them to stay if that's OK."

"The more, the merrier as far as I'm concerned," Max said, pouring a cup of water for himself and Amanda, and topping off the others as well. "Not the first time we've all sat around a table together. Of course this one is quite different, but I hope it has the potential to be just as profitable." The others were silent, just curiously studying Max. He said, "I hear you're having some operational issues here."

Les said, "Things have been better, but we're getting by. People are getting fed. Beds are getting filled."

"Of course. I'm sorry. I didn't mean to imply..." Max hesitated. "Let me start again. I should've said, I'm having some operational problems and hoping you might be able to help me." Max's different choice of words flipped the atmosphere from defensive to receptive. He said, "Several months back, I moved my operation to the old Western Hotel on Fremont. Since then, I've been plagued by two problems: I have too much space and not enough workers to fully utilize the space I am using. I'm not sure when your lease is up here, but I know rents are rising fast and will probably be double or triple what you're paying now. My thinking is, what if you were to move the Oasis to the Western? I have hundreds of unused rooms, a kitchen, and ample dining capacity. We could be up and running in no time. Truth be told, a hotel is probably better suited for what you're doing than what I'm using it for, but I think we could really complement each other and maximize the use of the space."

Les waited patiently for his turn, or at least for Max to take a breath and give Les a chance to pose the big question that he couldn't get past. He said, "If I can't afford this place, what makes you think I can afford space at your place, which is in even a higher rent district? I need to move farther away, not right into the middle of the action."

"That's the beauty of this," Max said. "I'll be able to keep your rent the same or maybe even lower it. You'll get better facilities in a better location at a better price. How many people can you accommodate here, thirty to thirty-five?"

"Forty," Bill said proudly, unable to stay out of the conversation. Like most people at the table, it was pretty obvious he didn't like Max, and he certainly didn't trust him either.

"Impressive," Max said. He motioned to Amanda to distribute what was in the folder. "Apologies for having only one copy." Amanda slid the drawing of the proposed changes across to Les. The others crowded around to see. Max pointed to the left side of the schematic. "You can see, our initial plan is to allocate fifty of the rooms on the Ninth-Street side of the hotel for mission guests. Each room will have two beds and its own bathroom. The kitchen area will be here." He drew a circle with his finger in another area of the drawing. "And the dining area for up to a hundred people here. So depending on how many people you decide to put in each room, you'll be able to serve anywhere between 25 and 150 percent more each night."

Crystal spoke up. "So what's in it for you? You have to be getting something out of it or you wouldn't be doing it."

Max was not unnerved by everyone's reluctance and distrust. He seemed to feed on it. Sitting back in his chair, he folded his hands on the table, rotating person to person as he spoke, even though the others weren't really part of the discussion. "Fair point," he said. "All good deals, if they are going to sustain, need to be win-win. As I mentioned, you'll get more and better than what you have, and I'll get additional tax breaks for subsidizing the mission, and potentially a solution to my second problem of not having enough people. Most of your guests don't have jobs, correct? What if we could give them not just food and a place to stay, but also a job? It would be a huge step toward independence."

Bill said, "I see what you're doing. You just want a cheap, live-in workforce."

Amanda stepped in. "Not at all. The workers would be employed and paid the same as other workers. They would just have a shorter commute."

"Obviously the employment option will not work for all of the guests," Max said. "It'll just be for those who have shown promise and consistency. Those who are successful will serve as examples to others. Just imagine as word travels that there's a place that will provide food and shelter and work for people to get back on their feet. Think of the good we could do."

Everyone was quiet. Amanda removed a document three-quarters of an inch thick from the folder and passed it to Les. "Here's the proposed contract that outlines all the details. Feel free to have another lawyer look it over and contact me, or I'm happy to sit down with you and go through, point by point, and answer any questions."

Max said, "I know we haven't had the most positive interactions in the past, and I'll take the blame for that and admit part of my motivation in this is to go in a new direction. I could outsource my production to a remote location, sell the building or the entire operation, and live a life of leisure, but I don't want that. I want to be part of what I've built and share the benefits with the community that provided the opportunities."

Les picked up the contract and flipped through the edge of the pages with his thumb. "I appreciate you bringing this proposal to me. I'm sure you can understand I'll need some time to go through the details."

Amanda took a business card from her purse and placed it in front of Les. "As I said, if you or your representative would like to discuss any changes or questions, please don't hesitate to contact me."

"Take all the time you need." Max stood and walked around the table to Les. "I'm not trying to sell you or asking you to trust me. It's all there in black and white. This is a good deal for both of us. Think of it like blackjack. We're not playing against each other. We're playing against the house. We can both win."

They all exchanged good-byes, and Max and Amanda showed themselves out. Everyone sat in silence, staring at the documents on the table.

Crystal looked over at Penny. "Did you know anything about this?"

"Me?" Penny raised her eyebrows, her tone escalating as well. "How would I be involved?"

Crystal said, "I don't know. Him knowing the place has been struggling, the timing of their arrival right when we were finishing, you volunteering to get the door, and your history of meddling all just fit together into a pretty hard-to-swallow coincidence."

"I wish I had thought of this," Penny said. "This seems like a great opportunity."

Les said, "It doesn't matter where it came from. Just as long as it's here."

"And that it's legit," Bill said. "Do you trust him? It just seems too good to be true."

Les stacked the drawing on top of the contract. "I guess we'll find out. I'll go through and run the numbers to see if it can work, and have an attorney look over the legal aspects. I should probably try to get a hold of Martin too, if I even can. He gave me full legal authority to make all decisions, but he started this place and ran it for twenty years. Just would feel wrong to up and move it without him knowing anything about it."

Penny said, "Well let us know if you need any help. I'd be happy to ask my lawyer in St. Louis to have a look."

Les smiled at her. "Thank you. I appreciate that. You all do so much for me already." He looked over at Bill. "Your son is an attorney too, isn't he?"

Bill nodded slowly. "He is, but I haven't talked to him since Darlene passed, and we didn't exactly leave things on such good terms. But I'll call him if you need me to."

"No that's OK," Les said. "There are plenty of other lawyers. I just thought if you were talking that might be the easiest option."

Chapter Fifty

Date: Monday, August 4, 2014

Dow Jones Open: 16,493.72

What Max had failed to mention in his pitch to Les and the others was his additional motivation for relocating the Oasis to the Western. Of course the tax benefits, extra labor source, and giving back to the community were legitimate reasons, and it wasn't like he had nefarious intentions of some kind. But a big factor was also the publicity it would generate. Not so much in the direct favor for his brand, but more in how he could use the positive public perception as leverage with McDonald's. The contract he had with them was clear, and he had failed. He had committed to producing 4.5 million units by June 30, and came in well shy of the mark. There was no arguing that.

His failure meant McDonald's had the upper hand, and that was without them knowing he was leveraged to the hilt and needed the deal to avoid bankruptcy. He probably could've negotiated a new deal based on the inventory they had finished, but it most likely would've been for less money and had more restrictions that further weakened his position. When he renegotiated, he needed a play that would tilt the game back in his favor. He needed to show them an ace, a strong enough move that the mere threat would force McDonald's to stand despite having the odds in their favor. They all knew McDonald's had the better hand. He just needed to convince them that they had more to lose and that their chance of losing was real.

The only opportunity for an advantage that Max had was in the court of public opinion. If he fought them corporation against corporation, he would lose because, well, they were McDonald's, and also because the contract was in their favor. Big corporations like theirs gobbled up businesses like his every day. On top of that, no one outside either of the companies really would care one way or the other. To the public, it would be just another billionaire arguing with a millionaire over more money than most people would ever see in their lifetimes.

With McDonald's being such a behemoth, no amount of charity or community service on their part could change the public's perception. Any good they did, they should because they have so much, and what they did do still probably wasn't enough. Any favorable situation they had over another, regardless of how legal or just, was simply another example of their greed and abuse of power. Max Doler Industries, on the other hand, was relatively unknown. He could portray himself as the scrappy upstart, a company just trying to get by and help the community along the way. The beauty of his plan was that once McDonald's saw his face card ace and the threat of negative publicity was real, much like the down card under an ace in a potential blackjack hand, it didn't matter what the card actually was; it only counted that McDonald's believed it was a strong enough card to beat them if he played it.

Max developed an elaborate strategy and communication plan to change the image of his company from the widely successful international seller of the Lapkin, Max Doler Industries, to the community-focused Max Doler Investing. When he first launched the company, he had used his image and personality to market and sell the Lapkin, but over time, after spending several hundred thousand on a high-dollar consulting firm to create a new marketing and branding strategy, he had distanced himself from the company image. With the new more innocuous MDI brand, he was behind the scenes rather than leading the charge. The consulting firm suggested by putting the products first, they would set the company up for more long-term success as he phased out of the business over time. Their contention was that if he was MDI and he pulled out of the business to focus on other interests, there would be nothing remaining. But Max was learning that people didn't care just about products, they cared about individuals, and if he didn't give them a reason to care, there would be no long term.

The first major action after the name change and the marketing and advertising campaign necessary to promote the change was the relocation of the Oasis to the Western. And it wasn't so much the physical move that was important, it was the press release that was drafted well before the move for Max to take to his meeting with McDonald's.

In the meeting, Max acknowledged upfront his failure to produce only 3.5 of the 4.5 million units, citing labor issues. It was another move he had learned early in his life: point out your own failures first and take away the opponent's ammunition. With the problem stated and out of the way, he transitioned to the solution by sharing the projections of how the deficit would be made up with an additional 333 thousand every month in addition to the million already promised.

The McDonald's team consisted of Jesse Cash, their chief brand and strategy officer, and Vicky Case, senior VP of product development, and several underlings whose sole purpose was to watch and learn. They all listened attentively to Max's presentation. Max could see restrained anxiousness in their eyes; they were just waiting for a chance to pounce. What they didn't realize was that Max had stacked the deck. He already knew their cards and the ones coming off the top.

After Max had given them the bait, he paused his delivery. He was by no means done talking yet. He was just giving them the opportunity to make their first anticipated play. Vicky jumped at the chance to finally speak. "Well Max, as usual, that's certainly an impressive presentation. It's really unfortunate that you weren't able to meet the quota and deadline as agreed. We know how difficult staffing challenges can be. But the bottom line is that you didn't honor your side of the contract, and if we were willing to renegotiate—and I'm not saying we are, but if we did—why should we believe you can produce one-point-three million in a month when you couldn't do a million before?"

"I'm glad you asked that, Vicky," Max said, ready to make his next move. "Definitely a valid question and one we put a lot of thought into." Max flipped to the next slide, titled Recovery Plan. "One of the exciting moves we have planned to help shore up our labor issues and elevate the awareness of what we're doing in the community is to relocate an existing homeless mission to an unused portion of our facility. We believe the combination of the mission guests who are ready to re-enter the workforce, plus the informal and formal publicity we'll get to attract new employees, will enable us to easily meet our employment needs and run all three lines for three shifts to meet our elevated production goals." He nodded to Amanda, who passed out copies of the new proposed facility and a draft of the press release. "We haven't announced this to the public yet, and before we do, we want to get your input."

Since branding was Jesse's main focus, he immediately read the press release. Vicky, still in attack mode and ready to turn Max's failure to their advantage, just glanced at the drawing and ignored the press release. She said, "While what you're proposing is a great and noble gesture, we're losing focus on the core issue, which is that you have failed to deliver as promised. We had a rollout plan based on 4.5 million units. If we're under that, we'll have to rework our plans, risking successful delivery to our stores. All this additional work and risk is going to cost us. I'm afraid the only way we could even consider renegotiating is at a lower price per unit. I'll have to discuss with the team and get back to you, but I'm thinking it will be somewhere around ten cents cheaper, at $1.40 per unit."

When preparing for the meeting, Max had run three scenarios. He thought McDonald's might go for as much as fifteen cents or as few as five, with the ten as the middle ground. That reduction meant for the 7.5 million units to be produced over the full term of the contract, their revenue would drop from $11.25 million to $10.5 million, approximately 7 percent. Sacrificing $750,000 to make over $10 million wasn't unreasonable. Max knew that, and Vicky certainly did too. The problem for Max was that the margins were already slim, and he knew that it wasn't just about the 7.5 million units. It was also about all the ones potentially after. If he set the price now at $1.40, that would be the starting point for all future negotiations. It wasn't just about what he would lose on this deal, but on all future ones. Once the price had been lowered, it would be an uphill battle to increase it going forward. The estimate to update the facility, relocate the Oasis, and subsidize the operation was only $225,000, much cheaper than reducing the price per unit, and with the additional labor and publicity associated with the Oasis relocation, they at least had a chance to meet the increased production numbers.

Max listened to Vicky intently, although there was nothing unexpected in her words. He was really just waiting for Jesse to finish reading the press release. Because Max's leverage was based on how the McDonald's brand would be perceived, he knew it would be Jesse, not Vicky, making the decision. Once Jesse looked up from the press release, Max interjected. "While I appreciate your offer to keep the deal by reducing the price per unit, I think we have to look past the dollars and cents. You can see in the draft of the press release that we give our partnership with McDonald's recognition as a driving influence for why we are able and want to relocate the mission. With all the positive work you do around the world, you are a shining beacon to smaller companies like us, inspiring us to do more and be more in our communities. Our margins on the Lapkin are already extremely thin. If we were to cut them further, we wouldn't be able to make this move and help those in need of help. While I understand you will incur additional costs in revising and adjusting the rollout schedule, won't you make that up in the positive press you'll get supporting us in this plan?" Max was careful not to mention the negative publicity they might get if they didn't. He didn't want his pitch to come across like an ultimatum. If they felt backed into a corner, they would fight without regard to cost or collateral damage, if for no other reason than just to prove they were in control. Max said, "We're not asking for any additional money than what we previously agreed to, just redistributing the volume over the time period."

At that point there was no was no reason to flip over rest of the cards and see who actually had the best hand. Max had already won. Vicky didn't want to admit it yet, because she wanted to go back to her boss with the $750,000 profit. Jesse was more than happy to back away from the table with exactly what they started with, plus the additional publicity for the brand. He leaned over and whispered to Vicky. They went back and forth a few times, then sat back in their chairs.

Jesse said, "At McDonald's we believe in being active in our communities and encouraging our partners to do the same. Provided you would be open to some suggestions on the verbiage of the press release, we fully support your efforts and are open to revising the contract to accommodate."

After they hammered out the terms and the McDonald's contingent had left, Max exited the meeting room feeling as good as he could remember. The past month had been busy with Les accepting the deal and relocating the Oasis to the Western and ramping up the production to meet the new targets.

All three lines of the second shift hummed along; forklifts scooped, carted, and stacked pallets of boxes of completed product ready for shipment; and through the glass wall separating the factory from the mission, he could see mission guests finishing up their evening meal.

He walked toward the door to the dining area, which also served his workers as well. In addition to the obvious cost savings, Max wanted his workers interacting with the mission guests as much as possible. In that way, they would be role models and examples of the opportunities available to the guests. It was also why he insisted on the glass wall between the factory and the mission areas. He wanted both sides to always be able to see the fine line between the two worlds and how easily one could cross over, forward or backward.

Stopping for a moment, Max looked across the production floor then back at the dining area. Les and Bill were sitting at a table talking to three men while they ate. At another table, Penny assisted two women filling out job applications. For the first time in months, he relaxed, feeling like he was finally on the other side of the problem. With the positive press and buzz they had already received in July, announcing the Oasis relocation and the first group of Oasis benefactors starting employment, they were able to have all three lines running for the first two shifts, and one of the lines running for the third shift. Production was still estimated to come in under the 1.3 million target, but with all the good publicity and the positive trend, he knew McDonald's wouldn't push back. In a few weeks, when an additional line would be operational during the third shift, they would be able to correct the deficit and meet the promised quota by the end of the month. By the beginning of September, they would have enough employees to run the last remaining line during the third shift, so for the first time, the facility would be operating at full capacity. The forecasts showed they would not only easily meet the McDonald's target, but they'd also be able to start accepting outside orders again and fill those on backorder.

Dow Jones Close: 16,569.28

Chapter Fifty-One

Date: Wednesday, September 10, 2014

Dow Jones Open: 17,016.05

Crystal was living up to her end of the agreement for the free room and board with Bill. She was staying clean and working full-time at the Oasis. Throughout the negotiation and subsequent construction and relocation of the Oasis, she noticed the relationship between Max, Les, Bill, and Penny seemed to be strengthening. They were slowly warming to him as he followed through on, often far exceeding, everything he promised. Crystal, however, still didn't trust him and avoided him as much as possible. When the others persuaded her to be more open, urging her that he had changed, she said, "I've seen the real him. People like that don't change. Just wait. He'll want something at some point." What they didn't realize was that he had already got what he wanted when he salvaged the McDonald's contract at the original price. They had already given him a great deal. He was merely trying to give back.

It wasn't like she was completely blind to the good he had done. She recognized that the Oasis's transition from the Arts District to the Western had been seamless, and Max was the main reason for the success. He had fulfilled his commitment to build out the facility at the Western with all new equipment: beds, kitchen appliances, dining tables, an office and live-in suite for Les, and even a van to replace the old truck. All of which were desperately needed because, working there, she knew firsthand that the stuff at the Oasis was well past its expiration date. Replacing everything also allowed no disruption in service. They were able to close the Arts District location after breakfast on August 1 and open for dinner that evening at the Western. Despite continually reminding the guests at the Oasis and posting signs all over and around the old location, a line still formed each morning and evening outside the door. To make sure everyone was looked after, Les had Bill or Crystal drive there every day and scoop up any stragglers in the van to bring them to the new location. Each day the number dwindled, and after a week, the van was coming back empty, so they stopped.

For continuity, they all agreed it was best to keep the Oasis name, with the addition of "at the Western," to distinguish it from its previous location. With all the publicity they received, there was some confusion exactly what type of place the Oasis at the Western was. Crystal had answered the phone on more than one occasion for people wanting to make reservations at what the callers assumed was a new resort property in the downtown area. Les didn't change the legal and nonprofit structure. He was still the sole shareholder. Max didn't even want to be part of the management team or on the board, which surprised Crystal because she expected him to want to have his greedy paws all over it. But he really did keep his distance. He was simply the property owner, leasing the space to the Oasis for a paltry $2,500 per month, and also a major donor.

On this particular evening Crystal was at the sink, scrubbing a pot from dinner. She wore capri jeans and a white apron that covered her front from her neck to her knees. Her gray T-shirt underneath was pulled up and knotted around her waist, exposing the small of her back from behind. A wide, white turban headband held back her thick, black hair bouncing in all directions as she sang "Rolling in the Deep" by Adele, pretending the spray nozzle was a mic. "Baby, I have no story to be told. But I've heard one—" She felt someone watching her. Glancing over her shoulder, she noticed Max behind her by the food serving line. Startled, she dropped the pot into the sink. "Geez, you scared me. I didn't hear you come in." She picked up the pot and continued rinsing it, this time in silence.

"Don't stop singing on account of me," Max said. He had on a seersucker suit with a white shirt and red tie. "That was beautiful. Who was that?"

Crystal put the pot in the drying rack and started on a new one, her back again to Max. "It was Adele."

"Never heard that one before. Guess I'm out of touch with what's popular."

"That song came out four years ago," Crystal said. Her head remained down, her arm buried inside another large pot.

"Sounds like I'm worse off than I thought." Max fetched a bottle of water from the cooler and walked over to the counter so he was at least talking to her side and not her back. "Can I give you a hand? I could at least dry or something."

"No, I can manage. I'm almost finished. Wouldn't want you to mess up your fancy suit anyway." She rinsed the pot and stacked it next to the other one on the counter. "You know, you really shouldn't creep around spying on people, even if you own the place."

"I'm sorry. I didn't mean to surprise you," Max said. "I was just taken aback by your singing. Wasn't aware you had those kind of pipes."

"Well, now you are." Finished with the pots, Crystal took the stopper out of the sink and let the water drain. She removed a towel tucked into her back pocket, dried one of the pots, and put it away, moving around Max like he was just another piece of furniture.

Max said, "You know, I'm not such a bad guy if you get to know me."

"Never said you were." Crystal whisked by him to retrieve the other pot.

"Well, what is it, are you embarrassed by what happened between us before?"

"Me? Embarrassed?" She laughed, shaking her head. "Typical. You should be the one embarrassed."

"Well, I'm different now. I've changed. We both have."

Crystal stopped on her way back to the sink, turning and facing him for the first time. Regardless of how hard she tried, even in this environment, with him in a nice suit and knowing all the good he had done for Les, she couldn't see past the drunk, obnoxious asshole she had experienced in the club so many times. "No, that's where you're wrong," she said. "We haven't changed. We're still the same people. We're just doing different things."

"But good things," Max said, widening his eyes. "That has to count for something."

He looked sincere, but Crystal had seen people fake it before. She said, "I think it's great what you've done here, and how you helped Les and all the people who need the Oasis, but I'm sure you're getting more out of it than what you put into it. People like you always do. Just like there has to be a reason why you're talking to me right now. It can't be just because you want me to like you and us to be friends. So why don't you save us both a lot of time and get to the point. What do you want from me?"

Max didn't respond. He just stood and stared.

Crystal said, "What, no witty comeback? No counter move to regain control?"

Max emptied his lungs, taking a long, slow breath to refill them. "You're right. I should just be honest with you. I heard what happened at Dino's and with the show and with your mom."

"Thought you said you didn't know I could sing! So you're a liar now, too. Not a very good start."

Max's voice rose in frustration. "God! Will you just be quiet for a second and let me speak? I wasn't lying. I did know you could sing, but I had no clue that you were so good. I just want to help you if I can."

"And there it is. I knew you were building to something. No, thanks. My performing days are over." Crystal folded the towel and placed it on the counter. She untied the water-soaked apron and tossed it in the laundry bin at the end of the counter. Noticing Max's eyes drop to her bare midsection, she untied the knot in her shirt and let it fall to her waist. "If you know about Dino's, then you know how things turned out the last time someone tried to help me with all that."

Max said, "I'm not interested in helping you perform. I want you to help other people." This time it was Crystal who was quiet. The anger and tension in her face faded. She tilted her head to the left and stared at Max curiously. He said, "Almost a third of this building is still not being used. I could, of course, convert it to offices and rent it out, but there's already enough available commercial space downtown. I want to continue what we started here and make it more for the community. I was thinking maybe converting the rooms to classrooms and offering some courses for my employees and people in the community. When I was talking to Penny about this, she told me about your singing and dancing and how your mother was a music teacher for preschool kids. I thought maybe we could put in a dance studio and have some sort of music-related classes. Was thinking you might be interested in teaching, or at least helping set it up. What do you say? Are you interested?"

Crystal's first thought was of her mom and how many kids she had helped, most of all her, over the years. Crystal had been so focused on getting herself healthy that she hadn't thought about much else other than staying sober and her responsibilities at the Oasis. Her performing days might be over, but that didn't mean she had to completely shut down that side of herself. But this was Max she was talking to. Nothing was ever as it seems with him. She looked back in his direction. His earnest demeanor softened her further. She knew she wasn't, and probably wouldn't ever be, completely cured, but she was feeling better. At some point, she would have to find more than the Oasis. His offer was just too much, too soon, though. She said, "I don't know. I think it's best if I just focus on me right now. But thanks for the opportunity."

Later that evening on the bike ride home with Bill, Crystal pedaled up alongside of him as they rode down Carson behind Container Park. She said, "Max came to me earlier with a pretty crazy idea."

Breathing heavily, Bill downshifted into a lower gear. "Oh yeah? What was that?"

Crystal slowed her pedaling to make it easier on him. She said, "He wants to use some of the available space at the Western for music and dance classes for kids."

"Well that doesn't sound very crazy at all. Don't think there's anything like that downtown."

They stopped at the traffic light waiting to cross Las Vegas Boulevard. Crystal stepped off the pedals and turned toward Bill. "The crazy part is that he wants me to teach them. Can you imagine that? Me! A teacher!"

"I think that sounds amazing." The light turned green, but both of them stayed where they were, straddling their bikes. "Wasn't your mom a teacher?"

"She was, but you know what she wasn't?" Crystal said. "A recovering drug addict, alcoholic, former stripper."

Bill said, "I hate when you say things like that. Is that what you think of yourself?"

Another bike rider heading in the same direction swerved around them, staring as he passed, complaining about them blocking the bike lane. They both walked their bikes over to the curb. Crystal said, "I am all those things though."

"But you're so much more," Bill said. "Why just focus on the negatives?"

Crystal didn't have an answer. She motioned at the light, which turned green again. "We should keep moving."

They rolled forward in silence, crossing Las Vegas Boulevard and continuing west on Carson. The sun was dipping behind the high-rise buildings that lined Third and Fourth Streets ahead, covering the road with long shadows. It was Bill who sped up to ride alongside Crystal this time. He said, "The only thing crazy about that idea is that you're considering not doing it. I know you and Max have got history, but like him or hate him, he is a damn good businessman with a pretty amazing track record. Do you think he would ever suggest something that would lose money or make him look bad?"

Crystal drew quiet again and just pedaled. They turned left on Third Street heading south to the Juhl. Dwarfed by the Regional Justice Center, the street was in complete shade and ten degrees cooler. She thought about what Bill had said. He did have a good point. Max would never put his reputation in jeopardy. She said, "I do miss singing and dancing, and my mom used to have me help her with her classes all the time, so I do have some experience. Maybe it's not so crazy after all."

Dow Jones Close: 17,068.71

Chapter Fifty-Two

Date: Wednesday, September 17, 2014

Dow Jones Open: 17,131.01

The drive to Los Angeles was the first time Penny had really been out of Vegas since moving there. She had hiked several times in Red Rock Canyon, done a loop around Lake Mead, and paid a visit to the Hoover Dam, but after doing those, she turned around and drove home. For this trip she wanted to leave and know she wasn't coming back that night. She needed different faces and different spaces. That was the main reason she drove. She could've easily taken the hour flight in the morning, met with Damon and the producer he had lined up, and flown home that evening, but she wouldn't have felt like she was actually away. She wanted to experience every minute of the five-hour drive, to see the landscape change from city to desert to mountain and back to city.

The onslaught of signs and billboards for the Mad Greek Café plastered along Interstate 15 and her pulsing head from not sleeping the night before forced a stop in Baker for a gyro and a Greek coffee. She should've known better than varying from her eating routine. Both ran right through her, triggering another stop in Barstow. Winding around a curve through the San Bernardino Mountains, her decision to substitute coffee for sleep caught up with her. Mountains towered on all sides. Beyond the guardrail to the left was only empty space. Vertigo overtook her. She rolled down the windows and slowed to forty miles per hour. The dizziness lingered. She navigated to the right lane. At least if she was going to pass out, crashing into the berm would be better than taking out the surrounding traffic. Cursing her decision to drive, she took long, slow breaths until she descended into Rancho Cucamonga and was safely on the long straightaway through the eastern suburbs. The closer she got, the more nervous she became about her meeting with Damon—the main reason for the insomnia the night before. She needed to get back to work and do something meaningful. She had been reluctant to get married because she never wanted to sacrifice her career. She had resented and blamed Alec for not supporting her after the loss of the baby, causing the affair with Fritjof and the loss of her job. Les helped her realize that it was her that gave it all away. To get her life back, she needed her career back.

Despite the importance of the meeting, when traffic slowed to a crawl on I-10 and she had to call Damon to say she would be late, she was secretly hoping he would suggest postponing it, just to have a little more time to prepare. But of course he had planned on her being late and had scheduled the meeting two hours later than what he had told her. With the traffic, the estimated drive time was increasing toward five and a half hours, giving her plenty of time to get in the right mindset and also to think about what she would say to the others.

She knew Max would gladly be on board. Anything that promoted him or his business that he didn't have to pay for was a windfall. Les would be pragmatic about the idea, balancing the benefits for everyone along with those of the Oasis. As long as everyone else agreed, he would be in. Bill would support her unless Crystal opposed, then he would probably stick up for Crystal. So it would all really come down to Crystal, and Penny knew how she would respond. That's also why she was so nervous. Crystal would never go for it. But the chances of CBS going for the idea were even slimmer, so Penny decided to worry about Crystal on the drive home.

The original plan was for Penny to check into the InterContinental in Century City, and Damon would swing by and pick her up. From there, they would head across town to the CBS offices in Studio City. But her delay thwarted that plan, and she had to go straight to Damon's office on Avenue of the Stars, which was conveniently around the corner from her hotel but still thirty minutes away from the Studio City meeting.

She pulled into the U-shaped drive in front of the towering office building. Ferraris, Porsches, and Range Rovers filled the lanes. It resembled the valet area of a luxury hotel rather than an office building. She loved her BMW 3 Series, but it didn't measure up to the other cars, much like she didn't really compare to the high-end talent that probably had driven the cars here. She waved off the attendant, informing him she was merely picking up. He directed her to a yellow area along the curb. While waiting, she rooted out her makeup and did her best to hide the lack of sleep and being captive in the car for most of the day.

Damon walked up and tugged on the passenger-side door handle. He was dressed stylishly, as usual, in an all chocolate suit and shirt with a champagne tie. Penny dropped the makeup into her purse and threw it into the backseat. Rolling down the passenger window, she said, "Come over on this side. You're going to have to drive. I need to change on the way." She sprung from the car, gave Damon a quick hug, and climbed into the back.

Damon slid behind the wheel and maneuvered the car onto Avenue of the Stars.

Penny rummaged through her bag for an outfit that wouldn't be wrinkled. "Looking at those cars, business must be good."

"Oh those aren't my clients," Damon said. "My clients have to park in the garage." His eyes occasionally flashed in the rearview mirror to connect with Penny's.

"Like me, you mean." Penny unbuttoned her pants and inched them down around her hips, catching his eyes in the mirror. She stopped, flipping her hand up at the mirror. Damon angled the mirror toward the roof of the car to give her privacy. She slipped the jeans off and tossed them on the floor. "So what do you think our chances are?"

Damon said, "Actually I'd say pretty good. The senior producer for *CBS Sunday Morning* I pitched the idea to liked it enough to set this meeting with the executive producer. Hopefully this one goes better than the last meeting we had." He turned his head to the right to show the smile on his face.

"Eyes on the road, buster." Penny pulled up her black pencil skirt and fastened it around her waist. "On the drive here, I about passed out from a panic attack, so it could get exciting." She replaced her T-shirt with a sleeveless lime-green top and cinched a thin black belt around her waist to accent her figure. "OK, you can have your mirror back."

Damon readjusted the mirror, smiling and nodding his approval at the transformation. "In all seriousness, are you sure you want to risk such a big project on people you just met and, well, to be frank, who have proven to be unreliable?"

"I'm willing to take that chance. I just really need to do something else. You said yourself, you have five sports jobs you could land me in tomorrow." She held up two different earrings to her ears and leaned over, checking to see how they looked in the mirror. "I just don't want to go backward. This is my break to branch out and do something more serious." She grabbed the black suede, pointed-toe pumps next to her, leaned up between the seats, and climbed through.

They winded along Coldwater Canyon Drive to Ventura, planning the strategy for the meeting, deciding who would say what, discussing the timeline to deliver if there was interest, and determining the type of deal they would push for. Despite all the stress from the trip, the hurrying up and slowing down in traffic, the freshening up and changing in the car, they actually arrived ready and five minutes early. An assistant to the executive producer greeted them in the lobby and showed them to the meeting room.

Penny was sweating profusely under the black jacket she had slipped on over her sleeveless shirt. She wanted to take it off, but was afraid the sweat rings under her arms would be visible. Damon sat in the middle of the long rectangular table facing the door. Penny paced behind him. Damon pulled out the chair next to him. "Have a seat and relax, or pretend to be relaxed. Remember they're buying you even more than the story."

"Sorry. Guess I'm just a little out of practice." Penny sat down next to him. She took one of the napkins next to the tray of pastries and fruit in the center of the table and dabbed first under her left arm then her right. The CBS contingent, consisting of three people, entered. Penny subtly crumpled the napkin and tucked it under her right thigh on the seat. Damon rose to greet them. Penny followed him around the table for the introductions.

From CBS was *Sunday Morning*'s executive producer, Lynn Chang. Penny recognized Lynn from her days as a correspondent on the nightly news back when Penny was in college studying journalism. Now in her fifties, Lynn had gray streaks in her silky-black hair, but she still had the penetrating stare and high cheekbones that always found a way to draw the truth out of people. Along with Lynn was Nila Rogers, a senior producer for the show. Based on the awkward professionalism between Damon and Nila, Penny thought it might've been more than the strength of the idea that secured the meeting. Nila was a natural beauty, the type that actually had to work to conceal it. She sported black-framed wayfarer eyeglasses, had her dishwater-blond hair pulled back in a ponytail, and wore minimal makeup. Her tailored black two-piece suit hugged the curves of her slender six-foot frame while covering her from shoulder to ankles, except for the small triangle of exposed skin under her neck from the single open button at the top of her white blouse. The other person was introduced only as "Lynn's assistant," and she slunk off to the side to take notes.

After the introductory chitchat, each person made a small plate of food, and the two sides took their seats across from each other. Lynn transitioned the conversation to the intended business. "I have to say, when Nila first pitched the idea to do a Vegas piece, I wasn't interested. Vegas is always changing but it never changes. When she told me it was about rebirth and second chances, though, I warmed to the idea. Why don't you tell me more about it?"

Damon looked at Penny and nodded. She steadied herself, keeping her back straight, shoulders pulled back, and arms at her side, just like she was on camera.

"The title is Community Money. It's a personal interest story about four people who moved to Las Vegas and how their lives became intertwined, and they learn to help each other. There's a former policeman who retired from New Jersey only to lose his wife and find himself completely alone in a foreign city; a talented singer and dancer who relocated from LA to perform in a show and had the show close before opening, forcing her to turn to stripping to make ends meet; a Catholic priest who left the Church to take over a homeless mission and was forced to rely on gambling to keep the doors open because of rising costs and shrinking donations; and a successful entrepreneur who overextended himself wanting to keep his business in Vegas, and as result faced bankruptcy."

Nila said, "And what's your connection to these people? What makes you the one to tell this story?"

"I guess you could say that I'm just like they are," Penny said. "I've witnessed it all happen firsthand. I met them at a blackjack table shortly after I moved to Vegas and have watched it all unfold."

Lynn said, "This is a little outside your style of reporting isn't it? I've seen some of your clips from St. Louis, and your background is all sports, correct?"

Penny shifted in her seat, feeling the power of Lynn's gaze directed upon her. "Yes, that's correct. But one of my motivations in coming west is that I want to transition away from sports into more human-interest pieces."

Damon said, "We think this could be the perfect vehicle and platform to launch this new direction."

"It sounds to me that you've forgotten one story, though: your story." Lynn plucked one of the grapes from her plate and popped it into her mouth. "This is about five people, not four. Telling their stories is your own rebirth."

The room fell quiet. Penny mulled Lynn's response. Breaking the silence, Penny said, "Well, I'd prefer to keep myself separate from the story. I don't want to take away from the others."

Lynn shook her head. "But you'd only be telling part of the story that way. You're not just a fly on the wall. You are the story as much as they are. It gives it credibility and integrity and another layer of emotion." Lynn paused, letting her words sink in. "Tell you what, you guys think it over and let us know. If you're willing to tell the complete story, then I think we can work something out."

Damon looked at Penny, who was just staring straight ahead, not responding one way or another. He said, "I think we're open to that. We don't need any more time, do we? Let's just hammer out the details right here. What do you say, Pen?"

Penny looked over at him. She didn't really agree, but she wasn't ready to blow up the deal over it. "Um, yeah, sure. Of course. If that's how you want to do it. I'm totally on board."

"Outstanding." Lynn stood from the table. "I'll leave Nila to work out the details with you. You tell us when you're ready for a camera crew, and we'll send one over. Let's target the rough footage to be done in no later than four weeks, and we tentatively air in eight to twelve weeks. This will tie in well with some other holiday stories."

After Lynn exited the room, Damon, Penny, and Nila went through the standard contract for independent contractors, all the release forms that would be needed from the others, and the production resources available to Penny to develop and execute the segment.

On the way to the car, Penny tossed the keys to Damon. "You can drive back, too. I'm way too excited."

"I'll tell you where I'm driving us—straight to a bar," Damon said, squeezing the key fob to unlock the car. The lights flashed and horn beeped two rows away. "I think this calls for a celebration."

"I'm down for that," Penny said, walking up to the passenger side door. "My only question for you is, how long you been banging her?"

Damon looked across the top of the car at her. "Who? Nila?" Penny smirked back at him. He said, "Is that what you think of me?"

"I saw the way you two were, trying to be all professional but unable to stop looking at each other. How long has it been going on?"

Damon smiled. "Off and on for about six months."

Penny said, "Well make sure you keep it going another few months or at least until the contract is signed."

Dow Jones Close: 17,156.85

Chapter Fifty-Three

Date: Monday, November 3, 2014

Dow Jones Open: 17,390.90

Bill and Les walked underneath the rotating Ruby Slipper and Lady Luck neon signs in the median outside the El Cortez on Fremont East. Les said, "Want to go in for a couple hands? Been a while since we played together." After the move to the Western, Les's free time had shrunk to basically an hour or two per day. He had known with the expanded capacity there would be more work—more cooking, shopping, cleaning—but he also had more help and a lot more donations. All the publicity generated from the relocation and the press release had brought in people looking both for help and to help. The people coming in for assistance wanted more than just a meal and a bed. They had heard they could also get a paycheck. Some of them were ready and most not. The ones that were, it was as simple as helping them fill out an application. Not so much for the others. They really didn't understand why they weren't ready. They needed a lot of coaching and counseling, which took up a lot of time. Most of it was spent delicately explaining why they weren't ready and what could be done to get them ready even though the chances of that were very slim. But this was the part of the job that Les was really enjoying. Sure, it took more time, but it was also more rewarding, despite the low success rate. Fortunately, with the additional volunteers and donations, he had a lot more resources at his disposal. Of course this cut into his gambling time, which meant less cash coming in, but he didn't need the money anymore. He did miss the analysis and strategy of the game, and occasionally got the itch for action, but he knew the game was always there, and if he didn't go today, he could always go another day.

Bill looked up at the white letters spelling *GAMBLING* vertically on the teal sign above the El Cortez entrance on Fremont and Sixth. At night the bulbs along the side blinked, trailing one another, drawing passersby. Today the sign was peacefully pasted against the sky as strings of clouds floated behind. He said, "Nah, it's a nice day. Let's just walk."

They ambled on, passing the block-long collection of bars and restaurants— The Beat, Insert Coins, Therapy, Vanguard, and Park—across Las Vegas Boulevard into the Fremont Street Experience, the five-block entertainment district. Bill pointed up at the ninety-by-fifteen-hundred-foot steel canopy that covered the historic street, now a pedestrian mall. "You know, we were coming here before any of this even existed. You could drive from one end to the next and even park right on the street."

Four zipline riders raced by overhead. Les said, "Now you can glide from one end to the next."

"Hard to believe how quickly it's gone by," Bill said. "After we moved, Darlene and I used to come down here every Sunday for breakfast and to gamble. Don't think I've been down here since."

Two feather-clad showgirls working for tips asked if they wanted a picture. Les smiled, holding out his hand to politely decline. He said to Bill, "Is that what's been troubling you lately? Missing Darlene?"

"Thought it would get easier," Bill said. "Just seems to be getting harder. Not sure what the point is anymore."

They wove around a crowd gathered around Paul Stanley and Gene Simmons lookalikes in full KISS makeup and costumes. Les said, "What do you mean? Look at how much you've helped Crystal, and there's no way I could've kept the mission open and pulled off the move without you."

"But we're past all that. Crystal has been sober for over five months and is stronger by the day. The help and support for the mission is really rolling in now. Penny has her secret project that she won't tell anybody about. Max is, well, he's Max. He's always got something going on. It just seems like now everybody has their thing. Mine was Darlene, and now she's gone."

"Maybe your thing is helping all of us with our things. I think you're underestimating everything you do. None of us would be where we are without you."

They stopped next to a large group of people encircling a contortionist in a straitjacket wrapped in chains, writhing on the concrete as he built the tension for his escape. Bill said, "That's nice of you, and I'm happy that everyone is finding their way. I really am. But in many ways, and I know this is terrible to say, it just makes me feel that much more alone. I hate feeling that I was better off when you were all struggling, and I felt like you needed me. What kind of person does that make me?"

"The normal human kind," Les said. "You lost the most important person in the world to you, and right after that some people needed you, so you pushed all those painful feelings down and helped us. As long as you were helping us, all the other stuff stayed buried. Now that some of that responsibility has been lifted, the pain that you buried is working its way to the surface."

They continued walking, passing Binion's, feeling the cold draft from the air conditioning streaming through the open front. Bill said, "But I was a cop for over thirty years, and I saw more ugliness than anyone should see in five lifetimes. It never bothered me. I was always able to keep things separate, deal with it, and move on. I just can't shake this. Everywhere I go, everything I see, all that I do, I'm reminded of what's not there: Darlene. I feel like my life stopped when hers ended."

"Maybe it's not Darlene at all," Les said.

"Well, it's not the job. I can tell you for sure that I don't miss that one single bit. There hasn't been one day that I woke up and wished I were going to work. It's just, as I'm going through my days, it's like air has been let out of everything around me. Not all of it. Just some, so that everything still has the same shape and coloring, but it's all droopy and dull. I just miss Darlene."

They stopped in front of Glitter Gulch, originally the nickname of the entire street due to the abundance of neon signs. Now it was attached to another low-end strip club. More zipline riders screamed above as the braking system abruptly slowed their trip into the station. Les and Bill looped around to the other side of the street in front of the Golden Nugget and turned back. Les said, "Did you ever consider that it could just be regret?"

"Nonsense," Bill said. "There's nothing more anyone could've done. The doctors said so."

A Leonard Nimoy Spock lookalike walked past, flashing the live long and prosper hand signal. Les nodded at him and turned back to Bill. "Not for Darlene, for Hughie. You could bring him back into your life. Seeing him when you and Darlene renewed your vows and talking to him when she was sick and after she passed unlocked all the old emotion. Instead of dealing with it, you channeled it toward us, but maybe it needs to be directed at him and his family, your family."

Bill bristled at the suggestion. "That's ridiculous. We've both moved on. He doesn't need me at all. We hadn't had any contact for over twenty years, and he turned out great. With the way our last call ended after Darlene passed, I think it's safe to say that it's over for good."

"It's only over if you want it to be," Les said.

A ten-year-old boy with a buzzed head and an oversized tan two-piece suit walked up and handed Bill a flyer that said, *He died for your sins. Will you live for Him?* The boy returned to a man and a woman holding an eight-foot wooden cross with the same two sentences written down and across the upright and transverse pieces.

Bill folded the flyer and tucked it in his pocket. "I guess what I'm saying is that I want it to be over. I'm not angry or upset. I'm just tired. I feel like I've done everything I was meant to do, and it's time."

"Time for what?" Les said. "You don't decide when it's time. That's for God to decide. He chose when to take Darlene. Maybe because you needed to be alone to do what you need to do. As long as Darlene was here, you would focus on her and not what you should be doing. He'll take you when it's time."

"That's what I'm asking. What if I do decide? Will you help me?"

Dow Jones Close: 17,366.24

Chapter Fifty-Four

Date: Thursday, November 6, 2014

Dow Jones Open: 17,491.66

Penny couldn't put it off any longer. The camera and sound crew were scheduled to arrive on Monday to start filming, and she hadn't even told the others about the piece, let alone gotten their permission. At first her excuse for not telling them was she wanted to make sure CBS was interested. Then it was that she wanted to have the script done, so she could show them the story and exactly what each of them would have to do. But each time she checked off a box and eliminated an excuse, others popped up, like, she was waiting for final approval on the script from Nila at CBS, or she couldn't find a convenient time to get everyone together, or she didn't want to burden everyone with extra stress until she knew exactly when the crew would arrive. But after all those things were taken care of, and Nila had just called confirming the start of the shooting on Monday and asking again for the release forms, Penny knew it was time.

Earlier that day Penny had asked the others to meet in the dining area after the dishes were finished and all the guests were settled in for the night. Even after everything they had done together, there were still two cliques. Les, Bill, and Crystal sat at one table, and Max sat alone at another, reading emails on his phone. All three production lines on the factory floor blurred with activity through the glass wall behind them.

Penny kicked things off, saying, "I apologize for being so aloof lately and springing this meeting on you all at the last minute, but we're all so busy these days, it's been tough to find a good time to get everyone together to share this really exciting news." She removed four copies of the ten-page script, titled *Community Money,* from her brown leather shoulder bag and handed a copy to each person. Crystal started reading immediately. The other copies remained on the table in front of the recipients. Penny said, "I must admit I wasn't completely honest with you about my trip to LA last month. I did go and do all the fabulous shopping and R&R stuff I told you about, but I also had a meeting with my agent Damon, who most of you met, and the, uh, well, the producers of the *CBS Sunday Morning* show to pitch them an idea." The reactions to her admission ranged from Max's indifference and continued preoccupation with his phone to Les's curiosity to Bill's confusion. She couldn't get a read on Crystal because all she could see was the top of Crystal's head as she flipped through the script. Penny continued, "The good news is that they offered me a job, or more of an opportunity, really, but it could lead to something more permanent."

The weight of the words finally sunk into Max. He stopped reading the emails and tucked the phone away in his pocket. He said, "Hold on a second. THE *CBS Sunday Morning* show? The one created by Charles Kuralt?"

Penny nodded. "That's the one. I can't believe it myself."

"That's terrific," Les said. "Of course you're going to take it, right?"

Penny looked down at the floor, her voice wavering. "Well, that depends."

Bill said, "On what? Do you have to move to LA?"

Crystal lifted her eyes from script. "No. It depends on whether we'll help her or not." She tossed the script in the center of the table. "The bad news she was referring to before is that the story she has sold is about us."

"That's not true. There really isn't any bad news," Penny said. "It's more of a good news, better news situation."

Bill said, "I don't understand. Why would *CBS Sunday Morning* care about us?"

Penny pulled out a chair and sat down facing the two tables. "It's not just about all of you. It's about me, too, how we all met and came together to help each other."

Max stood and moved over to sit with the others. "I, for one, love the idea."

"Of course you do," Crystal said. "You love anything that puts the Max Doler name out there for free."

Max said, "Easy there, tiger. It's not just my name anymore. It's also the Oasis and Miss C's Music & Dance. Don't be so shortsighted. This isn't just about what you want. Think about it. This could be huge for the school, too. You'll have people lining up to get in."

"I am thinking about it," Crystal said. "Who will want to send their kids to a class taught by a recovering drug-addicted ex-stripper? While that makes for a great story, I don't think that's the best advertising campaign."

Penny scooted her chair to their table and opened the script. "That's what's so great about this and why I gave you all a copy. We control the narrative. We decide what to include and leave out. If you look through the pages, you'll see, yes, I revealed some personal information but nothing bad."

Max said, "You can say whatever you want about me as long as you end with good stuff. People love a comeback, and they always remember what you did last, not first."

Penny interlocked her fingers and held her hands in front of her, pleading with them. "Just promise me, please, that you'll go home tonight and read through the script. If there's anything you don't like, we can change it." She hesitated, waiting for any objections. Max was in for sure, but none of the others seemed totally convinced. No one said anything though, so she continued. "After you read it, if you're OK with what's written, I just need you to sign and return the release form on the last page. The crew is scheduled to arrive on Monday to begin shooting the footage."

"As in four days from now Monday?" Crystal said. "Thanks for all the advance notice."

Les, in his typical measured way, said, "Crystal does has a valid point. It is odd that you've been working on this for a while now, and this is the first time we're hearing about it. We all have so much to do these days. I'm just concerned whether or not we'll have the time and energy for another thing."

"I bet she's been planning this all along," Crystal said. "That's probably why she had us all meet Damon months ago. It wasn't just me auditioning. It was all of us. Like a circus casting. Come meet all my weirdo friends."

"Why do you always have to think the worst?" Penny said. "That meeting with Damon was a legitimate singing audition for you. I was just trying to help you get started and asked the others there for support. All this came up in the past month after the Oasis moved and you accepted the offer to open a studio. I really did want to tell you sooner. Been dying to, actually. I just wasn't sure CBS was going to go for it. Then, when they did, I wanted to get all the details worked out, so you could see exactly what was planned. Honest, I'm only trying to help. If you don't want to do it, don't do it. There's no pressure. If you do it, the crew will be here all next week and will work around your schedules. We'll shoot a lot of video, but the entire piece will be only about four minutes, which will require each of you to be on camera answering questions directly only for sixty seconds or so, and that will be all of us in a group, seated around a blackjack table just like when we met."

"I have no problem taking this home and giving it a read," Bill said. "And I'll support whatever the group wants to do, but I just don't understand what I've done that is so great. I get it for the others. Les has the mission; Crystal, the studio;

Max, the factory; Penny, you have this story. But I'm just a boring retired guy with nothing better to do."

Crystal reached over and put her hand on Bill's. "The fact that you don't see it is what makes you so amazing. You've done more than any of us."

"That's one thing we all can agree on," Les said.

Penny stood up, leaning on the table. "So everyone will withhold judgment and at least have a look?"

Les looked around the table at the others. "I'll be the first to say I'm not comfortable in the spotlight and prefer to be behind the scenes with the Oasis out front, but we do have additional beds to fill and a lot of people in this community that could benefit. If this will help do that and help you all in the process, then I would be selfish to say no."

"You had me at free," Max said. "I just need Amanda to look over the release form before I sign it."

Crystal flopped back in her chair, folding her arms across her chest. "I guess I'll have a look, too, then. I just hope you all recognize that we each have some skeletons in our pasts. If anyone does any digging into our lives, this could all blow up in our faces, and we'll be worse off than before."

"Even if they do find out some of the negative stuff," Max said. "No one cares about rebuttals or retractions. Those stories always get buried."

After the meeting, Penny, knowing Crystal was the tough vote, talked her and Bill into leaving their bikes and taking a ride home. She knew if she could convince Crystal, the others would agree no problem. In the car, Bill sat in the back, insisting Crystal ride in the front seat. Driving up Ninth Street for the short ride to Bill's, Penny said, "So what do you think about doing the story?"

Crystal didn't hold back. "I think I made myself pretty clear before. If you're asking for an immediate answer, I'd have to say no."

"But why?" Penny said. "It can do so much good for all of us."

"You all assume attention is such a positive." She rotated in her seat toward Penny, looking back at Bill, who seemed more than happy to remain quiet. "Do you really want people knowing your business, about Darlene dying, about your son?"

Penny watched Bill in the rearview mirror shrug, lifting his hands at the same time. He said, "I don't really have much to gain and probably even less to lose, so it doesn't really matter to me."

Penny turned her head speaking directly to Crystal. "Let's go upstairs to Bill's and go through it page by page." She pulled the car into an open spot on the Garces St. side of the Juhl. "Anything you don't like we'll change."

"Actually I was hoping you would come up anyway," Bill said. "There's something I want to talk to both of you about." He opened the door and stepped out onto the sidewalk waiting for them. Penny and Crystal remained in the car, just looking at each other, surprised by his request. He had been distant lately and not very talkative at all, so for him to be initiating the dialogue, it had to be something important.

Penny removed her seat belt and turned the car off, speaking back through the open car door. "Of course, Bill. Is everything OK?"

Crystal raised her eyebrows and shook her head at Penny, indicating she didn't know what it was about either. Bill said, "Everything is fine. I just have a favor to ask you both."

They walked in silence into the building and onto the elevator. Penny used the captive environment to work on Crystal about the piece. "So tell me, why are you so skeptical? It really is a great opportunity for the music school."

"Too good, actually." Crystal said. "I don't care how much good Max does, I doubt I'll ever trust him completely, and if I'm being completely honest, I'm not sure I totally believe you either. It's all come up so suddenly. Things just fit together too perfectly, and you always seem to have a hidden agenda."

The elevator doors opened. Exiting into the hallway, Bill dug the keys out of his pocket. He said, "I don't know. I think that might be a little harsh. Penny's heart is always in the right place." He put the key in the door but hesitated before opening it, looking at Crystal. "And it does seem like things are working out pretty well for you. Maybe you just need to trust everyone." Bill opened the door and turned on the light. Penny and Crystal followed him into the apartment.

Penny stopped just inside the doorway in the small foyer area. Bill and Crystal continued into the apartment. Speaking to their backs, Penny said, "No, she's right. There is more. Les knows this. I might as well share it with you as well." She steadied herself. She was so good at hiding her feelings and just delivering what people wanted to hear, she wasn't sure where to begin.

Bill turned back toward her. "Well, come in and sit down. Let's talk."

"No, I think I'll stay right here." Penny remained in the foyer, her voice quivering with vulnerability. Crystal stood next to Bill. Penny said, "The truth is that I need this. All the drinking and carrying on I've been doing, that's not me. I'm completely empty and lost. I need more. I need to work. All I really have is my career."

"I totally get that," Crystal said. "The same thing happened to me when the show got canceled. But why us? Why can't you do a different story?"

"Believe me, I tried. Damon pitched a bunch of other ideas. It was the only one they'd go for. It's this or nothing. The only other option is to go back to the same stuff I was doing before or some stupid radio job. I just can't. I have to move forward."

Bill walked over and hugged Penny. She buried her head in his chest. He said, "Why didn't you just say that from the beginning?"

She turned her head to the side, pressing her cheek against his chest. "I don't know. It's not easy for me to admit I need help. I like to be the one helping. Why do you think I get up in everyone's business?"

Crystal took out the two copies of the script from her purse and tossed them on the kitchen table. She said, "But do you have to blast our lives across national TV to do that?"

Bill released from Penny and turned to Crystal. "I understand your reservations. Things are starting to go well, and you don't want to risk that. But for me, I really don't have much more to lose." He spread his arms, looking around the apartment. "I wouldn't exactly call this a life. I'm just putting in time now."

"Stop it." Penny walked over and grabbed his arm, pulling it down. "You can't honestly believe that."

"It's true. I feel like I'm sleepwalking most days." Bill slumped down into one of the chairs at the table. "The only thing that gets me though is knowing that each day I'm one closer to it all being over."

The downturn in Bill softened Crystal. She said, "So that's why you've been in such a funk lately? I thought you were getting sick of me being here and wanted me to leave."

"Not at all. You can stay as long as you like. My home is your home. You're one of the only bright spots." Bill heaved himself off the chair and walked over to the urn with Darlene's ashes that was perched on the mantel above the fireplace. "Like I said in the car, I do have a favor to ask of you two, though."

"Of course, whatever you need," Penny said, walking over next to him.

Crystal also joined them in the living room. "Now that I'm back on my feet and making money, I can start paying rent and chipping in on the bills."

"No, it's nothing like that. I don't want your money." Bill pulled the sleeve of his sweatshirt over his hand and brushed the thin layer of dust off the urn. "It's just, when I do go, I need someone to make sure my and Darlene's ashes are taken care of. My son will want to bury us back east, but we wanted to stay here in Vegas. Will you do that for me?"

Penny put her arm around Bill. "Of course we will."

Crystal stepped next to Bill in front of the mantle. Putting her arm around him, she leaned her head against his shoulder just like Penny was doing on the other side. "You know I would do absolutely anything for you. But we won't really have much say if your son challenges the decision. I remember my mom's funeral. There's no way anyone could've told me when or how she would be put to rest."

"Don't you worry about that." Bill wrapped his thick arms around both of them. "I can take care of all that in the will."

Crystal pressed the side of her face deeper into his arm. "OK, now let's stop talking about this."

Penny put her hand on Crystal's arm behind Bill's back, squeezing it in fear at the resignation in his voice. She composed herself, using her best soothing newscaster tone, the one she was taught to use when she knew things were not going to be all right, but she had to convince everyone they would be. " Crystal's right," she said. "We all know that's not going to happen for many years down the road."

"You never know." Bill looked over at the urn, pulling them both even closer. "I just want to be prepared."

Dow Jones Close: 17,544.47

Chapter Fifty-Five

Date: Sunday, December 14, 2014

Dow Jones Open: Closed

"Community Money" was scheduled to run on *CBS Sunday Morning* as part of their holiday show focused on giving. The Sunday before it was set to air, Max invited everyone over to his penthouse to watch the final cut of the piece.

In typical Max fashion, the gathering was more than a few friends drinking sodas, huddled around a bowl of popcorn and a bag of potato chips. He had a local restaurant cater the food, hired Birdie on his night off from the Parlour Bar at the El Cortez to be the bartender, and invited a wide assortment of people, ranging from downtown business owners to local media and city politicians. It was definitely overkill for a video that was coming in at four minutes and six seconds, but that was Max. He wanted to create as much buzz as he could leading up to the broadcast, and squeeze as much business and political goodwill as he could out of it. When Penny got there and commented on his "Go big or go home" party planning, Max said, "I went big, and I am home."

While Penny looked quite comfortable mingling, meeting the new people and talking about her work and life before and in Vegas, Bill and Crystal kept to themselves, chatting up Birdie at the bar and grazing around the food table with items like beef heart tartar, shishito peppers, ceviche, and other delicacies, most of which they didn't appear to recognize and probably would've never known the name of if it wasn't for the cards in front of each platter. Crystal was dressed for the occasion, wearing the same black spaghetti-strap dress from the night at Dino's, but she didn't seem too eager to meet anyone new. Bill had on one of his many short-sleeve checked button-downs with khaki pants. He had always been protective of Crystal and never liked crowds himself, so if she wanted to hang around the food, he seemed more than happy to do the same.

When Les arrived, he also looked surprised and overwhelmed by the magnitude of the gathering. He was wearing the same black T-shirt and jeans he usually wore, except for a few additional stains from the work he had stayed behind to finish. Max introduced him to several key people but, seeing Les wasn't really comfortable schmoozing, he angled him through the crowd toward Bill's and Crystal's familiar faces. Pulling at his T-shirt, Les said, "I had no idea there were going to be this many people. I would've at least put on a clean shirt."

Bill held up his bottle of beer and the plate mounded with all the different small-bite appetizers. "I'll never complain about free beer and food, even if I have no idea what most of it is." He plucked a stuffed mushroom and popped it into his mouth. "I know this one is a mushroom, but after that you're on your own."

Max walked in front of the sixty-inch flat screen mounted on the west wall of the open floor plan for the kitchen, dining room, and living room. He had on a blue blazer with a tuxedo-style lapel and crisp white dress shirt paired with jeans and black loafers. The windows that stretched across the entire northern wall featured a field of twinkling lights with a constant stream of car headlights winding out toward Gass Peak in the Las Vegas Range. Max flicked his finger against the side of his champagne glass, emanating a muted tone. The murmuring of the crowd lessened but did not stop entirely. He started speaking anyway. "Thank you all so much for coming, especially during this busy holiday time and on a school night. I know how all you city officials have to work in the morning and are never late." He hesitated amongst the groans and laughs as the joke settled in. "Someone asked me why I went to all this trouble when the segment will air next week and be available online for everyone to see. There are two reasons, really. One, I wanted to publicly recognize the people responsible for making this happen, and two, I wanted to share the moment with all of you who have worked so hard to resurrect downtown Vegas and build it into the thriving community it's becoming." Max stopped, prompting everyone in the room to clap. "To properly set up and explain the video we're going to watch, I'd like to introduce to you the inspiration, brains, talent, and as you can see, the beauty behind it: Ms. Penny Market."

The crowd applauded. Penny strutted up, seeming completely at ease. Her golden hair flowed around her shining face and over her shoulders. Her makeup was applied like fine art, all the colors specifically chosen and blended to accent her striking features. Max handed her a remote, whispering instructions on what buttons to press when she was ready. She calmly scanned the room, smiling and connecting with each person while she spoke. "Thank you, Max, for the lovely introduction, and most of all for opening your home and providing all the wonderful food and drinks. I must, however, correct you on one thing. I'm not the inspiration for this story." She waved her arm around the room. "All of you in the downtown community are the true inspiration for the story. I just got the opportunity to tell it." Applause rumbled through the room. "One of the things I noticed in moving here is that a lot of people who visit for the bachelor parties, work conventions, Super Bowl weekend, and all the other two- to three-day stopovers is that everyone thinks they know Vegas. While they witness a part of what has made this city the entertainment capital of the world, it's not what Vegas is. Vegas is about community, the people that are here when everyone else goes back home, the ones who bear the windstorms, the one hundred and fifteen-degree heat, and flash floods, and those who pull together in the time of need. While none of the five of us featured in the story were born here, we are transplants, like so many of you, who understand behind the glitter is the gold." Stepping to the side of the TV screen, she motioned toward the screen and pressed the button on the remote to start the video, while Max dimmed the lights. "Please enjoy this sneak peek of *Community Money.*"

The *CBS News Sunday Morning* logo appeared on the screen, with the show title in block letters. The screen faded into an aerial shot from the south end of the strip heading north, following the well-known landmarks along Las Vegas Boulevard all the way downtown to Fremont Street. Penny's mellifluous voice accompanied the video. "Las Vegas is a city known for its twenty-four-hour lifestyle, huge jackpots, extravagant accommodations, and, unfortunately, colossal, heartbreaking busts. But if you look beyond the glitter and the neon lights, you will find a community of people similar to those in most American cities." On the screen, children strapped with backpacks, on bikes and on foot, flowed toward a school. Busses and cars dropped off students in front. Penny said, "You have your neighborhoods, your schools, your families, people who were born here, and people who have relocated, some to escape and some to pursue a dream." Historical photos and clips of Vegas rotated on the screen, showing its early days as an encampment for miners and a stopover for western-bound travelers, then its rise as a resort town and entertainment capital, and finally its evolution into a full-functioning city.

Penny's voiceover continued. "Vegas has always been about the people, from the early pioneers like John Fremont, Helen Stewart, and William Clark, to the business trailblazers Mayme Stocker and Jim Cashman, to the organized crime influences of Ben Siegel and Moe Dalitz, to the corporate effect of Howard Hughes and the entertainment buzz from celebrities like Elvis Presley, Frank Sinatra, and

Liberace, to the impact of casino visionaries Benny Binion, Kirk Kerkorian, Jay Sarno, and Steve Wynn. While this story is not about anyone nearly as famous as those named, the message is important because it's the one that carries Vegas forward. It's about community money, how the resources are shared and always changing hands." Pockets of applause and cheers bubbled in the room. The Spanish mission façade of the El Cortez appeared on the screen. The camera shifted to the perspective of a person walking in. Penny's voice started telling the stories of the five of them. The shot transitioned to a blackjack table with the camera filming from the dealer's perspective and the five of them seated as they were that first night.

Across the room Max noticed Crystal whisper something to Bill and Les. After a few words, she headed for the door. He trailed behind her, following her into the hallway. Even though the door was closed, he spoke in a whisper. "Where you going? You know how bad it looks for you to leave in the middle? Not to mention how rude it is to Penny after she worked so hard pulling it together."

Crystal stopped halfway down the hallway, pivoting to face the accusations. Her cheeks blazed with anger. She didn't even attempt to lower her voice. Actually the more she talked, the louder she got. "Look, against my better judgment I did the piece. You know why? For Penny, for Les, for you. Don't even try to stand there and say what's going on inside is for us. That's all Max Doler, and I don't want to be a part of it."

Max spoke even softer. "Keep your voice down. This is a big night for all of us. Whether you like it or night, you are part of it. As long as you work at the Oasis and teach classes at the Western, you are connected to it all. The sooner you accept that, the better off we'll all be."

Crystal unloaded on him. "But why does everything always have to be such a big affair with you?" Max stepped back, surprised by her emotion. He was used to her being angry with him, but this was different. She was yelling and crying at the same time, pointing with the full thrust of her arm. The right strap on her dress slid down to her tricep. Adjusting it back to its proper position, she composed herself. "Why couldn't you just have us over and watch it together?"

"Because we would've missed a great opportunity to promote what we're doing in the community. These days it's not just about what you're doing. Other people need to know, and your message has to be loud enough to be heard above all the other noise." Max looked at his watch and motioned toward the door. "Now come on. Let's go back inside. The video is probably almost over."

Crystal didn't budge. "You could've at least asked us. Do you know how uncomfortable I am talking about my past and how hard it is for me to stay sober?

Every day is a new fight. To be in a room full of strangers asking questions with everyone drinking and carrying on is miserable. Do you know how many of those community leaders have come into the club and pawed all over me? All I can think about is having a drink and getting hold of some drugs. I can't be in there right now."

Max stood with his mouth agape. Finally finding words, he said, "Oh my god, I didn't even think about that. I'm so sorry."

Crystal dropped her voice to a whisper. "That's just it, Max. You never think about anyone but yourself." She turned and breezed down the hallway toward the elevator.

Max didn't say another word. He just stood in silence, watching the bottom of her black dress wave from side to side as she stormed away. His head slumped forward, realizing just how selfish he had been.

Amanda opened the door and stuck her head out. "What are you doing out here? The video is ending soon."

Max collected himself for a moment, nodding his head. "Yes, coming." He looked down the hallway one last time even though Crystal was long gone. He realized he had become the bully he had always hated, more interested in controlling than helping. Taking in a deep breath, he turned and walked inside.

From the TV, soft piano music played as the closing sequence of the kitchen and dining area at the Western filled the screen. The production lines bustled with activity in the background. Oasis guests sat at the table, eating. Crystal and Bill served food to a line of guests snaking toward the door. Les stirred a large stainless steel pot on the stove. Penny sprayed dishes and loaded them on a rack in the dishwasher. Max received the clean dishes on the other side and put them away. Penny's voiceover was warm and compassionate. "This may not be the jackpot people imagine winning when they come to Vegas, but this is the one the town was built on and the one still available today for those who contribute to one another."

Dow Jones Close: Closed

Chapter Fifty-Six

Date: Tuesday, December 23, 2014

Dow Jones Open: 17,971.51

Miss C's Music & Dance had been open almost two months. What had started as one class on Wednesday evening and two on Saturday quickly grew to seven classes following the *CBS News Sunday Morning* story. The classes were preschool dance, children's choir, song and dance for theater, jazz and hip-hop, and ballet ranging from ages three to fourteen. The jazz and hip-hop and ballet were separated in two classes, one for ages three to eight and the other nine to fourteen. The song and dance for theater and the older student ballet and jazz and hip-hop classes met three times a week on Monday, Wednesday, and Friday evenings. The other four classes were held just once per week on Saturdays. Crystal could barely keep up with the workload, and people were asking for more, wanting piano, guitar, and drum lessons and one-on-one tutoring. Max committed to further modifications for additional studio spaces and offered the help of his HR staff in hiring more instructors.

Max was really trying. Crystal could see that. After the *Community Money* party at Max's when Crystal and he had it out in the hallway, she did notice a difference, or maybe she just felt better because she was finally able to say how she really felt and for the first time, she knew that he had heard her.

The day after the party Max had stopped by her ballet class. Soft adagio piano music played through the speakers. Crystal was wrapping up the class walking around giving notes from the session to each of the nine to fourteen year olds, who were doing their best to hold first position. Crystal had been so focused on the class, she hadn't noticed Max come in. This is how it was when she was instructing, and why she was enjoying it so much. The rest of the world faded away, just like when she used to dance. The sadness and pain she used to feel when thinking about her mother were gone. Opening the school, working with the children, and singing and dancing almost every day brought joy back into her life. Her bitterness and resentment waned. The memories of her mother had become comforting companions. When teaching, she would remember the instruction her mother had given her and the stories she had shared from her own teaching at the pre-school. She no longer felt alone. Her mother was always with her, and for the first time in a long while that was a good thing.

Crystal had already let go of what happened the night of the *Community Money* party, but seeing him, she realized he obviously had not. She walked to the head of the class and curtsied to the students initiating for them to finish with a reverence combining port de bras with curtsies from the ballerinas and a bow from the one male in the class. Afterward they all clapped, and the students talked quietly amongst themselves moving to the side to collect their belongings.

Crystal walked over to the sound system and crouched down to stop the music and cue up the songs for the next jazz and hip-hop class, which was scheduled to start in thirty minutes. She heard the sound of the heels from Max's short steps on the wooden floor behind her. She just kept fiddling with the buttons and knobs on the receiver. He said, "Seems like the classes are going well."

Crystal stood and angled toward the square folding table and chairs she used as a desk. "The students are working hard. Good things happen with consistent effort." She sat down at the table and scribbled down notes in her notebook.

Max followed her, stopping at the table. He gestured toward one of the chairs. "May I?"

"By all means," Crystal said, not lifting her eyes from the notebook. "You own the place."

Max climbed up on one of the folding chairs. "I just wanted to come by and apologize for last night. You were right. It was selfish of me. I never thought how difficult that might be for you, how difficult any of this has been."

Crystal looked up from her notebook. "That's OK. It's over now. I survived, and Penny told me it went well, so that's good."

"I promise, it won't happen again," Max said. "From now on, we'll make the decisions that affect us, together." Crystal didn't say anything. She had heard him but wasn't sure she completely believed him. Max said, "Which is why I'm here. I have an idea I wanted to run by you."

Crystal folded her arms and sat back in her chair in a defensive position. "I'm listening."

Max leaned forward on the table. "I was thinking about how hard the students have been working and with the holidays approaching, it might be nice to have some sort of recital."

Crystal reacted like she usually did when he proposed anything: she balked at the idea. "This sounds like the party all over again, just another way for you to capitalize on the hard work and positivity of others."

"That's not the case at all," Max said. "I just want the students' effort to be rewarded and for the parents to see how good their kids are doing."

Crystal hesitated, thinking what her response would be if it was anyone other than Max sitting across from her. Nope. It was just too soon. She said, "But we've only been open seven weeks, and the majority of the students have just joined in the last few. Most of the classes are barely at the organized chaos level, let alone ready for public consumption."

Max leaned back and hopped down from the chair. "Well ultimately it's your decision. I'm not going to push. If you think it's too soon, then we can wait. Maybe do something in the spring."

Crystal looked at him skeptically, wondering if this wasn't just another tactic to get what he wants. "I do. What if the results don't meet the parents' expectations? I just don't want a bad showing to kill the momentum we're building."

And that was the last she had heard about it from Max. It was actually Les who convinced her to have the recital. What Les had to say would always be worth a little bit more to Crystal. He never had an agenda; he just let things unfold, asking questions to allow someone's perspective to shift rather than pushing it in a direction by saying what he thought. When Crystal was complaining one morning about Max showing up at class and pushing her to have the recital, Les asked her point blank, "Why does having a recital scare you?"

Crystal said, "I'm just worried the kids aren't ready, and it'll hurt their confidence and they'll want to quit, or their parents will think it's a waste of time and pull them out."

"Is your fear really based on their feelings and actions or your own?" Les asked in his even and calming tone. He likely had more he could've added, but he didn't. That was just Les. He always knew how to pick the one question that cut to the core of the issue and let the person sift through all the scenarios and rationale.

Crystal considered his words. It wasn't as if this were a preview or opening of a show like she was accustomed to from her theater days. There wouldn't be critics in the audience looking to grab attention with snarky reviews. These were just kids looking to have fun and hopefully just parents happy to see their children having fun, although she did remember some pushy dance moms who had much grander views of their children's talents than were really there. Crystal said, "I guess maybe it's a little bit more about my fear. I mean, I'm still really new at this. In front of the kids, I feel fine. But what if the parents see through me? I don't really have any training to be an instructor."

Les said, "But you grew up in a home infused with music and dance and have put thousands and thousands of hours into perfecting your craft. Aside from maybe some directors you have worked with, how many people have you met that actually know more than you do? I doubt any of them will be in that room, and if they are, they will see your brilliance and passion."

"I guess in the end it's about the students," Crystal said. "I'll ask them. If they want to do it, we'll do it."

Of course the answer from the students was a resounding yes. Any opportunity to shine in front of their parents and friends was a welcome one. The children became so excited and energized by the idea that Crystal actually felt guilty for having considered not doing it. The students' attention and effort in classes also improved once they had a goal. In addition, the sign-ups for new classes scheduled to begin after the first of the year had filled by the middle of the month. Max had been right, but Crystal would never admit that to him.

While the studio facilities were brand new and state of the art, they weren't suitable for a recital. There just wasn't enough room to put on a show and provide seating for spectators. Max used his connections with the City of Las Vegas to arrange for the Office of Cultural Affairs to procure the auditorium at the Historic Fifth Street School.

Originally called the Las Vegas Grammar School, the school had been built in 1936 to accommodate the increasing population due to the Hoover Dam construction and legalization of gambling. It had been referred to as the Fifth Street School almost since its inception, due to its location on Fifth Street, which was renamed Las Vegas Boulevard in 1959. After the school closed, it sat empty for several years before the city redeveloped it, preserving the mission style building and getting it added to the National Register of Historic Places. It was also conveniently located across the street from Bill's place at the Juhl so Crystal didn't have far to travel to and from the rehearsals and performances.

Tickets for the recital were ten dollars in advance and fifteen the night of the show. Children accompanied by adults got in free. Les and Bill ran the concession stand, with all the proceeds going to the Oasis. The program was scheduled for an hour and a half with each of the seven classes performing for three songs and a fifteen-minute intermission. Penny teased Crystal about the length of the dance sets being three songs. She said, "Which stage you training them for, the one you started on or the one you ended up on?" Crystal laughed it off. It was only six months ago, but she was so far away from it all. She had hardly even thought about those days anymore. It seemed like another life. When she had started stripping, she put her real life on hold, and now that she was ready to resume, she let go of it as if that person had never existed. The last thing she was going to do was allow the timeout she had taken for a few years ruin twenty-plus years of hard work and dedication.

Four hundred folding chairs were arranged in rows of twenty across the lacquered hardwood floor of the auditorium. A red velvet curtain covered the thirty-five-foot opening of the stage. Crystal and Penny and several of the parents spent most of the day of the recital decorating and setting up for the show. The students arrived at four to do final rehearsals. Most of them had never performed in an auditorium, so Crystal wanted them to experience the feeling of being behind the curtain when it opened.

During the rehearsal, many of the students froze looking out at the auditorium full of all the empty chairs. She told them it would be easier when the chairs were full, the lights were on the stage, and the auditorium was dark. She knew from her own experience that the first time feeling all the eyes on you and not being able to see anyone was actually worse. The pressure of the moment is what pushed you through…for most people. There were always a few who couldn't block it out and would run off stage, but she didn't tell them that part.

The ballet students went first, followed by the theater song and dance group, then the jazz and hip-hop, the preschool dance, and the children's choir wrapped up the show. She used songs from *Giselle*, the *Nutcracker*, and *Rosamunde* for the ballet; "Hard-Knock Life" from *Annie*, "Join the Circus" from *Barnum*, and "Freak Flag" from *Shrek* for the theater set; "Yeah" by Usher, "Mambo No. 5" by Lou Bega, and "Swagger Jagger" by Cher Lloyd with the jazz and hip-hop group; "Good Ship Lollipop," "I Feel Pretty," and "Penguin Cha Cha" for the preschool dance numbers, and finished off with a compilation of holiday songs by the choir. The pace of the show was set with the ballet music to ease into the evening, the theater songs to offer some humor, the jazz and hip-hop to pump up the energy, the preschool dance to lighten the mood and pull at the heart strings, and the holiday songs to round out the evening and put everyone in a festive spirit. Of course there were an assortment of stumbles, wardrobe malfunctions, forgotten and flubbed lyrics, and stage fright, as would be expected, but they only added to the charm and endearment of the show.

After each of the groups filed onstage to take final bows to the standing crowd, calls for Crystal echoed until she emerged onstage to take her well-deserved bow. She was honored and humbled, feeling her face reddening from the raucous reception. Of all the curtain calls she had done, the one for the show she hadn't even performed in meant the most. But it was the person who strode down the aisle carrying a bouquet of roses that unleashed the tears. It was her old agent and family friend Maura, whom she hadn't seen since her mom's funeral.

She stared at Maura in shock, almost as much as if her own mother had been standing in front of her. She closed her eyes and shook her head, opening her eyes slowly to see if the picture had changed.

Maura presented Crystal the flowers, tears welling in her own eyes. "You did good, kid. Your mom would be so proud."

Crystal swallowed hard, fighting off the emotion. "But how? Who?"

"Old Maura might be retired but she still has her connections. Let's talk after, kid. We have a lot to catch up on."

Crystal bent over and hugged Maura, almost pulling her up on stage in her own excitement. Maura squeezed her back. The auditorium swelled with applause.

When the last of the parents filed out with their wired performers still buzzing from the show, Crystal walked out from backstage and sat on the front edge, looking at Penny and Maura sitting together. With her legs dangling over the side, she leaned back, propping herself up with her arms. "Aha, now I see who your connection is, Maura. How on earth did you two ever connect?" She bounced her legs against the stage.

"It really wasn't that hard, actually," Penny said. "I remembered you talking about Maura before, so I asked Damon to see if he could track her down. She retired a few years ago, but she had a bit of a reputation as a tough negotiator in her day so some of the older agents in his firm knew of her right away."

Maura said, "What can I say? I guess I'm unforgettable."

"That you are." Crystal hopped off the stage. Bill and Les entered through the doors from the lobby, walking down the aisle toward them, after closing down the concession stand. Crystal asked, "How'd you make out tonight?"

Les patted the side of the steel box tucked under his arm. "Over five hundred in sales and almost another three in donations."

Bill held an unwieldy cardboard box pressed against his chest. When he got to the front, he dropped the box on a chair, shaking the contents back and forth. "Anyone hungry?" He took out a bag of peanut M&M'S and ripped open the package.

"Famished," Crystal said. "I haven't eaten since breakfast." She rummaged through the box and pulled out a bag of Twizzlers.

"Let's all grab a late dinner and celebrate," Penny said. "Where'd Max go?"

Les said, "He had to run to get to a late meeting, or maybe it was to get ready for an early one in the morning. I can't remember. You know Max, always on the go."

"If Maura's in, I'm in," Crystal said. "Bill, you're coming aren't you?"

"Think I'll call it an early night, too," he said, chomping on a mouthful of the M&M'S. "I'm tired, and with all the candy I ate tonight, I could probably stand to skip a meal or three."

Les reached over and rubbed Bill's belly. "I'm surprised we turned a profit with Billy minding the store."

"Just doing quality control." Bill emptied the rest of the bag into his mouth.

"Actually, I'm going to have to pass, too," Les said. "I have a full day tomorrow."

"Party poopers." Penny stuck out her bottom lip at them. She turned to Maura and Crystal. "Looks like it's just us girls."

The group said their good-byes with promises to meet at the Oasis in the morning to help with breakfast. The ladies went back to Siegel's 1941, the twenty-four-hour restaurant at the El Cortez. Penny had gotten Maura a free room at the hotel from the connections she developed while filming part of the *Community Money* piece there. Siegel's had vintage décor and archival artwork, hearkening back to the time when Ben Siegel and Meyer Lansky were calling the shots at the casino. The atmosphere, emotion from the evening, and three glasses of wine that Maura had during dinner triggered an onslaught of stories from LA, New York, and Las Vegas covering the sixties to the nineties, when Maura, as she put it, "finally had to settled down." Crystal knew Maura had never been married, but she hadn't been aware of her wild and colorful past. Maura mixed in stories about Valeria and Crystal as a young girl. Some of them Crystal remembered, and some were new or she had forgotten.

As the hour pushed past midnight and yawns surpassed the laughs, the mood became more serious. Maura said, "I was really sorry to hear about the show closing, kid. That was a tough break. I tried getting a hold of you to see if you needed help finding something, but you never returned my calls and eventually the numbers no longer worked. I must say I was a bit worried. I kept an eye on the trade news in Vegas to see your name pop up in a new show, but it never did.

Hearing from Penny was a blessing. To see what you have created and how you interact with those kids really makes me happy."

"I'm sorry for disappearing on you." Crystal looked down, stirring the straw in her club soda. "It's just after my mom's passing then losing the show—it was really hard on me. I went through a pretty dark period."

Maura reached over and stroked Crystal's arm. "All that matters is that you're happy now, and are surrounded by people who care for you." A playful smile curled at the edges of Maura's mouth. "Speaking of the people around you, what's the story with this Bill guy? Ha-cha-cha-cha."

Penny burst out laughing. "Oh Maura, you're quite the handful. I'm not sure he could handle you."

Crystal scrunched her face and plugged her ears, shaking her head back and forth. "Noooo, I don't want to hear this. It's like imagining your parents having sex." She became still, a pensive look hanging on her face. "You know, on second thought, maybe that's exactly what he needs. He's been so down lately." She looked at Penny. "He's become absolutely obsessed with what is going to happen after he dies. That's all he talks about." She turned back to Maura. "He made us promise that we'll take care of everything exactly as he and his late wife wanted it. He's even having a will drawn up so it's all legal and can't be questioned."

"I obviously don't know him," Maura said. "But I've seen many of my friends go through this. It's just a phase. They don't want to be a burden on anyone. Once they get everything taken care of, they let it go and forget about it."

Crystal shook her head glumly. "No, it's more than that. He's always talking about how he has lived his life and is ready to move on."

"Does he have any kids?" Maura asked.

Penny filled her in. "His son is married with kids back on the East coast, but they have been estranged for years."

"Maybe we need to change that," Crystal said.

Penny bobbed her head in shock. "What? Am I hearing what I think I'm hearing? The person who has vilified me for butting in and getting involved in other people's lives is suggesting we get involved?"

"I don't know," Crystal reached over and clutched Maura's hand. "I guess it works out sometimes."

Dow Jones Close: 18,024.17

Chapter Fifty-Seven

Date: Monday, December 29, 2014

Dow Jones Open: 18,046.58

Christmas had come and gone without much excitement. December was always a slow month in Vegas until the few days before New Year's. None of the group had immediate family to travel to, so they had spent the holiday serving others at the Oasis and delivering meals to homeless people in other parts of the city who weren't aware of the Oasis or couldn't make it in. On Christmas Day they served 117 people at the Oasis and delivered another 150 boxed dinners to people on the streets around the city.

Support, both volunteer and financial, for the Oasis was at an all-time high. Many of Crystal's students and their families had become regular contributors as well. Eleven of the mission guests had become fulltime employees for Max and were living on their own in apartments nearby. Of course, there was more than a fair share of problems, too. For every one success story, there were ten or eleven failures. It wasn't all sunshine and jackpots. People would start working and walk off in the middle of a shift, or leave one day and just not come back. Some would show up weeks later, back in line at the Oasis like nothing ever happened, and some they never saw again. Max was initially discouraged by the success rate, but he didn't really have the space to hire more people anyway. All the press and publicity had flooded MDI with applications. For every person that left, there were several external applicants willing to take their places. The program was still available to the Oasis guests, but Les and Max were just much more selective in the people they offered it to.

For being on the verge of bankruptcy midyear, Max ended the year in quite a different position. He had fulfilled the McDonald's quota every month and extended the deal for an additional five hundred thousand units per month for another year. He had also signed deals with the MGM Resorts group to supply Lapkins in their rooms and Darden Restaurants for all their Olive Garden, Longhorn, and Bahama Breeze restaurants across the US. The downside was that the online ordering had trickled to a halt. With the notoriety and success of the Lapkin, a proliferation of knockoffs became available. Max had initially gone after the impostors with legal action, but for every one he shut down, several more would spring up. He instead just focused on the corporate business. It was much simpler to ship bulk orders to one address anyway, and they wouldn't risk the potential damage to their brands buying from a cheaper but illegal supplier. Max had always known the Lapkin life cycle would run its course at some point. Until then he was going to ride that little magic napkin as far as he could.

To celebrate the good year everyone had had, once Christmas had passed and before things got too busy before New Years, Max invited everyone over to his penthouse for a holiday dinner. Afterward they all walked across the street to the El Cortez to play blackjack at a table Max had reserved with me as the dealer. Not sure if it was intentional, but they sat in the same order as the night when they first met: Crystal was at first base next to Bill, then Penny, then Les, and Max sat at third base. But unlike the first night, there was no drama or bickering. The mood was festive, especially for Bill, who was happier than he had been in a long while. But that could have been because he was winning, too. In a little over an hour, he had turned his hundred dollar buy-in into over $650. His usually conservative play of five dollars per hand had grown to twenty-five and sometimes fifty.

After he split fours against my six and pulled another four to expand his one hand to three, on a fifty-dollar hand, then got another seven on top of one of the fours to double down and increase his total bet to $200, everyone cheered when his twenty-one, nineteen, and twenty beat my eighteen. With a mound of green and red chips in front of him, I scooped up the $200 in green and paid him out in four black.

Penny said, "Somebody was obviously on Santa's nice list this year."

Max pointed at the lonely four red chips in front of Penny. "That would explain why you're down to your last four."

Penny snarled and stuck her tongue out at Max. "I didn't think Santa ever let his elves leave the North Pole."

"We're union now," Max said. "We get a week off after Christmas."

Bill sorted and stacked his chips. His bet circle was empty. I waited to deal, asking if he was playing another hand. He shook his head. "Nah, I think I'll call it a night." Immediate objections fired from all seats at the table. "Sorry to break up the party," he said. "I'm just tired. It's been a long day." He pushed his chips to the center. Eight hundred fifty dollars went back to him. He counted out three-fifty and slid it to Les for the Oasis and pushed the purple $500 chip back at me.

Crystal reached over and put her arm around Bill. "I knew we could convince you to stay."

I started counting out change to break up the chip.

"No, that's for you," Bill said edging it closer to me. "Happy holidays."

I nodded in appreciation, announcing it to the pit boss. "One purple tip coming in."

The others were quiet. Looks ranged from curiosity to concern. Penny said, "Come on, stay a little longer. This is the last time we can all get together before it gets crazy for New Year's."

"Nah," Bill said. "I'm going to get out while the getting's good."

Crystal slid her chips to the center of the table. "Think I'll cash in, too."

The others followed. First Les, then Penny, and even Max. For people who had played hundreds of hours by themselves and in varying combinations with each other, it was strange that no one wanted to stay if the others left.

"Don't leave on my account," Bill said. "Stay and enjoy yourselves. You're making me feel bad for breaking up the party."

Penny stood up and hugged him. "Come on, Bill. It's not a party unless you're here."

"Have a great New Year's, sweetheart." Bill squeezed Penny, holding her for an extended period of time. "Take good care of yourself."

"Don't be silly," Penny said. "I'll see you over at the Oasis before then."

"Never can say things too much." Bill broke their embrace, then moved down the line to Les. "Thanks for everything this year, my friend. Your friendship has meant everything to me." Les mirrored the sentiment and emotion. Bill didn't embrace Max, but extended his hand toward him. "For a miserable little prick, you sure turned out OK. Keep up the good work."

"You're not so bad yourself, for an ex-pig." Max pulled him close and reached his free arm around and patted Bill on the back several times. "Now get out of here before people think I'm a nice guy."

When Bill and Crystal got home, Bill, who hadn't said much on the way, asked her to sit down at the dining room table. His actions at the El Cortez had worried her. Now he was flat-out scaring her. The sentimentality had become seriousness. He retrieved a folder from his safe in the closet and sat across from her at the table. She couldn't hold back any longer. "What's going on with you? You're really freaking me out."

"I need to go over something with you." Bill took out a document from the folder and slid it to her. "My lawyer has the official copy, but I wanted you to have a copy and to explain everything to make sure you're OK with it."

Crystal looked down at the document, which said, *Last Will and Testament of William Bronson Price* on the top. Her eyes snapped back up to Bill. "Do we have to do this now?"

"I just don't want there to be any surprise or confusion if something happens."

Crystal said, "Why would something happen?"

"Can we just do this?" Bill asked. "It's important to me."

Crystal sat back in her chair, both her legs bouncing from the stress. "Look, I wasn't going to say anything, because we wanted it to be a surprise, but with the way you're acting I think you should know now. Don't be mad, but Penny and I contacted your son and invited him to come for a visit. He arrives tomorrow afternoon. Let's just wait and do this tomorrow when we can go over it all together. You may want to change it."

Bill didn't react at all. Crystal and Penny had decided not to tell him because they thought he would be angry. Now she wanted that anger. At least then she would know he still cared. Instead there was nothing. Just a monotone, dispassionate response. "You shouldn't have done that."

"Stop being so stubborn," Crystal said. "It's time you two finally talked and put all this to rest. You have been so amazing to me and to the others. He needs to see that side of you. You need that. Do you know what I would give to be able to have one more conversation with my mom? It's not too late for you two."

"I know your hearts are in the right place, but don't you think Darlene tried everything before? What makes you think if she couldn't do it over the years, you'll be able to now?"

"Well something's different," Crystal said. "He's coming here, isn't he?"

"I guess we'll just deal with that tomorrow. Can we at least go through this now?"

Line by line, they went through the will. Bill had bequeathed the apartment, household goods, furnishings, automobile, and other personal property to Crystal. Anything not wanted by Crystal and all of Darlene's belongings were to go to Hughie. The residue and remainder of the estate, after all payments, debts, expenses, and taxes, was to be divided. Half went to Hughie, one-fourth went into a trust for Bill's grandchildren, and the remaining fourth went to the Oasis.

Crystal was overwhelmed. "I can't accept this. You've already done so much for me."

Bill said, "Too late. It's already done. If you don't want it, then it'll go to Hughie, but it would mean a lot to me if you would accept it."

She looked at the will again. "OK, I'll think about it."

"That's all I'm asking." Bill turned to the second page. "Besides you haven't seen what I'm asking you to do."

Last Will and Testament

of

William Bronson Price

I, William Bronson Price, resident of 353 E Bonneville Ave, Apt 804, Las Vegas, NV 89101, being of sound mind and disposing memory and not acting under duress or undue influence, and fully understanding the nature and extent of all my property and of this disposition thereof, do hereby make, publish, and declare this document to be my Last Will and Testament, and do hereby revoke any and all other wills and codicils heretofore made by me. I declare this my last will and testament.

ARTICLE I:

    a.   I direct that all my debts, and expenses of my last illness, funeral, and burial, be paid as soon after my death as may be reasonably convenient, and I hereby authorize my Personal Representative (or Executor), hereinafter appointed, to settle and discharge, in his or her absolute discretion, any claims made against my estate.

    b.   I further direct that my Personal Representative (or Executor) shall pay out of my estate any and all estate and inheritance taxes payable by reason of my death in respect of all items included in the computation of such taxes, whether passing under this Will or otherwise. Said taxes shall be paid by my Personal Representative (or Executor) or Trustee as if such taxes were my debts without recovery of any part of such tax payments from anyone who receives any item included in such computation.

ARTICLE II:

    a.   The entire residue of the property owned by me at my death, real and personal and wherever situate, I devise and bequeath as per the following:

1. All tangible property including the apartment, household goods, furnishings, and automobile to Crystal Moore.

2. All personal family belongings and any property not wanted by Crystal Moore to Hughes William Price.

3. The financial holdings, including all retirement, banking, and other investment accounts are to be divided as per the following allocation:

    a. 50% to Hughes William Price

    b. 25% to my grandchildren Margaret Elizabeth Price and Samuel Edward Price.

    c. 25% to Lester Banks and the Oasis Mission.

a. If for any reason, property may not pass or does not pass by way of or through the before-mentioned, are specifically made a part of this Will by reference and all properties shall be held, administered, and distributed pursuant to the terms thereof, and the Personal Representative (or Executor) will assume and perform all of the duties of the Trustee.

ARTICLE III:

My Personal Representative (or Executor) is to act without bond and to the maximum amount possible without court supervision or control so that the estate can be settled as much as possible as a nonintervention proceeding. I nominate and appoint the following people in the following order of priority as Personal Representative (or Executor) until one such person qualifies.

1. My attorney, Amanda Burns

2. My friend, Crystal Moore

3. My son, Hughes William Price

4. My daughter-in-law, Grace Fortune Price

I grant to my Personal Representative (or Executor) full power to do everything in administering my estate that said Personal Representative (or Executor) deems to be for the best interest of my beneficiaries.

ARTICLE IV:

Of the provisions made herein for the benefit of my wife, an amount equal to the maximum allowable widow's (widower's) statutory interest in her husband's property, if any, shall be deemed received by my wife by operation of law as such statutory interest, and only the excess, if any, over such amount shall be deemed received under the provisions of this Will.

ARTICLE V:

If any beneficiary under this Will, or any trust herein mentioned, contests or attacks this Will or any of its provisions, any share or interest in my estate given to that contesting beneficiary under this Will is revoked and shall be disposed of in the same manner provided herein as if that contesting beneficiary had predeceased me.

ARTICLE VI:

Upon my death, I direct that my body shall be delivered as soon as after my death as practicable and to the full extent legally possible, without autopsy or embalming, to Wolf Funeral Home in Las Vegas, Nevada, where all fees and charges have been prepaid for my remains to be cremated. Following the cremation, my ashes are to be combined with my wife Darlene Renfield Price's and a small funeral ceremony is to be held. After the ceremony, the ashes are to be surrendered to Crystal Moore, Penelope Market, and Lester Banks and to be scattered in Red Rock Canyon, Nevada

ARTICLE VII:

This Will has been prepared in duplicate, each copy of which has been executed as an original. One of these executed copies is in my possession and the other is deposited for safekeeping with my attorney, Amanda Burns. Either of these wills is to be considered as the original. If only one copy of this Will can be found, then it shall be considered as the original, and the missing copy will be presumed inadvertently lost. Any clarifications or instructions concerning this Will may be obtained by calling the above-mentioned attorney who is requested to do everything necessary to implement the provisions of this Will.

IN WITNESS WHEREOF, I, William Bronson Price, the testatrix, sign my name to this instrument consisting of four pages this 14th day of November, 2014, and being first duly sworn, do hereby declare to the undersigned authority that I sign and execute this instrument as my Last Will and that I sign it willingly (or willingly direct another to sign for me), that I execute it as my free and voluntary act for the purposes expressed in it, and that I an 18 years of age or older, of sound mind, and under no constraint or undue influence.

_____

Testator

We, Aaron Finley and Joshua Reynolds, the witnesses, sign our names to this instrument, being first duly sworn, and do hereby declare to the undersigned authority that the testator declares it to be his Last will and requested us to sign as witnesses thereof, and that he signs it willingly (or willingly directs another to sign for him), and that each of us, in the presence and hearing of the testator and of each other, hereby signs this will as witness to the testator's signing, and that to the best of our knowledge the testator is 18 years of age or older, of sound mind, and under no constraint or under influence.

Witness:

_____

Residing: 1970 Alta Drive, Las Vegas, NV 89107

Witness:

_____

Residing: 119 Eleventh Street, Las Vegas, Nevada 89101

Dow Jones Close: 18,038.23

Chapter Fifty-Eight

Date: Tuesday, December 30, 2014

Dow Jones Open: 18,035.02

Crystal awoke early and looked at the clock. 7:15. Hughie wasn't scheduled to arrive until two in the afternoon. She hoped Bill would reconsider her objections about the will after sleeping on it. She pulled the covers up around her neck. The apartment was still and eerily quiet. Something was wrong. Bill was always up before her. She would hear the water running in the shower, the TV murmuring with *Good Morning America*, or just his lumbering gait as he moved from one room to the other. Even the mornings he went to help Les, she knew he had been up by the smell of the fresh coffee he had made and left warming for her. Today there was nothing.

She rolled over and checked her phone on the nightstand for messages. Only one from Penny: *Hughie's plane left on time. I'll pick him up and meet you guys at Bill's. Make sure you're there or let me know where you'll be.* She tossed the phone next to her on the bed and pulled the covers up over her head. The plan was so much easier when they had the element of surprise.

Not sure what she was going to do to change Bill's mind but feeling rested to take another run at him, she climbed out from underneath the covers and put on her bathrobe and slippers. Opening the door, she called out for Bill. No answer. Must've already gone to the Oasis, she thought. She shuffled down the hallway and into the bathroom. Brushing her teeth, she scanned the room nervously, recalling their conversation about the will. Her eyes fixated on a familiar item in the bottom of the trash. Dropping her toothbrush in the sink, she reached down and snatched the amber pill bottle. The label displayed the familiar name and prescription for Mildred Nickels. She rushed out of the bathroom toward Bill's bedroom. The door was closed, which was strange because even after Crystal moved in, he still never slept in there and barely ever even went in, except to fetch something out of the closet. She squeezed the empty pill bottle in her hand. Maybe he was out on the terrace. She walked into the living room. The pillows and blankets he usually used to sleep on the couch were stacked in the same position as when she went to bed. She knew they hadn't been used, because the fresh pillowcase from the laundry she had done was still draped across the pillow.

She walked over to the terrace door and pulled back the vertical blinds. A pigeon stood on the railing, looking back at her. They studied each other for a moment, then the pigeon flew away. Crystal let go of the blinds. They swung back and forth, rattling into one other. Flashes of light shot through the dimly lit room. Turning back around, she noticed the urn with Darlene's ashes missing from the mantel. Only an empty space remained where the urn had stood, a perfect rectangle outlined by the dust that had collected around its edges.

She walked back to her room to retrieve her phone and call Les. Bill had to be with him. On the way, she stopped in the hallway and stared at the door to Bill's room. She didn't need to call Les. She knew where Bill was. Plodding to the door, she rested her hand on the handle before opening it. The air rushed from her lungs. She turned the handle and pushed the door open.

Bill was there, reclined on the bed in a blue suit. The urn rested against the pillow on his left. He and Darlene were next to each other once again.

Crystal didn't enter the room. She knew he was gone, and that he had been for a while. She hadn't been able to save him then. There was no use trying now.

Her first call was to Les, then to Penny. They both came over right away. She didn't tell them about the pill bottle; she couldn't. It didn't matter anyway. They all knew Bill had just given up. In that moment, though, no one had an idea what to do. They thought about calling the police or 911, but it wasn't an emergency. Although Bill wasn't religious, Les performed the last rites. Penny looped in Max, who tapped into his network of contacts to get a doctor to come over.

When the doctor arrived, she was wearing a black doubleknit Adidas jacket and pants with white stripes down the arms and legs. Her brown hair was pulled into a ponytail with a thin white headband over the top of her head and circling around behind her ears to the back. She looked in her mid-thirties, but with her youthful attire and smooth skin and lean build, she could've passed for much younger. If it wasn't for the doctor's bag in her right hand, it would've been easy to mistake her for a coach or maybe even a player. She must've noticed everyone questioning her appearance because the first thing she said, tugging at the jacket, was, "Came right from the kids' soccer game. We won. Have to be back there for the next game in an hour." Les led her into Bill's room. She opened her bag on the bed and immediately started to examine the body, checking Bill's eyes, his temperature, for any signs of stress or marks on the body. She said, "Based on the body temp, he passed away about five hours ago. There doesn't seem to be any sign of trauma. More tests would have to be done to see if it was a heart attack. Most likely it was cardiomyopathy, which is a type of progressive heart disease. Over time, the heart tissue becomes thickened and stiff, weakening its ability to pump blood. I'm assuming from the urn that he recently lost his wife?"

Les said, "About a year ago. He had been doing fine, but the past month he became distant and frequently talked about death."

"It could've been building for a while," the doctor said. "Carrying that grief or stress can trigger your nervous system to release chemicals similar to the fight-or-flight response and make it difficult for your heart to pump blood properly."

"But he seemed fine last night," Penny said. "He was more emotional than usual, but he seemed happy and peaceful."

The doctor said, "That could be because he finally decided to let go and stop fighting. You see this in suicide patients, as well. Everyone is surprised by their death because they were so happy the day they died. But this is only because they finally decided to do it and weren't carrying the burden of decision any longer."

"What do we do now, doc?" Max asked. "Can you handle this or do we need to call the police or an ambulance?"

The doctor rose from the side of the bed, depositing the penlight she was using back into the medical bag. "To know the exact causes, we can run an angiogram to check the arteries and veins, but from what I can see I'm OK to say this was natural causes and complete the pronouncement of death."

"Well, I don't think we should do anything until his son gets here this afternoon," Penny said. "When he left New Jersey this morning, he thought his dad was alive. To arrive and hear from strangers that he had passed and was already at the funeral home would be too much."

Crystal became emotional. "So we're just supposed to let him sit here and rot?" She waved a copy of the will. "Bill left very specific instructions for how he wanted things handled. I think we should follow his wishes."

Max took the will from her and began reading. "Well now I know why he wanted Amanda's number."

Penny walked over to the nightstand and picked up a white envelope with *Hughie* scrawled in blue ink across the front. "He also left a note for his son. I think we should wait."

"Medically speaking, there are no problems with waiting until this afternoon," the doctor said. "Rigor mortis has already set in. There will be little change over the next several hours."

It was all too much for Crystal. She dropped to her knees, whimpering. "No, this can't be happening. I can't lose him, too."

Penny crouched next to her, rubbing her back. "You're going to be OK. You're not alone in this."

Les walked over and sat on the edge of the bed, taking hold of Bill's hand. "I think we should wait, too. We all need to make peace with this. Bill and his son had a complicated past. Let's allow his son an opportunity to read what Bill had to say in his presence and allow him to be part of executing Bill's wishes."

"We really don't have much choice but to wait." Max looked up from the document. "I don't mean to be cynical, but this already looks a bit fishy. If we rush him to the funeral home, it only looks worse. Think of it from his son's perspective. He arrives to find his dad has passed. A young girl, who is living with him, is also the executor of the will and a major benefactor."

Crystal's sobbing escalated. "You think I wanted this? I tried talking him out of it. I don't want this stupid apartment. I don't want any of this."

Penny pulled Crystal close, comforting her. "Come on. None of us wanted this. We all cared for him."

"That's not what I mean," Max said. "I'm just saying I think it's in everybody's best interest to wait."

So they waited. Four hours to be exact. During that time, Max finalized the pronouncement of death with the doctor; Les contacted the funeral home stipulated in the will for the cremation, the same one Bill had used for Darlene; and Penny consoled Crystal, who only felt worse as the day went on. She had never known her father. Bill was as close as she ever had. He was one of the only men in her life that had given to her and never expected anything in return. But the grief was also much deeper. Losing Bill stirred up the pain and sorrow she had only recently accepted with relation to her mother's death. She wanted to run. To hide. To not feel.

All four of them had planned to go to the airport together, but they weren't comfortable leaving Bill's body alone. No one could articulate why. Bill was right where he wanted to be—next to Darlene. But leaving him stretched out alone in the apartment just didn't feel right. That was one thing they all agreed on. Penny felt she should go, since she was the one who had talked to Hughie. They decided Les should also go, because he had the most experience and compassion in dealing with these situations. Crystal wanted to remain with Bill, but that only left Max to stay with her, which made her feel very anxious. They got along now, but were still like fire and gasoline. She didn't think that in her current emotional state she could handle Max's dispassionate businesslike manner. Thankfully everyone seemed to know this, because they eventually decided Penny should call Hughie when he arrived and let him know Max and Les were coming to pick him up, and she would stay with Crystal.

While Max and Les were on their way to the airport to pick up Hughie, Crystal showed Penny the will, pointing out the parts about what he left to her and how they were to dispose of the bodies. She said, "This is what he was talking about when he asked us for our help that night."

Penny read the will over several times while Crystal paced back and forth in front of her. Penny looked up from the document. "Did you know he was going to leave you so much?"

"Not until we got home last night. I told him it was too much, that he had already done so much for me. He said it was already done and whatever I didn't want could go to Hughie and his family. You have to believe me, I didn't want this."

Penny patted the couch cushion next to her. "I do, sweetie. Come sit down."

"I can't," Crystal said, increasing the intensity of her pacing. "Hughie has no clue what he's walking into. He got on the plane this morning thinking he was going to be dealing with one kind of stress and is going to be hit with something completely different." Her mind started to match the speed of her feet on the carpet. "He doesn't know any of us. What if he thinks I tricked Bill into doing this? Like I worked my way in and have been taking advantage of him."

Penny rose from the couch and walked to Crystal, blocking her path. She took hold of both Crystal's hands and positioned her face so Crystal had no choice but to look at her. "Listen to me. You are not alone in this. That's why Bill asked us both to help. We will get through this together."

In the remaining time they waited for Les and Max to arrive with Hughie, Penny convinced Crystal to sit down and together they reviewed the will, so they could agree on exactly how they would present it to Hughie. Much to their surprise, when he did arrive, his reaction was no reaction. He didn't say anything. His face showed no emotion. They could tell Les had already told him what had happened to prepare him for what he was walking into, but they at least expected some kind of reaction.

All standing together in the room around Bill's body, Les said, "He left a letter for you." Les walked over to the nightstand.

Hughie shook his head, puffing air through his nose in disbelief. "Of course he did. That's just like him. He gets to say what he wanted, and I don't. I'm not surprised though. I knew when Mom died, there wasn't much chance for us. She was always the link."

Les held the letter in his hand at his side. "It definitely seemed like she was everything to him, but I know he cared for you and was so proud of your achievements. He told me how he snuck into your graduations and the hospitals when his grandchildren were born, and followed your career. The link was never broken. He was always there. You just didn't realize it. He was a good man. He helped us all here so much."

Hughie cut him off, showing his first sign of emotion. "That's just it. My whole life, all I've heard is what a great man he is, how much he did for other people. But he could never show me. I always had to hear it from everyone else." He turned away from the body, scanning the room, looking at familiar objects from his childhood in this new, strange environment. "I'm in my parent's home, and I feel like I don't belong."

No one said anything. Everybody felt as uncomfortable as Hughie clearly did, like they were the ones that didn't belong. They just let him take it all in. He walked over to the wall covered with pictures. There Hughie was, with varying degrees of teeth and hair as he grew up, playing baseball with Bill as coach, with Bill at the Boy Scout Pinewood Derby, with both parents the night of a dance and a prom night, with Bill handing him the keys to a Jeep. Then the pictures suddenly changed. Bill was no longer in any of them. It was Hughie and Darlene at his college and law graduations, him and his wife and Darlene at his wedding, Darlene with him and his kids at their birthday parties. His whole life was on display in front of him.

Still with his back to everyone, Hughie repeatedly wiped his eyes then turned around. His face was red and tight, the muscles in his jaw bulging. He let out a deep breath and walked toward the bed. "I don't even care anymore. I'm just glad I can finally put it all to rest."

Max said, "According to the doctor, he went peacefully. He just lay down and never woke up."

Les extended the letter to Hughie. "He left this for you."

Hughie didn't take the letter. He just stood at the side of the bed, staring over the body. He reached down and rubbed Bill's gray, bristly flattop. "You know he had this same haircut as long as I can remember. Never changed it once."

Les nodded, still holding the letter for Hughie to take it. "We'll give you some privacy to read this. Take all the time you need."

Hughie looked up from the body. "No, I want you to stay. He obviously thought a lot of you all. And let's be honest, you all knew him a lot better than I ever did." The emotion Hughie had been fighting finally overtook him. He sat down on the edge of the bed, taking hold of Bill's hand with one of his and covering his face with the other and sobbing.

Penny walked over and sat next to him, rubbing his back. "You have to know how much he loved you and how proud he was."

This made Hughie cry that much harder. Everyone else just looked at each other, unsure what to do. No one wanted to be there, but they knew they couldn't leave either. Two things bound them: the awkwardness and their love for Bill.

Hughie looked up at Les. "Do you think you could read the letter? Quite honestly, I'm not sure I could get through it, and I really don't want to be alone right now."

"Of course," Les said. He peeled open the envelope and took out the two pieces of yellow stationery inside.

Dear Hughie:

I'm sorry I couldn't wait until you got here to tell you all this stuff or I couldn't bring myself to tell you sooner. I never had much growing up and was never as smart as you and your mother. All I ever had was listening to my gut. It wasn't always right, but it won me your mother's unwavering love and kept me alive on the job for over thirty years. I've always worried that if I stopped listening to it, I would lose my edge and something bad would happen to me, and I wouldn't be there for your mother when she needed me. I could never take that chance. Unfortunately your relationship with me was a casualty in that process. I wish I could've been the father you wanted, but I decided long ago that I would be the father you needed. If your well-being meant I had to sacrifice our relationship, then I was willing to make that choice.

Growing up, you were always a smart, independent, resourceful kid. I was proud of that. But as you got older, I started to worry about that and the direction it might take you. When you got into that trouble your senior year, I saw you going down the wrong path and I did what I thought was right to get you back on track. Once you turned things around, I thought about making amends, but things were working, so I didn't want to mess with it. The more time that passed, and the more you excelled, the harder it became for me to apologize. People thought it was my pride or my stubbornness, but it was really my love for you and the desire I had for you to be a good man.

Maybe it was selfish of me to leave like this, but once again I just listened to my gut, and it told me it was time to go. Staying around longer to see you when you got here would only complicate everything and make it that much harder on you. The true fact of the matter is life without your mother was not much of a life for me. She gave my life meaning and purpose. Without her, there would never be enough. I hope you can understand that because you have also found that in your wife. From what your mother told me, I think you have. I wish you all the happiness your mother and I shared together.

I know you will have questions about the will and the people in my life since your mother passed. Please trust me that they are good people and respect what I have specified in the will. I know with as good of a lawyer as you are, you could probably challenge and poke holes in it, but I'm asking you to accept it. These people have been here when I needed them, and I want to be there for them. Me not making you executor and not leaving everything to you, our sole heir, is not representative of my feelings for you. It's merely because I know you do not need it and it can be put to better use. Please also respect our burial wishes. Your mother and I both wanted to be cremated and our ashes scattered here in Vegas. You are welcome to join in as much or little of the proceedings as you would like.

I can leave this life in peace because of the man you have become. There is nothing left for me to do. My faithful devotion to your mother and you are my proudest achievements.

Love,
Dad

Dow Jones Close: 17,983.07

Chapter Fifty-Nine

Date: Tuesday, December 31, 2014

Dow Jones Open: 17,987.66

The flame blasted into the skirt of the balloon, warming the air of the half-filled envelope stretched across the empty field. With each thrust of propane, the envelope swelled in size, raising it off the ground and lifting the basket toward its upright position.

Most people were heading to the city on this, the busiest, most festive evening of the year in Vegas, but Max, Les, Penny, Crystal, and Hughie had gone the opposite way, to an empty field fifteen minutes to the west. It had been a rushed twenty-four hours before Hughie was scheduled to leave and the New Year's holiday commenced, but as was always true in Vegas, an express service was available. It required a few extra forms and dollars, but it was doable.

What no one had realized during the preceding months was that Bill had done a lot more than just talk about his death; he had planned for it, and not just with the will. He had actually scheduled his cremation with the funeral home to the point that they were expecting the call. How he ever knew for sure that he would pass the night that he did was a mystery...except for Crystal. But even the others had an inkling and knew it could've been solved with an autopsy if they really wanted to find out. Not every mystery needed to be solved though. In the end it didn't matter if his meticulous planning had included direct actions to ensure the scheduled departure. The result would not have changed.

With everything planned and taken care of in advance, Bill was picked up and cremated the same day he died. A short service was held the following morning at the funeral home, which also included Darlene's ashes, since a service had not been performed when she passed.

Crystal sang, "You'll Never Walk Alone" by Gerry and the Pacemakers, one of Bill and Darlene's favorite songs, according to Hughie. They played it so much when he was growing up that they wore out the album. When records went to tapes, then to CDs, it was one of the few that they rebought each time. Hughie performed the eulogy, speaking mostly about how Bill and Darlene met and their life together, which was nice for the others to hear because they really didn't know much about Darlene and that part of Bill's life, since he didn't like to talk about it.

As specific as Bill had been about all the other details, he didn't really establish where he wanted the ashes to be disposed. He had only stipulated that they be scattered to the west in Red Rock Canyon, where they had watched the sun set so many times together. It was Max who proposed, "Why don't we do it over Red Rock Canyon?"

Crystal said, "Let's just stick to the plan and drive out and pick a spot."

"We would be sticking to the plan," Max said. "We're just improving upon it and giving them a more honorable burial."

Penny said, "But will a plane or helicopter let us open the door and scatter the ashes?"

"A hot air balloon would," Max said. "I know a guy who I've used to do some advertising. He would definitely take us up."

Penny shook her head, laughing. "Only you would have a hot air balloon guy."

Max said, "Seriously, what better tribute could we pay than scattering the ashes floating above Vegas on New Year's Eve?"

Crystal deferred to Hughie. "What do you think?"

He smiled. "I think they would've loved the idea."

In the field, the hot air balloon, drifted upward, stretching the lines connected to the basket still anchored to the ground. The pilot pulled open the propane valve, shooting a final blast into the balloon. He nodded at Max. "We're all set. Hop in."

One by one, they climbed up the foot holes in the woven wicker basket and swung first one leg then the other over the side. Hughie lifted Max to help him over the side then handed over the rectangular green marble companion urn containing both Bill's and Darlene's ashes.

The pilot, in his fifties with silver hair, a bushy mustache, and sagging cheeks, released the lines and opened the blast valve, lifting them off the ground. With each burst of flame they climbed higher in the sky, rocking gently in the basket.

The pilot said, "We're climbing to about a thousand feet and will check the air. Plan to take you over toward Rainbow Peak."

Everyone was quiet, watching the objects on the ground become smaller and smaller. Cars raced in both directions along the I-15. The skyline of the strip flattened into its surroundings. Bands of red sandstone capped the upper portion of the peaks in Red Rock Canyon. The pilot pointed out Blue Diamond Hill,

Mount Wilson, and their destination, Rainbow Peak. To climb higher, he blasted fire into the envelope, and to descend, released the parachute valve, searching for the right air current to take them the way they needed to go. Drifting northwest across the valley, they passed above the affluent suburb of Summerlin, named after Howard Hughes's mother. They traveled across Calico Basin toward Icebox Canyon. Turtlehead Mountain was on the right. Mount Wilson, Rainbow Peak, and Bridge Mountain were straight ahead.

"I think this is a good spot." The pilot opened the parachute valve to drop down and hold their position. He said, "I don't want to get too deep into the canyon. The closer we get to the mountains, the trickier the wind gets."

Hughie picked up the urn from between his legs on the basket floor, cradling it under his right arm. He turned to Les. "Could you say a few words?"

Les nodded. "I think Ecclesiastes 3 is fitting." He unfolded a paper from his pocket and put a hand on the urn. "There is a time for everything, and a season for every activity under the heavens: a time to be born and a time to die, a time to plant and a time to uproot, a time to kill and a time to heal, a time to tear down and a time to build, a time to weep and a time to laugh, a time to mourn and a time to dance, a time to scatter stones and a time to gather them, a time to embrace and a time to refrain from embracing, a time to search and a time to give up, a time to keep and a time to throw away, a time to tear and a time to mend, a time to be silent and a time to speak, a time to love and a time to hate, a time for war and a time for peace..." His words mixed with the wind, blanketing those in the basket with comfort. Standing between Hughie and Penny, Crystal reached over and took hold of his free left hand and grasped Penny's with her other. Max interlocked his fingers and bowed his head. Les concluded the reading. "...All go to the same place; all come from dust, and to dust all return. Who knows if the human spirit rises upward and if the spirit of the animal goes down into the earth? So I saw that there is nothing better for a person than to enjoy their work, because that is their lot. For who can bring them to see what will happen after them?" He folded the paper and put it back in his pocket. "Darlene and Bill have returned to dust. In their lives, they knew all of these described times together and experienced eternity in each other's hearts. They were tested, and they were rewarded, finding satisfaction in their toil. And while their earthly lives may have ended, and they will not see what will happen after them, they carry on in each of us by how they touched and shaped our lives." He lifted his hand to make the sign of the cross. "In the name of the Father, the Son, and the Holy Spirit. Amen."

The others murmured amens.

Hughie propped the urn up on the edge of the basket and opened the lid. Moving over to the left side, he said, "Do you guys want to give me a hand?" Crystal moved to the right, Penny next to her, then Les, followed by Max. Hughie said, "On three. One, two, three." They tipped the urn over the side. A thick stream of ashes flowed, then fanned out over the canyon, blowing east straight back toward Vegas, disappearing into nothing.

Penny and Crystal embraced Hughie, the cross-breeze drying the tears on their faces. Les rested his hand on Max's shoulder, both continuing to stare back toward the city in silence.

Dow Jones Close: 17,823.07

Chapter Sixty

Date: Thursday, January 2, 2015

Dow Jones Open: 17,823.07

With the suddenness and emotion of everything leading up to New Year's, everyone needed New Year's Day to recover. Even though their situation was different than all of the hung-over partygoers', they all spent the day in a similar catatonic state, evaluating the flurry of events that led to their current realities. Hughie had caught the red-eye home New Year's Eve to be with his family on the holiday. He planned to come back the following week to go through Bill and Darlene's belongings with Crystal and decide what to keep and what to donate.

After what happened, Crystal couldn't bring herself to stay at Bill's. She had always felt like a guest there, and with him gone, she felt like an intruder. Once Hughie came back, and they had gone through everything, maybe it would be different. If not, she would have to sell the place. In the interim, Penny invited her to stay at her house.

She and Penny spent the New Year's Day in the living room, Penny on the couch, Crystal on the loveseat, eating pizza, ice cream, and whatever other junk food they craved that could be delivered, which included just about everything in Vegas. On TV were the college football bowl games. Penny tried to explain the rules to Crystal, who had never watched an entire game in her life. That day she watched four.

Les, of course, had his duties at the Oasis, which the others volunteered to help him with, but he declined. He knew everyone needed some time and space to process what had happened. Fortunately, the Oasis had grown to the point that there was enough consistent help so even he was able to delegate and step away from time to time.

Max spent the day bedridden, but it wasn't because of illness or injury. After the balloon ride, being the active member of the community he was, he had a full slate of events and parties to attend. It wasn't that he was any less upset or affected by what had happened; he just dealt with things differently. Emotion didn't have residual value with him. He felt what he felt, then he moved on. Whereas Penny and Crystal abated their grief with grease and sugar, Max won the affection of an attractive partygoer at Mayor Goodman's New Year's Eve gala, and the two of them celebrated until the early morning, spending the rest of the day in varying states of consciousness and arousal.

After the formal and requested funeral rites had been performed, and they all took their own personal time, they agreed they also needed to come together and send Bill off with a wake in a way he would approve of but was too humble to suggest in his planning: at the blackjack table.

Everyone met at the El Cortez and filled the open spots at my table one by one as people left either on their own or, after learning why the others were gathering, moved to another table. Once all were in their usual positions, they each threw in a twenty-five-dollar chip for Bill's buy-in, playing his hand exactly as he would've: minimum bet and never wavering from basic strategy. The mood was cheerful but somber, like everyone had just climbed into a car for a long drive. The excitement and anticipation were there, just buried underneath a layer of uncertainty. Nobody knew exactly how to act. For people who knew each other as well as they did, they were acting more like strangers.

"How about a round of drinks to get this party started?" Max said, stopping a cocktail server on her way by. "Can you bring me a cognac—you know what? Better make that two." He pointed at Les. "A hot tea for him. A Ketel rocks for blondie there." He looked at Bill's seat, which had been leaned up against the table to indicate a player gone but coming back. "A Miller Lite for our friend who stepped away, and for you…" He extended his hand toward Crystal.

"I'm good with club soda," she said.

We played several more hands. The waitress came by with the drinks. Max tipped her two green chips. He held up one of his cognacs. "To not what we lose, but what we gain." The others lifted their drinks and touched glasses in the middle of the table.

The game went on: winning and losing, up and down, five-card Charlies, backdoor Kennies, hard twelves, soft eighteens, mothers-in-law. Nothing was really new. Just like nothing was really that out of the ordinary about any of the people seated there. Oh sure, Max had made a few more bucks than most people who have pulled up a chair at my table over the years, but it hardly compared to so many of the whales who visit Vegas, regularly betting five, ten, fifty, a hundred thousand dollars a hand; Les was a compassionate, charitable man sacrificing his life to help those less fortunate, but nonprofit organizations around the world work tirelessly to feed, clothe, treat, counsel, educate, and shelter people in need; Penny was a shrewd, driven reporter with a nose for a good story, but countless journalists were churning out quality pieces every day to fill our twenty-four hour news cycle; Bill was a kind and caring man who had dedicated his life to protecting others and ended up alone, but there were retirement homes and communities all through Vegas filled with people who had much less and had lost even more; and Crystal was a beautiful and talented performer, but girls just like her arrive every day with hopes and dreams and get chewed up and spit back out by the tough lifestyle and breaks of Vegas show business. Were these five good people? Sure. Better than most? Probably. But what made them unique and why their stories have stuck with me was not what they did, but how they did it. They looked beyond their needs to create, to entertain, to protect, to inspire, to serve, and just helped each other. Their failures were their own, but their success was shared. They figured out that life is just a collection of days. Some are positive and some negative. It's not a linear progression. There are surges and slides, growth and decay, gains and losses. Most important thing is that, over time, people do more good than bad, and they invest in each other.

I dealt the cards around the horn: a thirteen to Crystal, an eleven for Bill, a seventeen for Penny, nineteen for Les, and two ladies for Max, all against my four of diamonds. Max looked at his pair, wiggling his fingers over his chips.

Recognizing his temptation to split, Crystal said, "Don't do it." He just smiled. She waved her hand over her thirteen. "I'll stay." She reached over into Bill's stack of chips and pushed another five to double down. Holding up one finger, just like Bill would've done, she said, "Facedown, please."

Concealing its identity as directed, I tucked an additional card under Bill's hand. Penny declined any help for her seventeen. "I'm good."

Les stayed with nineteen.

Max counted out ten chips into a separate stack and nudged them forward.

Crystal said, "Once a dick, always a dick."

Max laughed, pulling back the stack. "Geez, I'm just joking. Where's your sense of humor? You act like someone died or something." He looked over at Bill's chair. "Sorry, Bill. No offense." Penny giggled. Max looked at the others. "Too soon?" Crystal rolled her eyes. Max formed an X with his fingers over his cards. "Nothing for me. I'm staying."

I flipped over my card to reveal an ace of clubs. "Dealer has five or fifteen." The next card was an ace of spades. "Dealer has six or sixteen. Player would've had twenty-one if he split." Next card was a king of diamonds. "Dealer still has sixteen. Player would've had twenty on the second hand." I pulled the next card from the shoe, rubbing it facedown. I turned it over, revealing a six of hearts.

Twenty-two. Bust.

"Everybody wins."

Dow Jones Close: 17,832.99

Acknowledgments

I would like to acknowledge the following people, without whom this book would not have been possible.

The Litt family—Richard, Laura, Amanda, and Matthew. Thank you for taking me in and always providing love, support, and encouragement during my time in Vegas.

My longtime friend and old St. Louis roommate Lionel Handler. I'm happy we were able to reconnect in Vegas. Our weekly dinners kept me anchored and focused.

Josh Molina and Val Varela and the rest of the staff at Makers & Finders. Thanks for letting me camp out every day and for keeping me motivated. Your friendship and the lemon poppy seed muffins you added to the menu for me made all the difference.

Lyle Cervenka and Natasha Shahani. Your affection for each other and love for life fueled me in more ways than you'll ever know.

James P. Reza and Staci D. Linklater. Thanks for welcoming me into the downtown Vegas community and always pointing me in the right direction. Modern Holiday rules!

My research crew, who helped me navigate the Vegas landscape—even though that usually meant learning what not to do: Steven Tankersley, Adam Fleischmann, Joe "TS" Riordan, Marti Tsagrinos, Christian Gonzalez, Jessica Jones, Kevin Parritt, Steph Resler, Kevin James Ewing, Stephanie Smith, Mario Bonaventura, Megan Hubans, Colt Prattes, Angelina Mullins, Mark Black, Birdie, Matty, Josh, Cubes, and, of course, all the random people I encountered during one of those nights.

All the downtown Vegas businesses and locations that contributed either space for me to work or inspiration for content. El Cortez Casino, Downtown Grand Casino, Grass Roots, Velveteen Rabbit, Rachel's Kitchen, Gold Spike, Triple George,

Du-par's, Publicus, Pizza Rock, Atomic, Neon Brand, Las Vegas Metro Chamber of Commerce, Soho Lofts, BlackjackApprenticeship.com, and many more.

My beta reading team: Trisha Cooper Eblin, Julie Ririe, Pete Eliason, Bryan McCausland, Max Rubin, Chad Felton, Hollywood Dave, and Jay Moore. Thanks for reading early drafts and providing direction.

My freelance editors, Laura Garwood and Jeanne Thornton, who I first shared my work with. Your insight and magic are so greatly appreciated.

Tyson Cornell, Pat Walsh, and the team at Rare Bird Books. Thanks for your guidance and inspiration in the publishing process.

Brendan Bauer and Bryan McCausland. Thank you for investing in me. You epitomize the spirit of this story.

Readers Guide

1. The main characters of *The Investment Club* span the ages of 28-70 and come from diverse backgrounds. Why were they able to bridge such gaps and become so close? Who was your favorite? If you could have a conversation with any of them, which one would it be and what would you say?

2. *The Investment Club* is told in sixty one-day snapshots. How does starting and closing each chapter with the Dow Jones open and close from that day connect and add to the story?

3. Las Vegas is known for its extravagant strip, but minimal action occurs there. Why do you think the author chose to do this? How does setting the story in old downtown Vegas reinforce the themes and symbols of the story?

4. To be a good gambler, one must know when to cash in and walk away, but in life that is often seen as quitting or a sign of weakness. What is an example of a character cashing-in in *The Investment Club*? Was it an act of strength or weakness?

5. The author incorporates the rules and strategies of blackjack into *The Investment Club*. How do they apply to everyday life? Why is blackjack the perfect game to use as a metaphor for the story?

6. The narrator of *The Investment Club* is an older blackjack dealer who has lived and worked in Vegas his whole life. After all the people he has seen come and go, why did these characters and their stories resonate so much with him? How did he get to know such intimate details about them?

7. Significant events in the main characters' pasts shape and influence their current lives. Choose a character and explain how an event impacted their life. Was it positive or negative?

8. Vices play a major role in *The Investment Club*. Is it possible, as one of the characters says, to have addictive qualities without being an addict, or is that rationalization? Have you ever witnessed addictive tendencies in yourself? What did you do?

9. We often measure overall success by financial impact. What are examples of the non-financial dividends the characters receive for investing their personal equity in each other?

10. The author lived in Las Vegas while writing *The Investment Club*. What are some examples of details that he could've picked up only from living there?

11. A lot of action and focus in the book involves hand movements. How does this relate to the themes of *The Investment Club*?

12. Why does the author use alternate forms of content—an infomercial, press release, settlement agreement, and will—to convey information in *The Investment Club*? How do they reinforce themes in the story and provide insight to modern culture.

13. How do each of the main characters' names symbolize financial themes and symbols? How do the themes and symbols apply to modern society in general?

14. Investing in other people is a theme of *The Investment Club*, but so is accepting the help of others. Why is it often harder for the characters to accept help than to offer it? When helping others furthers their own cause, are they really being manipulative or selfless?

15. The opening and closing scenes of *The Investment Club* take place at the blackjack table at the El Cortez casino. What is similar and what is different? How have the characters changed?